BREAKING CONTACT

A Matt Sheridan Novel - Book Two

Robert Cole

Carentan Publishing

Ebook ISBN: 979-8-9875110-2-9
Paperback ISBN: 979-8-9875410-3-6

My mother, brother, and mother-in-law may no longer be here with us,
but I think they'd enjoy reading this if they were.

L.J.C
C.J.C
R.A.C

AUTHOR'S NOTE

This is a work of fiction. It is the story of a character who finds himself in a situation that no one in our world has ever experienced, and hopefully never will. This character has feelings, makes decisions, and takes action. He gets some things correct and others wrong. He does what he thinks is best. He is not perfect.

As the author, it is my job to attempt to bring this character, and others, to life and to tell a story that is engaging, entertaining, and perhaps even thought-provoking. Like the characters in the story, I get some things correct and others wrong.

Whenever possible, and to the best of my ability, I have attempted to make this tale as realistic as possible - or as real as an apocalyptic cataclysm could ever be envisioned. However, I have also taken significant license in the description of certain places, people, and events that may err from reality.

I have found that readers of apocalyptic fiction fall into two categories: those that enjoy a good tale, and those that know everything there is to know about surviving the apocalypse. If you're the former, I truly hope you enjoy this book. If you are the latter, I encourage you to put aside your preconceived notions of how these characters must act and simply enjoy the ride. After all, this is a work of fiction.

CHAPTER 1

September 26, 5:43am

Three days with no motorcycles.

Eighteen days since terrorists destroyed eight American cities.

Thirty-three minutes until the sun rose on a new day filled with stress and worry for his family. Thirty-three minutes. One thousand nine hundred and eighty seconds. Looking forward - an eternity. In hindsight - the blink of an eye.

Perched in the lookout chair, Matt's gaze failed to penetrate the dark outlines of the Vermont hills. His guard shift was almost over, and while his eyes traversed the darkened landscape, his thoughts were on the coming dawn: how the sun would soon bring color and clarity to his limited view, bringing to life the world around him that he could now barely discern in the dark of night. His thoughts wandered to the last eighteen days of uncertainty and how quickly the world around them had collapsed. He tried to reconcile how the cataclysm of eighteen days ago seemed like yesterday while tomorrow seemed so far away. The world had changed so much that he had no idea what kind of day this new dawn would bring.

In the bed behind him, Clare stirred with restless sleep. After fifteen years of marriage, he was still in awe of her beauty. He forced himself to look out the window rather than at his lovely bride, with her shoulder-length blonde hair framing her angelic face. Matt sipped lukewarm coffee from his insulated cup and knew his wife would awaken with the rising sun, as would the rest of the house. Over the last few days, he had volunteered for the 4-6 am guard shift, and he savored the morning's quiet solitude to gather his thoughts. Death was all around them, and his sole purpose was to keep his family alive. There were eleven of them now, and together they would overcome all of the challenges that lie ahead.

The sun was still below the horizon, its light soundlessly seeping into the world around him. Vague shapes transitioned to familiar terrain, and within minutes Matt had visibility over the entire front yard down to the hard-packed, rutted gravel of Sugarland Road at the end of the driveway below him. This was the avenue most likely to bring danger to his family. Matt picked up binoculars and scanned as far down the road as he could see while his ears strained to pick out the distant rumble of motorcycles. Aside from a quick drive-by three days prior, when two motorcycles had ridden past the house without slowing, there had been no sign of the Nomads.

All remained quiet outside the farmhouse as sounds within the farmhouse began to emerge. Matt could hear doors opening down the hallway, water running in the bathroom, and the rustling of sheets behind him.

"Good morning," Clare said from behind him.

"And a lovely morning to you, too," Matt replied, adding a cheer to his voice that he didn't necessarily feel.

"I'll take a quiet morning every time. Hungry?"

"A bit, yeah."

Matt heard the whoosh of the comforter being tossed aside and expected to hear the bedroom door open as his wife went to make sure the kids were up. Instead, Clare silently slipped behind him and wrapped her arms around him, nuzzling his neck. "Are we ever going to be able to just sleep in until noon like we used to?"

They both smiled, thinking of the weekends before kids when they'd stay in bed all morning binge-watching some home improvement or cooking show until their hunger dominated their laziness.

"Someday, honey. Someday soon, I hope."

"I think those days are gone, Matt," Clare uttered softly, their smiles disappearing with the knowledge that her statement was likely true.

Matt recalled waking up in the early morning hours of September 8th, thinking he had been awoken by a flash of lightning. The reality was that Islamic terrorists had detonated nuclear bombs in eight American cities. Due only to his quick reaction, an overabundance of caution, and good old Irish luck, Matt, Clare, and their two young children safely evacuated to Matt's brother's vacation farmhouse outside Woodstock, Vermont. On arriving, they had found his two nephews and a niece, along with two of their college friends, already vacationing at the farmhouse.

The two weeks after the nuclear attacks had unleashed chaos, uncertainty, and devastation the world had never seen. Beginning with the US President's disproportionate response to the nuclear attack in vaporizing the fifty largest Muslim cities across the globe and culminating with a weaponized smallpox pandemic that was estimated to have exterminated more than 96% of the world's population, the Sheridan extended family, now including their neighbor, Molly, and her granddaughter, Grace, had remained solely focused on survival.

Through a combination of pluck and luck, Matt and Grace had arrived at Dartmouth-Hitchcock Hospital, the closest major site to receive the re-engineered vaccine that could defeat this new strain of smallpox called the Black Pox. They arrived just in time to witness the highly-organized and lethal Nomad Motorcycle Club raid the hospital and ravage the small force of National Guard troops tasked with safeguarding the vaccine. Noticing several fleeing soldiers, Matt was able to successfully intervene and help the soldiers, who had fled with 10,000 doses of vaccine, evade the chasing gang members.

With the family successfully vaccinated against the Black

Pox, Matt attempted to repatriate the soldiers and their vaccine to the local sheriff's office in Woodstock, Vermont. They had been unaware that the real sheriff had been killed and replaced by an imposter from the Nomad MC. If it hadn't been for Clare, a former Army officer herself, coming to the rescue with his nephews, Matt and the National Guard lieutenant, Brent Langdon, would most assuredly have been killed.

Their string of luck had held so far, but with his wife's prophetic words had hit home. It seemed highly unlikely that things would ever return to normal, whatever normal was. He knew with certainty that he'd never take his son to an NFL football game or attend a father-daughter dance at his daughter's elementary school. *Jesus,* he thought, *did Tom Brady survive the cataclysm? What kind of world is it without Tom Brady leading the New England Patriots to a Super Bowl?*

"I think you might be surprised," said Matt. "We may never be able to lie in bed and watch reruns of Below Deck all day, but I'm confident life will evolve into some form of normalcy. Once the security situation works itself out, we'll be able to focus on more leisure activities with the kids."

"Yeah, I know. It's sad when I think of all that's been taken away from the kids and the fact they don't even fully grasp what they've lost."

Matt turned and gave his wife a kiss. "We still have each other and our family, and that's more than almost everyone else in the world can say. That, and I think we still have pancake mix, right? The world can't be that bad if we can still have pancakes and fresh Vermont maple syrup, right?

His wife smiled and chuckled. "Okay, okay, that's your hint that you're hungry."

"I'm starving, actually. But I'll make the pancakes. Dylan should be up to relieve me any minute. You go get dressed and get the kids. We'll eat pancakes in twenty minutes."

As if on cue, Dylan walked into the master bedroom to start his shift as the lookout sentry. Matt's brother's farmhouse in

Pomfret, Vermont sat on ten acres of land on a rural dirt road leading north from the tourist town of Woodstock. Perched on the backside of a small hill, the farmhouse provided a perfect defensive stronghold. With the master bedroom occupying the front of the 2nd story of the home, a sentry sitting in the front picture window had a perfect field of view down to Sugarland Road to their front.

Seventeen years old, 6'1", with longish brown hair, light eyes, and washboard abs, Dylan should have been calling plays on the gridiron and attempting to take his high-school team back to the state championships. Instead, he had proven himself a capable marksman and, along with his older brother Derek, was instrumental in Matt's plan to keep the family safe.

"Good morning, Dylan," said Matt. "How'd everyone sleep."

"Pretty good. It's six o'clock on the dot. Ready to be relieved?"

"Sure. I'm making some pancakes for everyone. I'll have someone bring you up a stack."

"That sounds awesome, Uncle Matt."

As Dylan sat in front of the window and picked up the binoculars, Matt headed out the door and downstairs. In addition to the master bedroom, the upstairs had a second bedroom and a large bunk room with a half-dozen beds. Matt's two children currently occupied the small bedroom, while the young adults shared the bunk room. So far, everyone was getting along well.

At the bottom of the stairs, Matt walked into the country kitchen, which opened into a dining room. A double-hearth fireplace dominated the space between the dining room and a formal living room on the other side. Down a short hallway from the kitchen, the branch opened into a massive family room with a sitting area large enough for ten, plus an enormous maple dining table most often used for jigsaw puzzles.

"Mornin' Molly," Matt said, entering the kitchen where Molly stood guard over a pot of coffee. "Any of your delicious coffee left?"

"Absolutely, Matt," replied Molly, as she reached for an empty mug. "How'd you sleep?"

"As good as can be expected with a sentry sitting at the end of your bed all night, I guess. I had watch from 4-6 am, so this is not my first cup of the day."

"Yeah, I was up with the sun as usual. Can I get you some breakfast?"

"I was thinking of making pancakes for everyone. Would you like some?"

"No, but I'm happy to help you make them." Molly handed Matt a steaming cup of coffee and then opened cupboards to pull out the pancake ingredients. Molly owned the farm to the north of Donald's and lived there for over forty years. Her husband had died several years previously, and her granddaughter Grace, a med student at the University of Florida, happened to be visiting when the cataclysm began. When the smallpox became a pandemic, Molly and Grace accepted Matt's invitation to join their extended family at Donald's farmhouse.

While Matt heated the griddle on the stove and Molly mixed eggs, water, and pancake mix in a large metal bowl, most of the younger crew wandered down to the dining room. First down were Derek and Brent, more commonly referred to as LT. Derek was his brother's oldest son, as well as his spitting image. Six feet tall with thick dark hair and a bearded scruff, Derek was still recovering from the loss of his girlfriend, Celeste, to smallpox. LT was a similar height to Derek but with the lean, sinewy build of an NCAA cross-country distance runner. He still had the short hair of an Army lieutenant and worked as an IT specialist before being called to active duty after the nuclear attacks.

"Mornin' gents," greeted Matt. "Grab yourself something to drink, and we should have pancakes for you in a minute."

"Sounds great, Uncle Matt.," said Derek, taking a seat at the dining room table.

"Yeah, that does sound delicious, Uncle Matt," said a new voice entering the kitchen. Matt turned to see his 22-year-old niece coming down the stairs. Her friend Amey and Matt's daughter Laurie trailed right behind her. Kelsey was tall, thin and almost always had her long brown hair pulled back in a ponytail. She was in her last year at Colby-Sawyer College, about forty-five minutes east of Woodstock in New Hampshire. She had brought her friend Amey to the farmhouse for a fun getaway with Derek and his girlfriend the day prior to the nuclear attack. Amey was mousy in appearance and quiet. However, Matt had been impressed by her analytical abilities as she helped keep track of all that was happening on the internet during the first few days of the cataclysm.

"Hey, Daddy," said his young daughter Laurie. She lept down the bottom three stairs and bounded into the kitchen. "I'm ready for pancakes!"

"Hi, sweetie," said Matt, turning towards his daughter. "Did you sleep..."

Before he could finish his sentence, they all heard the faint growl of motorcycle engines. Dylan's voice broadcast loudly from the handheld radio Matt had placed on the counter. "Motorcycles approaching, Matt. Coming from the south up Sugarland."

Everyone had already stood up from the table. "Okay, everyone. Grab your stuff and head to your assigned stations. Be quick," said Matt as he bounded from the kitchen and up the stairs, passing his wife and Grace on their way down.

"What is it?" Clare asked on her way down the stairs.

"Don't know yet. You're in charge of the ground floor as we rehearsed. The others should all know their positions. I'll update over the radio," Matt replied, not breaking stride and taking the stairs two at a time.

CHAPTER 2

September 26, 7:12am

By the time Matt reached the threshold of the master bedroom, the sounds of motorcycles were much louder. It still wasn't possible to determine the number of riders, but there was no doubt they were approaching up Sugarland Road and getting closer.

As he entered the room, he saw Dylan in the prone position with the binoculars propped up on the window sill, scanning to the south towards the sound of the approaching motorcycles. Matt enjoyed a brief moment of pride as this was precisely how Matt had taught everyone - keep a low profile while scanning for threats.

"See anything, Dylan?"

"Not yet, Matt. From the sounds of them, they seem to be driving pretty slowly. Not sure if that's because of the dirt road or if they're visually checking each house as they drive by."

"What's your estimate on how many motorcycles?"

"I think it's just a couple, Uncle Matt. The noise is steady, but it's not a roar or anything. Maybe two or three bikers would be my best guess. At this pace, I'm thinking three to four minutes before they pass us."

Matt started to reach for the other set of binoculars on the shelf but hesitated, reaching instead for the scoped Remington 700 propped against the wall. Dylan was more than capable as a spotter, and his position in the right-side window gave him the best angle on the approaching motorcycles. Matt sat in the chair directly in front of the open left window, six feet to Dylan's left. The sizable semi-circular picture window had sliding panes at each corner that opened fully. Matt knew that in the darkened room, he and Dylan were invisible to anyone approaching on the road.

Taking the ever-present handheld radio off the window sill, Matt spoke slowly and calmly. "Battle stations, battle stations. This is not a drill. I am in the Lookout; Clare has the first floor, LT and Grace to Alpha, and Derek and Amey to Bravo. OP1, get back to the house now. Do not rush, stay calm, and everyone check in when you are in position."

After the events at the Sheriff's office and the killing of the Nomads four days prior, Matt knew the motorcycle gang would be out for blood and searching for them all over the Woodstock area. He and Clare had had several discussions about fleeing the area altogether. Still, given what little they knew of the situation beyond the farmhouse, they both agreed this place offered the best chance for survival.

Consequently, Matt had spent much of the last three days developing a dynamic plan for defending the house and training the entire family on their specific roles. The house was ideally situated on the backside of a knoll that kept the structure almost completely hidden from anyone traveling along Sugarland Road to their front. The master bedroom window at which Matt and Dylan now sat provided 180 degrees of visibility across the front of the house and across the road. After walking all around the property and visualizing how he would attack the house, it became evident to Matt that two defensive positions, each about fifty meters to the sides of the house, offered deadly enfilade fire down the most likely approach routes as well as interlocking defensive fire tied in with shooters positioned in the windows on all sides. This 360-degree coverage would not allow the eleven of them to hold out against a large-scale siege, but Matt was confident they could repel almost any initial assault.

After staking it out on the ground, Matt used the backhoe

to dig the two defensive positions as well as shallow trenches leading from each position back to the side and rear of the house. Working as a family over the last few days, they used lumber and plywood topped with dirt and grass to camouflage the two fighting positions. Matt emplaced aiming stakes and drew detailed sector sketches so defenders could aim confidently along expected avenues of approach. The two outposts were referred to as Alpha (southern side of the house) and Bravo (north side), and all eleven family members had rehearsed getting to the positions and what to do in the event of an attack.

Inside the house, Matt had used sandbags to fortify three sandbagged fighting positions on the ground floor. Each fighting position was referred to by the cardinal direction they faced. "North" was the window overlooking the driveway, while "South" was between the living and dining rooms, where the telescope offered unhindered views down the valley to the town of Woodstock. "East" was a position set up by the sliding glass door overlooking the backyard and up the hillside to the rear of the house. The master bedroom lookout, similarly fortified with sandbags, would cover the front of the house. While the Lookout was technically West, it was still referred to as the Lookout. Taken as a whole, the positions provided 360 degrees of interlocking fields of fire, and Matt was confident no enemy could get within 100-150 yards of the building without coming under withering fire from at least two fighting positions.

Rifles, ammunition, and armored vests were stocked at each position, and over the last two days, Matt had drilled the entire family on various contingencies. Everyone knew their roles, and he had purposely set it up so that everyone felt comfortable defending from every position.

With the Remington 700 police sniper rifle across his lap, Matt noticed for the first time the crisp breeze entering through the open window in front of him. The leaves had begun to turn, the green of summer replaced by the orange, red and brown hues of autumn in Vermont. At this time of year, one might smell the faint whiff of a far-off wood stove or the manure from a freshly fertilized field carried on the Fall breezes. This morning, all Matt smelled was the fresh air, crisp and clean - accompanied by the increasing throaty and unwelcome rumble of approaching Harley-Davidson motorcycles.

Matt cycled the bolt on his rifle, calmed by the smooth action and the firm seating of a .300 Winchester Magnum round in the chamber. While Matt had brought his own Remington 700 from his home in Rhode Island, that weapon was currently downstairs as Matt felt the police versions they had liberated from the Windsor County Sheriff's office were more suited for the lookout. The version Matt held in his hands was a special tactical model for law enforcement and had a shorter barrel, an attached suppressor as well as a top-of-the-line Leupold 5-25 variable powered scope. This meant Matt could magnify objects five times their standard size at low power, all the way up to 25 times at full zoom. While suppressors in the movies make rifles sound almost silent, in reality, the suppressor attached to this rifle would only somewhat mute the sound - making it less distinct than the sharp bang of an unsuppressed rifle and more difficult for an enemy to distinguish the sniper's hiding location. Matt had test-fired and zeroed the weapon and was very confident in its accuracy and his ability to hit targets as far away as five hundred meters. As a U.S. Army sniper school graduate many years prior, Matt had once felt confident in his ability to drop targets out to over 1,000 meters, but those skills were perishable. While Matt was still a very good shot, he would need considerable practice to get back into proper sniper form. Practice was not something he could afford to do at the moment. Still, as there was minimal wind, the road less than 150 meters to his front, and he was shooting from a supported position, Matt had little doubt he could hit any target that presented itself.

"Alpha in position," squawked the radio, sounding like Grace.

"Bravo in position," seconded Amey from the position to the north of the house.

"Positions North, South, and East all manned." The last transmission was from Clare, who had control of the ground floor.

Matt donned his radio' earpiece and now keyed his mic. "Okay, everyone. The motorcycles are approaching from the south and should be in front any minute. Hopefully, they'll just drive on by, but no one is to fire unless they're directly fired upon or I give the order. Keep off the radio, and keep your head on a swivel. Out."

Matt chuckled as he let go of the mic switch and settled the rifle on the sandbags. Ending your radio transmission with "Out" or "Over" was required in the Army, but Matt's Army days were well behind him, and no one other than Clare and Brent had ever served in the military. He shook his head, realizing certain habits were hard to break.

The sound of the motorcycles was very close now, and Matt looked towards Dylan, who had a much wider angle of view to their south.

"Can you see them?" Matt queried.

"Just a sec. I think they're almost at the old school, and we should see them any second." Dylan referred to an old one-room schoolhouse on the side of Sugarland Road, five hundred meters to their south. "Okay, here they come."

Dylan focused the binoculars. "Looks like three motorcycles. Single riders on each. Driving maybe 5-10 miles an hour, tops." He paused. "They should be coming into view any second...."

Matt took up a solid shooter's position behind his rifle, set back a few feet from the window to keep the barrel from sticking out. He had the power on the scope ratcheted back to the lowest setting, giving him the widest field of view but still magnified plenty to see the three men approaching on motorcycles. Matt studied each of the men before him as his ears remained alert to any change in the pitch of their motorcycle engines, which would signify they were preparing to stop. He hoped they would cruise on by as the motorcycles had done several days prior.

The first thing Matt was looking for was to see if this group contained the leader of the Nomads. This was the man they had caught a glimpse of while fleeing through White River Junction with the case of vaccine vials along with LT Brent and his soldier, Smitty. The Nomad leader was an absolute monster of a human being, standing at least 6'8" and tipping the scales at well over 300 pounds. Matt surmised that none of these riders was the Nomad leader.

The three bikes approached in a loose formation with one rider out front and the other two gang members riding abreast about ten yards behind the lead rider. They were definitely Nomads, as Matt could see that each rider wore a sleeveless leather cut adorned with numerous patches. The lead rider had an assault rifle slung across his back, while the other two bikes looked to have rifle scabbards mounted vertically along their front wheel forks. It was impossible to tell what type of rifle each scabbard contained.

Matt's brain absorbed and processed all this information as he tracked them with the scope.

"I don't think they see us," whispered Dylan beside him.

Matt didn't respond, remaining focused on the passing motorcycles whose pace up Sugarland Road never altered. Within seconds they rode past their chained driveway entrance and continued up the slope to the north.

"Okay, everyone. They appear to be passing by. Everyone remain in position and keep alert. This could simply be a recon or a ruse to get us to focus on these riders. Keep scanning your assigned sectors."

No one replied, as Matt had drilled them, and he knew they were all alert and ready. Next to him, Dylan leaned to his left to keep the bikers in view as they rode up the hill to the north, towards Molly's farm. They could still hear the low, steady rumble of their engines in low gear moving further away.

Fighting position Bravo, located about sixty meters to the north of the farmhouse on the military crest of a small hill just higher than the house itself, had a slight view of the road up toward Molly's. Roadside trees obscured most of their view, but Matt had emplaced the fighting position at just the right spot to be able to see a sliver of the front yard of Molly's farm, about four hundred meters to their north.

"Derek, waddya see? Anything," Matt asked.

"One sec, Matt. They appear to be stopping at Molly's place." The reply came not from Derek but from Amey, occupying the hole with Derek. Matt envisioned Derek focused on his binoculars while Amey manned the radio.

"Matt," Amey's voice broadcast at a slightly higher pitch. "Matt, they're definitely stopping. The three motorcycles are stopped, and two of the bikers are walking up to Molly's front porch. The two have walked out of view, but one of the guys is still sitting on his bike in her driveway. Derek says it looks like he's lighting up a cigarette...actually...Derek thinks it's a joint. Still can't see the other two guys."

"Okay, thanks, Amey. Keep reporting anything you see. Everyone else, stay frosty. Watch your sectors."

Matt knew Molly must be pretty anxious, knowing these men were likely looting her home, a home that had been in her family for generations. The seconds ticked by like minutes. Matt wanted to ask Amey for an update, but he had always hated when his commanders pressured him for information, and he had confidence Derek and Amey would report anything new. In these types of situations, patience was a virtue second in importance only to vigilance.

"Matt, this is Bravo. All three bikers are now on their bikes, starting them up." As Amey's voice came through the radio, Matt could barely make out the distant revving of the motorcycle engines. "We think they're leaving. Okay, they're leaving...two are turning their bikes around. Yep, they're going." Pause. "Matt? Derek says the guy smoking the joint is still sitting there, but the other two are leaving."

"Which way, Amey?" Matt asked, a sense of urgency in his voice. "Can he see which way the two are going?"

Before Amey replied, next to him, Dylan spoke. "They're coming back, Matt! I can't see them yet, but the sound is definitely coming towards us."

"South, Matt! Derek says they are heading south toward us! Two of them." Amey squawked through the radio.

"Okay, everyone. Keep calm." Matt tried hard to keep his voice slow and steady. "They could just be heading back to Woodstock."

Matt swung his rifle to the right and picked up the two bikers as they slowly made their way down the road. They didn't seem to be driving much faster than before, and he hoped they would slide right passed the front of the farm's driveway.

"Shit," he muttered as both bikes stopped in front of the chain stretched across their gravel driveway.

"They're stopping, Uncle Matt," Dylan said, captain of the obvious.

Matt watched the two bikers through his scope. They didn't appear agitated as the one with the assault rifle slung over his back dismounted his bike, flipped down the kickstand, and began walking to the three-foot high post with the padlocked chain on the side of the gravel driveway. The biker tugged at the lock and the chain, realizing that nothing short of bolt cutters would allow them passage. Matt could see him speaking with the other biker and watched as the other guy dismounted his bike and leaned it on its kickstand.

Matt's brain raced, attempting to process the calculus of what to do next. He could shoot both bikers, but that left the third guy unaccounted for at Molly's farm. If he didn't shoot these two, they would be at the door to the farmhouse in sixty seconds.

"Derek. Do you have eyes on the biker at Molly's?"

"Uh, yes, Matt," Amey replied for Derek.

"Do you think you can take him down with your M4?" Matt mentally performed the calculations and knew that Derek was 350-400 meters away from the lone biker in Molly's yard. This shot would be challenging but doable for the average Army Ranger, but despite Derek being a very good shot, Matt knew the likelihood of him hitting the enemy at that range was slim at best.

"Ah, he's not sure, Matt," replied Amey. "But he says he will if you need him to."

"Tell him to hold his fire, Amey." With that, Matt turned his complete attention to the two bikers who had just stepped over the driveway's protective chain. The one biker had unslung his assault rifle and now carried it slung across the front of his body. In contrast, the other biker had what appeared to be a sawed-off semi-automatic shotgun complete with an external magazine. Matt knew these shotguns were vicious in close combat.

Matt's brain ceased working on processing information and trying to determine the best course of action. His decision made, Matt's breathing slowed as he centered the crosshairs on the chest of the lead biker. His mind played through the next few steps, and without further thought, Matt pulled the slack from the two-stage trigger, continued to squeeze gently, and saw the biker's chest explode almost simultaneously with the feel of the rifle's recoil and the sound of the suppressed shot. Before the second biker could react, Matt repositioned the crosshairs on the man's chest and squeezed the trigger a second time.

Both men lay unmoving on the ground. Wanting to be doubly sure, Matt quickly put a round into each man's head. The suppressed .300 Win Mag rounds were considerably muted compared to an unsuppressed rifle. While much of the sound would stay within the house, another reason for having his firing position well back from the window, Matt remained concerned that the sound would carry to the third biker sitting at Molly's farm.

"Amey, did the other biker react to the gunfire? Ask Derek what he sees."

Five seconds. No reply.

Three more seconds, and finally, the radio squelched. "The biker's gone, Matt. Derek took his eyes off him to look down the driveway at the other bikers, and when he looked back, the man was no longer there."

"Shit!" Matt muttered to himself, although Dylan could apparently hear him. This was approaching the worst-case scenario - a Nomad aware of their presence and free to vector his fellow gang members to attack the farmhouse. Keeping his voice calm and steady, Matt toggled the radio. "Okay, everyone. Maintain your positions and scan your sectors. We have one biker out there who could be approaching the house from any direction." Matt unkeyed the mic, taking a normal breath. "Derek, I want you behind the rifle and scanning towards Molly's. If you see the biker, you are free to engage."

"I don't hear his motorcycle, Uncle Matt," Dylan said, sitting next to Matt and not speaking into the radio. "At least he's not fleeing to warn the rest of his gang."

"Good point," said Matt. "Keep watching the road. I wonder what this dumb motherfucker is up to."

"Matt! Matt!" Amey's excited voice came through the radio. "We see him! He's on the other side of Sugarland Road and walking back towards the farmhouse. He's trying to stay hidden behind the stone wall."

"Roger," replied Matt. To Dylan beside him, "You see him? Scan the wood line there, maybe two hundred yards up, just before that copse of trees."

"I see him, Uncle Matt!" Dylan exclaimed. "Right there, right where you said."

Matt pivoted his rifle and, after a quick traverse, picked up the biker as he darted from the stone wall to stand behind a tree. He stood on the other side of the road about 200 meters away by Matt's best estimate. Matt was pretty confident the guy couldn't yet see the dead bodies of his two friends, but he likely could see their motorcycles parked at the foot of the driveway.

Matt thought of radioing Derek to see if he had a good shot, but instead, Matt put his left hand on the ring at the back of the Leupold scope and dialed the power up a few notches. At this power, the biker's torso filled half the lens, and placing the reticle on the center of the man's chest proved a simple task. Matt was certain the man did not wear body armor. Matt took a slow breath and exhaled casually while maintaining the reticle steady on the chest area of the man's leather vest. He used his finger to take up the slack in the trigger's first stage. As Matt exhaled and reached the natural pause at the end of his breath, he squeezed his trigger finger, launching a 190-grain bullet on a flat trajectory directly into the man's chest. Matt watched through the scope as the round entered exactly where he had intended. The round exited the man's back in a spray of red mist while the biker himself fell as would a marionette with his strings cut.

No need for a second bullet to ensure the man was dead.

CHAPTER 3

September 26, 7:19 am

"Enemy down. Enemy down." Matt spoke into the radio. "Listen up, everyone. We have a lot to do right now and not a lot of time to do it. I want everyone to quickly head straight back to the house. Leave your fighting positions ready to be reoccupied, but head back now. We'll meet in the living room in five minutes."

Without waiting for a reply, Matt turned to Dylan. "Great work, Dyl. You saved us this morning. I want you to stay here for a few minutes until I can get Kelsey and Laurie up to relieve you. Then head down to the living room."

"Uh, thanks, Uncle Matt. That was pretty crazy. Good shooting, by the way." Dylan was eighteen but had matured several years in the last few weeks. Matt knew the family's survival depended on Dylan and Derek doing much of the heavy lifting around the house, not just physically. But Matt also realized he could say the same thing about everyone.

"Good work, bud. I'll see you downstairs in a few," Matt said as he bounded out the door and down the stairs to the first floor.

As he got to the bottom of the stairs, he was met by his wife Clare, who he knew had been manning the North position and checking on Kelsey and Christopher manning the other first-floor fighting positions.

"Jesus, Matt. Do you think more are coming?"

"I don't know, honey. That's what I want to talk to everyone about. I think we need to proceed as if they were scouts, and a larger attack could be on the way. What do you think?"

"Yeah....Jesus. I don't know. I mean, maybe these guys were looting homes, and we got them before they could tell anyone?"

"Yeah," said Matt. "Let's gather everyone up and discuss. Would you mind getting me some water, please? I'm dying of thirst."

"I guess shooting people has that effect, huh?" Clare joked, although Matt could see she wasn't smiling. Matt watched as Clare dashed into the kitchen to get some water and hug Christopher as he walked by. Matt turned and headed into the living room.

The first to greet him was his daughter Laurie. Curly blond hair, deep green eyes, and seven years old, she saw the last few weeks' events much differently than the adults. This was more of a family vacation for her, although she was pretty in tune with the heightened stress level of the adults, especially when Derek was sick and quarantined in the driveway. Her role this morning had been to sit with Molly in the protected basement area, which had been designated the casualty collection and resupply point.

"Hi, Daddy! Is everything safe now? Molly says it's 'all clear.' Are we still going to work on the puzzle today? I think we can finish it." Her endless flow of questions indicated his young daughter was stressed. Each evening various family members would sit at the large table in the family room and work on a jigsaw puzzle. Laurie looked forward to these times, for while she wasn't the most focused puzzle-solver, her cousins often handed her pieces to see if they fit, and most of the time, they magically did.

"Of course, sweetie," Matt said, leaning down to give his daughter a kiss on the forehead. "Thanks for helping Molly in the basement. We have a lot of work to do today, so I'm sure people are going to need your help, but I think we should have some puzzle time after dinner."

Clare called to Laurie from the kitchen, and Matt took that as his queue to sit down in the chair he favored. His mind was still processing that three dead bodies were lying down by the road, and he raced to think of all the things they needed to get done as soon as possible. Laurie ran in with a large glass of water for him. He gulped it down in several chugs while listening to the rest of his extended family trudge up the stairs into the breezeway between the kitchen in the original part of the house and the large family room where Matt now sat, which was in the farmhouse's more recent addition.

Everyone looked tense and concerned, but their small talk ceased as they entered the room and found a place to sit. He looked around as several of them sipped from Nalgene water bottles.

"Okay, I want this to be a quick meeting as we have lots to do. First, we need to update our security posture. Amey, would you mind taking Laurie and heading upstairs to the Lookout to relieve Dylan? Don't worry. I'll be up to fill you in on things in a few minutes as I have a critical task for both of you. Please ask Dylan to come down here. Thanks." Shifting to look at his 11-year-old son. "Christopher - I'd like you to head up to OP1. This is really important. The telescope and binos are already up there, and I want you to focus on watching the stretch of road down by Sugarland Farm that you can see from OP1. Also, check to see if you can detect any vehicle movement in town. If you see any movement at all, call out on the radio. Okay?"

"Got it, Dad." Matt watched as his prematurely mature 11-year-old walked out of the room to be their main lookout on the hill behind the farmhouse. Christopher took after his father in his height, strength, and athleticism, but he had his mother's blond hair and brown eyes. From OP1, Chris should be able to detect any vehicles approaching their way and provide at least a five-minute warning.

With his children and Amey on sentry, Matt looked around at his assembled family. This morning's events had been stressful but not particularly taxing, and everyone looked pretty much as they had about an hour ago at breakfast. "We have a lot to do and little time to do it. I don't want to waste any time discussing strategy or what-ifs. The bottom line is that we have three dead Nomads and their equipment to clean up, and we need to prepare for a larger follow-on attack. We've been rehearsing this for the last few days, and I'm super proud of how everyone responded this morning."

Matt paused to take another long drink of water.

"It's not clear whether these guys were a recon party explicitly looking for us, but based on how they acted, I'm thinking they were out reconning or looting and happened upon Molly's house as a place that might have valuables. Something made two of them head back here - I'm hoping that it's just that they noticed our house from Molly's front yard after passing us by on the road. In any case, we need to get rid of these guys - the same way we did the others who tried to attack us last week. I didn't see any of these bikers carrying any type of radio, so it's doubtful they were able to inform their Nomad buddies.

"That said, at some point, their gang is going to come looking for them. I want them to disappear in the next thirty minutes. Derek, you're the best on the backhoe. Fire it up and dig a hole up on the knoll above Bravo, big enough for three Harleys and three bodies. Do it as fast as you can. We have at least an hour before anyone looks for these guys, but I want to minimize how long we are using loud machinery."

"Got it, Uncle Matt," said Derek. "Right next to the hole with the other bodies?"

"Exactly." Matt almost smiled, thinking that never in a million years could he have imagined talking with his nephew about burying bodies as if they were talking about stacking wood for the fireplace.

"LT, Grace, Dylan, and Kelsey - you're on body detail. Go pull the one guy out of the woods and put him next to the other two. Take anything useful off of them. Walk the two motorcycles in the driveway up to the hole Derek is digging if you can. If not, we can use the front-end loader to move them. Once Derek is done with the hole, bring the backhoe down and load up the bodies to dump them. Questions?"

The four of them looked at him, and then LT half raised his hand as he spoke. "What about the Harley still at Molly's?"

"Shit. Forgot about that! Thanks. Once you load the bodies onto the tractor, why don't you and Grace walk up there and take care of it? Just put it in the barn and cover it. No need to walk it all the way back here, and I'd prefer you stay off the road if you can. Good?"

"Yeah, sounds like a plan, Matt."

"Okay, you five, get going. Make sure you're armed and have radios."

The five young adults moved immediately to perform their tasks, leaving Clare and Molly with Matt in the family room. Molly was sipping from a cup of tea while Clare wrung her hands on a dishtowel she had brought from the kitchen.

"Matt, I'm not sure we can hold out against a full-on attack by these degenerate bikers. I mean...Jesus, Matt. I almost lost it this morning when I looked over at our 11-year-old son wearing Level IV body armor and sighting down an M4 behind sandbags in our goddamn living room! I mean, part of me was so proud of him, but the other part was absolutely horrified. This wasn't dress-up day at work. What kind of mother lets her kid carry an assault rifle?" Clare's hands continued to twist the dishtowel as Matt watched helplessly, unable to respond to his wife's rhetorical question.

Putting her tea down on the coffee table, Molly interjected, "The kind of mother whose family is going to survive all of this. That's the kind of mother, Clare. You do what you must to survive, and the two of you should be proud of how you're parenting this big family of ours." Molly leaned over to hug Clare on the couch next to her.

Matt still wasn't quite sure what to do, but after a moment, the spell had been broken, and he could see the two women looking at him to continue his taskings. "Okay, Matt. What about us?" Clare asked.

"I think we need to prepare to evacuate," blurted Matt, trying to look at both women simultaneously. "We've debated this almost every night since the incident at the Sheriff's office a few days ago. If the Nomads know we're here, how long can we realistically hold out? I mean, we're not a military unit. We can't think in terms of acceptable casualties, and we all know that any concerted attack by the Nomads will definitely result in some of us being wounded or killed." Matt paused to gauge any reaction. "You should have seen these savages at Dartmouth-Hitchcock. They took on an entire Infantry company and brutally defeated them. What do you think they would do to our little farmhouse?"

"I agree in principle, Matt," said Molly. "But where would we go? And could leaving make us more vulnerable?"

"Yeah, Matt, if they're going to catch us anyway, don't we have the best chance by staying here with all our supplies and defenses?" Clare added.

"Yeah..." Matt used both hands to rub his face, closing his eyes and massaging his eyelids with his pinkies while he tried to think. Matt knew from his prior combat experience that often, there was never a perfect solution to such a complex problem. "That's why I wanted to talk to you both. Right now, I think it's important the kids focus on our defensive posture and being ready to repel an attack. But I think we need a solid contingency to bug out of here, and we need to make sure we're ready to evacuate on a moment's notice. If a hundred bikers converge on this place, we simply aren't going to survive."

The three talked through several options while monitoring the progress of burying the bodies and began to outline what they thought was a solid plan. A more urgent radio call interrupted their conversation.

"Matt, this is LT. Matt, you there?"

"Go ahead, LT," said Matt into the radio mic clipped to the collar of his shirt.

"I'm at Molly's. We have a problem."

"What kind of problem?"

"This Harley has a CB radio, and someone keeps calling for the Grinch to answer."

CHAPTER 4

September 28, 5:47 pm

The last two and a half days had thankfully proven quite uneventful.

After receiving the radio call from LT and Grace, Matt had the two of them walk the motorcycle down the road back toward the farmhouse and up the driveway to park it next to the garage. While everyone was initially in a panic that the third Nomad had radioed in the farmhouse's location, it was clear to Matt, after listening for an hour, that his family had dodged a bullet.

The fact that "Nomad base" kept calling for "the Grinch" to reply told Matt that the Nomads now knew their recon team had gone missing but that they were not aware of the Sheridans' location. The Nomad headquarters asked for Grinch to check in and did not seem alarmed or agitated. In fact, after two hours, they stopped calling for the Grinch altogether.

Of greater significance, there continued to be sporadic chatter on Channel 13 - the chosen CB frequency that the third biker's radio had been set to. Occasionally, whichever family member was monitoring the radio would cycle through the other channels, but so far, no other transmissions had been heard. Matt was convinced that if the Nomads were concerned their team had been compromised, they would at least have switched CB channels. The fact that other gang elements were checking in sporadically and bragging about the loot they had found led Matt to believe they were in the clear. Clare, Molly, and the others agreed with Matt's assessment. However, the family continued to prepare and rehearse their defenses while simultaneously prepping for a contingency evacuation.

One other noteworthy piece of information they gleaned from eavesdropping on the CB radio was that it appeared the Nomads were still actively searching for the vaccine and specifically the "cowardly National Guard guys" that had escaped the attack at Dartmouth-Hitchcock Hospital. At no time were the Sheridans mentioned by name, and Matt took comfort in the fact that the biker gang believed they were chasing a team of soldiers who had fled from the hospital the week prior. To Matt, this meant the biker gang leader would not think he was up against an entrenched family but instead was seeking a few soldiers who were on the run in a part of Vermont they were unfamiliar with. The carefree way the three bikers had wandered up Sugarland Road reinforced this assessment - if they thought they were approaching a well-defended farmhouse, Matt figured they would have been much more cautious.

Since the incident, Matt had increased their security posture to having three people on sentry duty at all times. During the day, someone was always manning the main bedroom Lookout, OP1 behind the house, and fighting position Bravo on the north side of the house. This gave them 360-degree surveillance overall approaches to the farmhouse. Matt didn't want anyone as far away as OP1 at night so that position shifted to manning the house's first floor and roaming between all the different sentry spots.

In addition to the everyday chores that kept the house running, the others spent much of their time configuring the supplies for an emergency evacuation. The three vehicles were filled with gas and loaded with fuel, food, weapons, and ammunition. Everyone packed a small go-bag, but there were also items of clothing and other essential living supplies packed efficiently in all vehicles. Lastly, they planned out several escape routes as well as linkup protocols. Everyone, including young Christopher, studied maps of the area to the point that Matt was confident each family member knew where and how to link up should they be separated for any reason.

Matt was sitting with Amey, who had become his *de facto* intelligence officer. They sat at the family room table, pouring over maps of Vermont, New Hampshire, and Maine to select and refine potential locations to relocate. Matt liked two locations the most, one about twenty miles away and the other several hours' drive. Without communication or the internet, it would be impossible to know if either location was viable until they could put eyeballs on the sites, so it was important to Matt that he and Amey learn as much as they could with the information they had available.

They had been going at it for almost two hours, pouring over geological survey maps and satellite images Amey had downloaded prior to their loss of electricity and the internet when they were interrupted by a call over the radio.

"Matt, this is Grace up in the Lookout. There's something you need to see. I don't want to alarm anyone, but I suggest going to battle stations just in case."

"Roger, Grace, on my way," Matt replied, toggling the now ever-present radio mic attached to his collar. He knew Grace was as level-headed as anyone, and it was always better to be safe than sorry. "Battle stations, battle stations, everyone. We're not sure about the threat, but everyone should go directly to their battle stations. Who's on OP1?"

"That would be me, Dad!" The excitement in Christopher's voice was evident. "I don't see anything, Dad. Definitely no movement on the road to our north and south."

"Okay, buddy. You stay there for now. LT and Dylan to Alpha and Derek and Kelsey to Bravo." Matt got up quickly. "Amey, you take the North position right there by the window. I'll go talk to Clare on my way upstairs."

As Matt shuttled down the hall, he was met by his wife

coming up from the basement. “What is it, Matt?” she asked as she reached the top of the stairs, almost running into Matt in the hallway.

“I don’t know yet, Clare. You take the first floor, and I’ll let you know as soon as I can.”

“Got it. Go. Laurie and Molly are downstairs, and Amey and I will hold things down here.”

Matt took the stairs two at a time and bounded into the master bedroom, keeping low so as not to silhouette himself in the large plate-glass window.

“Whadda ya got, Grace?” He said to the back of her head as Grace was in the prone position behind sandbags, her eyes glued to the large maritime binoculars that were a permanent fixture of the Lookout. Matt slid into the prone next to her.

Turning on her side to face him, she handed him the binos. “This is really weird, Matt. It scared the shit out of me, but I’m not sure what to make of it. There’s a piece of paper tacked to a tree with a knife directly across the driveway, and I swear it’s never been there before.”

“What’s it say?” Matt said, putting the binos to his eyes.

“I don’t know. It’s like an upside-down V and an I, or a 1. Followed by some letters that don’t spell any acronym I’m aware of. RLTW, I think it said.”

Matt adjusted the binos to the width of his eyes and zeroed in on the end of the driveway. He found the 8.5 x 11 piece of white paper tacked to the tree. He visibly tensed for the couple of seconds it took to read and understand the writing, and then his body noticeably relaxed. So much so that Grace said, “What’s wrong? You clearly know what it means.”

Matt pulled the binos away. “Well, I’m not 100% sure who put it there, but I know it means we have some friends in the woods.” Matt grabbed his radio mic, “Okay, folks. Keep alert, but I don’t want anyone firing at all. I think we have some friends in the woods across the road, so don’t be alarmed. I’m going to walk down the driveway, so please make sure your weapons are on safe. Continue to scan your sectors.”

Turning back to Grace, Matt said, "Great job seeing this. Keep watching. I'm going to walk down there, and I expect someone to come out of those woods to meet me. Cover me with the rifle, but don't shoot unless you are certain the person is about to shoot me."

"Okay," replied Grace skeptically. "Who is it?"

"I'm not sure yet, but we're about to find out." Matt stood up and ran down the stairs where Clare awaited him.

"What did you see, Matt? Friends? What friends?"

"I'm not 100% sure, Clare," Matt said as he pulled on his FLC load-carrying vest with Level IV armor and grabbed the M4 that he kept at the bottom of the stairs. "The note was handwritten with Lambda Iota and RLTW for Rangers Lead The Way."

"Jesus," said Clare. "Who the fuck could that be?" Matt always got a kick out of Clare's swearing. It meant she was back in Army mode and fully dialed in. She knew that Lambda Iota was Matt's old fraternity from when he was an undergrad at the University of Vermont, and she was very familiar with RLTW as Matt and his fellow Rangers often used it as part of their sign-offs on emails or notes.

"I don't know, honestly. I'm hoping it's Pete, he's originally from just south of here, but I just talked to him a few weeks ago, and he was in DC." Matt finished putting on his kit, charging his M4, and ensuring a live round was in the chamber. "I'm going to walk out the basement door and slowly walk down the driveway to where I'm in view of the road. Whoever is there should see me and hopefully come out. I'd like you on the sniper rifle upstairs with Grace as your spotter. You know most of my friends from Lambda, so you have the best eye as to friend or foe."

"Pete? You think he's here? You sure, Matt? I mean, fuck, you don't really need to walk out there. Maybe we should post a reply note in the window."

Matt thought about it for a second. It was a pretty good idea - much safer than walking out there. But as he thought about he realized that it would be dark in thirty minutes. They didn't have time to wait to see if their note was read by whoever was across the road. Matt felt confident that this was a friend. No one else would take the time to write those letters, knowing they would mean so much.

"Yeah, I'm sure. I'll be careful. And I have you as my guardian angel." Matt gave her a quick kiss on the lips and then headed down the basement stairs.

Matt toggled his radio as he exited the outside door and walked around the side of the garage. "Listen up. I'm about to walk about halfway down the driveway. Alpha and Bravo, keep your weapons trained on the tree line across the road. I believe we have friends over there, so only fire when you are positive they are going to fire at me. If I'm right, one man will walk out of the woods, and he will be unarmed."

Matt walked down the driveway, carrying his M4 at the collapsed low ready position, his hands on his weapon but letting it dangle to his front, the barrel pointing towards the ground in front of him. He walked about forty yards to a point where the gravel driveway curved steeply downhill across the front of the yard. This was the crest of the rise that kept the farmhouse hidden from the road, and standing here, Matt had a full view of the paper sign posted to the tree. He also knew he would be visible to anyone in the woods. On a scale of one to ten, Matt's pucker factor had reached double digits.

Matt didn't want to toggle his radio, giving away the fact that he had backup. So he stood there and waited.

As expected, he didn't have to wait long. A man stood up behind the stone wall about thirty meters to the left of the paper sign. He held both hands high in the air, stepped over the wall, and began walking across the road toward the chained driveway. Matt recognized him instantly - his good friend Pete Rhodes.

Matt toggled his radio. "Do not shoot. Safe your weapons. This guy is a close friend. Keep scanning your sectors."

Matt thought of rushing down the driveway to greet his

friend, but he knew what Clare would say, so he waited and watched Pete approach. When he got to within about twenty yards, he could see the strain and exhaustion on Pete's face. Matt walked forward to close the gap with his friend, and they embraced in a powerful man hug.

"Man, am I glad to see you, Matt!" Pete said, clutching Matt tighter and clinging to him like a drowning swimmer to a life preserver. Matt knew immediately that one of his closest friends of twenty years had had a very rough few weeks.

"Jesus Christ, Pete. How the heck did you get here? Are you alone?" Matt pulled himself from the embrace and held his friend at arm's length, looking him up and down. Pete was dressed in civilian tactical clothes similar to Matt's, but he looked exhausted. He had lost quite a bit of weight since Matt had seen him a couple of months prior, and his funky smell was proof that he hadn't bathed in quite a while. Despite Pete's appearance, it was when Matt looked him in the eye that he realized the toll the last few weeks had taken on his friend. Pete's eyes had that shell-shocked look Matt had seen many times in teammates returning from an especially harrowing mission.

"Not alone. I'm with Liz and Stan White and his family. They're waiting just down this trail road behind us. Perkins Hill Road, the map says."

"What about Kelly?" Matt asked. As soon as the words left his mouth, Matt watched as Pete's entire face changed. Pete's stoic countenance evaporated, replaced by pure grief. His lower lip quivered, and Matt could feel Pete's shoulders tremble as he attempted to hold back his emotions. A tear fell slowly down Pete's cheek, carving a path through the grime caked on his face. The dam broke, and Pete sobbed into Matt's shoulder.

"She's gone, Matt. The fuckers killed her just outside of Albany." Pete regained his composure and wiped his eyes. He was not embarrassed to show emotion in front of his long-time friend, but he felt it was essential to keep a lid on his feelings. Matt could only imagine the heartache his friend was experiencing.

"Man, I am so, so sorry. Kelly was one of my favorite people in the entire world. Clare is going to be devastated. How's Liz holding up?" Matt said, hugging his friend tight again. Liz was Pete and Kelly's twenty-year-old daughter and also Matt and Clare's god-daughter. Matt had been in the waiting room when Liz was born and had remained close as she grew into a star volleyball player and current youngster Midshipman at the Naval Academy in Annapolis.

"She's tough, Matt. Way tougher than me. It's been a hell of a journey to get here. Literally, hell."

"Okay, man. Okay. I'm glad you're here, and now you're safe."

Matt broke their embrace and looked over Pete's shoulder down the road, where he could see the point where Perkins Hill Road intersected Sugarland Road about a hundred yards to their south. It was a rarely used dirt track that only showed on certain maps, but it eventually wound toward the Suicide Six ski mountain on the Pomfret Road. "I assume you have a vehicle? Let's get Liz and the others up to the house and figure out what's going on."

CHAPTER 5

September 29, 8:22 am

Rested and fed, the adults gathered around the family room table. Matt nursed the remnants of a cup of coffee with Clare sitting next to him in quiet conversation with two of their new guests, Liz and Marvi. Trays full of biscuits and mugs of steaming tea and coffee lay on the table for everyone to grab what they wanted. Matt grabbed a fresh cup of Molly's coffee, strong enough to walk into your cup on its own, and debated whether to snag another of her amazing biscuits. His brain said "no" but was overridden by his sense of smell which seemed to force his hand forward to grab one of the still-warm fat pills. As he took a bite, he surveyed the motley crew assembled around him.

Dylan, Amey, and Christopher were on guard duty, and it seemed everyone else was present, including their five newly-arrived friends. While Liz and Marvi sat to Matt's right on the other side of Clare, across from him sat Pete, Stan, and Juliet. Pete Rhodes was one of Matt's closest friends - a fraternity brother from the Lambda Iota fraternity at the University of Vermont. While Pete was two years older than Matt, they had shared countless fun times and adventures while in college and had stayed in close touch throughout the years. Pete, a dead ringer for Tom Cruise, had followed his penchant for dressing up for Halloween as Maverick from *Top Gun* or Lieutenant Kaffee from *A Few Good Men* by attending law school and joining the Navy as a JAG officer.

While serving in Hawaii as a young lieutenant, Pete had forged a close bond with Stan White, who was at that time a Lieutenant Commander and one of the Navy's rising stars. Stan was a former All-American basketball player at the Naval Academy who shocked everyone when he abruptly retired after serving his twenty years, even though he had been promoted below-zone to Captain, given command of one of the Navy's newest ships, and was undoubtedly destined to become an Admiral. At 6'6", his athletic build, dark skin, and good looks made many think he had gotten ahead by being African-American or good-looking. But Matt knew that Stan was one of the few true geniuses he had ever met and had turned down full computer science scholarships to MIT and Stanford to attend the Naval Academy. Upon retirement, Stan moved his family to Charlottesville and founded a tech company that had made Stan a billionaire.

Stan's wife, Marvi, was of Filipino descent with an undersized body and a supersized intellect. People often assumed they had met while Stan cruised the Pacific in the Navy, but they had actually met earning their MBAs at Stanford. While Stan was a computer genius, Marvi was the smartest one of the couple. She was one of the most interesting people Matt had ever met, having come from very humble beginnings and rising to found and lead several very successful companies. Matt had always enjoyed her company. Their daughter, Juliet, was a plebe at Annapolis and played on the volleyball team with Liz. Juliet and Liz had gone to high school together and were very close friends.

When Matt had started his consulting firm in Washington DC after grad school, Pete was in private practice in the city. He had helped Matt immensely as both an advisor, outside counsel, and unofficial lobbyist. Pete's connections in the government and private sector throughout the Beltway were extremely valuable in assisting Matt in growing his business. Five years ago, Pete had sold out his partnership in one of the capitol's leading law firms and moved to Charlottesville to become the general counsel for Stan's tech startup, QuAI. Quai, a word most frequently spelled as quay in English, was a play on the common definition of the "public street next to a ship, commonly referred to as a wharf," and the last two letters, AI. In a very short span, Stan and Pete built the firm to become one of the leading AI companies in the world, and Matt knew they performed a lot of Top Secret - Sensitive Compartmented Information work for various three-letter agencies of the US government.

Noticeably absent from the newcomers was Pete's wife, Kelly, and Stan's 20-year-old son, Emmett. Emmett had died of the Black Pox, and Kelly had been tragically killed by some rogue militia who attempted to stop the group at a roadblock outside Albany, New York. Pete had been too upset and exhausted last evening to tell them all the details, and Matt hoped to learn much more this morning.

As Matt watched Stan slowly eat a biscuit, he wondered how Stan and his family had gotten to this point. Matt had figured Stan would have been one of those invited to the President's bunker in Colorado or some other secure government facility.

"So Pete, I know you gave Clare and me a rundown last night, but for the benefit of everyone, would you mind telling your story again?"

"Uh, yeah, sure, Matt," Pete answered quietly, taking a sip from his mug and clearing his throat. "Well, on the morning of September 8th when the terrorists struck, Kelly and I were asleep in bed at our home in Charlottesville. Stan and Marvi were at their home down the road from us. Both our daughters were at school in Annapolis, and their son, Emmett, was at UVA across town. Sometime that morning, it's kind of a blur now and seems so long ago, Marvi invited Kelly and me over to their place to watch the news and be together. Emmett had biked the few miles home from college, and Stan and I kept trying to reach the girls at Navy. As you know, one of the bombs had basically wiped out DC, so we were concerned about what would happen to Liz and Juliet, who were only about fifty miles away from ground zero.

"We learned from the girls that they were being told they were going to bus all 4500 Midshipmen down to Naval Station Norfolk and stay there until things could be figured out. There were also rumors that they'd be offered leave, but no one really knew what was going on. Stan somehow got through to Admiral Ruck, the Superintendent, and finagled permission to have both girls take leave. By late morning Stan and I were on the company's helicopter en route to Annapolis to pick the girls up. The airspace had been shut down, but somehow Stan was able to get clearance - or maybe we did it without clearance, I don't know. We picked up three other Midshipmen who were from the Charlottesville area, and we were all home for a late lunch.

"As Marvi and Kelly can attest...." Pete winced, the raw sting of his wife's death still piercing his heart. Taking a sip of coffee, he pushed back the grief as Liz began sobbing quietly and Kelsey rubbed her back in comfort. "As Marvi can attest, Stan and I both have a bit of prepper gene in us, so we each had quite a cache of supplies. At the time, we were mostly concerned with loss of power and disruption of government services, so we decided it made sense for us all to hunker down at Stan and Marvi's for the time being. We all spent the first couple of days shuttling supplies and things from our house up the hill to Stan's.

"I know you and Clare have been there quite a few times, but for everyone else, Stan and Marvi have a pretty amazing house built on a hill a few miles outside of Charlottesville. It had plenty of space for all of us, seemed quite secure, and also had generator backup, as well as being pretty remote. As things deteriorated and the Black Pox became a reality, we realized we had made the right call, and Stan's place would be the best place to survive the apocalypse. Life was pretty normal for the first ten days or so."

"So, what caused you to leave?" Brent asked, sitting with Amey on the couch in the family room.

Another expression of pain crossed Pete's face. Before he could answer, Stan spoke first. "Initially the vaccine, but ultimately it was The Base and their reign of terror that forced us to flee."

"The Base?" interjected Amey. "Are they real? I had begun seeing rumors of them online before we lost the internet, but I thought they were in Pennsylvania or something like that?"

"Oh, they're fucking real," said Pete, taking back his position as narrator. "They killed Kelly, and I think it's just a question of time before they get to places like here." He paused, trying to remember where he had left off before Brent's question. "So before The Base, it was the vaccine that caused us to leave our little fortress in the hills. Emmett got sick...."

Everyone followed Pete's glance toward Marvi and immediately realized what likely had happened.

Pete continued, "We weren't 100% sure he had the pox, but he was showing a fever, and we knew he could have been exposed. This was right when the President gave his vaccine speech, and Charlottesville was still functioning somewhat. Emmett went into town a couple of times to trade for supplies we thought we were missing, and when he broke out with a fever, we didn't want to take any chances. The main National Guard unit in Virginia had a headquarters in Staunton, about thirty miles away, so Stan and I decided to make a road trip to see if we could score some vaccine. Emmett was quarantined in a bedroom over the garage, but we were also worried that all of us could have already been exposed.

"Did Staunton have the vaccine?" asked Matt, not having heard this part from Pete last night.

"Yeah. Yeah, they did. One of the Guard officers there worked at QuAI, so it was quite simple once she recognized us. Stan and I each received a vaccine injection right in their office. They gave us vials and needles to inject the entire family, and we spoke for a few minutes with the acting commander. While that armory itself was quite calm, everywhere else was a complete shit show. Their plan was to deliver cases of vaccines to major hospitals along the I-81 corridor - Charlottesville, James Madison in Harrisonburg, Lexington, Winchester, Hagerstown, et cetera. But evidently, this armed militia group calling itself "The Base" was attacking their convoys and the actual hospitals themselves and stealing the vaccine."

"They did that here as well," Matt said. "Except it was a motorcycle gang, not a militia."

"But why would they want to steal the vaccine?" asked Kelsey.

"Because it's the most valuable commodity in the world right now, my dear Kelsey," Pete replied. Everyone in the room sat back for a second in their chair, fully comprehending the reality of how valuable the vaccine was. The vaccine was like water in the middle of a desert - the only salvation for survival against the deadly Black Pox.

Not wanting more questions to distract him, Pete forged on, recounting their story. "So Stan and I received the vaccine right at the armory in Staunton, and they gave us a small glass bottle and a box of needles. They told us the vial contained fifty doses of the vaccine. We drove straight back to Stan's place and injected everyone. Emmett had a blazing fever, but we were hopeful he was going to pull through as he had yet to develop any of the pustules that come in the advanced stages of the pox." Pete paused to grab a water bottle from the center of the table, unscrewed the cap, and took a sip. "We were wrong. By the morning, Emmett's fever had spiked, and we knew we were too late. He died in his bed later that evening."

Everyone in the room had tears in their eyes, although most had never met Emmett or any of the White family. Clare hugged Marvi tightly, and Stan stared blankly down at the table. After a moment, Pete continued. "So, at this point, I think it was just about a week ago...."

"Six days. September 23rd," said Stan, barely above a whisper.

"Yes, right," Pete continued. "So the next day, the afternoon of the 24th, Kelly and I walked down the road to several of the neighbors and administered the vaccine. Like us, these people had basically been hunkering down. At the fourth house we went to, we had a conversation with a guy through the door as he wouldn't open up. He was an older gentleman, had full-blown pox, and told us it was too late for him. His wife had just died that morning, but what he told us was extremely interesting. He said Charlottesville was now controlled by The Base and that this militia - many wearing full Army uniforms and quite possibly defectors from the Guard - were disarming people and keeping all the females under forty or so in town. Men were allowed to go home and could keep one hunting rifle, but any pistols or assault rifles had to be turned in. He also said they had pardoned all the inmates in jails across the state."

"Why were they keeping the females?" Matt asked, his voice neutral.

"Well, the old guy told us that the militia said they were keeping the girls and women safe as there were roving renegades throughout Virginia who were still looting and raping, especially in small towns. The neighbor said he knew the militia was lying, but he was glad his daughters lived in California and outside the reach of these hooligans."

"That's pretty fucked up," blurted Derek as all the younger people around the table nodded their heads in agreement.

"Well said, Derek, it most certainly is," said Stan. "Obviously, Marvi and I are completely devastated by Emmett's death, but I think it's important to also understand that we had a lot more information than what we heard from this neighbor." Matt and Stan had become quite close friends socially over the years and had also worked together on occasion as their businesses had overlapped on several very Top Secret projects. Stan's QuAI was on the IT and intelligence side, while Matt's was operational. The three couples - the Whites, the Rhodes, and the Sheridans - got along extremely well, and the three families had vacationed together several times. Christopher, now on watch upstairs in the Lookout, was absolutely devastated to learn of Emmett's death, as Emmett was one of his heroes. "After the nukes destroyed eight US cities, followed by the retaliatory nuclear attacks as part of Operation Hellfire, we activated a contingency plan at QuAI that secured the entire facility against any possible incursion. There is zero chance that an unauthorized person can access the QuAI data center and its artificial intelligence deep-learning capabilities. The only way to gain access would be a significant amount of explosives, and any successful breach would result in the complete self-destruction of the entire facility. That said, I maintained a very robust remote access capability from my home - a capability that is portable and now currently stored in the back of the Range Rover outside."

"You can get online now?" Amey asked.

"Well, technically yes, but it's not quite that simple. Why don't we table that for now, as I think it's important you understand our journey and how we ended up here," continued Stan. "As the Black Pox pandemic began and the internet was still mostly functional, QuAI offered us the ability to gather real-time information from across the globe and synthesize this information into our data center. Using our deep learning algorithms, we were able to both draw conclusions and make reasonably accurate predictions about what was happening.

"A few things became obvious to us. First, the world's population was dying off rapidly, and the vaccine had almost entirely failed to curb the death toll. QuAI predictions were that somewhere around 95% of the world's population would be dead by the end of September. The models predicted a continued slow decline stabilizing at 3.7% of the world's population by the end of the year. In numerical terms, we're talking about the global population shrinking from 7.8 billion people to under 300 million. That's globally! In the United States, less than 15 million people would survive out of the 330 million Americans that populated our country in August. About 500,000 people remaining in New England and 20,000 in Vermont. These numbers were absolutely staggering."

"Those are in line with Amey's and my estimates that we've

been using as well," said Matt. "Sorry to interrupt. Please continue."

"Yes, well, the population estimates were pretty straightforward, and most people listening to the President's speech and doing the calculations would come up with similar figures. What QuAI provided us that no one else had was the ability to continue to collect an absolutely enormous amount of data from the internet - scouring the globe but primarily focused on the United States and putting all of these tiny, disparate bits of data together into a cohesive information framework. The internet was down in many places, but QuAI still retained some access through satellite connections, as well as a tremendous data bank collected before things went dark. From this, the AI computer could learn and continue to develop conclusions and projections. In simple terms, QuAI could tell us what threats we were likely to face in the coming weeks and months so that we could plan our defenses. And what kept coming up repeatedly was, you guessed it, The Base.

"I can get into as much detail as you want, but for now, QuAI offered up several conclusions that completely blew our minds. First, The Base was a centrally-led group focused on exerting complete control over the mid-Atlantic and southern New England States. Second, it was initially organized before the attacks of September 8th, and third, The Base's origins and leadership are Islamic fundamentalists cloaked as American patriots."

Most in the room looked at Stan as if he had sprouted a penis in the middle of his forehead. Matt, unsure how to respond, took a sip from his now cold coffee. Clare couldn't tell if the grimace on Matt's face was from the remnants of the brew or the stink bomb Stan had dropped on them. She'd been quiet all morning and decided to speak up.

"Okay, Stan. We obviously have no reason to doubt the veracity of those conclusions. Putting the implications of this bombshell aside, what made you all leave the safety of your home in Charlottesville? It seems like you were quite well situated there."

"Great question, Clare. And the answer, I'm afraid, goes back once more to QuAI. With all the information downloaded to the servers in the data center and the internet's footprint dwindling significantly as most of the US and the world went dark, I began querying QuAI's deep learning to have it make some informed predictions. Please remember, because of our contracts, QuAI has not only access to all open-source information but also a significant amount of classified intelligence as well, so its output includes information that no one else in the world has full access to. Additionally, QuAI doesn't access the internet like most computers. Her system uses dedicated fiber optic lines, cellular as well as satellite. Even with the power out or unreliable throughout much of the world, QuAI still retained some access to data resources and collection sensors such as satellites.

"In very brief terms, QuAI made it clear that The Base was focused on completely dominating the swath of territory from Massachusetts to Maryland and had plans to create the equivalent of a totalitarian caliphate in this area prior to expanding outwards. It would be outwardly secular, with none of the religious trappings normally associated with Islamic fundamentalism, but its rule would make the Taliban look like progressive Democrats. They wanted full control over the female population as forced labor and wives and had very organized plans for rebuilding the economy and exerting influence over the rest of North America. And lastly, according to QuAI, their plans were very likely, almost certain, to succeed. At least in the short term."

"Why choose this part of the US? Because it's the most densely populated? Access to the eastern seaboard?" Matt asked.

"Actually, it was selected for one simple reason. These states all have the lowest percentage of gun ownership per household and were seen as the most likely to support a strong, centralized government offering them protection."

Matt and the rest of the family sat back, continuing to be stunned by each revelation.

"You mean they think New England and the Mid-Atlantic states are sheep?" Derek asked.

Stan chuckled for the first time in several days. "Well, that would certainly be oversimplifying it, but generally speaking, you are correct."

"Okay," said Matt. "So why would you want to drive into this area? Why not stay in Virginia? Or head south?"

As Stan started to answer, Pete spoke over him, taking back control of the conversation. "Partly because of you and Clare, but mostly because QuAI said northern New England was likely to be somewhat safe through next year and that heading south with no real connections to an established safe haven would be extremely risky for our families. Driving through the Carolinas or heading West was fraught with a tremendous amount of violence, risk, and uncertainty. The computer models suggested that if we could get through Pennsylvania and north of New York and Massachusetts prior to The Base solidifying its hold, we would have the best chance for long-term survival."

"But Clare and I were in Rhode Island when the bombs went off. What made you think we were here? I mean, we're happy to have you, but I don't know why you'd make such a long journey to come to a place you didn't know we'd be at?"

"Did you forget I'm from Vermont, Matt?"

"Shit, yeah, I guess I did. I think of you as a true Beltway bandit!" Matt joked.

"Touche! Yeah. After going through all the scenarios with Stan, it made sense to head for Vermont. If we struck out here, we had options to head toward St. Johnsbury or even over to northern New Hampshire or Maine."

"So what happened on the trip? What route did you take?"

"Well, we really didn't make this decision until after Emmett died, which coincided with The Base's presence really starting to be felt throughout the Blue Ridge Mountain area of

Virginia. Once we started planning for this seriously, we came up with a pretty circuitous route. Basically, we cut west to West Virginia and then up through the center of Pennsylvania to near Binghamton, New York. Then we'd drive over to the west side of Albany before turning east through southern Vermont. QuAI plotted a route of secondary roads though the least populated areas and farthest away from reported violent incidents."

"I know you told Clare and me last night about what happened to Kelly, but would you mind sharing that with the group? Most of you have met Kelly quite a few times, but for those of you new to the family, Kelly was one of Clare's and my dearest friends and Laurie's godmother."

"And my soulmate," said Pete softly. Clearing his throat, Pete continued. "Everything went surprisingly well. We traveled from before dawn until after dark each day, following the route planned by QuAI. We had selected our 4-door Jeep along with Stan's Land Rover Defender to go in a 2-vehicle convoy and added a small trailer behind the Land Rover that we filled with fuel cans and supplies. We made great time following a route that was generally along US 219. The first night we made it as far as a state forest just north of State College, Pennsylvania. We parked in the middle of nowhere, and Stan and I stayed up most of the night pulling guard duty.

"We departed before first light the next morning with the goal of making it to somewhere past Cooperstown, New York. On this second day, we traveled quite a bit slower as we were seeing signs of more people. Two of us would go first in the Jeep, with the Land Rover following about two hundred yards behind. We had radios for comms. One of the best things about working at QuAI is that we had some excellent portable battery solutions, so power wasn't an issue. Remind me to show you all that stuff later today. We were on schedule, having traveled over three hundred miles in about fourteen hours when it started to get dark. We were northeast of Cooperstown, approaching the small town of Cherry Valley, when we came upon a roadblock. It was just Kelly and me in the Jeep, and I immediately radioed for Stan to stop before coming within sight of the roadblock. At first, I thought maybe the guys at the roadblock hadn't seen us and we could back up, but two motorcycles raced out from behind the roadblock and braced us between them, their headlights illuminating our Jeep. I told Kelly to keep her AR-15 below the open window but to be ready to use it, and I slowly stepped out with my hands raised. These guys clearly were not up to any good and forced me at gunpoint to put my hands on the hood while the other guy pointed a gun at Kelly. A third guy walked up from the roadblock. They were all dressed in old-school Army BDUs with woodland camo pattern but had civilian boots and no insignia or rank. One guy said that they were, quote - *the military representatives of The Base, the constitutional authority that governed all of New York* - endquote, and then informed me that he was confiscating both my vehicle and my female passenger. I had the distinct impression that I was not going to be left alive, and my mind was racing with how to get out of this jam. Suddenly a shot rang out, and the man closest to Kelly dropped like a stone. Knowing it was Stan in overwatch, I lunged for the guy covering me as more shots shattered the night's quiet. I wrestled with my guy, somehow able to pull my K-bar and stick it through the back of his skull. I pulled my pistol and jumped up to look for other targets. Both men were down, and I could see Stan running up along the side of the road."

Pete paused, looking down at his hands. Clearly, he was reliving the moment and having difficulty finding words. Stan began to speak, but Pete waved him away. "It's okay, Stan. I'd like to finish. I owe it to Kelly to tell her friends how she died."

Pete continued looking up and scanning to make eye contact with almost everyone in the room. "When I looked to the passenger seat, I saw that Kelly had been shot. One of these fucking barbarians had shot her point blank in the throat. I jumped through the driver's door and tried to apply pressure, but I knew it was too late. There was just too much blood. It was everywhere. Kelly was trying to speak, her eyes glued to mine, pleading...."

"It's okay, Pete. It's okay," said Matt, leaning forward. Stan had his arm around Pete, and Kelsey walked over to hug him. Pete began sobbing silently.

They all sat there, most looking down, thinking about their lost friend. Matt slowly and subconsciously shook his head, knowing full well that events could have easily gone differently for his family over the last three weeks. Matt was not a praying man, but he was grateful he still had all of his loved ones around him.

Matt was about to ask Stan a question when Pete emerged from his thoughts and continued the story. "So I made the decision to bury Kelly there, knowing it made no sense to travel with her body. Stan and I looked at the map and saw Glimmerglass State Park on the shores of Lake Otsego was only about ten miles away. I remembered the lake from a trip Kelly and I took to the Baseball Hall of Fame in Cooperstown, and I thought it would be an appropriate spot for her last resting place. We drove her there, buried her overlooking the lake, and then cleaned the Jeep as best we could with lake water. We then drove the hundred and eighty miles from there to here, sticking almost solely to dirt roads. It took almost twenty-four hours, but now we're here."

"She was an amazing woman," said Clare, then turned towards Liz. "I know how proud your mother was of you, Liz. You're almost all she spoke of. You are now fully part of this family. All of you."

"Yeah," Matt added. "Pete, we've been brothers since UVM, and you and Liz have always been a part of our family. Stan, Marvi, Juliet - you are now part of this clan as well, for as long as you like. There are sixteen of us now, and together we *will* survive this cataclysm." Matt looked at every person in the room, making eye contact until everyone nodded in the affirmative. "Okay, we have lots to talk about and even more to do. Stan, Pete, and Marvi, Clare, and I'd like to give you a full tour of the property and our preparations. While we're doing that, Molly, maybe you could take everyone not on guard duty and help integrate all the supplies and other new items we have?"

CHAPTER 6

September 29, 2:14 pm

Matt sat in his little command post in the basement, his feet propped on Donald's old desk as he looked at the whiteboard on the wall in front of him. The last few hours with Pete and Stan had been extremely enlightening, and Matt's brain was revving with the myriad options, possibilities, and risks that lay before him and his now 16-strong extended family.

He could faintly hear Clare, Molly, and Marvi outside his door as they organized items in what they now referred to as the "supply room" portion of the basement. Marvi, in addition to her Stanford MBA and engineering skills, was an accomplished chef who had not only written numerous cookbooks but had invested in several successful restaurants. Her experience with food storage and meal planning was welcomed openly by Clare and Molly, and they were now sorting through and integrating the supplies the newcomers had brought. Everyone else not on sentry duty was upstairs, either working the newest jigsaw puzzle or napping.

Matt idly twirled a dry-erase marker with his fingers, tapping each end lightly on the desk as it completed a rotation in his hand. The metronomic tapping of the marker helped focus Matt's thoughts as he stared at the blank space he had recently created by wiping clean the left side of the whiteboard on the wall before him.

The new arrivals had added significantly to the Sheridan clan's capabilities to survive. However, in keeping with Matt's personality and overactive mind, he was constantly trying to plan further into the future to ensure success. After spending the morning with Stan and Pete, Matt was taking a quiet moment to mentally absorb all the new capabilities into the survival plan he had been refining since the moment they had fled their house in Rhode Island.

The QuAI computer was a potential game-changer, but only if they could somehow get it back online and connected to whatever was left of the internet. Similarly, not only did the newcomers give them five more workers, sentries, and shooters, but the combined expertise of all five significantly added to their capabilities. All aside from Marvi had military training, although Matt joked to himself that he wasn't sure if the Navy really counted as military, and the combined intellectual horsepower of the Rhodes and White families was incalculable.

After staring at the whiteboard and contemplating silently for about thirty minutes, Matt finally felt that he had refined his thoughts to the point he could capture them on the wall. Standing up with his green dry-erase marker, Matt stepped over to the whiteboard and wrote three bullets:

- *Nomad = The Base ???*
- *Comms*
- *Winter*

Stepping back to look at his words, he reached out and jotted two additional items below the bottom bullet: *Smoke* and *Snow*.

Matt dropped into Donald's plush leather desk chair, leaned back, and put both feet up on the desk again. This was basically the same pose he had held for the previous thirty minutes, but instead of tapping the dry-erase marker on the desk blotter, Matt tapped the green marker aimlessly against his lips. Deep in thought, admiring the words on the board and trying to see if there was anything to add or if these bullets accurately captured their current predicament.

Before Matt had cleaned the whiteboard to make space

for these new bullets, the board was filled with other words such as defensive perimeter, weapons training, rationing plan, and evacuation, among other dry-erase notations in various colors. Nodding his head subconsciously, Matt was satisfied these three new bullets, *Nomad, Comms,* and *Winter*, were the three most important things they needed to now address.

The first bullet was crucial to every aspect of their future survival. *Were the Nomads a part of this new "The Base" group that Stan and Pete had described?* As an outlaw motorcycle gang, Matt was somewhat confident they could elude, deter, defend, and possibly even defeat any rogue marauders that might continue to target his family. Matt also knew that their group was now large enough to consider offensive raids and ambushes that would keep the Nomads away from Sugarland Road and the family safe in their current hideaway.

However, if the Nomads were an actual subsidiary of The Base, it would be a completely different situation altogether. Whereas Matt felt the Nomads motorcycle gang would get substantially weaker and less organized throughout the winter, it was clear from Stan and Pete that The Base was only getting stronger. Once The Base had a complete stranglehold on Massachusetts, Connecticut, and New York, it was just a matter of time before they continued their expansion into southern Vermont. With the Nomads a part of The Base, Matt no longer had the option of killing the Nomad leadership as a means of cutting the head off the snake, for The Base would simply continue to replace the leadership group - likely with ever-more ruthless leaders. Instead of withering away, a Base-supported Nomad gang would get stronger through the winter and seek out and destroy any opponents they felt were threatening. Confirming the linkage between the Nomads and The Base was critical to Matt's future plans for survival.

The second bullet, *Comms*, could possibly help answer the question posed by this first bullet. Upon returning from giving Stan, Pete, and Marvi the tour of the farmhouse's property and defensive positions, Matt watched Liz supervising the setup of the QuAI servers in the workbench area of the basement. A cyber-security major at Annapolis, Liz had been interested in computers her entire life. Now she ran cables between the four stacked server racks connected to two laptops and what appeared to be portable SSD hard drives stacked on top of one another. Two large, hardened plastic cases sat open on the floor, and Matt could see from the foam cutouts that all of this equipment had been packed securely in these crates for movement. As he watched, Liz started a running commentary about the cost and capabilities of this portable QuAI machine, most of which Matt immediately forgot. He did retain that each rack cost more than a quarter of a million dollars and contained eight of the latest NVIDIA graphics servers. Networked with external hard drives, this AI learning machine could provide a stunning array of information on virtually any subject. When connected remotely to the main QuAI data center, this was one of the most powerful computing machines in the world. Given all that had happened over the past three weeks, Matt wondered if this were perhaps *the* most powerful computer in the world, right here in his brother's farmhouse basement. They could only run the computer system for short periods of time because of the drain on their generator. Still, even in short increments, the benefit the information QuAI could provide would be incalculable.

Other than maps, graphics, and historical information, the QuAI computer was not extremely useful to the farmhouse's defense or the family's survival. However, based on earlier comments by Stan and Marvi, there was the potential to use this portable machine and some satellite telecom equipment Stan had packed to connect their computer to existing satellites. If successful, this would allow them to search for other communications stations worldwide. This communication could be instrumental in directing their path to survival and connecting with similar groups in the US to build alliances. Matt knew the sixteen of them could only stand their ground for so long on their own. At the moment, their key to survival was remaining hidden from any force stronger than themselves.

This brought Matt to bullet point number three - *Winter.* On the 8th of September, Matt's goal was to have enough resources and supplies for his family to survive the thirty days of chaos Matt expected after the terrorist attacks. With the Black Pox pandemic, Matt refined his planning to ensure they could survive at least six months - and there was no doubt that they currently had the food, fuel, and supplies to easily make it through to April of next year. With less than 5% of the population surviving, Matt felt confident in their ability to forage for shelf-stable food in nearby homes and stores and to keep food on the table by butchering local cows, keeping hens and chickens, and fishing the pond on the property. These food sources would allow Matt's family to survive indefinitely, and this wasn't even factoring in their ability to initiate farming on their own property next spring.

The two aspects of winter that concerned Matt the most were *Smoke* and *Snow*. When most people think of winter survival, they think of shelter, food, and warmth. These were not issues for the Sheridan family as they had plenty of food, almost a full tank of propane for cooking, and a dozen cords of split firewood that would last them several winters. These issues were dealt with in Survival 101, and Matt knew he had progressed well passed the Ph.D. level when it came to surviving in today's world. The existence of the Nomads and The Base, both possibly searching for Matt's family and the case of vaccine they currently possessed, added a dimension to survival that deeply concerned Matt. *How to remain hidden when the temperature drops?*

The nights would begin dipping below freezing by the end of October, and by mid-November, they could expect regular snowfall. By mid-December, it was almost certain that the ground would be covered by snow, and this snow cover would last until March. The need to heat the house came with freezing temperatures, and burning wood in the wood stove created smoke. This smoke could be seen for miles during the day. Even if Matt restricted the use of the wood stove to the evenings when the smoke would be invisible, the smell of burning wood was likely to permeate the surrounding area, and anyone passing by would know there were survivors nearby.

The problem created by snow was even more daunting. Once snowfall accumulated and remained on the ground, the family's movements would be severely restricted. Any footprints or vehicle tracks they created would be impossible to erase and would lead directly back to the farmhouse. While Matt came up with several ideas to reduce or obfuscate these tracks, no matter how much he racked his brain, he could not devise a method that would allow them to leave the property without leaving some form of trail for an enemy to follow.

Whereas Matt initially thought he had until spring to come up with some long-term solutions, he now realized he likely had less than a month before winter made things infinitely more difficult for his family to survive.

CHAPTER 7

September 30, 11:31 pm

Matt lay prone on the flat roof of a one-story commercial building on the northwest side of Route 4, on the east side of the downtown area of Woodstock. Matt realized he was only about two hundred meters from the Windsor County Sheriff's Office, where he had almost met his demise the previous week. Matt was in a comfortable spot that afforded him views to the northeast along Route 4 and felt confident he could both see and hear someone coming with at least several minutes of warning. He breathed deeply, savoring the fresh evening air, a sharp contrast to the putrid smell of the buildings in town that he and Dylan had searched last night. This was his second night on patrol, and in a few minutes, he expected to hear on the radio that his crew was entering the town.

Yesterday afternoon, after spending considerable time strategizing future plans, Matt gathered the family and discussed what he felt were some of their highest priorities. At the meeting, he also welcomed input from the newcomers and found many of their comments and ideas extremely useful. The result was that all agreed that Matt and Dylan would do a 24-hour reconnaissance of Woodstock to get a better feel of what was happening a week after their clash with Tate and his Nomad crew at the sheriff's office.

Last evening the two of them had dressed warmly and loaded up with weapons, optics, some food, and a couple of poncho liners. They had used the rising moon's light to noiselessly bike down Sugarland Road, past Billings Farm, and into the heart of downtown Woodstock. Their first stop was the First Congregational Church on the corner of Elm and Pleasant streets, which Matt was reasonably confident would be empty and provide both a place to stash their mountain bikes as well as an excellent view from the top of the church's historic clock tower. They found a perch on the open-air railed landing above the clock, almost five stories above ground, and spent the next four hours scoping every inch of downtown Woodstock and its approaches.

Matt had selected Dylan as his companion and spotter even though everyone else had also volunteered for the mission. Matt knew this was potentially an extremely hazardous mission, and to him, Dylan seemed the obvious choice. Dylan was extremely athletic and had tremendous strength and endurance, but he had also proven himself a steady spotter and capable in combat. Most importantly, by taking Dylan, Matt left all of the experienced adults to defend the farmhouse and the family. If something were to happen to Matt and Dylan, the family's best chance of survival was to have the most experienced decision-makers and gunfighters back at the house.

Just after 2 am, after spending almost four hours and seeing nothing but nocturnal animals, Matt decided it was time to start looking around on foot. He and Dylan had already decided on the route they would take, and their goal was to get to the Windsor County courthouse no later than 5 am. The courthouse, situated directly on the south side of Route 4 west of the center of town, was another historic building with a steepled tower that Matt felt would make a great sniper perch to spend the daylight hours. The primary goal of this excursion was to recon for the presence of the Nomads or any other hostile or potentially friendly forces that might be present in town.

Matt and Dylan leapfrogged down Elm Street to Route 4, which was referred to as Central Street in the downtown area of Woodstock. Gillingham's General Store still had its green awning proclaiming its existence since 1896, but that was now about the only part of the store still existing. The front windows were shattered, the door completely missing, and a glance inside from the sidewalk showed that it had been completely looted. The rancid smell of decaying food made Dylan retch as they walked by. Across the street, the block of buildings where the bank and Bentley's restaurant had been was now just burnt husks, the result of the big fire Matt had seen through the telescope after the Black Pox pandemic had begun. Matt was disappointed that the Yankee Bookshop was also completely gutted as he had hoped to pick up some detailed maps. They could also see another block of a half-dozen burned buildings across the street, but the shops further down Central Street on both sides appeared intact.

They planned to recon slowly up Central Street to the east as far as Mac's Market, then turn south and double back through some neighborhood streets to the Woodstock Inn and the elementary school. Matt felt confident this route would provide them evidence of anyone remaining in Woodstock, friend or foe. The late-September night was brisk, and as the pair progressed east, the breeze carried the faint scent of decay. They walked very slowly, mostly weaving through driveways and open areas on the north side of the road to avoid walking straight down Central Street.

The pre-cataclysm population of greater Woodstock was about 4,000 people. Given the 4% survival rate Stan and the QuAI computer predicted, less than 150 people likely remained in Woodstock. That said, Matt was pretty confident that the current town population was exactly zero, as anyone remaining would likely have been taken by the Nomads or National Guard. Those with the intelligence to survive and the capability to flee would have left the town weeks ago for a more secure place in the surrounding mountains.

Matt and Dylan made note of a couple of stores that might prove useful; otherwise, Woodstock was completely abandoned, destroyed, and otherwise useless to them. As they crept up on Mac's Market, the only grocery store in town, Matt knew that it, too, was not going to provide anything useful. The windows were smashed, and even from his position across the street, the putrid smell of rotting food was overpowering. Matt could see almost a dozen human bodies littering the small parking lot and knew that any non-perishable food items had likely been looted long ago. He and Dylan turned south and tread carefully towards Lincoln Street, leapfrogging each other using bounding overwatch positions, then turned back west to follow Slayton Terrace over to High Street. Turning due west on Cross Street would then bring them along the back side of the Woodstock Inn, and Matt figured this and the Woodstock elementary school across the street would be the most likely center of any remaining activity in the town.

As he and Dylan stealthily made their way behind a parking lot and through some neighborhood yards to a position about a half-block due south of the back of the Woodstock Inn, they both began gagging from the stench. Matt covered his mouth and nose with the bandana wrapped around his neck and gestured for Dylan to do the same. Not quick enough, Dylan dropped to his knees and tried to wretch as silently as possible, unable to push down the queasiness in his stomach and prevent himself from vomiting. With Dylan continuing to dry-heave a few yards to his right, Matt took a knee behind a stone wall and began scoping the back of the inn.

Utilizing the AN/PVS-30 night vision sight acquired from the Sheriff's armory, Matt could see quite clearly into the rear of the Woodstock Inn, albeit through a green tint. Two ambulances were parked haphazardly on the grassy area beside what appeared to be several large rectangular military tents. Matt instantly realized that this area had likely been set up as a triage or collection point once the Black Pox pandemic began. Traversing his sight to the right, Matt could see what appeared to be body bags stacked next to several shipping containers. With his knowledge of emergency responses to a pandemic, Matt surmised this area was a temporary morgue and knew instantly the source of the overpowering stench that was making Dylan gag. Without power, the mobile morgues were unable to keep the corpses cool, and over the last week or two, the bodies had begun to decay significantly.

Sensing rapid movement to his left, Matt shifted his rifle to be able to see the source, wondering if he and Dylan had been spotted. After a few seconds of traversing his scope, Matt watched as several dogs sprinted across the open ground dragging what appeared to be the upper torso of a human body. The makeshift morgue had become a cafeteria for the wild animals in the area, and Matt knew there must be large numbers of abandoned dogs that were now becoming feral after being abandoned by their owners, left behind either intentionally or through death.

Not wishing to stay in the zone of putrid death behind the inn, Matt zeroed in on the elementary school across South Street as well as the surrounding buildings. Besides a few more roving animals, Matt could not spot any indications of human life anywhere in the town of Woodstock. This confirmed the previous afternoon's consensus at the family meeting and allowed Matt to move on to their next objective.

After reconning the town, the plan was for Matt and Dylan to set up in the wooden cupola atop the Windsor County courthouse a block to the northeast of the Windsor Inn. Providing long-range views to both the east and west along Route 4, this was the position Matt and Dylan planned to remain for the entirety of the coming day. Matt hoped the prevailing winds would remain coming from the east, relieving him and Dylan from having to withstand the smell of rotting flesh throughout the heat of the day.

Based on the information they gathered from Tate about the Nomads, Matt knew that the Nomad headquarters was apparently located at Dartmouth College. He assumed that the Nomads had control of the I-89 bridge across the Connecticut River in West Lebanon as well as a likely presence in White

River Junction - all places well to the east of Woodstock. The goal of this part of the recon was to see if anyone approached Woodstock from the west.

The pair had bedded down in the tower of the courthouse by 4 am, and Dylan had quickly fallen asleep, with Matt taking the first two-hour watch. After an uneventful shift, the two had switched places, and Matt had slept soundly until nudged by Dylan's boot. Matt glanced at his watch. 6:52 am.

"Matt, wake up," whispered Dylan, trying to be quiet and urgent at the same time. "A vehicle's coming."

Instantly awake, Matt sat up and looked to the east, where Dylan was gesturing. Sure enough, he could hear the approach of a diesel engine. The sun was up, and the morning was quite cool, but without any competing manmade sounds, he and Dylan could distinctly hear the engine's whine as its transmission cycled through gears heading through town. Matt immediately recognized the sound as coming from a military HMMWV (pronounced "Humvee"). He had hundreds, if not thousands, of hours riding or sitting in one, and the sound of a HMMWV to an infantry soldier was distinct.

The railings around the cupola allowed Matt and Dylan to remain in prone positions and still have excellent east and west views down Route 4. They both watched from a hidden position as the vehicle approached, and Matt was confident there was no possibility they would be seen. With no traffic, the HMMWV drove at what Matt estimated to be about forty miles per hour through town, from east to west. He was expecting the vehicle to slow at some point, with Woodstock being its likely destination, but the HMMWV kept coming and zoomed right by their position above the courthouse. Watching it speed westward, Matt lost sight of the vehicle within seconds.

As the sounds of silence returned to Woodstock, Matt told Dylan, "Looked to me like a New Hampshire National Guard soft-shell Humvee with open back - driver, TC, and four passengers. Vehicle-mounted 240 Bravo and pax all had M4s."

Dylan stared back at him, his mouth hanging open slightly. "Ummm, if you mean a Hummer with five people and some guns, then I agree."

Matt laughed quietly. "It's Humvee, bud. Hummers are the yellow SUVs that Yuppees drive - a High-Mobility Multi-Wheeled Vehicle or Humvee is what the military uses."

"Gotcha. My bad," replied Dylan, eager to learn but also not caring too much about military terminology.

"So what else did we see? And what did we learn," queried Matt, wanting to use this as a teaching opportunity.

"They were Nomads."

"How could you tell?" Matt asked, already knowing the answer.

"The driver had one of those leather cuts on like the others wore."

"That's right. Good job. What else?"

"Mmmm, they weren't that concerned about anyone attacking them."

"And what gave you that conclusion?"

"Because they had a machine gun mounted on the roof, but no one was standing behind it, like in videos from Iraq and Afghanistan."

"Exactly!" Matt concurred. "Good job picking all that up in just a few seconds. That's the key to being good at recon. Anything else? Could you tell where they were going? Or where they were coming from?"

Dylan thought for a second, a slight frown on his face. "Ummm, no. They came from the east, but I don't think we know if they were coming or going or anything like that."

"Okay," replied Matt, "Fair enough. We can't tell where they're going, but I do think we can surmise that it's somewhere local."

"How can you draw that conclusion?"

"Well, it was an open-sided HMMWV with doors down and an open back cargo area. They had a full house - driver, a guy riding shotgun who's also referred to as the TC or the tank commander. I know, it's not a tank, but that's what he's called. Plus two guys in the rear passenger seats and two on the cargo floor in back. Did you see any bags? Or fuel cans?"

"No, just five guys and most seem to have an AR-15 or M4. No bags."

"Good. I agree. So to me, that likely means they're going somewhere fairly close and likely not planning to stay too long. Otherwise, they'd bring fuel cans - no more gas stations, right? And also likely bags."

"Yeah, good point," agreed Dylan. "So how did you know the vehicle was from the New Hampshire National Guard, Uncle Matt?"

Matt laughed lightly. "Well, that's something you'd know if you were in the Army, but I wouldn't expect anyone non-military to look for. Every vehicle has the unit stenciled on the front and rear bumpers. In this case, it was easy to see it said NHARNG on the bumper. I think it said 1-103, but I'm not sure what kind of unit. LT might know."

"Okay."

"So what do you think it means that Nomads are driving National Guard vehicles and seemingly unconcerned with security?"

"It means they control this place. Maybe all of this part of Vermont and New Hampshire." Dylan's mouth was dry, the repercussions of this conclusion settling in.

"Yeah, I agree," said Matt, also trying to process what this meant for his family's safety. One thing he knew for sure was that it wasn't a good sign. It meant the Nomads were powerful enough to seize Army equipment and secure enough to drive around without worrying about the Army trying to take it back. But it also didn't appear that these Nomads were on a high alert status - this seemed almost like a milk run, and they didn't appear to be paying much attention to their surroundings. Hopefully, this meant that maybe, just maybe, they weren't terribly concerned about finding the Sheridans or the missing Nomads currently buried on his brother's property.

Matt and Dylan talked quietly for a few more minutes to ensure they each gleaned all the information they could from the quick drive-by of the Nomad vehicle.

"Sshhh!" Dylan hissed. "Do you hear that?"

They both strained their ears, and Matt soon heard the sound of an approaching engine. It sounded to him like the Humvee was returning down Route 4 from the west of town. Dylan and Matt hunkered down a little bit more. Matt reached over and pulled an additional 30-round magazine for the M4 he had propped next to him, then sighted down the barrel of his Remington 700. He was confident there was no way the Nomads in the passing Humvee had spotted them, but he also didn't know why it was returning so quickly.

Dylan and Matt watched as the Humvee entered the town from the west and saw that it was the same vehicle that had passed exactly eight minutes prior. Matt looked carefully through his scope and tried to see any identifying features of the occupants. The driver and guy riding shotgun were the same, but it was clear that at least two passengers were different. While Matt hadn't paid too much attention to the occupants on the first pass, he was certain that the two people in the back had been white males. On this return trip, a very large black male and a woman with her hair in a ponytail were facing each other in the open rear cargo area of the Humvee. The black man wore a leather cut over what looked like an Army BDU shirt, and the woman wore a filthy, green Dartmouth sweatshirt. From the tattoos on her forehead and the multiple piercings of her ears, eyebrows, nose, and lips, Matt surmised that she might not be a Dartmouth grad.

The vehicle maintained the same steady 40 miles per hour pace as it entered the town, handled the curve to the right that Route 4 took in front of the courthouse, and then continued east through town in the direction of the Interstate and the towns of White River Junction, West Lebanon, and Hanover.

Matt and Dylan kept watch until they could no longer hear

the diesel engine, and the birds chirping became the only sound in Woodstock.

"Okay, that was interesting. What did you notice, Dylan?"

"Well," said Dylan, still processing. "I think the people in the back were different people."

"Exactly!" Matt replied. "And what does that mean?"

"Mmmm, I don't know, honestly...I mean, I guess it means they dropped some people off and picked up some new people. Because there was still only five of them in the Hummer."

"Humvee."

"What?"

"It's a Humvee. Sorry, man, I can't let you go through life calling it a Hummer. Your girlfriend gives you a hummer; you ride in a Humvee."

Dylan choked back his laugh in an attempt to be quiet. "Ah, yeah, okay, Uncle Matt. Whatever you say."

"But you're right about them dropping people off. What else do we know?"

"Well, it only took them eight minutes from the time they passed us. So wherever they dropped people off, it's not more than four minute's drive to the west."

"Exactly, Dylan. Great deduction. And in reality, it probably took at least 1-2 minutes to unload and load, possibly even as much as five minutes. So somewhere, one-to-four minutes' drive to the east, there are now two Nomads and possibly four. Doing what, we do not know."

"Roadblock?" Dylan said in a guessing tone.

"Good guess. That's kind of what I was thinking. You know this area better than me; what's a one-to-four-minute drive down Route 4 that way?" Matt asked, gesturing to the west.

"Nothing, really. There's like an ice cream snack bar place maybe a mile down the road." Dylan thought for a second. "Oh shit. The high school. The high school is about two miles due west on Route 4, maybe a tad under two miles."

"Bingo!" Matt said. "That's gotta be it. They must have some kind of outpost there." Now it was Matt's turn to think.

After almost a minute of silence, he continued, "I think it's a roadblock or checkpoint like you said. It doesn't make sense to bring four people out and then return with four people if there's a big outpost at the high school. They'd just manage their own guard rotation. I'm betting they have four on at a time and rotate. I don't know how long their rotations are, so maybe it's eight people, and they rotate four at a time. But I don't think it's a large outpost."

"Makes sense," said Dylan. "Are we going to check it out?"

"Not this trip. We continue as planned and spend the day here. I'm gonna call this into the farmhouse on the radio right now, but I think we Charlie Mike unless something changes."

"Charlie Mike?" Dylan asked, looking at his uncle as if he had spoken a foreign language.

Laughing, Matt replied, "Sorry! Being in a sniper hide is making me revert back to Army lingo. Charlie Mike means Continue Mission. It's from the phonetic alphabet for the letters C and M."

"Ah, okay," said Dylan, in a tone that made Matt feel old.

"So let me call this into the house and let them know what we saw, and then I'm going to catch some sleep until it's my watch."

Matt called their observations into Clare, who happened to be manning the radio. The rest of the day was completely uneventful until exactly 6:49 that evening. It was after sunset, but there was still quite a bit of ambient light, and they saw headlights on the horizon about the same time they heard the engine. It was the same Humvee with six people, who all appeared to be Nomads wearing some mix of leather cuts and Army woodland camouflage uniforms. This time, the return trip took slightly longer, and it passed them going back east at 7:04, its headlights piercing the night as complete darkness was about to set in.

"Okay, definitely a changing of the guard," said Matt quietly to Dylan. "See anything new or different."

"No, only that I think it was the exact same people that came back this morning. I recognized the black guy and the woman in the back on their first pass, and I'm positive it's also the same driver and guy riding shotgun."

"Excellent. I agree on the passengers and glad you noticed the driver, as I was focused on something else. I did notice one thing very interesting."

"What's that, Uncle Matt?"

"The 240 Bravo wasn't loaded?"

"What do you mean?" Dylan asked. "How could you tell?"

"Well, the M240 Bravo is a belt-fed 7.62-millimeter machine gun. It's an open-bolt-fired weapon, unlike the M4s we have. Basically, this means the bullet sits locked in place, with the bolt pulled back. When the trigger is pressed, the bolt slams forward and fires off the round. The gases from the firing bullet then push the bolt back to fire again and again, up to several hundred rounds per minute. The bullets are all linked together with metal clips and feed in one after another as long as the trigger is held down. The way they have the 240B mounted, there should be an ammo can mounted there with the belt feeding into the feed tray of the machine gun. They didn't have an ammo box or any ammo belt, as far as I can tell."

"Doesn't it take a while to load the ammo belt?"

"Exactly! Either they don't have ammo, or they are so sure of their security that they don't feel it's even necessary to have the belt loaded for a quick reaction to an ambush."

Matt called this new info up to the farmhouse, this time speaking with Pete over the small handheld radio. Pete was the designated leader of the two-vehicle group they planned to send down into town later that evening. If the town was empty, as Matt and Dylan now knew with some certainty, the plan they had all agreed upon yesterday was to raid the hardware store on the east side of town for some items they felt critical to their future long-term survival. Matt ended the radio call by saying tonight's mission was a "go," and they'd rendezvous at the linkup point.

At 10 pm, Matt and Dylan had walked the mile or so east

down Route 4 to their overwatch positions to await the arrival of Pete's group. Dylan was positioned about 300 meters south of the hardware store at the point where Route 4 takes a sharp turn to the north, while Matt found a spot on the roof of a landscaping business to the north of the Ace hardware store. They'd been lying in position for almost an hour when the radio chirped.

"Matt, this is Grace. At Billings Farm, no issues."

"Roger. All quiet here," replied Matt. Dylan and Matt had walked the entire route through town and noted no obstacles in the road. They now had significant night vision capability, with what they had liberated from the Sheriff's office and what Stan had brought with him, so the plan was for the drivers of the two SUVs, Pete and LT, to wear PVS-14 night vision goggles while those riding shotgun used a thermal monocular. They would drive a steady 10 miles per hour with the idea that they would be virtually silent and undetectable as they drove through town with no headlights.

"Turning onto Pleasant Street," Grace's voice whispered through his radio earpiece. Instead of replying, Matt clicked once for the affirmative.

"Approaching Mac's."

"I have visual," replied Dylan, murmuring into his mic. The plan was for the vehicles to pause and pick up Dylan en route to the hardware store.

Within a minute, Matt heard the slow, almost silent crunch of vehicle tires on gravel and turned to his right to see Pete's Jeep Wrangler and his brother Donald's old Suburban pull into the parking lot of the Ace Hardware, backing up so their rear ends faced the front door.

"In overwatch at Ace," Dylan said over the radio. This was Matt's cue to link up, and he lowered himself down the trellis he'd used to access the roof and jogged across the street to the hardware store. As he approached, he saw Dylan standing between the two parked vehicles and using his night vision to surveil the road in both directions.

"All good?" Matt asked Dylan as he approached.

"Yep. They're all inside already. I have overwatch if you want to go help. I'll let you know over the radio if I see or hear anything."

"Sounds good. Let me know if you see anything at all." Matt put his pack and sniper rifle into the back of the Jeep and then went in through the hardware store's front door. Actually, Matt realized there was no longer a front door, just an opening where the door had once been.

They knew that the hardware store would definitely have been looted, but the hope was that the items they needed most were those things unlikely to be important to looters at the start of the cataclysm three weeks ago. *Had it only been three weeks?* Matt thought to himself.

As Matt walked into the store, he could see the beams of several flashlights in two separate areas. As agreed upon at the family meeting yesterday, the purpose of this raid was to gather supplies for perimeter security and fuel. Matt walked down the nearest aisle and saw Liz holding a flashlight while Derek pulled down spools of wire. Matt could already see a shopping cart in the aisle full of all types of batteries, especially the larger 12-volt ones - dozens of them. Derek began loading a second cart with several large spools of wire in various colors.

"All good, Liz?" Matt asked.

"Yeah, Matt," replied Liz, somewhat out of breath. "Tons of batteries and wire. We're gonna go check the electronics section after we load this stuff in the SUV."

"Okay, sounds good," said Matt. "I'm going to check on Pete and Grace." Matt jogged down to a cross aisle and found Grace two aisles over.

"Where's Pete?" Matt asked.

Startled, Grace looked over at Matt. "He ran the first cart out to the car. No large fuel cans as we thought, but we did get a half-dozen 2-gallon cans. He also got a couple dozen 5-gallon buckets with lids. And we hit the mother lode with the fuel stabilizer. They had several unopened boxes on the top shelf no one seemed to notice."

"Great. What are you looking for now? What can I help with?"

"Can you help me with this spool of tubing? I already found two siphon pumps. I think this tubing should do it." She shined her flashlight on a rack containing several spools of clear vinyl tubing in various diameters. Matt reached up, pulled down a full spool of 1" and 1/2" tubing, and threw them in Liz's shopping cart.

"Anything else?" Matt asked.

"Nope. Our team is done. Meet you in the car." Not waiting for a reply, Grace pulled her shopping cart into a quick 180-degree turn and walked rapidly toward the front of the store. Matt followed her to the front of the store, but instead of heading out to the parking lot, he grabbed his own cart and headed down one of the aisles. He'd been thinking all day about some other items that he wanted, and he knew it was going to take them five minutes at least to pack the vehicles with everything they had pilfered. He walked up and down the aisles, grabbing things off shelves and tossing them in his cart. Before long, the cart was full, and Matt headed toward the exit - his cart full of items such as dozens of rolls of duct tape, empty sandbags, glass cutters, Flex Seal, spray paint, rope, and a variety of hand tools.

Matt turned down an aisle intending to head for the front door when he saw Pete approaching, pushing a similarly-laden shopping cart. "All set?" Pete asked.

"Yeah. I think I'm good. Did we get everything we needed?"

"Oh yeah," said Pete. "And then some. Liz and Derek went a bit overboard. C'mon, let's get this stuff loaded and get out of here." Nodding, Matt followed Pete up the aisle and out the front door.

In minutes they were all loaded and headed back through town and home. Matt couldn't wait to see his family and hopefully get some much-needed sleep.

CHAPTER 8

October 1, 10:08 am

"Look what the cat dragged in!"

Walking into the dining room after waking up, Matt smiled at Pete's greeting. Pete was sitting at the dining room table next to Stan and across from Clare, each nursing a cup of coffee. Matt grabbed a clean mug off the counter and poured a cup from the half-full French press sitting on the table.

"Good morning, Sunshine," Clare said, leaning over to give Matt a quick kiss on the cheek. "Enjoy your beauty sleep?"

"Yeah, yeah," Matt grumbled, enjoying the banter. Banter meant everyone was in a good mood and not stressed out.

"We were just enjoying the morning and waiting for you to wake up," said Stan. "Clare figured you needed the rest after being awake for almost two days. Dylan's still sleeping as well."

Matt savored his first few sips of the strong coffee, despite it not being terribly hot. Seeing some muffins on a plate in the middle of the table, Matt grabbed one. Before he knew it, he was reaching for a second one, having already devoured the first.

"I can cook up some eggs if you want them. You must be famished," offered Clare.

Pausing to chew so as not to respond with his mouth full, Matt replied, "Thanks, honey. I think I'm good. These muffins are doing the trick." He took another sip, looked around, then grabbed a third muffin. "Where is everyone?"

"Well, it seems like everyone's kind of broken into their own groups," said Clare. "Christopher's at OP1, and I'm sure you saw Amey at the lookout when you woke up. LT and Dylan are working outside on adding sandbags to some of the fighting positions. Molly, Marvi, and Grace are reorganizing supplies downstairs, while Liz and Derek are doing something with the computers in the basement. Kelsey, Juliet, and Laurie are over in the family room. The three of them cooked breakfast and cleaned up this morning. Your daughter is turning into quite the chef!"

Matt was still always surprised at how normal Clare could make things feel. The world as they knew it had basically ended, but Clare was able to keep people motivated and occupied as if it were just another day at the farmhouse.

"So, Pete, Stan - now that you've had a couple of days to get settled, I'm quite keen to hear what you think of our situation, especially long-term. Since your arrival, I've just assumed that you're here for the duration, but I guess maybe that's the first question I should ask. Are you planning to stay? Or do you have plans for moving on?"

Pete immediately answered. "We're all in, Matt. You and I've been brothers since college, and Liz and I are 100% part of this family for as long as you'll have us."

All eyes turned to Stan.

Stan looked at Matt and then turned his gaze to speak directly to Clare. "Clare, I haven't known you near as long as you've known Pete, but I think you know Marvi and I have always enjoyed spending time with you and your family socially over the years. What you may not know is that I have always held your husband in the highest regard professionally. His military record, which I'm sure you know but most people will never know, and the things he's done for our country as a *consultant*," Stan emphasized this last word by drawing air quotes with both hands, "have proven without question that he's an elite planner, operator, and warrior. While I may have been a Navy O-6 and made a lot more money, there is no question in my mind that your husband is a better leader than

I will ever be. If it's okay with you, I'd love for Marvi, Juliet, and myself to be considered part of your family. We will contribute everything we have and serve in any capacity you need for the good of the extended family."

Clare broke eye contact with Stan and glanced at her husband sitting next to her. Matt could see a tear forming in his wife's eyes. "Of course, Stan. Of course. We are so very sorry about Emmett, but you, Marvi, and Juliet always have a home with us."

Stan nodded and looked toward Matt. "Matt, there's absolutely no doubt that our greatest chance for long-term survival is under your leadership. I know this is a family and not a military unit, but what you've done here in the last three weeks is simply incredible. I don't know how much prior planning you put into everything, but I feel confident we can ride things out here for as long as necessary. Years, in fact."

Matt looked at Stan, humbled by his words. Matt had always felt similarly about Stan and would follow Stan just about anywhere. However, given all that had transpired, the fact that most of the group were Sheridans, along with Matt's experience in combat and survival situations, it made sense for him to lead. "Thanks, Stan. Obviously, it goes without saying that you are all welcome, and as far as I'm concerned, I've thought of you as members of the family since the moment you arrived. Two weeks ago, I was extremely concerned about our chances for long-term survival, but at "Sixteen Strong" we are an extremely capable and formidable force.

"Okay, shifting the subject a bit, let's talk about areas of concern. It's October 1st. It'll get colder throughout the month, with the first snowfalls and freezing temps likely by mid-November. We can expect steady freezing temps and accumulated snow by mid-December. What are your greatest concerns for the safety and survival of our families here?"

Matt looked at all three around the table, and Pete decided to speak first. "The Nomads, Matt. Our biggest concern must be defending against the Nomads and other human predators out there. You've done an incredible job on survival supplies. Even with sixteen mouths to feed, Molly mentioned that we easily have enough food supplies until next summer. Our fuel is sufficient through the winter, both propane for cooking and wood for heat, and our water supply is reliable, and for the most part, limitless. But the Nomads could attack at any moment, and we have no idea how big a force we might be up against. Stan, d'you agree?"

Stan stroked his growing stubble, still not used to not shaving every morning. "Yeah, Pete, you're spot on. I think the next sixty days are the most critical as far as the Nomads are concerned. If we make it to winter without being attacked, I think it's probable the biker gang will hole up for the winter and not be overly concerned about finding us. They appear to have freedom of movement, but they also have many more mouths to feed and people to keep warm. With no electricity or supply lines, they're going to need to spend a considerable amount of effort making sure they simply survive the cold winter months.

"My one caveat to that, though, is the vaccine. We have to assume the Nomads know you have it, and the Black Pox vaccine may be the most important commodity on earth. Those that aren't vaccinated must continue to stay isolated in perpetuity. I'm also assuming the Nomads likely found another source of vaccine, possibly one of the other National Guard shipments. However, if they want your case badly enough, they will search high and low until they find it."

"Agreed," said Matt. "Clare? Your thoughts?"

"Well, you and I've talked about this quite a bit. My biggest fear is always about the kids. When we fled Rhode Island on September 8th I had two kids I felt responsible for. Now I have ten. Pete and Stan, I'll tell you what I tell Matt almost every day. My preference is to go to a place where we will never be attacked and where we can focus on rebuilding our lives and forging a future for our children in this fucked up world. But honestly, I don't know where that place exists or how to get there. So until such a place makes itself known, I feel like this is the safest spot for us all."

"Amen," said Pete.

"You all bring up some excellent points," said Matt, keeping everyone on track. "And for the record, I agree with everyone. This is the safest place for now, but I think we need to spend considerable effort planning, preparing, and rehearsing various contingencies. I also think there are two things we need more of."

"What's that?" asked Stan.

"Information. And weapons."

"What kind of information? And don't you think we have enough rifles and ammo?" This time it was Pete who asked the question.

"For information - everything we can get access to. Stan, I'd really love to see what your ability is to get access to the QuAI mainframe or to establish satellite comms or internet. Locally, I think it's critical we gather as much intelligence as possible regarding the Nomads and any other threats in our surrounding areas. Simply put, we need to know what we're up against. Stan, any thoughts?"

"Yeah, plenty. Liz and Juliet are downstairs right now with Derek working on accessing the QuAI data center. We can go down after this and see their progress. I also have two satellite phones charging downstairs. I'm not sure who we can call that still has a working sat phone, but we can start figuring that out. I agree it's important to understand these Nomads. Are they just some violent, rogue biker gang, or are they more organized and have a greater agenda than raping and pillaging? From what you've told us, they appear more than just a simple outlaw motorcycle club."

"Yeah, I'm certain there's more to them than meets the eye," said Matt. "The Nomads appear as a bike gang, but act much more organized. That Tate guy was something else, and the way they're relieving their outpost every twelve hours smacks of some serious organization and structure. Which is why I want to ambush the outpost at Woodstock Union High."

"Ambush?" Clare asked, her voice rising in pitch. "Why the fuck would we ambush them? They aren't posing us any direct threat."

"Okay, okay. Let me clarify. I want to conduct another recon to see their outpost, with the goal of planning a successful ambush. If we do it right, I think we could gather a lot of information about the Nomads and also get our hands on the weapons I think we're missing."

"Yeah, you mentioned weapons a second ago, Matt. What do you think we're missing?"

"I want a crew-served machine gun, and their vehicle had an M240B mounted on it. I'm assuming they might have some other things at the checkpoint as well, given that it appears they've taken over the equipment of a National Guard unit. Grenades, claymores, maybe even a radio. These are all things that we'll need if we're to all survive a concerted attack on this farmhouse."

Everyone looked at each other, fully realizing that Matt was correct in his assessment. Matt continued, nailing his point home. "We can run if we want and try to find a safer haven, but if we want to stay, then we need to be prepared to fight. And as every Army Ranger will tell you: if you're gonna fight, plan to win and win big. We don't have the luxury of taking losses. One casualty to us means one of our family members has been killed. That's simply not acceptable. We need to be smarter, faster and more vicious than the fucking Nomads. And I have some ideas on how to do just that."

CHAPTER 9

October 1, 2:10 pm

Matt sat on the flat stump in the backyard that they used for splitting wood. The first day of October turned out to be beautiful. Mid-sixties, sunny, with a deep blue, cloudless sky the color of lapis lazuli and zero humidity. Matt thought it was perfect football weather, then realized with sadness that he'd never experience the joy of taking Christopher to see the Patriots. *What kind of a fucking world is it with no NFL football?* He thought to himself. *And where the hell is Tom Brady right now*? Matt wasn't a praying man, but the one deity he did hold dear was Tom Brady. *I hope you're on a fully-stocked Caribbean island tossing a football with Giselle and the kids, TB12!*

Snapping out of his short reverie, Matt looked down at the black Iridium satellite phone in his left hand. He had searched his computer and found a sat phone number for Rob, his former chief operating officer who was holed up on Matt's company's isolated estate on the southern cape of South Africa. He had last communicated with Rob by email several days after the nuclear attacks, and Rob had provided some significant early intel regarding the Black Pox.

Three weeks into the cataclysm, Matt wasn't sure whether Rob would be monitoring his sat phone or even if Rob were still alive.

Matt flipped up the bulky antennae on the side of the phone and pressed the speed dial button he had programmed with Rob's number. He let the phone ring and counted twelve rings before an automated voice informed him that the Iridium subscriber was unavailable. There was no option for voicemail. With no other options, Matt pressed the speed dial button and called again.

Ring, Ring

Ring, Ring

Ring, Ring

"Hallo?" A female voice answered in a gritty South African accent, one Matt instantly recognized.

"Lucy? Is that you?" The connection was solid, but with a one-second delay, it was slightly awkward.

"Yes. Is this Matt?" Relief flooded through Matt. There were other survivors halfway across the world. Maybe things weren't as bad as they feared.

"Yes, Lucy." Matt found himself speaking very loudly. Even though he knew it was just a standard phone call, subconsciously, he spoke louder with the knowledge that Lucy was geographically so far away. "It's Matt. How are you doing? Is everyone safe?" Lucy was Rob's wife. She was from a very wealthy Cape Town family and was the main reason Rob had pushed to locate the company's training center in South Africa.

"Rob, myself, and the kids are safe and healthy, Matt. We've been very fortunate here on the estate. But we're completely isolated." The estate she was referring to was a 800-hectare property northwest of the seaside resort of Plettenberg Bay on the southern tip of South Africa. The estate included a very large plantation home, a training and conference center, as well as more than a dozen guest cottages and small homes for the more than thirty full-time employees and their families.

"That's great, Lucy. I'm so glad your family is safe. Is Rob around?"

"Yes, Matt. I've sent Amila to fetch him. He's been working in the armory and should be here any second."

Before Matt could respond, he heard a quick shuffle over the phone, followed immediately by Rob's voice.

"Matt? Is that you, bru?" Rob had grown up an Army brat,

and while his accent was pure American, spending most of the last few years in South Africa had added some very South African lingo to his conversations.

"Yeah, Rob, it's me. We just got access to a sat phone. Glad to hear you're safe."

"Yeah. Same here. How are Clare and the kids? How are you making out in Vermont?"

"We're good, Rob. A few adventures, but overall we're doing quite well. The US, at least as far as we can tell, has completely collapsed. They didn't really get the vaccine out, so best estimates are less than a 5% survival rate here."

"Yeah, Matt. It's all gone to *kak*. The world is fucking gone, bru. Just gone. The pox is killing or has already killed, just about everyone. Frankly, I think it's only a matter of time before it gets us all."

"Are you vaccinated? Were you able to get the vaccine?"

"No, Matt. No vaccine made it to South Africa. We don't have the means to make it, and I think we were pretty far down the distribution list. How about you? I heard some places got it in the US and Europe, but for the most part, the distribution was too late."

"We got some. It was a fiasco, but we were able to secure a pretty large quantity of it. The whole family is vaccinated. And we're up to sixteen people now. Remember Pete Rhodes? He and Stan White showed up with their families a few days ago."

"*Haibo*! THE Stan White, from QuAI?"

"Yes, the very same. They had quite an adventure getting here from Virginia. What're you hearing, Rob? Anything?"

"Nothing to hear, bru. Not sure anyone is left. I flew down here on the evening of the 12th just as Joburg was completely shutting down. I talked to Martin a couple of times by sat phone, the last time being on September 19th I think. He said the pox was rampant in England and Europe and that the vaccine they were administering was not working. Apparently, the US was modifying the vaccine specifically for the Black Pox, but none of those batches were likely to make it outside the US because international travel had been shut down."

"Okay. That makes sense with what we've seen here. How about there? What infrastructure remains, Rob?"

"Well, all the infrastructure is here, but the people are all dead. From what we heard before the last radio station stopped broadcasting, it looked like 96-98% of the population would die either from the pox, violence, or lack of food. I think the cities here are dead. Completely."

"How many do you have there at the lodge? Have you been in communication with anyone else?"

"We have twenty-four here at the lodge. Eleven adults and a few more teenagers; the rest are under twelve. We've been in contact with two distant neighbors, one a large farm and the other a game preserve. Between the three places, we have almost a hundred people. But due to the pox, we're not mingling. We've set up some exchanges of needed goods just this week and also sharing a bit of information. So far, we've been spared any violent attacks. What about you?"

"Yeah, it's just the sixteen of us here now, but there's a lot more violence here. We've had several run-ins with an outlaw motorcycle gang that seems to have taken over this part of Vermont and New Hampshire. So far, we've managed to win all the encounters, but they are our biggest threat."

"Holy Christ, bru. That's a fucking nightmare. We're preparing for a similar situation here, but so far, we haven't seen any gangs. It's just a question of time, though. Survival of the fittest and all that, right?"

"Yeah. Definitely the world we live in now. Have you heard anything else? We've no idea if any of the world's governments still exist."

"Remember Roy Brownley from the Agency?"

"Tex?"

"Yeah, the one and only. Well, I talked to him briefly by sat phone maybe ten days ago - the days are all now kind of a blur. But it was right after things went to *kak* with the

Black Pox, and the President had gone public saying he was distributing a new vaccine. Roy's still with the Agency and apparently got pulled to Cheyenne Mountain when the first nukes went off. He admitted the federal government has lost total control over the eastern US. Apparently, the active and reserve military forces had all been called out to instill order after the nuclear attacks. These guys bore the brunt of the initial waves of Black Pox as they were so intermingled with the community. A few military commanders even went rogue. The 4th ID and some JSOC and Air Force units were diverted to protect Cheyenne Mountain, and some of the larger military installations in Texas, Southern Cal, and Washington state received the vaccine early enough and basically circled the wagons with much of their community intact and the means to protect themselves."

"I can see that. What about the rest of the world?"

"Tits up, my friend. I think when Hutchinson bombed the Muslim world back to the Stone Age, he opened up the door for others to do the same. China invaded Taiwan, which fought back a lot harder than anyone figured. North Korea nuked South Korea, and then it was basically 'game on.' I imagine all that has petered out now as no one but the Americans had the ability to produce a vaccine so quickly. Tex said the 98% fatality rate the President mentioned might be *low* if you can believe that! I think Mother Nature hit the reset button."

"Shit, man, this is all pretty crazy. We're still not sure how lethal this motorcycle gang is. We might be forced to bug out of here, maybe sooner rather than later."

"Where to, bru?"

"Not sure yet. I have a couple of ideas. I'll let you know if we do decide to leave."

"Well, Matt. You know you're always welcome here. This isn't a terrible place to make a new start. But the hard part's getting here. You might be able to find a plane and someone to fly it, but not sure about fuel or what condition any of the runways here are. And you could always sail. Keep that in mind."

"Yeah, thanks for the offer, Rob. It's enticing, but I think we're gonna try to stick it out here if we can.

"Roger, Matt. I completely understand. Let's talk every week, okay?"

"Sounds good, Rob. It was good speaking with you, and I'm glad you, Lucy, and the kids are safe. I'm going to keep this phone charged and monitored 24/7, so call whenever. Talk to you soon."

"Take care, brother. Talk soon."

Matt sat on the stump, looking at the satellite phone in his hands. While it was heartening to know his friend was safe and alive, never had Matt felt quite so alone. He looked up at the hillside behind the house, the trees a fiery mix of orange, red, and brown. Mother Nature was always going to win. Anyone who thought humans could destroy the planet was foolish - all humans could do was make it uninhabitable for humankind. And it seems in the last three weeks humans had done just that.

The government was gone, along with the rule of law.

There was no cavalry to ride in and save the day.

The good guys were not going to win.

Matt, not for the first time in the last couple of weeks, felt the tremendous weight on his shoulders of constantly having to make the right decisions and stay one step ahead of every single thing out there that could possibly harm his family. *If my children are going to have a future, it will be up to Clare and I to provide them one*, Matt thought to himself.

Lost in his thoughts, Matt had no idea how long he sat there until he felt a firm hand on his shoulder. Turning his head, Matt saw the imposing figure of Stan White standing behind him.

"Matt, sorry to disturb you. There's something I'd like you to see," said Stan, not bothering to wait and simply turning toward the basement door with the unsaid expectation that Matt would follow.

CHAPTER 10

October 1, 2:44 pm

"So I just talk, and it will answer?"

"That's right, Matt. But you'll have to speak directly into the microphone here," answered Liz, pointing to the microphone balanced on a small tripod on the workbench in front of them.

Matt had followed Stan into the part of the basement where Liz, Derek, and Juliet had been working on the various QuAI servers and laptops. It now looked like a futuristic computer with a long rack of servers to the left, several open laptops to the right, and a large screen computer monitor in the center of the bench at chest height. It looked to Matt like the same monitor on the house computer upstairs.

"You brought all this with you?" Matt asked.

"Well, everything but the monitor," said Liz. "We snagged that from upstairs." Made sense to Matt.

When he had first walked in, Stan had gestured to Liz, and she had clicked the mouse to initiate a video playing on the large computer screen. It was a map of the world with the continents and countries outlined along with dots of light all over it signifying the world's population. Across the top was a running figure that had started at over eight billion, along with the date and time. The date at the top began at September 7, and as Liz clicked the start button, the time scrolled rapidly forward. On the morning of September 8 the dots of lights noticeably dimmed in the eight US cities hit by nuclear bombs, a black hole appearing in the center of each metropolis signifying massive loss of life. The overall global population tally didn't change much until an hour later when large black dots began showing up mainly across the Middle East, North Africa, and South Asia, with a few of these black dots of death in East Africa and Indonesia. Matt knew this coincided with the death rained down upon dozens of Muslim cities as part of Operation Hellfire. The tally at the top of the screen ran backward until the first number became a 7, signifying the population had been reduced by more than a hundred million people. *Jesus Christ,* Matt thought. He knew all those people had been killed, but seeing all that death reduced to a running number on the monitor was something else altogether. *A hundred million people, gone, just like that.*

The video continued to run but the lights remained fairly constant, as did the total global population figure dancing at the top of the screen. On September 16th the lights across the map signifying population centers began to noticeably dim. The time-lapse seemed to equal one second per hour, as it took about twenty-four seconds to progress through an entire calendar day. They all watched silently as the video sped through September 16th, then the 17th, and 18th - all while the millions of lights across the globe seemed to dim and be replaced by darkness. By the 25th of September, the world map was almost completely dark, and when the video ended with the date at September 30 there were only about three dozen lights, and these were all in the United States and Canada.

"Those lights?" Matt asked. "Does that mean those are the only places where people are left alive? It doesn't seem like there's a light anywhere in New England"

"No, Matt," replied Juliet, answering before Liz could. "The lights are population centers, and I think there needs to be a concentration of at least 1,000 people in a square mile or something like that. So I'm pretty sure those are areas in the US where QuAI estimates there are still more than 1,000 people per square mile."

"Exactly," chimed in Stan. "We watched this while you

were on the phone, Matt. Those dots appear to be located in places like Denver, Killeen, El Paso, Seattle, San Diego, Clarksville, Savannah, Toronto, Montreal. Mostly places with major military bases, and also places likely to have received new batches of the vaccine."

"How do you explain Montreal and Toronto?" Matt asked.

"Great question, and one I don't have the answer to," said Stan. "Best guess is that it's a combination of vaccine availability, lack of weapons in the hands of private citizens, and maybe just an overall willingness to get along in an emergency."

"How about they have the largest Muslim populations in Canada, about 10% each?" Matt asked.

A look of concern replaced Stan's initial blank look at not having a ready answer. "That's an incredibly astute observation, Matt, one I hadn't even considered."

"I raise the question only because of what you told me about The Base."

"Yeah, Matt. I get it. I think your observation has merit. It's certainly worth looking into."

"Looking into?" Matt said, his eyebrows raised. "The internet's dead, Stan, and Toronto might as well be on the moon. The world that matters to us right now has been reduced to this farmhouse and the surrounding environments."

"But that's the point I brought you here for, Matt. Our information sources aren't dead. We're now linked into QuAI," said Stan.

"You mean you're connected to the main computer and data center in Charlottesville? It's still operational?" Matt asked, a bit incredulous that something so advanced and requiring so much electricity was still operational.

"Yes, it is. For the most part."

"Wait a sec, Stan," interrupted Matt. "Derek, would you mind going upstairs to round up Clare and Amey? And if you see Marvi, Pete, Grace, or LT you could probably ask them to come down as well if they're not doing something important. There's no sense in having Stan tell this more than once." With a nod of the head, Derek bounced out of the room and up the stairs in search of the others.

Matt turned back to Stan and Liz. "While we're waiting, how are your main computers up and running? Your backup generators had to have run out of fuel by now, haven't they?"

"We built QuAI specifically to be able to run almost indefinitely, with a few restrictions. It doesn't use fossil fuels to generate power."

"No fuel? What does it use for electricity?"

"Well, you remember visiting our data center right?"

"Yeah, how could I forget? It's like Fort Knox fifty feet underground."

"Exactly, Matt. Except it's not fifty feet, it's more like 150 feet. Most people think it's built into the side of a mountain, but it's actually built well below the mountain. We actually use a high-speed elevator just so people feel like it's only one or two stories down, while in reality, it's more than ten. And what only a few know is that under that mountain runs an underground river, an offshoot of the Rivanna River."

"Okay?" Matt said, not fully understanding.

"We spent a lot of time, effort, and money to ensure the AI machine learning system we built would not rely on traditional power sources. Underneath our data center is basically a generator and battery room that uses hydropower turbines built into the underground river to harness the river's flow to generate and store electricity. We use modified Tesla Powerwalls to store sufficient electrical power to run the data center and then some."

"The entire data center? Forever?"

"Well, there are some complicated nuances. It should run for at least ten to fifteen years but with some limitations. The AI computer manages its output alongside the available stored electricity and will turn servers on and off, as well as go to a low-power mode with most of its capability shut down until the batteries are recharged. Based on our usage pattern, QuAI will learn how to best manage the stored electricity."

"That's fucking genius, Stan."

"Well, I can't take the credit for it. Some very smart people came up with that one. But it does two things that are critically important now. One, the river runs 24/7, so we should have access when we need it. Two, and most importantly, unlike other alternative power sources like solar or wind, our generators are over two hundred feet below bedrock. They are 100% secure from tampering."

"Wow. No wonder you're a billionaire," said Matt, only half-jokingly.

Just then, Derek dashed down the stairs followed by an entourage of Clare, Marvi, Grace, Pete, and LT. "I got everyone, Matt. The gang's all here."

"Please gather round, everyone," added Matt. "There's no sense Stan and Liz briefing this more than once." Turning to Stan, "The floor's yours, Stan."

"Okay, everyone. Feel free to get comfortable sitting on those boxes or chairs. Wherever you can sit and still see the screen." Stan stood to the side of the large computer monitor while others shuffled around to get comfortable. Matt remained standing.

"I was just telling Matt that based on Liz, Juliet, and Derek's hard work, QuAI is now fully up and running, connected to our primary data center in Charlottesville. I won't get into the details, but QuAI was purposely built to withstand just about any man-made or natural catastrophe and to keep operational for years using its own power source. Liz put together a quick time-lapse data graph that shows how the world population is likely now 2-4% of what it was a month ago. But that is a general overview. This next video, which I'm glad you're all here for, is quite a bit more specific. Liz?"

At Stan's direction, Liz used the mouse to click a few things on her laptop screen and select a file entitled HawkEye360. A video popped up on the large monitor that everyone could see.

Like the original video, this one portrayed all the continents flattened across the width of the screen and was also in time-lapse, although at a much faster pace. The world was covered in green and blue dots, possibly millions of them, spread across the population centers of Europe, Asia, and North America. Matt at first thought this was another video showing the population dropoff until he realized a large number of the dots were spread throughout all of the oceans. The footage ended by showing a timestamp of last night, and while 99% of the colored dots had disappeared, there remained several thousand green and blue dots worldwide.

Matt was about to ask what the dots represented when Stan spoke first. “Folks, these green and blue dots represent radio frequency transmissions across various spectrums. The green dots generally represent transmissions from things such as UHF and VHF radios, cell phones, and satellite phones. Blue dots are various types of radar transmissions, emergency beacons, and things like that.” Stan paused to let everyone absorb this new information.

Amey was the first to react and raised her hand to ask a question. Stan nodded at her, and she asked, “How do we have this, Stan? I mean, is this a simulation, or is this real data? The internet is dead, right?”

“Excellent question, Amey. I’ll answer your last question first. The internet really isn’t a physical thing. It’s more just a series of computers linked together. We think of the internet as a Cat7 or coaxial cable coming into our house somewhere from an internet service provider, but in reality that’s just how most people’s computers access the internet.” Stan used his hands to form air quotes as he spoke the last word. “We use different website addresses to access the specific type of information we want, or we just Google it, and Google finds the right computer where the information we’re searching for is stored.

“So the short answer is that the internet is mostly dead because most of the computers hosting websites are now without electricity, and therefore, the information they contain is no longer accessible. However, there are repositories of information that still have electricity, and fortunately for us, QuAI has access to many of these. I'm specifically referring to satellites. Most of these are still online and likely will be for at least months to come, if not years."

"They run out of power that soon?" Clare asked.

"Clare, it's not so much the power as it is the position and time." This time it was Liz who answered. "Most satellites in orbit receive regular position adjustments to keep them where they need to be. They also receive time updates for their internal clocks. You remember when you were in the Army and used frequency-hopping, right?"

Clare nodded, remembering how her vehicles' radios, called SINCGARS, required their clocks synced to the second in order to hop frequencies a hundred times per second at the exact same time the radio she wanted to communicate with was hopping.

Liz continued, "Well, it's basically the same thing. Satellites communicate through radio transmissions, as do cell phones and sat phones. There are about 5,000 satellites actively orbiting Earth, and while they serve a variety of purposes, they all communicate through radio transmissions. As their base stations are likely inoperable, it's a matter of time before their orbit slips out of the location our computers are looking for it, or its internal clock loses sync with clocks here on Earth. Space time is not the same as Earth time, and satellites continually need updates to stay synced. Some satellites may have already ceased working, some will last for months, and others may still be useful for years."

Seeing as how everyone understood the basics, Stan brought the conversation back to the video they had watched. "We downloaded the data for this video from the HawkEye system of satellites. It's a private system contracted with the US Department of Defense, but as QuAI is the aggregator of information for the DOD, we have access. I asked QuAI to put this together, and this map shows us the most advanced communities remaining."

"What about all the dots on the oceans? There must be thousands of them," LT asked.

"You're right, Brent. Depending on the size, purpose, and speed of the vessel, ships carry between ten and sixty days of fuel. On a normal day, more than 50,000 merchant ships crisscrossed the oceans at any given time. I haven't asked QuAI this, but I think a quick estimate is that maybe 10% of those ships are still at sea. They're likely searching for a safe port and trying to figure out what to do given what they may or may not know of the Black Pox pandemic. Those blue dots are mostly their search and navigation radars."

"How about US Navy ships, Stan?" followed up Brent.

"Well, US aircraft carriers are nuclear-powered, which means they could technically remain at sea for years. However, at some point, they'd need resupply for their people, especially food. I think France has one nuclear carrier. The US has about 60 nuclear-powered subs, the Russians maybe 30, and China, UK, and France less than a dozen each. Again, while these will all have power for years, they must resupply on land every month or so at least. That's something we can get QuAI to look into."

"Stan, is it possible to zoom into that map? To maybe see the radio transmissions in our area?"

"Yes, one sec," replied Liz. She typed for a few moments on her laptop keyboard, and the map on the large monitor zoomed into an area depicting New England from the Canadian border down to New York City. The date time stamp in the upper right corner of the monitor now showed "Last 24 Hours."

"Holy shit," said the previously silent Pete. "That's way more than I thought." There were hundreds, if not thousands, of primarily green dots all over the map.

Matt studied the map carefully, along with everyone else.

Stan spoke first. "Let's remember what we're looking at

here. Each dot is a radio transmission occurring in the last 24 hours. If one stationary radio were to transmit fifty times, the dot would grow in size but it wouldn't move. A handheld radio in a car, with the driver keying the mike every mile over a ten-mile drive would put ten dots on the map."

"Can you zoom in further, Liz?" Matt asked. "Like maybe just a fifty-mile radius around our location?"

Liz typed more on the laptop, and the map on the monitor zoomed in further, centered around Woodstock. The map now showed an area including the Hudson River to the west, Lake Sunapee to the east, and the Vermont towns of Barre and Springfield to the north and south, respectively. Dozens of green dots appeared on the screen. The largest dot by far was centered on the Dartmouth campus, but other large clusters dotted the map in Lebanon and Hanover. Most in the room focused on the several dots located on the property where they now sat - realizing that these were the handheld radio transmissions they had made in the last 24 hours to speak with OP1.

Matt, however, was focused on several other clusters - one approximately a mile and a half west of downtown Woodstock at a point Matt knew to be Woodstock Union High School. For Matt, this confirmed that this was indeed a Nomad checkpoint. Matt also noticed similar-sized clusters in Randolph, Thetford, Hartland, and Springfield in Vermont and in Enfield, Georges Mills, and Newport, New Hampshire. These transmission clusters formed a circle with roughly a thirty-mile radius from the center of Dartmouth College in Hanover, New Hampshire.

"Okay, everyone. This is our situation right here. We can see our radio transmissions, and it's safe to say these others are likely Nomads. The good news is that there don't appear to be any transmissions near us at all. The bad news is that it looks like the Nomads have some form of control over this entire area of Vermont, so we definitely need to keep our eyes peeled at all times."

There weren't any more direct questions, so Stan told

the group that they would be querying QuAI to see what other information they could come up with. Within minutes, everyone but Matt, Stan, and Liz left to go back to what they were doing.

Matt was fascinated by the capabilities of QuAI and realized it was something that ultimately set them apart from everyone else in the world. "Who has access to this other than you?" Matt asked Stan.

"Just this terminal here. Before we left, I intentionally activated the protocols that would allow remote access only from these two tokens." Stan pulled a chain from around his neck that had a small electronic fob on it. Liz pulled a similar chain from around her neck. "There are only three. Marvi and I are wearing them, and when we made the trek up here, I gave the third one to Liz as she was in the other vehicle."

"What about Cheyenne Mountain? Can they access it? You have a lot of DOD and other US government classified information, don't you?"

"Yes, the data center contains very classified information, but no, they can't access it. When we left Charlottesville, the protocols I enacted make it seem as if the data center is completely offline."

"Okay. I think I understand. So we're the only ones with this information?"

"Well, we're the only ones with the information contained within the QuAI data center. That's almost a yottabyte of data. However, QuAI has access to information outside our data center - like the HawkEye satellite system, for example. We do not have exclusive access to that system, and it's possible Cheyenne Mountain has partial access. If they're still online."

"Well, it certainly looks from the previous map that Cheyenne is still online."

"True," agreed Stan. They both had seen the concentration of green dots outside Denver.

"Shifting gears a bit. Liz, can you scroll across this map like you can with Google Maps? Like basically follow a route while keeping the map zoomed in."

Liz thought for a second before responding. "Not exactly, but I think I can accomplish what you're looking for. Just tell me the route, and I can tell the program to shift coordinates. It will take a few seconds for the system to adjust and then visually portray the data on the monitor."

"Okay, can you give me a snapshot of northern Vermont and New Hampshire? Same scale as you have now, but centered on say, Littleton, New Hampshire?"

"Comin' up." Liz typed away on the keyboard, and in less than ten seconds, the screen refreshed.

"Oh, is it possible to pull up the last three days and not just the last twenty-four hours?"

"Sure thing, Matt." A few more keystrokes and Liz gestured to the primary monitor where the date time stamp changed from "Last 24 Hours" to "Last 72 Hours."

"Perfect," said Matt, stepping up and studying the computer screen. There was a noticeable lack of any colored dots, with the exception being a few in Littleton and some more down toward the north end of Lake Winnipesaukee and one of the lakes to its west. "Okay, how about shifting once more to the east, centered on Augusta, Maine."

Liz nodded. Stan, who'd been watching Matt as much as the monitor, finally asked, "What are you thinking, Matt? Anything you care to share?"

"Mmmm," replied Matt, closely examining the refreshed map showing central and coastal Maine north of Portland. "No secrets, Stan. I'm just thinking of possible contingencies. I'm still not 100% sold on this being the safest haven for us, and I wanted to see what the rest of northern New England looks like. I have a cousin from the Lewiston area, and I was checking what the coast of Maine looked like as far as radio transmissions."

Stan and Matt both looked at the map carefully. There was a smattering of green dots across the map, but none in any significant quantity. It looked like maybe there were a couple of groups using UHF radios around several lakes, including Rangely Lake, Sebago Lake, and Great Pond. Matt assumed these were likely extended family groups like his or possibly even ham radio operators. There were also a dozen or so blue dots along the coast of Maine that was visible on the map, with the assumption that these were boat radars.

Interesting, Matt thought. *Very interesting.*

CHAPTER 11

October 3, 7:57 pm

The six older adults gathered around the dining room table while the younger group, those not on sentry duty, played games in the family room on the other side of the house. Matt and Pete had cooked dinner for everyone that night, and after cleaning up, Matt had asked Clare to gather Pete, Molly, and the Whites for a conversation over coffee.

The screen door was open, allowing the cool night air to sweep away the room's stuffiness. It had been an unseasonably warm afternoon for early October, and the crisp evening breeze coming through the door was welcomed by all. A small battery-powered lantern lit the table as the generator had been turned off after dinner. Matt could see the dim light of the larger lantern used by those in the family room penetrating the hallway between the two rooms. He knew the first floor could not be seen from the road and felt reasonably confident that this small amount of light was an acceptable security risk.

"I know it's been another long day, and we're all just about ready to hit the rack, but I thought it was important to discuss all that we learned today as a group," said Matt. For the next few minutes, he brought everyone up to speed on the details of his conversation with Rob, as well as recounting what they had learned from QuAI. "So with all that," Matt continued, "the biggest issue facing us remains the Nomads."

"Without question," replied Pete.

Matt looked around the table and saw everyone nodding

their heads in the affirmative. "Given that, I think that at some point the Nomads will stumble upon us. We've been extremely fortunate up to this point, but any moment could bring these animals to our doorstep. And while we're more formidable and better prepared today than a week ago, we're still no match for a concerted attack by a group of Nomads."

"So what are you proposing, Matt?" Molly asked. Molly was usually quite reserved, so when she spoke up Matt knew that everyone agreed this was a critical problem for them to resolve.

"I'm proposing we raid the Nomad checkpoint at Woodstock Union High. I've been thinking about this a lot the last couple of days, and I think we can pull off a very successful raid that could have enormous benefits for us. First, I think we can do this without any casualties. Second, I think it's likely that we can seize at least two machine guns with ammunition which will considerably upgrade our ability to defend ourselves. Third, there is the potential for stealing one of their radios which would let us listen in on their communications. Lastly, if we do this right, I think we can plant some misinformation that will lead them to search for us in an entirely different direction."

"I agree with Matt," said Pete. "Every day, we wait for someone to drive up this road and find us. We need to do something to even the playing field a bit."

"But what if we're not successful?" Clare asked. "It's not like we're a military unit. What if one of us gets killed, or even wounded? Is it worth that risk?"

Clare's point was a good one. Matt thought of how Kelly had been killed and knew from experience that no matter how well he planned the raid there was a significant possibility that one of his family members would be wounded or killed.

The silence became awkward until Molly spoke quietly. "I don't think we really have a choice, do we? We watched those three bikers come by the other day, and we were very lucky they didn't radio in their position. Our location isn't that remote, and sure as rain, whether it's next week, next month, or next year, one day a group of Nomads is going to come up that road and attack us. If we're still here, we need to be able to defend ourselves. Period."

Matt saw all heads were again nodding in the affirmative, even Clare's.

"So what exactly are you proposing, Matt?" Marvi asked.

"Good question, Marvi," replied Matt. "Here's exactly what I have in mind."

As he outlined his plan, he saw several smiles and knew his strategy would work.

CHAPTER 12

October 6, 2:21 am

Matt lay prone at the corner of a small house and looked through the ACOG sight of his M4 rifle. He lay directly across the street from the Nomad checkpoint in front of the Woodstock Union High School entrance, and in one minute, the raid was about to commence.

The previous evening he and Dylan had left the farmhouse on a new recon mission to find out everything they could about the Nomad roadblock. They'd driven along dirt roads to a point east of Route 12, the main road running north out of Woodstock, and in the middle of what was known locally as the Woodstock Town Forest. They parked the SUV here, a bit more than a mile north of the roadblock, and took an hour to slowly work their way to a position in the second story of a home about eighty yards behind where Matt currently lay. They spent the entire night watching the checkpoint, noting every aspect of the Nomad's routine, and then watching the shift changeover at approximately 7 am yesterday. During the night, with Dylan in overwatch, Matt had reconnoitered a 360-degree circle around the Nomad checkpoint, keeping about one hundred yards away at all times so as to remain completely hidden.

The Nomads had built a rudimentary but effective roadblock. Using a total of four police cruisers - three Sheriff's vehicles and one state police SUV - the Nomads had positioned these perpendicular to the road in such a manner that the vehicles stretched from the guardrail on one side of the street to a steep ditch on the other side, with only a ten-foot gap remaining in the middle of the road. With two vehicles on each side of the gap, the Nomads then parked a hard-shell Army Humvee to solidly fill the gap. Similar to the Humvee the Nomads used for resupply, this Humvee also had a pedestal-mounted M240B 7.62mm machine gun atop the turret. Unlike the resupply vehicle, this machine gun was always loaded and manned by a Nomad gang member. The vehicle and a lone occupant in the turret faced the road to the west, with a clear field of fire toward any vehicles approaching along Route 4 from that direction.

The result of the recon allowed Matt to refine his tactical plan. Leaving Dylan in the small house they had used for overwatch, Matt had returned alone to Donald's farmhouse to brief the entire family. With everyone on board with the updated plan, the raiding party had spent yesterday afternoon rehearsing the raid repeatedly until Matt was highly confident that they had the best chance for success. Dylan maintained eyes on the checkpoint to let them know if anything had changed. Matt hated leaving him there alone, but he knew one of the principles of reconnaissance was to keep eyes on target as long as possible prior to the attack.

After ensuring everyone going on the raid was fully rested and fed, the raiding party had left the farmhouse in a three-vehicle convoy before midnight and followed the same route Dylan and Matt had taken the previous night, leaving the vehicles hidden in the forest approximately a mile north of the Nomad roadblock. Matt led the ten-member raiding party down the dirt road to the back of the overwatch house, linking up with Dylan. This position was about 140 yards from the checkpoint. While the second-story windows offered unobstructed views of the checkpoint, Matt knew their gathering spot behind the house was well hidden from the Nomads.

Matt's plan for the raid was straightforward and directly

out of the Ranger Handbook. He dispatched Grace and Juliet to provide flank security behind the now-abandoned Woodstock Fire Station #2, about two hundred yards to the east on Route 4, closer to the center of Woodstock. From this position, the two women could see east almost to the edge of the town center. This would give the assault team several minutes' notice should someone attempt to reinforce the Nomads. The eight remaining raiding party members were equally divided into two elements: an overwatch team and an assault team. The overwatch team consisted of Clare, Liz, Pete, and Dylan. Clare and Liz were two of the best marksmen with the long rifle, Dylan had the best knowledge of what could be seen from the overwatch, and Pete was there to be both a spotter and overall coordinator on the radio.

Matt, Stan, LT, and Derek comprised the assault element. Matt knew from extensive experience that assaulting an objective required two traits above all else: fearlessness and violence of action. Based on the terrain and the setup of the Nomads, the assault team would have to take their initial shots from a concealed position where Matt now lay and then rush across approximately sixty yards of open terrain to close with and kill the enemy. With the adrenalin pumping at the highest levels humanely possible, these sixty yards would feel like a mile. The four assaulters would have to move in two-man teams from covered position to covered position, all the while keeping a steady flow of bullets going downrange and hopefully into the bodies of the defending Nomads.

With four Nomad defenders, Matt's plan should result in all four being neutralized almost immediately with the first volley of fire. However, Matt also knew that no plan ever survived initial contact with the enemy and that it was very possible that he, Stan, LT, and Derek were going to have the fight of their lives to win this battle. Stan, despite a background steering large Navy ships, was a very accomplished 3-Gun competitor, as was Matt. "3-Gun" was a multi-gun competition in which participants carried three guns, normally an assault rifle, a shotgun, and a pistol, and maneuvered through various courses and stages where they were required to engage targets in a variety of positions and with a specific weapon. LT was an Army officer who, despite having no combat experience, had still completed significant Army training in small unit tactics while in ROTC and his Officer Basic Course. Matt chose Derek for one simple reason: he was a fearless stud. Having been an all-state linebacker in high school, Derek had the "never-quit" gene, and Matt knew he would definitely be an asset to the assault element.

With everyone in position, Matt looked at his watch. It was 2:21, and the plan was to initiate at 2:22.

Toggling the throat mic on his radio, Matt spoke quietly and calmly. "Assault team in position. We can see three of the four Nomads. Do you have the fourth?" Matt could see one Nomad in the Humvee turret speaking with another, as well as a third man standing in the open door of the Vermont State Police SUV. The guy in the Humvee turret was a sizeable Black guy, and it clicked that this was likely the same guy Matt had seen a few days prior while sitting in the cupola above the courthouse in the center of Woodstock. He didn't appear terribly alert or concerned and instead was leaning on the side of the turret and talking with the guy standing below him.

"Roger, Matt," said Pete through the radio. "We have two by the Humvee and two by the state police vehicle on the left side. One person is sitting in the police vehicle, and we don't have a direct shot. Per the plan, our targets are the two gentlemen standing in the open. Standing by."

"Okay. Assault team, focus all your fire on the state police SUV." The plan Matt had briefed was simple. He wanted the four best marksmen to have pre-planned targets. As the only US Army-trained sniper in the family, Matt would initiate by firing first, and both he and Stan would prioritize their first rounds at the turret gunner as this individual posed the most significant threat. Clare and Liz, using Remington 700s with night scopes from approximately 140 yards away, would each immediately fire a round into the chest of their designated target as soon as Matt fired, and hopefully before these Nomads could react. They would follow up their initial shots with a kill shot on their initial targets and then switch to anyone else left alive. Matt and Stan would fire at the turret gunner until he was dead, while Derek and LT would shoot rapid-fire directly into the state police SUV.

Once they thought everyone was neutralized, the entire assault element would move forward under the watchful eyes of the overwatch element.

That was the plan.

In about five seconds, Matt knew the plan would be useless.

"Okay, on my mark." Matt sighted through the clear glass of his ACOG. With a magnification power of four and plenty of ambient light from both the moon and the two gas lanterns the Nomads had on the hoods of their vehicles, Matt could see the man in the turret clear as day. He lined up his reticle on the chest of the man who appeared much closer than the sixty yards away Matt knew him to be.

"Three." Matt calmed his breathing.

"Two." Matt slowly tightened his finger on the trigger.

"One." Matt squeezed gently, surprising himself as his rifle fired.

Matt knew his first shot had hit the black man under his armpit and directly through his heart. Matt registered the man slumping over with the left side of his head blown away from Stan's first round, killing the man a second time if that were possible. Matt shifted his fire to the state police vehicle and placed three quick rounds through the rear passenger door, followed by three more rounds through the driver's door.

Matt could hear the assault team to his right continue to fire quick shots while also hearing steady shots from the overwatch position behind his left shoulder.

"Cease fire, cease fire," Pete said calmly through the radio. "All targets down."

Everyone stopped firing, and Matt used his ACOG to sweep

the objective. In addition to the man dead in the turret, Matt could see two bodies lying lifeless on the ground.

"I only see three. Do you have a visual on the fourth?" Matt asked.

"Roger, Matt. The fourth is in the driver's seat of the state police SUV. We can now see him clearly from here. He's dead."

Matt realized the initial plan had gone off like clockwork - all four Nomads had been killed without being able to return fire. "Okay, everyone. Assault team moving forward. Overwatch, keep us covered. Pete, start the clock."

They had agreed that they would take no more than ten minutes on the objective, and preferably not even that. Spread out about ten meters apart, the four members of the assault element broke from the covered positions and began walking toward the Nomad roadblock. Matt had explicitly warned them all against running, as that's how people break an ankle.

Within thirty seconds, they were looking down at the dead Nomads on the ground.

"LT, Derek, grab the M240 machine gun and all their ammunition. Stan, check out that guy to the left. I'll check the two over here," directed Matt. He walked to his right and saw the guy on the road. It looked like at least a half-dozen rounds had hit the guy in the upper chest and head. It was clear at least two of the bullets had been from the ladies in overwatch based on the large exit wound in his back and the fact that he was missing his entire lower jaw. Although he had seen it many times before, probably too many times, Matt was always stunned by the destructive power of a .300 Win Mag round.

Matt had authorized everyone to use flashlights as there was no longer any reason to keep in the dark, and speed was a more critical factor. Matt had a SureFire tactical flashlight mounted on his M4, and he clicked it on to see into the open door of the police vehicle. He expected the body in the SUV to be that of the tattooed woman he and Dylan had seen the other day. Matt waved his flashlight over the body slumped over the steering wheel, and could see that it was a man with a long goatee and tattoos on his arms, neck, and face. It was not the pony-tailed woman in the Dartmouth sweatshirt.

Matt triggered his mic. "Hey Dylan, the fourth person here is a guy. I was expecting the woman we saw with the face tattoos?"

There was a pause as Dylan processed Matt's question. "That makes no sense, Matt. She was definitely on the last Humvee and got off with the black guy and two others."

Oh shit, Matt thought. At the exact same instant, he heard the buzz-snap of supersonic bullets snapping past his head. Matt saw Derek and LT fall to the ground like sacks of potatoes as he and Stan pivoted to their left and brought their rifles up to a firing position.

"Target left. School entrance." Matt heard Clare say over the radio, her voice calm as ever. Matt could not hear their suppressed rounds being fired, but he knew she and Liz were engaging this target. His scope settled on the man as their bullets impacted his torso. He was about fifty yards south of the checkpoint and standing in the middle of the road leading into the high school parking lot.

"Target down." Both Clare and Pete said simultaneously over the radio. Matt looked around, and he and Stan rushed over to Derek and LT, who were scrambling to get back on their feet.

"Are you hit?" yelled Stan. "Stay down. Where are you hit?"

Derek and LT ignored his advice and continued to stand, brushing off the front of their cargo pants. Matt heard a quick chorus of "I'm good" and "I'm not hit." Matt rushed over and patted Derek down, ensuring himself that Derek was indeed not injured. *Holy fuck!* Matt thought. *How fucking stupid am I not to put security on the far side of the objective.* Matt could almost hear the Ranger Instructor in his head saying, "You fail, Ranger. You fail."

Once Matt assured himself that both men were not injured, he knew it was time to continue the mission.

"Time?" Matt called to Pete over the radio.

"Four minutes gone. Six remaining."

"Okay. Keep scanning the school parking lot." Matt released his mic, then toggled it again. "Grace, how's the flank?"

"All clear, Matt. Nothing moving."

"Roger."

Turning to Derek and LT, Matt said, "Guys, grab that machine gun and anything else of value. Let's get ready to get out of here." Turning to Stan, he continued, "Stan, let's you and I go check that guy out and maybe take a quick look at the high school. I wonder if they have a base in there. Maybe a radio?"

"Good idea. I'll follow your lead."

Matt began walking down the road and turning into the driveway of the high school. The school was set back about fifty yards from the road with a parking lot between the school buildings and the road. The parking lot was almost completely empty, but Matt thought he could see several motorcycles parked by the nearest entrance to the school. Within seconds Stan and Matt had walked up to the man on the ground. Like his fellow Nomads, this guy was unmoving and clearly dead. He was wearing a black baseball cap and had an M4 slung on a two-point sling, a MOLLE tactical vest stuffed with 30-round magazines and M67 fragmentation grenades.

"Stan, can you grab his rifle and ammo. These guys have fucking grenades. I'm going to take a quick look at the school."

"Will do. Be careful."

Matt walked up the school's driveway, his rifle butt firmly in his armpit and carried in the depressed muzzle position. This allowed him a clear view over the front sight post of his weapon, with the ability almost instantly to acquire and dispatch targets. Using the flashlight had ruined Matt's night vision, so he decided to trigger his rifle's powerful tactical light and illuminate the front of the school. While his light gave the enemy something to shoot at, Matt figured anyone in the school could already see him so he might as well be able to see them clearly as well.

He noticed two Harley-Davidson motorcycles parked by the

front entrance, and his brain registered a slight movement behind them.

Is that a...? Matt thought.

Bang! Bang! Matt's rifle bucked in his hands as his reflexes were faster than this thought process. He saw movement and fired two quick rounds at the position fifteen meters away where he felt a person could potentially have hidden.

At this distance, Matt heard the never-to-be-forgotten sound of bullets impacting human flesh. The soft *thwack* the supersonic 5.56 bullet made on impact was unlike any other sound. In this case, it was immediately followed by grunts of pain, followed by a low moaning sound. As Matt stepped to his right, the angle allowed him to see the tattooed face of the ponytailed woman from the Humvee illuminated in the beam of his tactical light.

Matt sensed Stan running up next to him and could see the beam of Stan's rifle-mounted tac light merge with Matt's own light in illuminating the wounded Nomad female.

"Cover me," said Matt calmly. Without waiting, confident Stan was covering him, Matt stepped to his right to not put himself between Stan and the woman, allowing Stan a clear shot at all times. Matt sprinted forward, his rifle trained on the woman. He could tell both his rounds had hit her in the torso, one high on the side of her shoulder and the other low in the center of her abdomen. She was holding her stomach and rolling on the ground; her eyes squeezed shut in pain.

Careful so as not to put himself in Stan's lane of fire, Matt reached down and snatched the woman's M4 carbine, yanking the sling harshly over her head. Seeing that she had a holstered pistol, Matt reached down and grabbed that as well.

He waved Stan forward while simultaneously keying his mic. "Time hack, Pete?"

"Four minutes remaining, Matt. Plenty of time."

"Okay. We have two more Nomads. One KIA that you can see, and one wounded female by the school entrance."

"Got it, Matt. We can barely see you through the trees from

our overwatch."

"Okay. Hey LT, how's it going with the Humvee?"

"All good, Matt," LT replied, sounding out of breath. "Got the 240 Bravo and a ton of boxed ammo. Also, some other goodies I think you'll enjoy. I need two more minutes to get all the goodies."

"What goodies, LT? Something we need?"

"They have claymores, Matt."

Wow! Thought Matt. It made sense, but he hadn't ever considered that. "Okay, LT. Game changer. Get them all."

Unkeying his mic, Matt spoke directly to Stan. "Check in there, Stan. I bet there's a radio. See what else they have that we might want. I'll cover her and see if I can get any info out of her."

"Will do," said Stan, moving to clear the entranceway to the school. The door was gone, and they could see with their flashlights that the foyer had a lot of stuff in it but otherwise appeared unoccupied. Matt covered Stan from where he stood and watched as Stan entered the doorway, his tac light illuminating the large foyer. "You gotta see this, Matt. Now." The excitement in Stan's voice was evident.

Matt sprinted into the open door, looking down at the woman to see that she was still writhing in pain but also definitely wounded severely enough that she was no longer a threat. Between his light and Stan's, the contents of the room were plain to see. In front of him were two army cots, a small cook stove, several empty bottles of bourbon, and some porn magazines strewn over the floor. As Matt swung his light to the left, his breath caught in his throat. Crates of ammo, a rack with at least a dozen rifles, and what appeared to be several boxes of fragmentation grenades and explosives were stacked along a wall. Further along the same wall, Matt noticed three six-foot-high stacks of MRE cases. Matt whistled as he swept his light over to the right. He noticed two portable generators and at least a dozen 5-gallon jerry cans of fuel.

"God damn," muttered Matt.

"Exactly," said Stan. "This is all stuff we could definitely use."

"Eight minutes!" Pete called over the radio. "Move out in two minutes!"

Matt's mind raced as he tried to devise a plan, looking at Stan and seeing that he was probably doing the same thing.

"Yeah, Stan, we can't pass this stuff up." Looking around, Matt made up his mind and keyed his mic. "LT, Derek, see if that Humvee will start and how much gas it has. Also, see if either police SUV has keys and will start. They had to have a way to move those vehicles."

"Roger, Matt," replied LT. "Checking now."

Matt turned to Stan. "I don't think we have time to get our own vehicles, and I don't want to drive them down that dirt road and leave tracks."

"Agreed," replied Stan. "I hadn't thought of that, but that's an excellent point. Fingers crossed on those vehicles starting." Just then, they could both hear the faint revving of a diesel engine and noticed headlight beams out on Route 4.

"Humvee works, Matt. Looks like about 1/4 of a tank of diesel."

"Okay, how about the SUV?"

"Yeah, Derek said the state police one is pretty shot up, a couple rounds had ruined the dashboard and windshield, but the keys are in the ignition and he thinks it will start." A pause. "Yeah, SUV started, Matt. He says fuel the tank is at less than a 1/4 full."

Matt saw how this would make sense to a Nomad. They had all this fuel, but they probably maintained the Humvee with very little fuel with the idea that if they came under fire, it was less likely to blow up. The reality, as Matt knew from experience in Iraq, is that a regular bullet would almost never ignite a full fuel tank as it was all liquid. However, the fumes in an empty take were a bit more likely to ignite. Those trivial facts were meaningless at the moment.

"Okay, everyone, listen up," Matt said into his radio. "We

have found a significant supply depot here, and I'm changing the plan. Clare, Pete, and Liz - you can head out now to the vehicles. Dylan, I want you to run down to link up with Grace and Juliet. You three will cover us against any reinforcements coming through Woodstock. As soon as we're loaded, you three run back up to where we stashed our vehicles, where the overwatch team will be waiting for you. When you're all together and Pete and Clare have a good head count, I want everyone to head home. Got it?"

"Roger, Matt," replied Clare. "What about you? Is it smart to leave you out there without overwatch?" Matt knew Clare was worried.

"Yes, Clare. We need this stuff, and I think it's best to get most of you headed home. Time is still critical here." Matt paused, switching gears but still speaking into the radio. "Derek, bring that SUV over here to the school. LT, load the M240 back on the pedestal and put the rest of the supplies back into the Humvee. Keep the engine running. When you're loaded, I want you to cover us from the turret. Call Dylan and Grace and give them the green light to head out once you can cover us."

"Roger," answered LT.

"Okay, everyone. I want to be out of here in less than ten minutes."

With that, he and Stan began moving ammo boxes to the front entrance. Derek arrived shortly, and the three of them shuttled supplies into the SUV until it was stacked full of ammo, fuel, and weapons. The rear end of the SUV was riding noticeably low, its rear springs fully compressed with all the weight stacked in the cargo area.

"Jesus, Uncle Matt," said Derek. "That's a lot of stuff. This SUV is basically a rolling bomb."

"Yeah, I guess you're right. I'm sure we're violating every rule in the book transporting gasoline with explosives, but you gotta do what you gotta do."

They all smiled, realizing this raid had garnered much more

than they ever thought.

LT had already taken overwatch and relieved Dylan, Grace, and Juliet to return to their stashed vehicles in the woods. As Matt and Stan loaded the last crate they thought they could fit, Matt heard Pete call over the radio that all six were accounted for and that they were headed back to the farmhouse.

"What now?" Stan asked.

"Okay, I have an idea. It's not going to pleasant but I think you'll like it. Do either of you know how to ride a motorcycle?"

CHAPTER 13

October 6, 2:58 am

Moving dead bodies was hard work.

Matt sat on a picnic bench at Coolidge State Park, sweating in the cool night air while collecting his thoughts and staring at the wounded woman he had propped up against a tree before him. This far into the state park, he was not worried about sound or light discipline, and he had placed her so she was sitting directly in the beams of the Humvee's headlights. He could hear LT pushing the Nomad's Harley deep into the brush about thirty yards off to his right.

Matt's plan was simple: try to make it look like maybe the Nomads had turned on each other, and three of them had killed the other two and left with their supplies. They had thrown the Nomad killed on the school's driveway, along with the muscled black guy, onto the hood of the Humvee and strapped them down. The wounded woman had been thrown into the back seat with Stan sitting beside her. At that point, the woman had yet to utter a word and was still in considerable pain while Matt stood in the open rear-passenger door looking down at her.

"Which Harleys belong to the dead guys on the hood?" Matt asked her.

Her hands still clasped tightly over her abdominal wound, she looked up at him and spit. Her mouth was dry, so no sputum came out, but her defiance was apparent.

Calmly, Matt grabbed his M4 hanging to his front on its two-point sling. Bringing up the barrel and aiming point blank at her chest, Matt flicked it forward and pressed it sharply into the woman's shoulder wound. The effect was like sticking her with a cattle prod, and her entire body jumped in the seat as she cried out in pain.

"I'm not going to ask twice," said Matt. While Matt was by no means a skilled field interrogator, he knew the key was to show no emotion and leave no doubt that he was capable of extreme violence.

The woman attempted to breathe away the pain and looked up at him, clearly thinking of spitting again. Seeing the resolve on Matt's face, she thought better. "The Softail on the left is Billy's, and Jumbo, the big black guy, doesn't have a bike here. We came in on the resupply Hummer." Mustering some resolve, she continued, "Thor is gonna fuck you up; you have no fuckin' clue who you just fucked with!"

Matt looked down at her calmly. "It's not called a Hummer," he said, closing the Humvee door on any further reply she might have.

While Matt had little experience riding motorcycles, luckily for them, LT owned a motorcycle and said he was completely proficient. The key to the motorcycles had been left in the ignition, and Matt used his K-bar knife to slash the tires of the other bikes. Briefing LT and Derek on how to get to Coolidge State Park, Matt told them to follow him in the Humvee as he jogged over to get into the vehicle's driver's seat. With Stan in the back seat guarding the wounded woman, two dead bodies on the hood, and being followed by a grossly over-laden state police SUV and a Harley-Davidson, Matt pulled out of the Woodstock Union High School entrance. He stopped briefly to jump out and puncture the tires of the three remaining roadblock vehicles, and then the small convoy sped west on Route 4.

It took them about ten minutes to get to the state park south of Route 4 on Route 100A. Stopping at a campsite, Matt had directed LT to ditch the Harley while he and Derek pulled the bodies off the hood and tossed them to the side.

Stan pulled the woman out of the Humvee and propped her against a tree.

"What about her, Uncle Matt?" Derek asked.

"Why don't you go grab LT, and both of you wait in the SUV, Derek," answered Matt, who sat at the picnic table with his full attention on the wounded woman. Derek hesitated for a second, about to ask a follow-up question. Thinking better of it, he simply turned and walked over to the SUV parked about twenty yards to the rear of the Humvee.

"What's your name?" Matt asked the woman. She just sat there looking at him. While she held her hands tightly against the bullet wound above her pelvis, there was very little blood. Matt had found no exit wound and knew the M4's 5.56 bullet was designed to tumble and ricochet when it entered a human body. Without immediate and extensive surgery, this woman had zero chance of surviving to see the dawn.

The reality, as both Matt and Stan knew, was that the woman was not going to survive this conversation.

"I already told you I don't repeat my questions," Matt continued.

She looked up at him, a mixture of pain and hatred on her face. "Butchie...but you can call me Jessica, you fuckin' pussy."

Matt smiled, admiring her attitude in the face of certain death. "Okay, Butchie, tell me about this Thor and the Nomads. Is he going to come all the way out here from his perverse playground at Dartmouth to kill me?" Matt guessed Thor was the monstrosity of a biker gang leader that he had seen while fleeing Dartmouth-Hitchcock, and who the fake Sheriff Tate had referenced was the Nomad leader who was based out of the Dartmouth green.

Butchie smiled up at Matt. "You have no clue. No fucking clue at all who we are. Do you, Pomfret boy?"

Matt's blood ran cold as Butchie started laughing. *The Nomads knew where we live,* he thought. *They fucking know where we are!*

"Cut the bullshit. You have no clue where we are from."

"He has no clue who we are," Butchie said, talking to herself and grinning. "This motherfucker has no fucking clue. We could take him out in a minute if he were a priority. But I guess he probably just became a priority!" And with that, Butchie started hackling with laughter despite her pain.

"Matt!" Stan called from where he stood at the passenger door of the Humvee. "Come here. Quick."

Leaving Butchie giggling in pain, Matt rushed to Stan.

"Listen!" Stan said.

Matt distinctly heard the crackle of a radio transmission followed by *"Checkpoint Blue, all good."*

Matt looked at Stan. "Shit, they're checking in?"

"Yeah," said Stan. "It's exactly 3:00 am. Must have hourly check-ins."

"Checkpoint White, all good."

"Checkpoint Green, all good."

"Fuck, what color do we think we are?" Matt asked Stan.

Shrugging his shoulders, Stan said, "Who knows? Your guess is as good as mine. The first call was Checkpoint White."

"Checkpoint Yellow, all good."

"Checkpoint Green, all good."

"Fuck!" Matt said in frustration. He turned toward Butchie. "Hey, what color is your checkpoint?"

She looked up and started laughing again, almost hysterically. "Ha! Ha! You motherfucker. Now they know! Now they know! They'll be on you like stink on shit!"

"Checkpoint Black, this is Base. Did you fall asleep?"

"Never mind, we got it. Black, huh?" Matt said to Butchie. Stan reached into the Humvee, grabbed the mic, and said, "Checkpoint Black, all good." There was no reply.

Butchie continued laughing. "They are gonna skin you alive, motherfucker. For real. After they rape you!"

Matt stared at her, expressionless. She looked up and stopped laughing. The smile on her face was replaced with a look of fear as she watched Matt slowly grip his slung M4 and aim at her. Without a word, and with no extraneous movements, Matt fired a single round into her forehead. He didn't even bother to watch her slump to the side, her brains painted on the tree behind her.

"Let's go. We need to get home." Matt said to Stan, moving to get into the front passenger seat of the Humvee as Stan slid in behind the wheel.

CHAPTER 14

October 6, 8:09 am

"Could you repeat that, Liz? Did you say a six-minute delay?" Matt sat in one of the two sitting chairs against the side wall of the upstairs master bedroom, with Liz occupying the other chair. To his right, Christopher and Kelsey sat as sentries in the Lookout. Christopher was looking through binoculars while Kelsey sat behind the sandbags and scanned across the front yard.

Matt was utterly exhausted. He hadn't slept a whole night in several days, and last night had been exceptionally tiring, especially the last few hours preparing for a Nomad attack.

Liz leaned forward in the adjacent chair. "Yes, Matt. As near as I can tell, the HawkEye 360 system is on about a six-minute delay. Technically it's real-time information, but it takes a certain amount of time for HawkEye to process the RF signals it's receiving. Then it takes a few minutes more for QuAI to query the HawkEye data, reformat it into a format we can use in our system, and then update the map we are seeing on our monitor. So yeah, about six minutes from when a radio transmits to when we can see it on our map. Pretty amazing, huh?"

"Okay. Yeah, definitely amazing. Except it only takes about five minutes to drive from the center of Woodstock to our front yard. So any transmissions the Nomads make will have to be out on Route 4. Otherwise, the map won't update until after they're shooting at us. Do I have that right?"

"Uh, yeah, Matt. Put that way, yeah, I guess you do have it right."

"Liz, don't get me wrong. What you're doing here is unbelievable. But we need to factor that six minutes into our reaction time. So I want you to raise the alarm if you see any RF signals to our north, up past Sugarland Farm on either Stage Road or Old Kings Highway. And also, any signals at all on Route 4 between Quechee and Bridgewater. Okay?"

"Got it," said Liz.

"And what about from the Nomad roadblock we raided? Still nothing after the chaos around 4:30 this morning?"

"Well, HawkEye captured dozens of transmissions along Route 4 and at the checkpoint just after 4:30. As we discussed earlier, this was likely their reaction force. We know that our radio in the captured Humvee didn't pick up any of this traffic, so we assume they know we have a radio and have changed frequencies. There have been two additional RF bursts from that location, one at 6 am and the other at just after 7 am."

"Ah, so they've put replacements at the roadblock."

"Yes, Matt. That's our assumption."

"Okay, anything else out of the ordinary?"

"No, not really. There doesn't appear to be any search of the surrounding area, at least based on the radio transmission locations. And before you ask, nothing at all from around Coolidge State Park. I have a special query in QuAI that will sound an alarm if there are any RF transmissions from the park."

"Okay, good. Because if we see a radio transmitting there, we can assume they found the bodies and our ruse didn't work."

"Got it. Anything else, Matt?"

"No, thank you, Liz. And please pass that on to your Dad and Juliet. That computer is giving us an advantage I would never have thought possible. Have you eaten? Go get some breakfast and then get some sleep."

Liz nodded, and Matt watched as she got up and walked

into the hallway and down the stairs. He sat back, closed his eyes while pinching the bridge of his nose, and tried to think of what he was forgetting to do. There was always something. Always.

He spent the next few minutes reviewing all that had happened since returning to the farmhouse at about 4:20 that morning.

Upon pulling up the driveway, they were met by everyone who had returned from the raid. Clare had decided to leave the sentries in place but have everyone else waiting to unload the supplies they knew were coming. When the Humvee and state police SUV were parked, everyone began unloading and stacking things in the driveway next to the open garage door. Matt was sure some people expected to see a wounded Nomad prisoner, but no one said anything when she wasn't present.

Matt watched Clare as she helped unload boxes of MREs. Clare looked over, and their eyes met, Clare nodding almost imperceptibly. Matt knew this was her acknowledging that he had made the right decision for the family.

Matt had already seen what supplies and munitions they had in the SUV, so he went to the Humvee to see what LT had initially loaded in the back. *God damn!* Matt thought. These were game-changers. Matt counted eight bandoleers he knew contained claymore mines complete with firing wire, an electrical blasting cap, and M57 firing device. Matt also saw at least ten 7.62mm ammo cans which Matt knew each contained two one-hundred round belts of ammunition for the M240B machine gun still mounted atop the Humvee. Quite a few other cans and crates were stacked around the back cargo area, and a glance showed these to contain 5.56mm ammo, M67 fragmentation grenades, and M443 40mm grenades. These last items were high-explosive dual-purpose grenades meant to be fired from the two M320 grenade launchers that were lying loose on the cargo bed.

This morning's raid has increased our firepower by at least ten-fold. Considering we took no casualties, I would rate that an overwhelming success! Far in excess of what I originally envisioned. Matt thought this to himself as he continued to take a mental inventory.

It was 4:30 in the morning, and Matt knew that if their earlier radio reply pretending to be Checkpoint Black had worked, then best case, they had until about 7 o'clock before the relief shift found the destroyed roadblock. Worst case, the reaction force was already at the high school trying to figure out what had happened.

You have no fucking clue at all who we are. Do you, Pomfret boy? Butchie's words echoed in Matt's mind.

We could take him out in a minute if he were a priority. Matt wondered if this were true. *Did the Nomads know about the farmhouse on Sugarland Road?* Matt thought that maybe the Nomads figured they were in Pomfret, but Pomfret was a big place, and Matt couldn't believe that the Nomads knew precisely where his family was.

But I guess he probably just became a priority! Butchie had a point there, Matt thought. This was likely true. Unless this Nomad leader, Thor, fell for Matt's ruse. By taking the Humvee and the Harley, along with three of the bodies, Matt thought that the Nomads might initially conclude this was an inside job. *If they fall for it, we just might be in the clear. At least for now.*

Now Butchie's voice in his head was replaced by Matt's old company commander, Captain Monahan. Monahan used to say, *"Hope is not a course of action. You can hope for the best but must plan for the worst."* In his mind, Matt could hear his commander saying this clear as day and knew exactly what they had to do.

From 4:30 until now, Matt had been a whirling dervish of activity. Re-orienting the defensive positions, training people on new weapons, ensuring each position had adequate ammo, and rehearsing the plan in case of attack were all tasks critical to the family's defense. The last hour had been what Matt considered to be the most important - emplacing the claymore mines.

The claymore is considered by many to be the most lethal anti-personnel mine in the US military's arsenal. Widely used by US soldiers during the Vietnam War and every conflict since, the claymore was a command-detonated device that sprayed 700 steel balls in a 60-degree arc that killed or maimed everything in its path out to over fifty meters. The mine was hardened plastic the size of a hardcover book, angled backward slightly at each edge to form a convex surface. In its infinite respect for the intelligence of the US soldier, the US military had stamped "Front Toward Enemy" in large, raised letters across the front of the mine. Many often joked about this, but in Matt's experience, those who joked had never sighted in a claymore during the dark of night with an enemy force approaching. Lying on the ground thousands of miles from home with the pucker factor about as high as it can get, Matt always appreciated being able to run his hands across the front and feel that lettering, knowing that in the heat of the moment, he hadn't made some stupid-ass mistake that was going to get himself or his teammates killed.

In its standard emplacement, the claymore used an electrical blasting cap placed in one of the two plastic wells at the top of the mine. The bottom of the mine came with a pair of scissor-like metal spikes that allowed the mine to be staked into the ground. These worked great in the jungle, but the manufacturer likely had failed to consider the concrete-like consistency of the sunbaked earth outside an Iraqi village or the rocky hardscrabble of Afghanistan, in which sinking these spikes proved a bit more difficult. Matt knew the claymores were the perfect defensive tool for Donald's front yard, and he allowed himself a quick smile, wondering the reaction his brother would have, knowing three claymores now covered the approaches to his front driveway.

With all these measures implemented over the last few hours, Matt currently had the house at 75% security. Twelve pulled sentry across the various fighting positions while four rested or worked on a project.

If the Nomads were going to come, Matt expected them in the next few hours. Matt dozed in the chair, one ear alert to the slightest hint of alarm from Kelsey or Christopher manning the Lookout.

CHAPTER 15

October 6, 4:55pm

"Dad, wake up."

Matt's eyes flew open, and he registered his son standing before him, tugging on his shoulder. "What? Are they coming?" Matt sprung out of the chair and knelt behind the sandbags in front of the window. He expected to see Kelsey there, but it was Amey.

"No, Dad. No one is coming. Mom said to let you sleep, but now she told me to wake you to go downstairs."

"Okay," Matt said, noting the time on his watch and gathering his thoughts. "Okay. I, uh, I'll head downstairs then. Thanks, buddy." Matt tussled his son's hair as he walked by, thought for a second, and then turned and embraced his son in a huge hug.

Christopher hugged him back. "What's that for, Dad?"

"Nothin' buddy. Just thought I'd give you a hug."

"Uh, okay, Dad." Christopher stepped out of his father's embrace and turned to Amey, slightly embarrassed. "Need anything, Amey? I'm off shift but thought I'd see if anyone needed anything."

Matt turned and walked out into the hallway toward the stairs, proud of his son but also a bit sad that his childhood had been stolen by the cataclysm. Instead of tossing a football, his young son was standing guard duty. As Matt walked downstairs, he knew that as long as they were at this farmhouse, his children would never have a normal childhood.

As Matt reached the bottom of the stairs and entered the kitchen, he noticed Clare standing there, putting some things away in the cupboard. Since he was in a hugging mood, he decided to give his wife one as well. Walking up, she turned, saw him approach, and stepped into his hug. What Matt expected to be a cursory hug turned into a a deep, crushing embrace with his wife clinging to him and burying her head in his shoulder.

"It's okay, honey," he whispered. "Everything is going to be okay."

Clare pulled back from his embrace and looked him in the eye. "It's not going to be okay, Matt. We've been lucky. But the day's not always going to end with a happy ending."

"Hmmm, is today going to end with a happy ending?" Matt asked facetiously, a smile on his face. He knew immediately Clare was not in the mood for humor as a dark expression clouded her face.

"Is that all you can think of, Sheridan? A happy ending?" Clare was clearly not enjoying his attempt at humor.

"Um, I'm sorry, honey," said Matt, backpedaling. "I was just trying to be funny. I mean, hell, we're in the apocalypse, and we just stole a bunch of weapons and explosives from a deranged biker gang. Can't a guy make a joke?"

Clare's expression softened slightly, and Matt could tell she wanted to smile but wouldn't let herself go that easily. "Okay, Matt Sheridan. Okay. But no happy ending for you tonight. Unless it's self-performed." She turned back to the sink, and Matt could tell she was smiling at her own wit.

Mission accomplished, Matt changed the subject. "Have you seen Dylan and Liz? It's time to put out OP2."

"Yeah, they're downstairs and ready to go. I think they're with Stan and LT. Everyone else is on watch."

"Great, thanks. I'm going to take them out there and should be back in about an hour. I'll call in when we're heading out and when I'm heading back."

"Okay, honey. Please be careful. I know this is necessary, but

I don't like the two of them being out there alone."

"I know. I feel the same. They'll be fine." Matt turned and walked down the hallway toward the stairs that would take him to the basement. Before descending the stairs, he slung his tactical vest over his shoulders, buckled it in place, and grabbed his M4. He didn't see anyone in the basement, so he walked through the door that would take him to the garage. As he entered, everyone turned at his presence.

"Hey, Matt," said Stan. "Get some sleep?"

"Yeah, I did. Thanks. It was definitely needed."

"Liz and Dylan were going over the claymore one more time," said Stan. "They're ready to go."

"Okay, thanks," Matt replied, stepping up to stand before Dylan and Liz. Matt took a moment and looked at each of them thoroughly, visually inspecting the gear they had on. Liz and Dylan were dressed almost identically, wearing brown cargo pants and a woodland camouflage BDU shirt. He could tell they each wore something heavy, probably a sweatshirt for warmth, underneath the camo shirt. They each wore a tactical assault panel with bulging pouches and several 30-round magazines protruding from the back of each pouch. Matt ensured each had an IFAK, or individual first aid kit, firmly affixed on the left side of their harness. Both Liz and Dylan had a small backpack, and Liz had a large, OD green bag slung over her neck and one shoulder, the bag itself hanging under her left arm.

"Water? Ponchos? Poncho liner?" Matt asked.

"Check," replied Liz, followed immediately by a similar response from Dylan.

"Fresh batteries for the handheld radios?"

"Check," replied both simultaneously.

"And you've double-checked the claymore, Liz? LT?"

"Check," replied Liz.

"Roger," said LT. "We've gone over it several times and double-checked the dual-initiation systems. It's good to go."

"Okay, folks. Let's do it," said Matt as he fished his earbud out of one of the pouches on his vest, put it in, and clipped the toggle switch to the left shoulder of his harness. "Alpha, this is Matt, party of three departing to the south."

"Roger, Matt," replied Derek over the radio. "Stan briefed us earlier. Let us know when you're on your way back."

With that, Matt nodded at both Stan and LT and then walked out the open garage door and headed toward the bridge over the stream behind the house. He never looked back, knowing that Liz and Dylan were following him. When he crossed the bridge, Matt turned to the right and headed south, traversing the side of the hill. Looking to his right, he could see the back side of position Alpha and the yard sloping gently downwards to the south.

Matt followed a small, unmarked footpath until he reached the end of Donald's property, marked by a low stone wall before a large, fallow field. Instead of crossing the field, he skirted it to the east to remain inside the wood line. He turned back south after a few hundred yards. At this point, he was walking straight downhill, and the going was relatively easy. He looked back and saw Liz and Dylan easily keeping pace, each about five meters apart.

Matt's route was parallel to Sugarland Road, albeit about two hundred yards to the east. The woods prevented them from seeing the road, but in the dell off to Matt's right, he could make out the famed Sleepy Hollow Farm. This farm was located almost one kilometer, or six-tenths of a mile, south of Donald's. The area Matt had selected for OP2 was another five hundred meters, putting it exactly one mile south of Donald's farmhouse.

Matt followed the footpath that made walking relatively easy. He was glad the trail existed as it would make Liz and Dylan's return trip much simpler to navigate. Dylan was familiar with these woods, one of the main reasons Matt selected him, but Liz had never stepped foot here before tonight.

In less than ten minutes, Matt knew they were getting quite

close as the trail veered to the right, on a westerly heading to directly intersect Sugarland Road. The three of them walked up to the edge of the road.

"Know where we're at, Dylan?"

"Sure, Matt. I know exactly where this is."

"Think you guys could find your way back, even in the dark."

"No problem, Matt. I've walked that path before. The trees we walked through basically bisect two fields, so we can't get lost as long as we stay in the trees. Eventually, we'll hit the stream behind our house."

"Okay, good. So the plan is quite simple. You're OP2. We're going to find a good spot about thirty meters back in the trees, allowing you good road visibility. See there; we can see almost down to where Sugarland Road ends at Old River Road. You'll be able to see and hear anyone approaching the road. And that's your job. You keep a good lookout all night, alternating one awake and one sleeping. Understood?"

They both nodded affirmatively.

"Good. Radio checks on the hour every hour, but also feel free to call with any questions at any time. The only bad question is one you don't ask. Capisce?"

"Yeah," said Dylan. Liz just nodded.

"Dylan, stay here and keep an eye out down the road. Liz and I are going back to find the best spot for OP2." Dylan nodded, taking a knee behind a large maple tree. Matt and Liz retraced their steps to a spot that provided an excellent view of Sugarland Road to their front and a much longer stretch of the road along a field several hundred meters to the south. Any person or vehicle traveling up Sugarland Road would be easily identifiable.

Matt knelt and gestured for Liz to do the same.

"This is now OP2. You can see Dylan to our front, and down to the left, you can see a wide stretch of the road. That stretch of road is your main focus. We'll put the claymore up where Dylan is, but you'll see anyone coming well before they get into the kill zone."

"Got it, Matt," said Liz, taking off her pack and finding a good spot to set up shop. Matt could see this was an ideal observation post, tucked in behind a low stone providing cover and concealment.

"Okay. Let's go put in the claymore. Hand me the bandolier, please?" Liz reached down and unslung the claymore bag from around her neck, handing the entire bag to Matt. Matt slung it over his neck, reached inside, and pulled out a thick wire spool. He handed this to Liz. Matt then pulled out the claymore mine, looking it over to ensure it had no cracks. Satisfied, Matt put his hand out for the spool of wire, which Liz promptly handed him.

"We should have plenty of wire, but it's important to always start at your position and move forward to the road, not the other way around." Matt unspooled several feet of the wire, made a small byte by doubling up the cord, and then tied it off to a small sapling next to their position. "This will keep the one end secure so it will stay in place as we unspool the wire up to the road. And if you ever do this again, always make sure the initiating device, in our case the manual clacker and the battery, remain in the bandoleer. We're going to arm the mine up there, and the last thing we want is to leave the ability for someone to accidentally set it off while we're up there. Got it?"

"Got it," said Liz, nodding.

"Now, let's walk this up to where Dylan is." Matt began walking back toward the road, unspooling wire as he walked and letting it fall loosely to the ground. As they arrived at the road's edge, he still had about ten meters left of the wire. Dylan knelt behind a three-foot diameter maple tree, and Matt walked around to the front of the tree a few feet off the road's edge. Matt flopped down on his stomach, looking down the road to the south from this prone position.

"Perfect," he said. Pulling the claymore out of the bag, Matt unscrewed one of the threaded caps at the top of the mine and handed it to Liz, who was now standing right beside him. He then unfolded the scissored spikes at the bottom of the mine, separating each pair so they pointed straight down from the mine, at about a thirty-degree angle to each other. He firmly stuck the spikes into the ground and pushed down until three-quarters were embedded in the loam in front of the tree. The claymore was now firmly in place, seated about two inches above the ground, slightly higher than the roadbed. Matt canted his head so his face was directly behind the claymore, his eyes aligned along the knife-edge sight. Matt used his hands to tilt the mine just so, and after a few seconds, he seemed satisfied.

"Okay, you two. See that birch tree about fifty yards down the road on the other side of the road?" Matt looked up and saw that both Liz and Dylan were nodding. "This thing is aimed right at that. When you clack this thing off, everything between this tree and that birch will be absolutely shredded."

Liz reached into one of the pouches on her vest and pulled out some red surveying tape. "Matt, Clare handed this to me earlier. She told me to give it to you when we put in the claymore. Said you'd know what to do with it."

Matt smiled, knowing he had forgotten something. As usual, Clare was two steps ahead, and Matt knew what the red ribbon was for. This wasn't a war zone, and they were not required to be stealthy and leave no markings that might give their position away. Surveyors marked trees all along these rural roads. "Dylan, take this tape and go down and tie a couple of loops around that birch tree, about chest high. You want to be able to see it from the woods back there, where OP2 will be."

Dylan grabbed the roll and jogged down to the tree, returning in a minute after tying a loop around the tree. To anyone driving down the road, it would be a simple surveyor's mark, maybe a property boundary or a tree marked for cutting.

"Okay. Now this is the fun part. Liz, hand me that threaded plastic cap."

Matt took the electrical blasting cap from the inside of the spool and gingerly pulled it free. The blasting cap was a two-inch long aluminum cylinder about the circumference of a #2 pencil. Matt knew these electric blasting caps were stable, but he still always handled them carefully. Taking his time, he slid the wire into the slot cut into the side of each of the small, threaded plastic caps and pulled it tight so the blasting cap was seated inside the well of the plastic cap. He then turned this upside down and pushed the blasting cap into the corresponding well at the top of the claymore, screwing in the plastic piece so that it fit tightly. The result was an electrical blasting cap seated firmly into the top of the claymore mine attached to the wire that ran back to OP2.

"Okay, folks," said Matt, getting to his knees and then using the tree trunk to stand up. "This claymore is now live. Remember, when this thing blows, it will shred everything in a 30-degree arc to its front, out to about fifty meters. Any questions?"

Dylan and Liz nodded - the immensity of the situation fully setting in. They had just emplaced a live anti-personnel mine on a road in Vermont and were expected to kill people with it. Matt let the moment sink in. He knelt and grabbed two handfuls of leaves, spreading them gently over the front of the mine until he was satisfied no one would spot it. Matt turned and walked back to OP2, Liz and Dylan following behind.

At OP2, the three knelt behind the stone wall. Matt reached into the bandoleer and pulled out a green plastic device that looked like some kind of rudimentary square stapler with a small lever held in place by a metal clip.

"This is your M57 firing device," said Matt. "I had LT test it before we left, as I didn't want to get down here and find it didn't work. You simply flip open this clip and then mash it down as hard as you can, over and over, until the claymore explodes. It's electrical, so you create an electrical current when you mash down the lever. The Army teaches you to clack it three times quickly; I tell everyone to keep mashing it until it goes off." Matt demonstrated by clacking the device. He then passed it to Liz and Dylan and had them practice clacking it themselves.

"When the claymore goes off, it's gonna be the loudest thing you've ever heard. You can expect a backblast of rocks and debris to come flying all the way back here. So when you clack this off, you must bury your heads in the dirt. This isn't the movies. Don't watch it blow up because it will be ten times bigger and louder than you can imagine. Understood?"

"Yes," said Dylan and Liz simultaneously.

Matt took the M57 from Liz and knelt on the ground. Leaving the wire knotted to the tree, Matt pulled free the end of the wire, which had several feet of play, and clipped the wire into the rubber gasket on the front of the firing device. He double-checked that the metal clip was in place and set the device on a flat rock.

"This is ready to rock and roll, guys." Matt looked at the two young adults in front of him. "Trust me. I picked you both for a reason. There are dumb 18-year-old privates who set up ambushes and kill the enemy all the time. I have every confidence that you both are more than capable. Juliet and Stan will be monitoring QuAI all night long. Liz, as you told me earlier, we are hopeful that we'll have some indication if the Nomads are coming because, hopefully, they will use the radio en route. If things go to shit, though, I want to be very clear about your orders here at OP2. Now listen to me."

Matt paused to ensure they both fully understood the moment's importance.

"First, at least one of you must always maintain eyes on Sugarland Road. Second, you are to radio any observations, especially any people you see, whether or not you think they're Nomads. Third, if you see Nomads, the plan is for you to initiate the claymore when the first vehicle gets to the marked tree. Hopefully, multiple vehicles will be in the kill zone, but we want the first vehicle to stop cold right here. If, for some reason, the radio is out, and this is important, if you don't hear from me and know those are Nomads, you kill the first vehicle. Understood? If we lose radio contact, you kill the first Nomads, and that will let us know they are coming."

"We understand," said Dylan.

"Good. Now last item. When you clack off that claymore, the two of you are to turn and run up to OP1 as fast as possible. Do not go to the house, as by that time, we'll likely be in direct fire contact with the Nomads, and I don't want anyone to worry about identifying you approaching the house. Stick to the woods, and get to OP1. As fast as you can. When you get there, wait there for me. Got it?"

"Got it," said Dylan.

"Yeah, we got this, Matt," said Liz.

"Okay! I love you both, and I'll see you soon. Try to do one-on and one-off so you get some sleep. I'll change you out tomorrow afternoon if nothing has happened. Stay frosty!"

Matt patted them each on the shoulder and then melted back into the woods, heading back to the house. He thought he'd be worried about leaving these two alone, but he felt pretty confident. Liz and Dylan were both extremely capable, more capable than any Private he'd ever had under his command, and he knew they'd perform their task well.

Now he had to put in place the rest of the plan.

CHAPTER 16

October 6, 10:41 pm

Matt sipped his coffee at the dining room table, watching Stan and Pete pouring over the map in front of them and discussing various options. Upon returning from OP2 at around 6 pm, Matt and LT took the Humvee, minus the M240B machine gun, and parked it in its new position. This was another part of the strategic plan they had all agreed to that morning. Marvi, Clare, and Molly were down in the garage making final adjustments while everyone else was either on sentry duty or sleeping.

"So...are we ready?" Matt asked the other two.

Looking up, Pete was the first to reply. "Getting there, man. Should be fully ready by morning if we work through the night."

"Okay, I think we need to get everything ready as soon as possible. They may not attack tonight, but we need to be ready when they do."

"What if they don't attack tomorrow, Matt? Or the next day? Or the next week?" Stan asked.

Pete answered before Matt could reply. "Second thoughts, Stan? I think we execute the plan tomorrow evening, no matter what. You were the one who proposed that this morning if I remember correctly."

"No, don't get me wrong. We've made the right decision. I'm 100% in favor. I was simply asking the question in case we should hold off for a few days and see what happens with the

Nomads."

"Stan, you make a valid point," said Matt. "But we hashed this out this morning, and we all know how Clare, Marvi, and Molly feel. As soon as we are fully ready to execute, we hit the "Go" button. And it makes perfect sense to do that tomorrow evening, Nomads or not."

"Yeah, agreed," Stan said.

"But I want to be ready by morning. That little voice in my head is screaming that these fucking barbarians are coming tomorrow - and at the slightest indication they're coming, we need to put the plan in motion. As we discussed, the only thing of real value that we have is our lives - and I'm not gambling with that, hoping for a few more days of peace."

"We're all on board, Matt. Everyone has been working their asses off to get ready," said Pete.

"I know. I know. We've all had to make life-or-death decisions, and we all know this plan is the best chance for our long-term survival. All of us, not just most of us." Matt felt the pressure of command, knowing everyone was relying on his initial plan. He'd been working on it in various pieces for the past few days, mostly involving Liz, Clare, and Marvi. Since this morning, however, when all the adults gathered to discuss Stan's phone call with Cheyenne Mountain, everyone had put in their two cents to improve the plan. Not only was everyone on board, but Matt was confident their plan was an excellent one.

Ever since Matt had spoken with Rob several days before, Stan had been trying to reach out to his contacts in the federal government in Cheyenne Mountain. This morning he had finally gotten through to someone on a satellite phone, and the discussion reaffirmed everything Rob had told Matt during their previous call.

The federal government now consisted of six geographically separated enclaves spread throughout the United States and operating under military command. President Hutchinson had died - not from the pox but a heart attack. The stress of the cataclysm had taken its toll on the man. The Vice President had been killed in the nuclear blast that wiped out central Washington DC. The president had nominated General Donovan, chairman of the Joint Chiefs, as the new Vice President, and this was approved by what remained of the Congress. Donovan, the former commanding general of the famed 101st Airborne Division, was now the President of the United States. Both Matt and Stan respected the man, but there was only so much that could be done with the entire world in such a state of collapse.

The first enclave under government control was the thirty-mile radius around Cheyenne Mountain and Colorado Springs, Colorado. This area was functioning with some degree of normalcy, but as close as Denver, it was still complete anarchy. The spread of Black Pox had decimated every community across the country. For the most part, society had devolved into small pockets of upstanding citizens banding together to protect themselves from those who sought to take advantage of the situation.

The five other enclaves were all centered around military installations that had been reinforced by both military firepower and a supply of the updated vaccine. Four of these enclaves were in the western part of the United States. San Diego and Seattle had been quick to establish martial law with a robust military component of soldiers and marines, along with dissemination of the vaccine. Oahu, an island with a large Navy and Army presence, was also able to seal itself off and vaccinate its residents. Fort Hood was the fourth enclave in the West but had significantly more difficulty than the other enclaves. Fort Hood had no natural geographic boundaries to support its defense outside Killeen in central Texas. As such, it had proven difficult to seal itself off fully. The result was having to defend 360 degrees amid significant levels of desertion. Small unit commanders, unhappy with a micro-managing commanding general, were leaving in droves with their families to seek greener pastures outside the confines of the Fort Hood complex.

Norfolk, Virginia, was the only enclave east of the Mississippi. The President, soon after the bombings, had ordered both the 2nd Marine Division and 82nd Airborne Division, both stationed in North Carolina, to immediately establish a cordon around the military installations in Norfolk and Virginia Beach. Knowing that Naval Station Norfolk was the key to the Atlantic Fleet, this area was deemed of critical importance, and the reinforcement by two infantry divisions ensured its protection in the ensuing chaos of the Black Pox pandemic.

These six areas were all that remained under the control of the federal government of the United States. Stan had spent the remainder of his phone conversation pumping his contact for information about what was happening in New England.

Stan's contact confirmed their previous knowledge of The Base and provided further details on how pervasive and evil this group was. The Base was a cross between the Taliban and the Gilead forces from The Handmaid's Tale, all disguised as freedom fighters for a new American republic. While Cheyenne Mountain had incomplete information, there were reports of widespread massacres, forced incarceration, and kidnapping of women for war brides and breeding. Stan's initial information that The Base had a foundation of Islamic fundamentalism was confirmed by intelligence gathered at Cheyenne Mountain. The Base had completely decapitated, both literally and figuratively, state and local leadership throughout the mid-Atlantic and southern New England states and, by all accounts, had established rigid control from Massachusetts to Maryland.

In northern New England, a line had been drawn from Portsmouth, New Hampshire west to Manchester and upwards along Interstate 89 to Burlington, Vermont. This was the current northern line of control of The Base. It was unclear whether The Base intended to push north of this line, as most efforts focused on solidifying control of their current territory.

Stan had asked about the situation in northern New England, and the reply he received was bleak. The vaccination efforts initiated by the President had failed across much of the country, but in particular in the mid-Atlantic and New England. The Base had focused its initial efforts on seizing the vaccine and had been highly successful in their efforts. Manchester, New Hampshire, had been the central hub for vaccine dissemination in northern New England, and The Base seized the airport right after LT had flown to Dartmouth-Hitchcock. Aware of The Base's seizure of Portsmouth and Manchester, the governor of Maine had relocated her state government to the city of Portland and had ordered all of the small numbers of national guard units in the state to protect this port city. What was left of the New Hampshire national guard also fled to Portland. Stan's contact confirmed that the Nomads were simply one of the many criminal groups The Base had co-opted to do their bidding in seizing control.

Based on all the information they had about the Nomads, from both their own experiences and the information provided by Cheyenne Mountain about The Base, they refined Matt's long-term strategic plan and settled on their next course of action. As Stan had concluded, the biggest question facing them now was whether they executed it of their own accord or under pressure from an impending Nomad attack.

Matt got up from the table and headed to the basement to see if Clare and the ladies needed help. He knew their part of the plan was ultimately the most critical at this stage, but he also felt confident they had the three most intelligent individuals in the family entirely in charge of that aspect.

CHAPTER 17

October 7, 9:29 am

Matt was sitting with Christopher on the sandbags of the new fighting position they had just finished in the woods above the creek behind Donald's. The spot was below OP1 and gave them a panoramic view downwards over the top of the house. They could see where the driveway met Sugarland Road and could also see the open field in front of position Alpha down to the wood line.

"Matt, they're coming!" Juliet's voice came through the earpiece, her tone a bit frantic. "HawkEye has dozens of RF transmissions that appear to be moving east on Route 4. They are just outside Quechee."

"Okay, everyone," Matt said as calmly as he could. "This is it. *Execute. Execute. Execute.* I want everyone in their assigned place by 9:30. That's six minutes."

Matt looked at his son, the fear evident on his young face. "It's okay, buddy. I trust you to care for your Mom and Laurie, right?" He could see tears beginning to well in his son's eyes.

"Yes, Dad," said Christopher, wiping his eyes before the tears could fall. "Don't worry about us. Just take care of you!"

"Deal!" Matt said, grabbing his son for a quick hug and then helping him stand up to jog down to the house. Everything was in place. They had rehearsed several times earlier this morning, and Matt knew six minutes was plenty of time.

As they arrived at the back of the house, Matt saw a hive of activity in the driveway. He nudged his son toward his mother, who was buckling Laurie into the back seat of their Chevy Tahoe, then clicked the toggle on his radio mic. "OP2, this is Matt. Did you copy Juliet's report? Nomads are just west of Quechee heading into Woodstock."

"Roger, Matt," replied Liz over the radio. "OP2 is ready."

"I want one of you with binoculars searching down to Old River Road. Give me a sitrep with numbers of vehicles and whatever else you can see."

"Okay, Matt. We're on it."

Matt stood in the driveway, not wanting to get in anyone's way. He watched as Stan and Marvi shuffled to the back of their Range Rover, carrying one of the crates in which the QuAI computer servers were stored. Right behind them came Pete and Juliet toting a similar case, this one likely loaded with hard drives.

As they loaded the cases into the back of the Range Rover, Derek and LT came bounding out of the garage. Unlike the others who did not appear suited for battle, Derek and LT wore armored plate carriers stuffed with level IV ceramic plates. Multiple pouches stuffed with 30-round magazines protruded from the front of the plate carriers. Additionally, they each wore a cut-down ballistic helmet with radio earmuffs, several they had liberated from the Windsor County Sheriff's Office two weeks prior. They looked ready for war.

"All set, guys? You know what to do. Any questions?"

"Negative, Matt," said LT.

"Ready, Uncle Matt," chimed Derek.

"Okay. Get to your positions. The new position on the hill is called Charlie, and I'll be there in a few minutes. I will initiate any fire. You hang tight until I shoot first. But when I start firing, you let loose and kill everything you see. LT, remember: six-to-nine-round bursts. I'd rather have you go longer than shorter. They call it a machine gun for a reason, right?"

"Got it," said LT.

"And when I yell 'fall back', you fucking fall back and run up to OP1. No hesitation - and I mean *none*! And LT, don't forget to bring the pig with you up the hill!" Matt said, using the euphemistic term of endearment machine-gunners used to refer to the M240B. "Now go. And be careful!"

As the two young men jogged to their positions, LT to Alpha and Derek to Bravo, Matt walked over to where Clare stood by the open driver's door of their Tahoe. He glanced at his watch and saw it said 9:34. Matt could see Christopher sitting in the front passenger seat, an M4 rifle cradled in his arm and pointing out the passenger window. Laurie sat in the back, almost lost in the sea of equipment and supplies that surrounded her. Clare, Marvi, and Molly had spent all night packing each vehicle with a carefully prepared list of items they would need. Matt was glad to see that his wife had made both his son and daughter wear full body armor and helmets.

"You should wear body armor as well, Clare. Just in case."

"We don't have enough, Matt. Only four sets, and those go to Derek, LT, Christopher, and Laurie. Besides, we're going to be fine." The glass was always half full for Clare, a trait Matt loved dearly.

"I love you," said Matt. Clare stepped forward and kissed him deeply.

"I love you too." Clare stepped back from the embrace, not wanting to get emotional. "We'll see you in just a bit. You're the one who should be careful!"

"We'll be fine. The plan is just to keep them occupied so you guys get far away. I'll see you at the linkup."

"Be careful, Matt. No heroics. Just get everyone to the linkup site." She turned and got into the vehicle.

Matt looked around and saw that all the vehicles were loaded, and everyone was giving him the thumbs up. He jogged forward to where Pete sat in his Jeep Wrangler, the lead vehicle of the four. Pete had his window rolled down, and Matt saw Grace sitting beside him in the passenger seat. Like Christopher, she also had an M4 in her lap.

"Don't worry about us, Matt. We'll be fine."

"I know, man. I have complete faith in you and everyone."

"You're the one we all worry about. You take care of yourself and get the five of you to the meeting point as soon as possible. We'll probably be out of radio contact, but try us when you're about five miles out."

"Will do. Be safe, brother," said Matt. Pete nodded, started his engine, stuck his arm out, and twirled his hand like a cowboy signaling the wagon train was leaving. Matt stood there and watched, the gravel crunching under tires as the SUVs drove by him. He waved as everyone gave him a thumbs up.

As the last vehicle, Donald's Suburban, turned north on Sugarland Road, Matt looked at his watch - 9:36. He looked up at Donald's house, his family's home for the last month, and realized there was nothing left inside that he needed. Everything of value was loaded up, and the memories were all securely stored in his head.

Matt ran across the bridge in back of the house and up to his overwatch on the hill at position Charlie. He suppressed his urge to ask Liz for a sitrep, confident she would call in as soon as she saw something. Settling behind the sandbags he and Christopher had emplaced, he took stock of his equipment. His M4 leaned against his pack behind him while his Remington 700 sniper rifle was propped against the sandbag to his front. From this perch, Matt could engage targets on the road and the likely foot approaches across the fields in front of both positions Alpha and Bravo. Matt could see LT standing in his fighting position, looking over the top of the M240B, while Derek was in position Bravo to Matt's right, using binoculars to scan both up and down Sugarland Road.

Matt's initial weapon for this battle sat on the sandbag directly to his front. This weapon consisted of two large 12-volt batteries taped together, sitting next to two black wires with the copper leads exposed. Matt knew that this wire led to three claymores daisy-chained across the house's front yard, capable of obliterating anything along a hundred-yard front of Sugarland Road.

The other weapon Matt had handy was the small M320 grenade launcher. Looking almost like a futuristic toy gun, this single-shot weapon could lob 40mm grenades up to 350 meters away. The stand of trees below Alpha, exactly 160 meters away, was the most likely foot approach by the Nomads, and Matt was confident he could drop grenades onto them with devastating effect.

"This is OP2. We see them, Matt. Just turned onto Sugarland," Liz said, her voice raised with excitement. Before Matt could reply, she spoke again. "Jesus! We can't count them all. It's motorcycles! Dozens of them."

"Okay, Liz. Are there any Humvees or trucks?" Matt asked, keeping his voice calm and hoping it would rub off.

"Yeah, four Humvees! In front. Followed by maybe thirty motorcycles." The hysteria in Liz's voice had risen considerably.

"Okay, Liz. You and Dylan know what to do. Should be about ten to fifteen seconds. Clack off the claymore when that first Humvee gets to the red ribbon."

"Roger..."

Matt waited a few seconds then heard a tremendous *Crump!* in the valley below and turned to see a large cloud of gray smoke rising above the treeline. He listened carefully but did not hear any small arms fire. This was a good sign. Hopefully, Liz and Dylan had bugged out as instructed.

"Matt, we did it!" This time it was Dylan speaking through the radio. He was clearly out of breath, and it sounded like he was running. "We've left OP2 and are running up the path. We should be at OP1 in about ten minutes."

"Roger, Dylan. Great job, you two!" Matt said.

"I'm pretty sure they didn't see us." This was Liz, also panting a bit as she jogged. "We definitely got them, though. I looked back and could see the first Humvee fucking trashed. I think we fucked up the second one too." Matt had to smile just a bit. This was the high of combat that only those who've been in it can understand. Going from being scared out of your mind to feeling like you just won the Super Bowl in seconds was an indescribable series of emotions. One second wondering if you're about to die, and in the next moment, knowing that you not only survived but have just won the ultimate contest of wills. You were still breathing while your opponent had given up his rifle for a harp. Coupled with the massive surge of adrenaline, Matt knew the high Dylan and Liz were on would fuel them all the way to OP1.

"LT, Dylan, get ready." Matt realized his radio call was unnecessary as the roaring sound of Harley-Davidson motorcycles hit them like a shock wave. The motorcycles were coming fast, maybe only seconds away. Matt knew it was likely that at least two Humvees would arrive in front of the roaring motorcycles, and he expected them to pull up right in front of the driveway. He grabbed the battery and the wire, prepared to initiate the daisy-chained claymores and rain hell onto these barbarians.

Matt watched the lead Humvee coming up from the South on Sugarland Road. It had to be traveling nearly 50 miles per hour, and Matt expected it to slam on its brakes at any moment. Matt could see a black-helmeted, leather-clad Nomad in the turret, holding on tightly to the pedestal-mounted machine gun in front of him. A second Humvee appeared behind the first, and Matt could see dozens of motorcycles following in a cloud of dust.

What the fuck!!! Matt thought. *The Humvee didn't stop!* Matt couldn't believe his eyes. The Humvee flashed by the front of Donald's house and continued up Sugarland Road. The Nomad battle group seemed intent on speeding to their location, but Matt realized the gang wasn't focused on Donald's farmhouse.

Matt's mind raced, attempting to assess the possibilities. *Where are they going? They clearly came up Sugarland Road for a reason. Oh my god! Are they chasing his family's convoy? How could they know about them?* All these thoughts flashed through Matt's mind, only to be interrupted by a sustained burst of machine gun fire - a burst that went on so long Matt knew the gunner was extremely inexperienced and not likely to hit anything.

Molly's!!!

"They're shooting up Molly's, Matt!" Derek spoke over the radio a split second after Matt came to the same conclusion. "They think we're at Molly's!"

It suddenly occurred to Matt how likely it was that the three bikers from last week may have called in their address, and the Nomads figured they were holed up at Molly's farm.

"Okay, guys. Hold tight. Let's see what happens." Part of Matt was hoping the Nomads might find Molly's house empty and pass them by.

"Driveway!" Matt heard Derek shout into the radio, followed by rapid-fire shots from position Bravo. Matt looked down and saw what must have been almost two dozen motorcycles bunched at the bottom of the driveway, at least six of which had maneuvered around the chain and were riding up the driveway. It looked to Matt like the gang members were trying to flank the Humvees and using Donald's property to approach Molly's farm from that direction. Unfortunately, that meant going right over the top of Derek. *Fuck!* Matt thought, immediately realizing that they were indeed fucked. The entire plan was based around an attack from the south! The farmhouse blocked the M240B in position Alpha from firing to the north. *What a fucking shit show!*

Matt had no choice but to fire the claymores to prevent Derek from being overrun. He touched the wires to the exposed battery terminals and was rewarded with an almost instant detonation. The deadly sheet of ball bearings from three claymores flew across the breadth of the front yard and driveway, eviscerating everything in its path. The devastation was unlike anything Matt had witnessed this close. Those bikers closest to the claymores were blown off their motorcycles, while many of those idling on the road simply dropped to the ground like marionettes with their strings cut. Except in this case, it wasn't strings but dozens of ball bearings shredding their organs. Motorcycles fell over like dominoes, and as the cloud of dirt and debris settled, almost all of the gang members were killed or severely wounded.

Holy fucking shit! Matt thought. *That definitely worked!*

Before Matt had more time to gloat, Matt heard a change in the firing of the Nomad's Humvee-mounted machine gun while Derek yelled over the radio. "They got me pinned down, Matt. Do something!"

Matt looked to his right and could see the rear Humvee was still on Sugarland Road, about halfway between Donald's and Molly's. While the vehicle still pointed north, the turret gunner spun his gun around and was now shooting directly into the sandbags in front of Derek's position. Derek was completely pinned down, and if he poked his head up, it would be blown off.

The closest weapon to Matt was the Remington 700, so Matt grabbed it and tucked it into his armpit, sighting through the scope. The Humvee was only about 200 yards away, so Matt instinctively knew that no yardage adjustments were necessary. Putting the reticle directly on the torso of the gunner, Matt pulled the trigger. He followed it up with two quick shots and saw that the gunner was dead, hanging limply in the turret.

"Machine gun dead. Engage targets, Derek. Focus on the enemy along the road."

Matt knew the claymores had taken out many but not all of the Nomads, and Matt had no idea how they would hold off those remaining. The plan had been for a quick strike and then falling back to OP1. While Matt knew all plans go to shit, he never thought it would go to shit this badly.

"They're trying to rally at the front. I got 'em," said LT into the radio, followed a second later by the chatter of his M240B. Unlike the Nomad gunner's sustained burst, LT fired controlled bursts of six-to-nine rounds into targets he could see along the road. Firing like this, Matt knew the M240B was lethal.

Matt saw the Nomads in the rear Humvee pulling their dead comrade out of the turret, with another Nomad stepping up in replacement. Matt dropped the sniper rifle and grabbed the M320. Estimating the range at 200 meters, Matt fired a high-explosive dual-purpose round at the vehicle. The 40mm was a low-velocity round, and Matt watched its trajectory like a baseball flying through the air. He immediately knew that it would be short, and he watched as the grenade exploded about ten meters in front of the Humvee. While not lethal, the explosion was enough to pepper the vehicle with shrapnel and cause the gunner to drop into the turret. Matt reached down to the bandolier laid in front of him and pulled another of the gold-tipped HEDP rounds, loading it quickly into the open breach of the grenade launcher. Using Kentucky windage and adding a bit of distance to his previous shot, Matt pulled the trigger and watched the round arc directly toward the Humvee. It hit the vehicle's hood and exploded through the windshield, shredding the occupants.

"North, Matt! Molly's!" Matt heard Derek yell into the radio. Matt looked to his right and saw the lead Humvee driving off-road into the shallow draw separating Donald's and Molly's property. In seconds the vehicle would crest the ridge and plunge fire down into Derek's position. Derek wouldn't last five seconds.

Matt loaded another HEDP grenade and was about to fire when he heard running steps coming up behind him. He whirled, expecting to see Nomads flanking his position. He breathed a sigh of relief when he saw it was Dylan and Liz.

Ignoring them momentarily, Matt lined up his M320 leaf sight onto where he estimated the Humvee would appear. The sniper in him estimated the range at 250 meters.

"Grab some grenades and prepare to hand them to me!" Matt yelled to whoever had flopped down next to him, realizing immediately it was Liz. Matt saw the nose of the Humvee crest the ridge and fired his grenade. He had aimed at a spot about twenty meters in front, hoping this accounted for the vehicle's forward speed. The three seconds it took for the grenade to impact was agony, but Matt was pleasantly surprised when it exploded under the right front tire of the Humvee. He grabbed another round from Liz and reloaded. As he lined up for another shot, he was aware that Dylan was rapidly firing at the Humvee with his M4. Now stationary, Dylan's rounds were on target. The turret gunner was nowhere to be seen, and Matt could see Dylan's bullets punching through the front windshield.

Matt took a breath, lined up carefully, and fired. The three watched as the grenade arced and exploded on the front bumper, devastating the Humvee and its occupants.

"Keep putting rounds on target, Dylan. Watch for anyone opening the doors and trying to flee."

Dylan didn't reply, but he kept firing.

Matt noticed a lull in the firing to his front. LT was occasionally letting loose with a burst of machine gun fire, but otherwise, the shooting had stopped.

"Break Contact! Break Contact! Derek, LT, both of you fall back now!" Matt said over the radio. Turning to Liz, "Keep your eye on the road. Put rounds into anything that moves. Call out if you see a muzzle flash."

Their firing seemed to cease from across the road. Matt watched as Derek and LT stayed low inside the shallow trench and ran toward the small wooden bridge spanning the creek below them. Matt knew from walking the terrain that the two of them should be completely hidden from view by anyone down on the road. Now that the Humvee in the north field had been destroyed, Derek and LT should be able to safely run up to OP1.

"Okay, you two," Matt said beside Dylan and Liz. "Let's get to OP1 and meet those two knuckleheads." Matt handed the M320 to Dylan and then slung the bandolier of the remaining 40mm grenades over his shoulder. He grabbed the Remington 700 and turned to throw his small rucksack over his shoulder and pick up his M4.

Dut-dut-dut-dut! Dut-dut-dut-dut-dut! Dut-dut-dut!

The unmistakable sound of 7.62mm machine-gun fire from the road made Matt, Liz, and Dylan all dive for cover. Over the continuous fire came the roaring sound of more Harley-Davidson motorcycles revving to a stop in front of the house. Matt realized the machine gun was not aimed at them in OP2 but was peppering the front of Donald's house. The bikers, most still sitting in the saddles of the motorcycles, were also firing rapidly into the house. The sustained rate of fire was incredible, and anyone in the wooden house would have been completely suppressed if not outright killed in the onslaught.

Except the house was empty.

"Don't fire!" Matt hissed at his companions. "They don't know we're here, and I don't want to give away our position." Matt pulled the sniper rifle into his armpit and settled himself into a prone-supported firing position using the sandbags to his front. A quick scan of the back of the house proved that LT and Derek had already crossed the bridge and must be running up the footpath to OP1.

"Both of you, head back to OP1. Now! Link up with Derek and LT and get ready to roll. I'll be right behind you, but I might be coming in hot!"

"I'll stay here with you, Matt. We need to take these fuckers out," said Dylan, lying down beside him.

"That's an order, Dylan. I got this. You and Liz get back. We're not fighting here. We're breaking contact. I just want to see if I can disable that machine gun." Dylan looked at him for a second, then nodded, jumped up, and began moving up the hill to catch up to Liz.

Sighting through the Leupold scope, Matt's goal was to take out the Nomad in the Humvee's turret and then slip away to OP1. The machine gun was still hammering rounds into the farmhouse as Matt lined up his rifle's scope. This was an easy shot, and Matt began to squeeze the trigger.

What the fuck is that! Matt thought, catching a glimpse of something before putting enough pressure on his trigger to send a round down range. *Is that a fucking giant!*

Matt adjusted the scope slightly to zero in on a man standing in the Humvee's open driver's side door, the side farthest away from Matt as the Humvee faced north up Sugarland Road. *This must be Thor!* Matt thought, taking in the giant of a human being standing there. The guy must have been close to seven feet tall and big enough to have eaten his brother. He was extremely muscular, his biceps bulging in his sleeveless leather cut as he pointed out windows for the machine gunner to target. He wore a black ball cap on backward, under which his blond hair was pulled back into a ponytail, and the sides of his head were shaved. Spittle flew from his mouth as Thor screamed and gestured to his remaining bikers to keep firing.

Fuck this guy! Matt thought. He slowed his breathing, keeping the reticle centered on Thor's nose. *This fucker's head's so big it's probably the size of the average man's torso!* Matt squeezed the tip of his right index finger and was startled when the rifle fired, a sign to Matt of an accurate shot. He watched in the scope as the 180-grain bullet hit Thor's upper lip at just under 3000 feet per second. The back of Thor's neck exploded in a red spray of blood, and Matt could see Thor's eyes roll up into his head as the man dropped to his knees and fell to the side.

Unsure whether the machine gunner had noticed Matt's muzzle flash, Matt cycled the bolt on his rifle, aligned his scope onto the gunner's chest, and put a round into him, followed by another to the gunner's head as he lay splayed out on the top of the Humvee's roof.

When the machine gun stopped firing, so did the rest of the Nomads along the road. Matt watched for a few seconds as two Nomads crawled over to check on Thor. Matt considered putting another round into the giant's skull, as Matt could see the top half of Thor's head poking out by the Humvee's front left tire. But Matt could also see Thor's dead, vacant eyes and figured the man was already on his way to Hell instead of

Valhalla.

Matt wasn't sure how many of the Nomads remained or if there were reinforcements on the way. *Now's as good a time as any to break contact.* Matt gathered up all of his equipment and headed up the hill to OP1.

CHAPTER 18

October 7, 10:51 am

Matt sat in the front passenger seat of the Humvee as they sped north on Howe Hill Road south of Sharon, Vermont. After killing Thor, Matt ran back up the hill to find everyone at OP1 waiting for him. From there, the five of them had jogged through the woods exactly one thousand meters, or one klick, due east of OP1. This was the location he and LT had stashed the stolen Humvee.

The jog was mostly uphill and a bit of an ass-kicker as they jogged about as fast as Matt could go, strapped down with several weapons. With Liz and Dylan in the lead, it occurred to Matt that he was no longer the best athlete in the group. Used to always being one of the strongest with the most endurance, he was a bit embarrassed seeing how fleet of foot both Liz and Dylan were. They were barely breathing hard while Matt was sucking in huge lungfuls of air, trying to keep up. *In my defense*, Matt thought, *I am carrying two rifles, a backpack, and a bandolier of 40mm grenades.*

Matt stumbled a bit, and LT, running right behind, said, "Are you alright, Matt? Want me to carry something?"

Matt shook his head and kept running. *That young motherfucker is carrying the 240 Bravo and has the balls to ask if I need help!* Matt smiled, realizing he was getting old but proud that his team, his family, was so strong. The knot in his side disappeared as he began to recognize the terrain and knew the Humvee was less than a hundred yards ahead.

Arriving at the vehicle, LT climbed into the turret and mounted the M240B onto the pedestal. The ammo box was already full, and he opened the feed tray, aligned the first round, and slammed the cover down. Everyone else threw their packs and extra gear into the rear cargo area and jumped into their assigned seats. Dylan was the designated driver, and Matt sat in the front passenger seat. Liz was behind Dylan, with Derek behind Matt and LT standing in the turret.

As Matt was the last to slam his door shut, he yelled, "Let's go!" Dylan sped out down the cow path and through the open gate into a large pasture. At the end of the field, he turned left on a gravel road, heading north. This road ended at the last farmhouse on this road, and Dylan swerved to the left, up a small embankment, and onto an open track with major power lines above them. Dylan had been selected as the driver because he was most familiar with the area and knew that this trail followed the power line up to where it crossed Old Kings Highway, approximately three miles to the north. At Old Kings Road, Dylan turned left and made two quick rights to put them on Howe Hill Road.

While the speed limit was posted at 35 mph, Matt told Dylan to push it a bit, and they were now cruising at just under 60 mph. Howe Hill Road led north, approximately eight miles to Sharon, Vermont.

Using the radio transmission info provided by the HawkEye system, along with detailed satellite imagery from QuAI and the maps Amey had previously printed before losing power, Matt had spent quite a bit of time yesterday plotting the exact route they should all take for their evacuation.

Their first priority was to break through the ring of roadblocks the Nomads had emplaced in a circumference around their Dartmouth headquarters in Hanover. If the Nomad territory were a clockface with Dartmouth at the center, Donald's farmhouse in Pomfret was located halfway basically at the end of the little hand as it was pointing to ten o'clock. The RF map clearly showed the location of each Nomad roadblock, and the two roadblocks they were concerned with were located along I-89 to the north in Randolph and on I-91 south of Thetford. These two roadblocks, located on the outer ring at 11 o'clock and 1 o'clock respectively, were strategically positioned to control traffic along the major routes to Hanover's north and northwest. Matt's plan was to use back roads to slip through a gap in the middle right at the 12 o'clock position.

The key to traveling east from Pomfret was crossing the White River; there were only a few places this could be done by car. Looking at the Hawkeye RF display, it was clear that the River Road bridge in Sharon had zero radio transmissions in the last two weeks. The decision to evacuate most of the family just before the attack was based on this assessment. In discussing the "breakout," Matt wanted to give the SUVs the greatest chance of crossing the White River undetected. By leaving immediately prior to the Nomad assault, they all agreed it was less likely the Nomads would have random patrols and instead would likely have massed their forces for the attack on Donald's farmhouse. When the family convoy departed earlier that morning, their goal was to cross the White River in Sharon, stop a few miles north of town, and wait for Matt and the others.

Matt looked up from his map and saw they were now less than a mile south of the bridge, putting them a few miles from the laager position where Pete was supposed to have stopped the convoy.

"Pete, Clare…this is Matt. Do you read me?"

"Yes!" Clare replied instantly. "Is everyone alright?"

"All good. Not a scratch on us. Can't say the same for the Nomads."

"Great. Where are you now?"

"Just coming up on the bridge. Are we clear?"

"Yes," answered Clare. "Road was all clear. No signs of Nomads or anyone else in Sharon. We're at the designated linkup spot."

"Roger. See you in a few."

CHAPTER 19

October 7, 12:16 pm

Matt stood in the open passenger door of the Humvee, binoculars pressed to his eyes and scanning the far bank of the Connecticut River. Derek was now manning the M240B and trained the weapon straight toward the bridge before them. A large sign beside the vehicle indicated that the Newbury-Haverill Boat Launch was "Temporarily Closed."

After linking up and exchanging hugs and tears of joy with the rest of the family in the driveway of a small horse farm on the north side of Sharon, Pete had led the convoy north on Fay Brook Road toward the village of Stafford. Stan, Liz, and Amey had meticulously planned this part of the route to the last detail. After more than an hour of driving, they were parked in Newbury, Vermont, overlooking a small, two-lane bridge over the Connecticut River into New Hampshire.

Matt had been scanning the far bank for any sign of movement for several minutes. The bridge and Route 10 on the other side appeared to be clear.

"Seems clear, Pete," Matt spoke into his radio. "We're in a good overwatch position here. Go ahead and cross the bridge and push through until you're parked on Route 10. Once you give us the go-ahead, the rest of us will follow."

"Roger," replied Pete.

The black Jeep Wrangler carrying Pete and Grace, idling quietly a hundred meters behind the Humvee and outside the view of the bridge, accelerated down the road and across the bridge. Matt lost sight of the Jeep on the far side, but Pete's calm voice immediately broadcasted that the far side was clear and gave the green light for the rest of the convoy to follow.

They were making great time en route to their first stop, which they had selected outside the small town of Shelburne, New Hampshire. Located almost exactly on the New Hampshire-Maine state border, this would put them just shy of halfway to their final destination.

Matt jumped into the Humvee and motioned for Dylan to move out. As they approached the two-lane bridge over the Connecticut River, Matt checked the side-view mirror to ensure the three SUVs behind him were following. Once across, they turned north on Route 10, and Pete's Jeep took back the lead position.

"Should be the next right, guys. Follow signs for Route 116 or Easton Road." Matt said on the radio.

"Roger." This time the reply was from Grace, riding shotgun with Pete. Matt was doing the navigation so that Grace and Pete could keep their eyes focused on identifying any dangers ahead. Matt also knew that Grace was probably rolling her eyes at the moment, as she had a Garmin GPSMAP handheld mounted on the dash in front of her, displaying every twist and turn of their route. Stan and Pete had brought two of the Garmin GPSMAPs, and Dylan also had a less-sophisticated Garmin model he used for hiking the Appalachian Trail. While Matt appreciated the simplicity and accuracy of the GPS, at heart, he was old-school - hence the roadmap resting on his thigh. Redundancy was fine with Matt; he would much rather Grace be annoyed than the convoy miss a turn.

Matt had been on Route 116 before and knew they had approximately twenty miles on a narrow two-lane road with very few homes. The rural road skirted the west side of Kinsman and Cannon mountains, the latter being one of Matt and Clare's favorite skiing destinations. Thoughts of this morning's battle crept into Matt's mind, only to be purposely tamped down as Matt did not want to dwell on how lucky they'd been. Or, looked at differently, how close they had come to catastrophe. The Nomad's inability to find the right farmhouse had completely shredded his defensive plan. Without the claymores and M320 grenade launcher, Derek and LT would likely have been killed, if not Matt himself.

Forcing his mind to change subjects, Matt thought of what lay ahead. Matt resolved that Vermont was the past as they sped toward Franconia, New Hampshire. Maine was now the future.

Matt turned to see if Liz was sleeping in the seat behind the driver. A glance showed she was awake, staring blankly out the side window, her mind likely 80 miles back in Pomfret.

"You awake, Liz?" Matt asked, needing to raise his voice a bit to be heard over the noise of the Humvee's diesel engine and open turret.

"Yeah," she replied, snapping out of her reverie. "What's up?"

"I know we all agreed to bypass Littleton, but did you and your dad come to any conclusions about all the radio traffic there?"

Liz paused momentarily, thinking of the detailed conversations they had all had while planning the route to the Maine coast. Littleton, a small town of about 6,000 people in northern New Hampshire where Interstate 93 crosses into Vermont, showed by far the most significant radio traffic in northern New Hampshire and Maine, although it was still not much of a cluster. In fact, the HawkEye system had shown that there was hardly any concentrated radio traffic above the capital city of Concord.

"No, which is why we pushed for the route that would circumvent Littleton. There's a large state police barracks there and a National Guard armory, but we couldn't be sure if this radio traffic was a product of good guys or bad guys. We know they set up roadblocks and a refugee containment area in Littleton off I-93, but we also think it's highly likely the police and soldiers were some of the first to get smallpox. My dad felt there was too high a probability that Littleton might be a northern outpost for the Nomads.

"Got it," said Matt. "Well, I think we made the right call. The spot you selected in Shelburne looks perfect for tonight. We should be there in just over an hour, and we can set up camp, review what happened earlier, and plan for getting to the coast tomorrow. Tomorrow's drive is only about 3-4 hours."

"Yeah," replied Liz somewhat listlessly, still mostly staring out the window.

Matt turned and snapped his fingers. Liz turned to look at Matt, focusing on him for the first time in this conversation. "You did good today, Liz."

"Did I?"

"Yeah, you really did. You can't dwell on it, though."

"That claymore killed a lot of people, Matt. *I* killed a lot of people. Just by clicking a lever on a plastic box."

"Yeah, you did, Liz. And if you hadn't, those people would have killed you, your dad, Clare, Laurie, everyone. There's nothing to feel guilty about."

"Oh, I don't feel guilty. I feel the opposite. I'm proud of what we did today. I was just thinking though - it could easily have been us on that road. Like right now, we could be driving through someone else's ambush. It's all so random."

Matt had seen this reaction before. After someone's first experience with combat, real combat, where you deliberately act to take someone's life, soldiers often have one of two reactions. The first was guilt, although this was quite rare in Matt's experience. Maybe it was due to modern military training, but soldiers didn't often feel guilty about killing the enemy. They were almost always glad to be alive, glad the other guy was dead and mostly proud of their actions. In conventional wars such as World War II or even Vietnam, soldiers were more likely to feel empathy towards an enemy combatant. The "there but for the grace of God go I" mentality, or sorrow for causing grief to a soldier's family who likely wasn't aware that you had just killed their loved one.

The second reaction Matt had seen was much more common. This was when a soldier came face-to-face with their own mortality and the randomness of surviving a battle. Once the adrenaline wore off, soldiers most often thought of why they had survived, and others had not. In the case of losing a comrade, this sense of lack of control over one's destiny and concept of luck often led to survivor's guilt or even reckless behavior, knowing that nothing one did made any difference to the fickle finger of fate.

"Look, Liz, we can talk more about this later, but there's one thing you need to understand right now. Look at me. Battlefield outcomes aren't random. The things we do, the precautions we take, the training we put ourselves through, the planning and the preparation - these all directly impact whether we live or die. Yes, people get randomly struck by lightning. But in battle, the strong and the prepared survive. Period. Those guys died today because we were better than them. Understand?"

"Yeah," said Liz. "I guess you're right."

"I know I'm right, Liz. I've been there and seen this more times than I can count. I've taken lives, and I've lost close friends. In almost every situation, those who make the fewest mistakes win. The reason we're alive today is because we prepared, we planned, and we made fewer mistakes."

Liz was now fully paying attention, so Matt continued. "We're driving down this road right now not because of fate but because you and your father chose this route. We've done everything we can to be as safe as possible in a very dangerous world, and we're going to survive. Maybe not all of us, but most of us. And that's why we do it, Liz. We win in battle not so that we can go home but so that our buddies can go home, and have a home to return to you."

"Okay, Matt. I think I get it."

"Liz, what you do every day will decide whether or not you survive. And more importantly, it's going to impact whether Christopher and Laurie survive. It's not random, and it's not fate. Let these Nomad fuckers believe in fate as they stupidly ride their motorcycles into battle, but that's not fate. That's dumb. And there's no reason to feel guilty, or like it could have been us. We're not them."

"Yeah, you're totally right."

CHAPTER 20

October 8, 3:44 pm

Matt kneeled and peered through his binoculars over the battlements of the Stone Mountain tower atop Mount Battie on the outskirts of the seaside town of Camden, Maine. The panoramic view over Penobscot Bay was breathtaking. For a moment, Matt was lost in a memory of hiking to this very point with Clare years ago when they were first married. At that time, the top of Mount Battie had been swarming with tourists eager for a picture atop the tower, the greenery of the dozens of Maine's islands in the background in sharp contrast with the aquamarine Atlantic Ocean.

Although shaped like a small fort, the stone tower was a war memorial to the young men of Camden who fought in World War I. A famous young poet had once penned a long poem expressing wonder about death, nature, and God. While Matt had been forced to study the poem in high school and never much cared for it, he had always loved the first stanza enshrined on a plaque at the bottom of the stone tower.

"All I could see from where I stood
Was three long mountains and a wood;
I turned and looked another way,
And saw three islands in a bay."

Matt now looked at these three islands and, unlike the young Edna St. Vincent Millay's penchant for death, Matt thought of life and the future of his family.

Vinalhaven.

That was the name of the large, low island spanning the horizon about ten miles distant, toward the southeast. Directly to his front was Vinalhaven's smaller sister island of North Haven, and to Matt's left and much nearer, maybe three miles offshore, was the island of Isleboro. These were three of the almost two hundred islands dotting Penobscot Bay, most of which were uninhabited stretches of shrub and lichen-covered rock.

More than a dozen Penobscot Bay islands had villages with year-round populations, but Vinalhaven was probably the most populated, with more than 1,000 full-time residents. It was also one of the largest islands at over 160 square miles. This sounds vast, but the island was roughly a circle measuring eight miles in diameter. The rocky coastline consisted of hundreds of small coves and inlets, while the shore was protected by dozens of tiny islands lying several hundred yards offshore, many smaller than a football field. Across a narrow channel on the island's north side was the sister island of North Haven, and to the south stretched thousands of miles of the Atlantic Ocean.

It was along an inlet on this south coast where the actual village of Vinalhaven was situated. In addition to a well-protected harbor with several piers and dozens of lobster boats, the village had everything you'd expect from a small island whose full-time residents were mostly fishermen, and whose population more than doubled in the summer with tourists and seasonal residents. There was a general store, several small restaurants and shops, and an inn.

As Matt scanned the distant west coast of Vinalhaven from his perch above Camden, he recognized for the first time how fitting Vinalhaven's name was to their current situation. This was the location they had selected as their final haven - the place to carve out an existence and raise his family in this post-cataclysmic world.

Matt had not selected Vinalhaven on a whim nor based upon a detailed map reconnaissance. Matt and Clare had spent considerable time vacationing on the island over the previous twenty years while visiting Matt's cousin and her husband, who owned a small cottage on a postcard-perfect inlet on the island's east side. When fleeing their Rhode Island home over a month ago, Matt seriously considered driving to Vinalhaven instead of his brother's farmhouse in Vermont. Matt sincerely hoped that his cousin and her husband were safe and secure on Vinalhaven, and it was to their property that he planned to go to when the time was right.

But today, the plan was to watch. And to wait.

They had fled Vermont in a hurry, but the family was no longer in a rush. The plan was to simply watch the rest of today and all of tomorrow. From this perch atop Mount Battie, Matt not only had a clear view of the offshore islands but also could see for miles up and down Route 1, the main coastal road of Maine. To the north, Matt could see to the small village of Lincolnville, and to the south, Matt could easily see into the major town of Rockland, about eight miles south of where Matt knelt.

Rockland was the largest port on the Penobscot and was home to the daily car ferry service to Vinalhaven. While Rockland was closer to Vinalhaven, Matt had selected Camden as he felt it would likely have a minimal population. Mount Battie also offered commanding views over the entire area.

"Mind if we join you?" Matt turned to see Stan and Pete ascending the stone steps to this lookout. Stan appeared to be carrying several lawn chairs, while Pete had an armful of MREs.

"Absolutely. Come enjoy the view," answered Matt.

Stan propped open three lawn chairs and motioned for Matt and Pete to join him while he sat down. "Courtesy of the RV from Massachusetts," said Stan.

On arrival at the hilltop parking lot of Camden Hills State Park, where they now sat atop the Mt. Battie Tower, several vehicles appeared abandoned in the spacious parking lot. Pete and LT had cleared each vehicle, finding them all empty. One of the vehicles was an older motorhome, which contained at least several lawn chairs.

"How's everything coming along down there?" Matt asked.

"Great," said Pete. "The vehicles are all backed into the edge of the parking lot above the cliff, and the Humvee is parked in front with direct fields of fire down the access road. No one can approach us from behind without us hearing them, so overall, it's a pretty good spot. Clare had the boys move two picnic tables over, and they've set up camp at the tower's base."

"Sounds good," said Matt.

"Yeah, Matt. I have to admit; this is as safe a spot as any. And the view here is stunning. Marvi and I had always wanted to visit here," said Stan.

Matt handed him the binoculars. "Have a look, Stan. That's Vinalhaven to the southeast, in the distance." Stan took the binos, adjusted their width, and scanned their surroundings.

"You think Michelle and Dave are out there?" Pete asked, referring to Matt's cousin and her husband. While Pete had never been to Vinalhaven, he knew Michelle and Dave quite well. Matt's cousin lived in Washington DC for quite a few years and often participated in social gatherings with Matt, Clare, Pete, and Kelly. Dave was a criminal investigator with NCIS and had recently retired to his and Michelle's hometown of Lewiston, Maine - about an hour and a half drive to the west of Camden. Matt sincerely hoped that his cousin had fled to the protection of their small cottage on Vinalhaven to wait out the aftermath of the nuclear attack and Black Pox pandemic.

"Yeah, Pete. I do. Dave's a pretty forward-thinking guy, and I think he would have bugged out of Lewiston at the first sign of trouble."

"You think they've got enough supplies on the island?"

"Good question. I know they kept at least thirty days of emergency rations there, and if they could get the car ferry over, he had at least one full vehicle's worth of supplies. Plus, whatever might be available on the island itself. So I'm guessing they're good, at least for another month or so."

"So you still want to wait here until the day after tomorrow?" Stan asked, still holding the binoculars to his eyes and now scanning the road and harbor directly below them. From this perch, they could see directly down into the town and could easily spot people walking or driving. So far, Matt had seen no signs of life.

"Yes, Stan. We're in no rush, but once we make our move onto the water, we become extremely vulnerable. I think it's important we see what's out there. Hawkeye showed some marine RF signals intermittently throughout Penobscot Bay, so we inferred that it was likely survivors fishing or lobstering. But we won't know for sure until we put eyeballs on them. I think we watch all day today, all through tonight, and all day tomorrow. Then we can begin to make our move. That was the plan we all agreed to - still agree?"

"Yeah, Matt. You make a good point. I don't love being in the open up here, but I think it's way more secure than rushing out to steal a boat and head to an island we know nothing about."

"Okay, good," said Matt. "Speaking of eyeballs, I'm going to get the telescope out of the Tahoe. I think that will let us see some serious detail in Camden harbor and the town itself."

CHAPTER 21

October 10, 7:20 am

The harbor looked calm, almost too calm.

Matt had been lying prone in a concealed position at the top of Camden's outdoor amphitheater for almost two hours, watching the harbor closely. Pete and Liz were in similar positions behind him, facing opposite directions to cover their flanks.

After watching the town and harbor closely for over thirty-six hours, they had all agreed it was time to do their first seaborne reconnaissance. Pete, who had owned boats his entire adult life, and Liz, a Naval Academy midshipman well-versed in handling small watercraft, were the obvious choices to accompany Matt on this trip. The plan was for the three of them to find a suitable boat and head out to Vinalhaven after first light.

They had departed their redoubt on Mt. Battie at around 4:30 am and driven Pete's Jeep slowly into Camden. They were not worried about being attacked as everything about the town was peaceful. They parked several hundred yards short of the harbor, leaving the Jeep in the driveway of a house on a side road off Camden's High Street.

During the thirty-six hours of observation, they had seen only two people - a young couple with their dog that had driven into town from the southwest. The two appeared to know exactly where they were going and had parked directly in front of the Camden police station but had entered the building next door, which appeared to be a hotel. The two did not appear to be concerned with their safety. Through the telescope, Derek thought that the man might have had a sidearm, but he was positive that neither individual carried a long gun. After twenty minutes in the hotel, the two left carrying a stuffed rucksack and several bulging pillowcases. Matt, who was sleeping when the individuals were spotted, agreed with the others that this was likely a canned food run by the couple, who departed southwest down Route 1 the same way they arrived.

Everyone had discussed the incident over dinner last night, with no real consensus on any conclusions. Seeing the couple meant that people were still alive in the area, but seeing only the couple meant that, in all likelihood, very few people remained in the Camden area. A four percent survival rate of Camden's pre-cataclysm population should have resulted in approximately 180-200 survivors. However, as Derek pointed out, FEMA and the state agencies had been encouraging people to seek out public shelters. The fact that there were no police cruisers parked at the Camden police station indicated that maybe they had been called elsewhere, and maybe that's where survivors were located. Lastly, they could not discount the fact that, as the couple was wearing surgical masks on their faces, the spread of the Black Pox virus may have been especially lethal in this community.

As Matt had carefully walked into town toward their preselected overwatch position at the amphitheater, Matt was captivated by the unmistakable scent of the sea. This tangy, salty aroma lingered on the early morning breeze. While unnoticeable atop Mt. Battie, here, the ocean's presence was ever-present, and Matt could almost taste the salt on his lips as he inhaled. As the dawn broke, the colors of the various boats occupying the small harbor were quite stunning.

After more than two hours of lying in wait, Matt was ready to get things moving. He pulled himself up to a kneeling position and was immediately joined by his two companions.

"You two ready to rock and roll?" Matt asked, with both Pete and Liz nodding affirmatively. "Pete, you still think that navy blue boat is the one we want?"

"Yeah, Matt. I'm pretty sure that's a Hinckley 35. It's like a million-dollar yacht."

"Seriously?" Liz asked.

"Yeah, at least a million," said Pete. "But that's why we want it. It's a quality boat that we can cruise probably at least thirty knots an hour out to Vinalhaven. It'll handle pretty much all seas. And most importantly, it has two outboard engines."

"It seems like a pretty expensive yacht to have outboards," said Matt.

"Yeah, well, it is. But for us, outboards are important. At least today. They're quiet and a bit more reliable for what we seek. In all likelihood, this boat hasn't been turned on in well over a month, so we need it to crank on the first try. I don't want to have to mess with an inboard engine for our first trip. Once we know everything's secure, we can choose any boat we like."

"Got it," said Matt. "Let's spread out and head to the warehouse as we planned. Keep at least fifteen meters between us."

Matt stood up and led the trio down the grassy slope of the outdoor amphitheater. They turned left on Atlantic Ave, then took a quick right onto Sea Street and walked a block down to the parking lot in front of the Lyman-Morse warehouse. The navy blue boat was tied to the floating dock along the stone and wood pier in front of them, wedged between two much larger sailboats. The floating dock, about six feet wide and running the entire length of the more than one-hundred-yard-long seawall, rose up and down with the tide. At its current height, with the tide almost in, the floating dock was about ten feet below the level of the parking lot. In the middle of the harbor, several rows of floating docks floated on the tide, most with one or two boats tied alongside.

"Okay, Pete. Liz and I will cover you from here. Go check out our new ride."

Pete walked forward nonchalantly, confident that they were alone. It was difficult to break the fear and cautiousness instilled by their interactions with the Nomads and The Base, but they all felt pretty safe here on the coast of Maine. At the edge of the pier, Pete cinched down his 2-point sling and then walked down the floating dock's shallow ramp and hopped onto the boat's rear deck. Even from thirty yards away, Matt could tell this was an exceptional vessel. Pete referred to it as a Hinckley 35, so Matt assumed it was thirty-five feet long. Matt knew this type of boat was called a picnic boat, though he wasn't sure if the moniker applied to this particular Hinckley. It was sleek, with a long forward bow and a large covered cockpit in front of a spacious rear deck. Pete had mentioned that there was an interior cabin that would have a small galley, bathroom, and bedroom.

Matt had a decent amount of boating experience but by no means considered himself a yachtsman, whereas that title was more appropriate for Pete, with his extensive boating acumen. He watched Pete inspect the cabin and then, after a few minutes, jump back up on the dock and walk toward where Matt and Liz stood at the corner of the building.

"No keys," Pete said as he approached. "I think we should check this building here. Looks like the marina's office."

"Okay. Liz, stay here and keep watch." Matt followed Pete around to the front of the building to a door with a placard above it stating "Office." As expected, the door was locked. Matt unslung his small rucksack, dropping it to the ground before him. Reaching inside, he pulled out a 15-inch claw bar courtesy of Woodstock's Ace Hardware store. Jamming the end into the door frame above the door handle, Matt hammered the other end with his gloved fist and pulled back rapidly and violently. The lock popped easily, springing the door open. Pete strode into the open office and went right toward a board behind the counter on which hung multiple keys. Looking at the board for a few seconds, Pete reached up and grabbed a key fob and key hanging from one of the hooks.

"This should be it," said Pete, walking out the door and toward the Hinckley. Matt took a brief look around the office, noting that everything seemed in its place, indicating the owners had not departed in a hurry, nor had the place been looted.

Walking out toward the edge of the pier after closing the office door behind him, Matt watched Pete get familiar with the boat. He was clearly enjoying himself, this likely being the first time he had helmed a million-dollar yacht. Pete reached into a panel and flipped some switches that Matt assumed turned on the yacht's batteries. He turned the key in the ignition, bringing the Hinckley to life. Matt could see the large monitor in the cockpit turn on and show a detailed map of Penobscot Bay.

Pete pressed a switch, and Matt heard a wine from the rear of the yacht. Turning, he saw the twin outboard motors lowering into the water. Pete then put his hand on the keys, which he had already seated in the ignition.

"Okay, this should start the outboards right up." With a twist of his wrist, Matt heard the outboard engines catch instantly and maintain a low rumble. He was amazed at how quiet the engines were, figuring that Liz probably couldn't even hear the boat from thirty yards away.

"Crazy how quiet it is," said Matt.

"This is what you get for a million bucks. Wait 'til you feel how she rides out in the open water. These twin 300-horse Yamahas should let us cruise easily at thirty-plus knots. This baby's a true thoroughbred."

From his perch on the seawall above the floating dock, Matt looked around the spacious cockpit and rear seating area, admiring the quality of the workmanship. Pete sat in the right one of two padded white captain's chairs in front of a wood-paneled dash centered with a large flat-screen monitor. To the front of the left captain's chair was an open doorway leading to the berthing area. The cockpit behind Pete featured dual banquets of seating surrounding a teak table mounted on a pedestal. The banquets were covered with plush blue and white-striped cushions and could easily fit 6-8 people. The open area on the rear deck contained additional seating covered in more blue and white-striped cushions that could seat an additional eight people, some facing aft and others forward.

"Full tank of fuel, Matt. So we won't need the tube and pump after all," said Pete, referring to the coil of surgical tube and the siphon pump Pete carried in his rucksack. "We're ready to roll. I'll need you to untie us when you're ready."

"Okay. Let's do this," said Matt. Matt jogged down the aluminum stairs, onto the floating dock, and stepped onto the Hinckley. Turning to Liz, Matt motioned for her to leave her spot and join them on the boat. Liz sprinted over to the pier's edge and down onto the dock.

"You want me to handle the lines, Dad?" Liz asked. Pete looked at Matt, who nodded affirmatively, realizing Liz knew way more about being a mate on this yacht than he ever would.

"You got it, Liz," said Pete. "Cast off front and rear lines."

Liz moved to the bow and undid the black rope from the cleat on the dock, loosely coiling and then tossing the rope onto the front deck of the Hinckley. She walked back to the rear of the boat and leaned down to unwind that rope from its cleat. Instead of tossing it, she coiled it and kept it in her hand as she effortlessly stepped down onto the gunwale of the yacht and the rear deck.

"You're clear," Liz called to Pete. Pete looked around the boat and then put his hand on a small joystick in front of the two chrome throttle control levers. He moved the joystick slowly to the left, and the bow of the boat began moving away from the deck, followed slowly by the rear. With the bow about ten feet from the pier and the rear end drifting several feet away, Pete clicked one of the throttle levers forward, and Matt heard one of the outboards click into gear. The bow began to turn faster, moving the entire boat away from the pier and accelerating slightly forward. The yacht easily cleared the large sailboat tied up to the pier in front of the Hinckley, and Pete steered the boat into the open water of the marina. As the boat turned fully perpendicular to the pier, Pete flicked the throttle levers to put one engine forward and the other inverse, causing the boat to turn in place so that it was now facing in the opposite direction that it had been tied to the pier.

Matt grabbed the binoculars from his rucksack, putting them around his neck while dropping the ruck on the banquet. He sat in the left-side captain's chair while Liz plopped down in the curved, padded banquet at the very rear of the boat, scanning the marina's perimeter for any threats. Matt could see the Camden Yacht Club to his left and the blue waters of the outer harbor stretched out before him through the large front windshield of the Hinckley.

"Okay, I'm going to go very slowly until we're through the outer harbor," said Pete. "I need to get a feel for this boat and don't want to take any chances."

"Roger, you're the captain," said Matt. "We're not in any rush. You watch where we're going, and Liz and I will watch everything else. I need to check in with Clare and the others."

Matt reached down and clicked his radio mic. "Clare, this is Matt. How do you read me?"

Clare's reply was instant. "Lima Charlie, Matt. We are watching your progress through the telescope. Nice boat!" Matt smiled at Clare's reference to the Hinckley and her use of the Army phonetic slang. "Lima Charlie" referred to the letters L and C and stood for "loud and clear."

"The range on these radios is supposedly twenty miles. I'll check in every few miles to see if they work all the way to our destination."

"Roger, Matt. Be careful."

"Aren't I always?" Matt smiled again, hoping Clare was smiling as well but realizing she probably wasn't. While Camden seemed safe, there were still so many unknowns that everyone's stress level remained quite high.

Pete nudged the throttles forward slightly, and the Hinckley surged to a speed Matt estimated to be under ten miles per hour. As they moved through the harbor, they were surrounded by dozens of colorful boats moored on buoys, bobbing peacefully and oblivious to the collapsing world around them. Matt still couldn't get over how quiet the engines were; sitting in the cockpit of the Hinckley was quieter than Pete's Jeep Wrangler. In the morning breeze, Matt could hear the symphony of the tinkling of the grommets on the sailboat masts as they motored by, almost as if these boats were acknowledging his passing. As they cleared most of the boats in the outer harbor, Matt felt the boat turn slightly to the right, and through the windshield, he could see they were on a heading to pass to the north of a lighthouse on a small island at the mouth of the outer harbor.

Matt leaned over to look at the display monitor in front of Pete. Curtis Island. That was the label on the small island passing by on their right. The Garmin GPS still worked.

"So what's the capability of this radar system? It looks like it's showing all these boats moored in the harbor," said Matt.

"Yeah, this thing is pretty incredible. Again, you get what you pay for - and for more than a million dollars, this yacht has a pretty significant radar system. That dome on top is the radar, and it is painting all the objects it sees on this screen," answered Pete, tapping the large touch-screen monitor on the wooden dash. "It'll show us all the objects above the water, including land masses, boats, and even rain."

"Seriously? What's the range?"

"Well, the radar will sweep out to 48 nautical miles. However, in my experience, its accuracy is based on line of sight, so with smaller objects like boats, it is much more accurate closer up."

"So we can see any boats coming at us?"

"Yes. Definitely. Unless they're hidden behind a land mass, of course. This system even has what's called target tracking. Moving objects will show their heading and speed."

"Very cool, Pete. A game changer actually." Matt looked out the window in silence for a moment, lost in thought. "So let me ask you. Could we use the boat's radar as a sentry? Moor the boat in a place where it can see approaches to the island. We'd be able to see any boats coming, right?"

"Yes. Great idea. The key will be where to place the boat to give it the best view unobstructed by land masses. Remember. Radar basically works by sending radio signals out in a 360-degree circle. When the signal hits an object, it bounces back and produces a signature that the radar translates with the software into an object on this screen. Based on the signature, the software can tell what type of object it is and color-code it as a boat, land, rain, et cetera. The radar beam can't see through objects, so when it hits something, it bounces back - it doesn't see what's on the far side of objects higher than the radar dome. With all these tiny islands, we'd need to make sure we had a clear view or at least understand where our blind spots were."

"Okay. I understand. Good to know."

Pete looked up and then glanced around through the windshield. They had cleared the Curtis Island lighthouse and entered Penobscot Bay proper. There was a slight ocean breeze, but Matt was surprised at how calm the sea was - more undulating swells than choppy waves.

"You guys ready to see what this baby can do?" Pete said to both Matt and Liz.

"One sec," said Liz, getting up from her seat at the stern and sitting inside the cockpit area in the bench seating behind Matt. "Okay, hit it."

Pete slowly moved both throttle levers forward. The effect was instantaneous. As the engines surged, the bow rose slightly then settled back down as the yacht accelerated onto a plane. The ride was incredibly powerful and smooth, and Matt realized how well-engineered this yacht was compared to the average pleasure boat Matt had experienced. The Hinckley was in a class of its own, and Matt could now see why it carried such a high price tag.

Matt looked over to the dashboard monitor and saw that their speed had settled at thirty knots. Colorful buoys flashed by on both sides of the boat, signifying the locations of lobster pots. Maine was considered the lobster capital of the world, and Penobscot Bay had thousands of lobster pots scattered throughout. The various color schemes on the buoys were unique to each lobsterman.

"We still thinking about 30 minutes?" Matt asked, still amazed at how quiet it was inside the cockpit. It was louder than before they hit cruising speed, but holding a normal conversation was still quite easy.

"Yeah. We should be passing south of Vinalhaven in about 25 minutes."

Matt sat and watched out the windshield as they cruised through Penobscot Bay. After the stress and uncertainty of the last six weeks, he enjoyed this brief interlude of serenity. For a few minutes, Matt could almost pretend he was enjoying a day on the ocean with his life-long friend, cruising in a million-dollar yacht on a crisp, clear October morning without another boat in sight. The boat hit a slight wave, jarring Matt out of his daydream. He looked down, saw the scratched bluing on his M4 rifle, and realized he wasn't in Kansas anymore. This wasn't a pleasure cruise but a dangerous recon mission to see if the island of Vinalhaven was safe for his family.

CHAPTER 22

October 10, 8:38am

The trip took closer to forty minutes. The route the yacht's GPS had plotted mirrored the ferry's route to Vinalhaven and had them pass through a maze of small islands off Vinalhaven's southwest coast and then along a narrow channel that bisected Vinalhaven's south coast and the uninhabited Greens Island. As this route would have their boat traveling within a hundred meters of the coast, Matt felt it more prudent that they stay farther ashore, Matt urged Pete to detour a bit to the south to keep their distance from the shoreline.

With the seas reasonably calm, the offshore route was no obstacle for the Hinckley, and Pete navigated them south of Hurricane and Greens Islands before turning due east and keeping a half mile off the coast. As they passed the southern entrance to Vinalhaven's main harbor, Matt used the binoculars to see if he could spot any activity. The portion of the docks that were visible appeared lifeless.

"Clare, this is Matt...Ruby...how copy?"

"I copy: Ruby. A bit fuzzy...still readable," came Clare's static-filled reply. Realizing that their handheld radios were not secure, Matt had put together a list of code words to reference specific locations to prevent anyone eavesdropping from knowing where they were. In this case, Ruby referred to Vinalhaven's harbor. Their destination, codename Garnet, was another mile due east, up and around the island's southeastern edge to a small inlet labeled on the map as Carvers Cove.

Liz popped her head out of the doorway in front of Matt's knees. She had stepped down into the hatchway about ten minutes prior to tour the berth area, and Matt assumed to use the bathroom as well.

"This boat is unbelievable," said Liz, stepping back into the cockpit. "It has everything. Bed, toilet, microwave, sink, stove. And everything is polished teak. Crazy."

"Yeah, I checked it out when we first came aboard. It's definitely nice. Maybe you should get your dad to buy one!"

"He's too cheap," smiled Liz, punching her father on the shoulder as she walked by.

"Hey, sweetie. I was going to say I'd buy this one for you, but if you're going to be mean, then no way," said Pete, rolling with the joke. Turning to Matt, his voice now turned serious. "Matt, I'm keeping us well offshore and at a steady 30 knots. You see this red marker?" Pete pointed to the GPS screen on the dashboard. "I'm going to turn due north here and head for the coast. The water is deep enough to keep this speed right into Roberts Harbor. I'll then slow down, and we can slowly cruise into Carvers Cove."

"Okay. That works."

"Once we turn north, we'll be within small arms range of the shoreline and at certain points less than a hundred meters."

"Got it. Keep the speed up until we get to Roberts Cove. We haven't seen any threats, but a boat going thirty knots is much harder to shoot at than one traveling wake speed." Pete nodded, and Matt turned to Liz. "Why don't you set up in the rear? All threats will come from the left side, so..."

"You mean the port side?" Liz said, a serious look on her face.

Matt stopped and looked at her, staring into her eyes until she cracked a smile and started laughing. "Yeah, okay, squid. All threats come from the port side. So stay low."

"Aye, aye, captain!" Liz smiled, turning to take her spot at the stern.

Matt had worked extensively with the Navy throughout his military and civilian career, especially Navy Seal Team 6 or DEVGRU, and had developed a love-hate relationship with them. Mostly he loved to hate them.

Thinking of the Navy made him think of his cousin Michelle and her husband, Dave. Michelle was a year older than Matt, and they had always been close when they were young but had lost touch as they both went off to college and followed separate career paths. When Matt and Clare moved to Washington DC after the Army, Michelle and Dave welcomed them to the city they had called home for several years. Michelle was an attorney, and Dave an NCIS agent.

While Dave worked for the Naval Criminal Investigative Service, he was not in the Navy. In fact, Dave was a former paratrooper with the 82nd Airborne Division and loved nothing more than making fun of sailors, especially in comparison to Army airborne rangers. While Michelle and Dave called Lewiston, Maine their home, Dave's family had owned a cottage on Vinalhaven for generations. Matt sincerely hoped that Michelle and Dave had chosen this spot to hunker down after the nuclear attacks across the U.S.

Looking through the windshield, Matt could see they were rapidly approaching a natural harbor protected from the Atlantic by a small low-slung island of about fifty acres. From the monitor, Matt saw that the island was labeled Sheep Island. On the left, about two hundred meters off the bow, Matt could see a small cottage perched above the rocky coast, inside a wood line of spruce-fir trees and juniper shrubs. Matt studied the house and property through his binoculars and saw no signs of life.

Pete turned the boat hard to port, toward the northwest, while simultaneously pulling back smoothly on the throttle levers. The Hinckley eased back in the water and slowed to about ten knots.

Matt pivoted the binoculars forward and traversed across

the frontage of Carvers Cove about a kilometer to their front. They passed through Roberts Harbor, a small, naturally protected harbor approximately four hundred meters across, with Sheep Island guarding its entrance. At the back of Roberts Harbor, in the upper northwest corner, was Carvers Cove, a small inlet five hundred meters long but only one hundred meters wide. At the very back of the cove sat Dave and Michelle's cottage.

The tricky part for Matt was that their security situation would significantly worsen once they entered the cove. While there were over a half dozen homes along the cove, three or four per side, the inlet required them to go relatively slow. They would be sitting ducks for anyone on either bank who wished them harm.

Matt saw no alternative. Making contact with his cousin required them to slowly navigate the length of the cove, dodging several moored boats and dozens of lobster buoys.

"Okay, Pete. Nice and easy. Let's bring it back to wake speed. Just fast enough for you to steer." Matt reached into the rucksack at his feet and pulled out a white t-shirt he had brought for this purpose. Holding the shirt in his lap, he carefully scanned both banks of the cove, ensuring himself that no one was present.

They were now halfway into the cove, and Matt focused his binoculars on Dave's cottage. *There!* Matt could not see any individuals, but Dave's blue Ford Expedition was tucked up next to the shed behind the house.

"Okay, Pete. I think they're here. I see Dave's truck. Can you put us in neutral and try to keep us in position right here?"

"No problem," said Pete, clicking the outboards into neutral.

"Okay, here goes nothing." Matt handed the binoculars to Pete and unslung his M4. With the t-shirt balled up in his hands, Matt stepped up onto the rear bench seat and then onto the left side gunwale. Holding the handles on the Hinckley's hardtop roof, Matt slowly waved the white shirt over his head.

"I think I see movement!" Pete yelled. "Definitely someone

moving behind the glass of the front porch windows."

Matt kept waving the t-shirt slowly and calmly, knowing that if Dave and Michelle were present, they would immediately understand the significance. He wasn't sure they'd recognize him at this distance but was hopeful they had binoculars.

"Keep an eye on our flanks," Matt called to Liz.

"The side door is opening," said Pete. They watched as the door came open, and a woman walked warily across the front lawn toward the water. She was tall, thin, with light brown hair straight down to her shoulders. Matt could tell it was his cousin Michelle even though she wore an N95 respirator. In her hands was an AR-15 rifle.

"How close can you get us, Pete?" Matt asked.

"Pretty close, I think, it's getting near to high tide, so I think I can get up within twenty feet or so of the rocks."

"Okay. Take us in slowly." Matt walked along the gunwale until he was standing on the small bow of the Hinckley. Michelle recognized him and began walking faster toward the shore. The cottage was set back about fifty yards, so she arrived about the same time the Hinckley hovered ten yards away.

"Michelle!! Are you guys safe?" Matt yelled.

"Matt! What the hell are you doing here? Are you okay?" Michelle yelled back after pulling down her respirator. "Don't come any closer though. Please. We've made it this long and don't want to take any chances. It's great to see you, but you'll have to quarantine for two weeks before you can get near us."

"Is Dave with you? Are you both okay?" Matt replied, ignoring her quarantine comment.

"Yes. Just a sec." Michelle turned and waved back toward the house. The side door immediately opened, and Dave came trotting out. Bald-headed and standing only 5'7", Dave may not have been gifted with height or a full head of hair, but he more than made up for this in the gym. Pound for pound, Dave was probably the strongest person Matt had ever met - an attribute that had allowed him to succeed as a paratrooper, police officer, and member of the NCIS SWAT team. Dave was dressed very similar to Matt, with a full chest rig of 30-round magazines and a suppressed M4 carried at the low ready across his chest. Like Michelle, he also had an N95 respirator which he wore pulled down around his neck.

Matt waved to Dave and waited for him to get close before speaking. "We have a lot to catch up on, guys. But first. I have vaccines for both of you. I think that should be the first thing we do."

"Hey Matt! Great to see you." Dave yelled, stepping up about five yards to Michelle's left, still a little bit wary. From this position, he had an angle that allowed him to see everyone in the boat. "Hey, Pete! Is that you, Liz?" He called out. Dave and Michelle knew the Rhodes family well; the three couples often socialized together in Washington DC. Pete and Liz both waved hello.

"First thing's first, Matt. Flash!" Dave roared, emphasizing the last word.

Matt's stared blankly at his close friend and cousin's husband, thinking maybe Dave had lost his mind. Then it hit him. "Thunder!" Matt yelled in reply.

Dave immediately dropped his M4 to be held by his 2-point sling. "Man, is it great to see you! Sorry about the Flash-Thunder thing, but I wasn't sure if maybe you were here under duress. It was the only thing I could think of!" Flash-Thunder was the running password and reply used by the American airborne forces during the D-Day invasion, as the Germans could not pronounce the "th" sound. When approaching an unknown position, the first person would say "Flash," and the response was "Thunder." Any other reply would be met by withering gunfire. Matt was glad he had remembered!

"Goddam man, I barely remembered that. I hope you weren't going to shoot us!" Matt laughed.

"Nah. But I wanted to make sure you weren't being forced to take someone here and have a bunch of bad guys waiting in the berth of your yacht there. Speaking of yacht, where the fuck did you get a Hinckley?"

"Hey, Dave!" Pete interrupted. "I hate to break up the party, but it's not the easiest keeping this thing positioned here with the tide coming in. I suggest we get you both vaccinated first; then we can chit-chat about the Hinckley."

Matt laughed again, ecstatic to see his cousin but realizing they had a lot of work to do. Walking back along the gunwale to the side of the cockpit, he turned to his crewmates. "Pete, pull us in as close as you can. Liz, I'm going to lower myself over the side here; when I'm in the water, could you hand me this case, please? Thanks."

Matt removed his chest rig and M4, laying them on the banquet seating. He then hopped up on the rear gunwale and lowered himself overboard. Right when he decided the water was going to be over his head, his boots hit the rocks. He was neck deep, and cold. Reaching up, Liz handed him a small plastic box containing a vaccine vial and a dozen syringes. Holding it over his head, Matt walked slowly towards shore, taking his time not to slip on the seaweed-covered rocks beneath him. Within seconds he was on the shore and scrabbling up the rocky embankment.

When he reached within fifteen feet of them, Michelle said, "Are you sure that's the vaccine, Matt? How are you sure?" Matt could tell she was petrified, and he realized what it must have been like to live the last month in fear of catching the Black Pox.

"Yeah, Michelle. I'm positive. This is the latest version of the updated vaccine. We've all been inoculated with it."

"Okay. We trust you, Matt. It's just...."

"I know, Michelle. I know. But please trust me. We're so glad to see you, but please let me help you. This vaccine is the real deal."

"Michelle, honey," Dave interjected. "We have to do this. We can't live the rest of our lives like this. Trust him." Dave stepped forward without waiting for her reply and pulled his chest rig over his head. Before Matt knew it, Dave had taken off his button-down shirt and was yanking up the sleeve of his t-shirt. “Hit me, brother.”

Matt chuckled, unzipping the small case and pulling out a vial and a syringe. By the time he finished injecting Dave, Michelle had her sleeve rolled up, and Matt injected her with a new needle. The first thing she did after getting the injection was wrap Matt up in a giant bear hug. Her entire body began shaking as she broke down crying. Matt let her cry for almost a minute, looking over at Dave and seeing that he was also highly emotional.

Matt patted Michelle’s back and eventually pulled gently away. “Hey cousin, you have no idea how glad I am to see you both. We have a lot to discuss.”

Michelle pulled back, her arms still wrapped around him and looking Matt directly in the face. “Clare? The kids? Are they...are they...?” She became choked up, unable to finish the question.

“They’re fine. They’re all fine, Michelle.” Relief washed across her face, removing all the stress she had been holding in. “In fact, they’re waiting in Camden to see you guys?”

“Camden?” Dave asked.

“Yeah,” said Matt. “Everyone’s camped on Mount Battie, waiting for us to bring them here if everything looks safe. Speaking of safe, have you heard from Max and Daphne? Are they okay?”

The smiles disappeared instantly from Dave and Michelle’s faces. Daphne was twenty and stationed with the Air Force in Japan, while Max was eighteen and a Private First Class infantryman in the 101st Airborne Division at Fort Campbell, Kentucky. “Not a word from either of them since two days after the bombings. Daphne sent an email saying she was fine and not to worry, and Max called to say he was being deployed to the outskirts of Atlanta to assist with the aftermath. We haven’t heard anything since.”

“I’m so sorry,” said Matt, reaching out to hug his cousin Michelle again. “I’m sure they’ll both be fine. We might even have a way to open communications with them. But before we get into everything, and there's lots to tell, what should I do with Pete and the boat? Should they moor it?"

Dave looked out at Carvers Cove, nodding. "Hey, Pete! See that little green and white lobster boat moored about fifty yards out?" Pete looked out and then nodded affirmatively. "That's ours. On the far side of it is a mooring ball with a dingy. Tie into that and row yourselves back here. Row over to the inlet to my left, and you'll see our dingy on the shoreline."

"Got it!" Pete yelled back, putting the Hinckley in reverse and turning it towards the mouth of the cove.

It took Pete and Liz about ten minutes to moor the yacht and row the dingy back to shore. During that time, Matt called Clare on the radio. The static was considerable, but they could understand each other as Matt called in "Garnet" and informed Clare that Michelle and Dave were safe.

With everyone gathered in the yard, Michelle took over as host. "C'mon, everyone, let's go inside. We have a lot to catch up on."

CHAPTER 23

October 10, 10:42 am

The five sat around the cottage's large kitchen table, drinking iced tea. Matt looked at his iced-filled glass of sugary liquid.

"I can't believe you actually have electricity," said Matt. "And ice cubes!"

"Yeah, it's the main reason we came out here after the nukes," said Dave. "Vinalhaven has had a submarine cable to the mainland since the 1970s, replacing an old coal-fired electrical generation plant that's been on the island since the early 20th century. About ten years ago, though, someone had the bright idea of harnessing wind energy. The island's energy co-op installed three big windmills on the northwest side of the islands. I mean big ones, something like 380 feet high. They produce more than enough power for both Vinalhaven and Northhaven, even in the peak of summer."

"Incredible. So you never lost power? At all?"

"Not that we know of. They have these crazy statistics. Like in the last four years, we average something like four hours of downtime per year. That's it."

"I have to say, Dave," said Matt. "Clare and I both thought of Vinalhaven as a perfect spot to evacuate long-term, and that was before I found out about the electricity. I still can't really believe it. This is going to make starting over so much easier than we thought."

"We are so unbelievably glad to see you. What's your plan

now?"

"Well, in a nutshell, we need to go back, get everyone and bring them here. Then we figure out how to live long-term and build a life on the island. There's so much to tell you, Dave, but the highest priority's getting everyone here safe and sound."

"Well, we're happy to have all of you, but sixteen is going to be a tight squeeze for this two-bedroom cottage. We can figure something out while you're getting them."

"Have you had any contact with others on the island? Know how many are still alive? I know Vinalhaven's population is something like 1200 people, but how many are left?"

"Yeah. There's twenty-eight people left on the island that we know of."

"Twenty-eight? That's it?"

"That's it," said Dave. "After the attacks, they started having daily meetings in the center of town to keep people informed. I went to the first couple but then stopped going. They didn't know any more than we did, and I'm not a big fan of centralized meetings. There were a couple of hundred people at most of those gatherings, and it turned into almost a farmer's market with people selling and bartering things. In those days, the ferry ran at least a few days a week, and the lobster boats went out regularly. But then the Black Pox hit. It just wiped out the island."

"Jesus," said Pete.

"Yeah, I'm not sure where Jesus has been the last six weeks," said Dave. "I believe there are only eight different family units left on the island, plus us."

"And do you communicate with these people?" Matt asked.

"Sort of," said Dave. "Twice a week, we try to meet in town at noon. People either drive, walk or ride their bikes. There's usually only five or six of us, and we keep at least ten meters apart and yell to be heard. For the last couple of weeks, we haven't really had much to say. Everyone has food and water, and we have electricity."

"Okay."

"Yeah. So we've basically been hunkering down at the cottage here, chopping wood, catching a few lobsters, doing some fishing. Keeping an eye out for strangers who might want to come here. That's about it."

"Any sign of the Nomads or The Base?"

"Nomads? Sorry, man, not sure what you're referring to."

"Some bad actors we came across in Vermont. They're taking over from Maryland to Vermont, and we're not sure how far they are into northern New England," said Matt.

"Sounds bad. But we haven't seen anything like that. As far as I know, no one on the island has made any attempt to travel to the mainland, and only one family arrived here after the first couple days. They've been here a couple of weeks and seem harmless enough."

"Okay. That's good to know," said Matt. The relief on Matt, Pete, and Liz's faces was evident. "So, we plan to head back and bring everyone back here probably late this afternoon or first thing in the morning. Any thoughts?"

"It's so amazing to see you, Matt," answered Michelle, who had been silent for most of the conversation. "We've been so isolated here, but we've also felt safe. Dave keeps wanting to check out Rockland and see what's happening on the mainland, but I've convinced him there's nothing we really need, and it's not worth the risk. Now that you're here, it changes everything."

"Yeah, Matt," agreed Dave. "It's so crazy to see you right now; it's hard to process it all. Michelle and I've made all these lists of all the things we need to do for long-term survival, but with your families coming here, it really does change everything. We could actually build a life here in the aftermath of all this death."

Michelle stood up and walked behind Matt, wrapping her arms around his chest from behind and kissing him on the cheek. "I'm so glad you're here, Matt. How about Don? And your parents? I know we have time to catch up later, but you haven't mentioned them."

"As far as I know, everyone is okay, but we haven't heard from them since a few days after the bombs. Donald and Tracy are actually in Ireland with Kirstie, so hopefully, they're doing well. My mom and dad were okay in Florida, but I don't know if any of them have survived the pox."

Everyone's mood turned somber, thinking of all the friends and family whose well-being was unknown.

"So, Dave," said Matt, knowing there would be plenty of time later for catching up and attempting to keep things focused. "What about the others on the island? How do you think they'll respond to our arrival?"

"Good question. I only know a few of them somewhat well; most I've just had a couple of quick conversations from ten yards away. They should be damn fucking grateful you're bringing the vaccine, so I wouldn't worry too much. How do you want to handle that? Our next scheduled pow-wow is in two days, on the 12th."

"Okay, good," said Matt. "That gives us plenty of time to get everyone here and sort some things out logistically. What do you recommend for housing? We have some tents for a couple of days, but ideally, we need to take over some houses."

"We'll figure that out," answered Michelle. "Why don't you guys go get Clare and the others and try to get back here tonight? Dave and I will figure out the housing situation. This cove alone has six homes that we can choose from."

"Yeah," agreed Dave. "Let us give that some thought while you're getting everyone over here. What's your plan for bringing everyone back?"

"We have to figure that out," said Pete, who'd been silent for most of the conversation. "There were some very nice boats in the Camden harbor. We'll likely find one more boat, which should give us plenty of room for everyone, plus all our supplies. It's going to be pushing it to get back here this afternoon. Low tide is around 5 pm, and I'm not sure we want to come into this harbor close to dark and at low tide."

"Good point, Pete. There's an old stone pier a few hundred

yards down on the north side of the cove.

"Yeah, we saw it. Is it accessible in all tides?"

"Yes. This was once a pretty substantial commercial pier over a hundred years ago, and we should be able to get two boats in there to offload everything. I'll go over and make sure it's all good."

Matt looked at his watch and did some mental calculations. "Okay, sounds good. Unless something's changed in Camden, I think it's best we push our return until tomorrow morning. There's no rush, and I'd much rather come in here near high tide and also have a full day to offload and get set up. Trying to do all that at dusk and get everyone settled is just asking for trouble that we don't need right now."

Everyone around the table nodded.

CHAPTER 24

October 11, 7:51am

The office in the Lyman-Morse warehouse building was a treasure trove of information. Sitting at the same desk where they had found the keys to the Hinckley, Matt looked through various documents that told him a lot about the last days before the shipyard had closed post-cataclysm.

A printout on the desk gave details of each boat moored on the Lyman-Morse side of the harbor, and Matt and Pete had used this document to select their second boat for the trip back to Vinalhaven. Right away, Matt knew it was the boat for them based solely on the boat's name - *Screaming Eagle*. The nickname of the famed 101st Airborne Division, where Matt served as a new 2nd Lieutenant, Matt felt it a solid omen of good fortune. Pete liked it for its utility and seaworthiness. *Screaming Eagle* was a semi-custom boat built at the Lyman-Morse shipyard and was listed on the paperwork as a "custom commuter yacht." After going out to see the boat, Pete explained that it was built specifically to ferry up to fifteen passengers for a resort on one of the Great Lakes, and its deep "V" hull and the utilitarian, all-weather cabin would be perfect for both passengers and supplies.

Pete had verified that its fuel tank was full, and the boat appeared in top-notch condition. He was now supervising the cross-loading of supplies and equipment with Clare and Marvi.

Matt, Pete, and Liz had said their goodbyes to Michelle and Dave and set off for the return trip to Camden after noon yesterday. They arrived in Camden Harbor without issue, retrieved Pete's Jeep, and went up to Mount Battie to brief the rest of the family. Everyone had been ecstatic and spent the evening sorting gear and planning for the trip back to Vinalhaven.

As of yet, they had only seen the one couple with their dog, and that was on the first day. Matt had LT and Juliet pulling security on the Humvee parked at the road entrance to the harbor while the rest of the crew shuttled supplies from the cargo areas of the four SUVs to one of the two boats that would make the trip to Vinalhaven in a couple of hours.

The Lyman-Morse manager had used his large desk blotter calendar to take detailed notes regarding boatyard activities. Of particular note, the diesel and gasoline fuel storage tanks appeared to have been topped off on September 9th, the day after the nuclear attacks. Matt instructed Liz to add the appropriate amount of fuel stabilizer to each tank to ensure the fuel supply would remain usable for at least another year, possibly longer.

A paper flyer from the Camden police department, dated September 19th, urged all residents to remain in their homes until further notice based on guidance from the National Command Authority to limit the spread of smallpox. The last notation on the calendar was on September 20th and simply said, "Closed shop. Sent everyone home. Not feeling well." Another item on the desk was a glossy folder containing what looked to be detailed renovation plans for the boatyard area. A complete remodel was planned, adding a couple of restaurants, office space, and shops. The artist renderings completely transformed the metal-sided warehouse/workshop into a modern, seaside entertainment district. *Just one more dream in all this devastation that would never come to fruition*, Matt thought.

Because Camden had appeared virtually deserted over the last three days, Matt assumed that almost all the residents had fled or succumbed to the pox. There were undoubtedly a few remaining, like the young couple they had seen previously, and Matt hoped at some point he'd be able to deliver vaccines to them before it was too late.

"Matt, this is Pete," Matt heard over the radio.

"Go ahead, Pete."

"Have you decided where you want to park the vehicles? We have everything emptied onto the dock and should be loaded in about fifteen minutes. With all of us working, it's taken hardly any time at all."

"Great, Pete. Yeah. Have everyone drive around to the backside. I'm going to open up the garage door, and my thought is to park them right inside. There's plenty of space for the four SUVs plus the Humvee. I think they'll be as safe as any place here."

"Sounds good. I'll have them drive around."

"And Pete," added Matt. "Could you have Liz bring two of the trail cameras in?"

"Wilco."

Matt got up and walked through the workshop to one of the large overhead garage doors in the back. Pulling hand-over-hand on the chain at the side of the oversized door, Matt watched as the four SUVs slowly drove around the side of the building and came to a stop in front of the door. Once the door was raised about eight feet high, he motioned for the vehicles to enter. Matt had them split sides, with two vehicles parked on each side of the door. This left plenty of room for the Humvee to park in the middle.

Liz was one of the drivers, and Matt could see she held two of the small trail cameras they had picked up at the hardware store in Woodstock. Used chiefly for spotting game by hunters, the motion-activated cameras could be set up almost anywhere and would record any movement within their field of view. Because they were motion-activated, the batteries could last for months, depending on the activity level. As Liz approached, Matt saw Derek get out of one of the other SUVs.

"Hey, Derek!" Matt shouted, loud enough to be heard across

the large warehouse. "Do me a favor. There's a bunch of toolboxes all over this place. Grab a crescent wrench and unhook the negative terminal from each of our SUV's batteries. Not sure how long we'll be gone, but this'll keep the batteries from dying on us."

"No problem, Matt," replied Derek. Matt watched as Derek grabbed Dylan and Clare, the other two drivers, and motioned for them to help him with his task. Liz walked up, and Matt instructed her to position one of the cameras inside the warehouse and another on the outside of the building where they would be able to see if anyone had walked onto the docks. The cameras would simply record activity on a tiny SD memory card because there was no electrical power in the building. While not providing real-time feedback, they'd at least be able to recover the chips on their return trip and view any activity. This could prove extremely helpful in identifying any threats on the mainland.

"Matt, Pete. We're all loaded and ready to depart," Pete said over the radio.

"Okay. Let's go! LT, this is Matt. Please bring the Humvee around to the open garage door. Everyone else, load up!"

CHAPTER 25

October 11, 5:12pm

For the first time in over a month, Matt felt truly relaxed. There was still a tremendous amount of work to be done, but sitting in the overstuffed leather chair and gazing out the large plate glass window, Matt could feel the tension and stress of the previous five weeks ebb out of his body like the receding tide.

Through the window, Matt could see most of his extended family enjoying the late Indian summer afternoon amid the peace of Vinalhaven. Derek, LT, and Grace were finishing setting up the last of the three large tents the family had been sharing atop Mount Battie for the last few days, while Dylan tossed a football with Christopher along the edge of the bay. Kelsey and Juliet sat in Adirondack chairs around a large solo stove, laughing as Laurie performed some sort of silly dance for them. In the kitchen behind him, Matt could hear the ladies preparing what sounded to be an absolute seafood feast of lobsters and clams. *It sure beat another day of MREs*, thought Matt.

When they'd arrived in Carver's Cove earlier that morning, Dave and Michelle had been waiting for them along the old stone pier at the cove's opening. Situated on the north side, maybe three hundred meters east of the Reed's cottage, the pier was a natural breakwater separating the cove from the larger Robert's Bay, itself protected by Narrows Island to the north and Sheep Island to the east. Liz, with her small-boat skills recently acquired at Annapolis, had expertly steered the Hinckley into the dock, where they had unloaded the yacht. As Liz moored the Hinckley further into the cove, Pete helmed the 42-foot Screaming Eagle alongside the pier. As most of the supplies were loaded on this vessel, it took the entire extended family almost a half-hour to unload and stack everything they had brought from the mainland.

While they unloaded and stacked the supplies, Dave gave everyone an oral history of this part of the island. In the last 1800s, Vinalhaven was one of the most important granite quarries in the United States, and many of the prominent buildings and structures in Boston, New York City, and Washington DC were built using granite loaded onto ships from this very pier. Young Christopher was especially fascinated by Dave's historical commentary, particularly when he learned Vinalhaven granite was used to build the Washington Monument, the Boston and DC courthouses, and served as the base of the Brooklyn Bridge.

While the granite industry and the pier's usefulness died in the 1920s, a large farmhouse remained a hundred yards west of the pier and right on the cove. Michelle and Dave had verified that the house was no longer occupied and still had functioning electricity and water. They recommended this as an initial staging base for everyone as it was halfway between the pier and the Reeds' small 2-bedroom cottage. The home, a white clapboard colonial complete with a cedar shake-sided barn and surrounded by fifteen acres of private land, was owned by a wealthy family named Bannon, who lived in downtown Boston. Given the first nuclear explosion's location and the fact that no one had been here since earlier in the summer, Dave was pretty confident no one would be returning. Matt agreed, and they had spent the last few hours making this a temporary home.

The house was recently renovated, with a large, open downstairs and five bedrooms upstairs. The barn's large, red-painted doors opened to reveal plenty of space to store everything, as well as a late-model Ford F-250 pickup that started on the first crank of the engine. Using the Bannon's pickup and Dave's SUV, they shuttled all of the supplies to the barn. While the boys worked with the supplies, Clare and Molly led the ladies on a whirlwind cleaning expedition to ready the house for sixteen new occupants.

As there weren't enough bedrooms for everyone, Clare had implemented a plan where the adults - meaning Matt and Clare, Stan and Marvi, Molly, and Pete - would each have a bedroom in the main house. The ten members of the younger generation would share tents out in the front yard. Young Christopher and Laurie had initially been assigned to sleep on couches in the family room, but Clare had warily acceded to their desire to sleep outdoors with the "other big kids."

Matt sat enjoying a moment of peace, sipping his first cold beer in weeks. The family room where he now sat took up half of the downstairs and had two large sitting areas. The rear area, where Pete and Dave had a map of the island laid out on a low, mahogany coffee table, was separated from the front part of the room, where Matt sat by a giant stone fireplace that could be accessed from both sides. With the fireplace to Matt's right, Matt could look left out the wall-to-wall picture window and view directly out to Sheep Island. He noticed the Hinckley and Screaming Eagle bobbing gently on their moorings in the cove.

Taking another slug from his cold glass of Allagash White beer, a twelve-pack of which had been found chilling in one of the two kitchen refrigerators, Matt had a brief moment of anxiety as he realized this was the first time they had completely let down their security. While he, Pete, and Stan still carried holstered pistols, all other weapons had been secured in either the barn or the home office on the other side of the house. Dave and Michelle had assured them that no human threat existed on the island, but Matt knew it would take some time for him to stop feeling naked without having his M4 within arm's reach.

Stan walked into the room, pouring a bottle of beer into a pint glass as he sat down on the couch across from Matt.

"How's things coming in the barn?" Matt asked.

"Surprisingly well. I was able to do a full authentication, and Liz and Juliet are running the computer through its diagnostics as we speak." While the downstairs of the barn was a large open bay with several small rooms off of it, the upstairs consisted of a large game room area complete with ping pong and card tables and large rooms off each side of the main area. On the left was a home theater that could seat twelve in large, overstuffed recliners, while the right side of the building contained a soundproof recording studio. Dave had mentioned that one of the owners was a woman who had several hit records in the 1980s, and clearly still had a passion for music. Stan had suggested that the recording studio would be the perfect place to set up the QuAI computer system, and Matt had urged him to do that as a top priority. Learning more about what was happening in their surroundings and the world in general was of critical importance to Matt.

"That's great. No issues with power?"

"None at all. When they renovated this place, they spared no expense. Everything is first-class."

"How about connectivity? I assume no internet, right? Just the BGAN satellite system?" Matt asked, referring to the laptop-looking terminal that was basically an advanced satellite phone for high-speed data transmission.

"Yes, just the BGAN. The good news is that, so far, the connection is solid and reliable. The downside is that it's pretty slow, at least compared to the high-speed data we've become used to before the cataclysm."

"Okay. That's good. Tomorrow we can talk more about QuAI and using her to figure out what's happening everywhere."

"Definitely. There's some things I want to show you tomorrow that I think you'll like. QuAI is going to be a huge advantage for us in the long term," said Stan, drinking deeply from his beer.

"Yeah, definitely."

"I think Vinalhaven is going to work, Matt. I mean, we still have an awful lot to do before winter sets in, but for the first time in a month, I actually feel safe," said Stan.

"Agreed. I was just thinking the same thing. What're your thoughts on sentries for tonight? I was thinking maybe one person awake at a time, either sitting outside by the fire or up in the barn's game room, which gives views over the bay and also the road approaching the house along the shoreline."

"Yeah, at least for tonight, I agree. Liz reminded me that we snagged a half-dozen driveway motion sensors, as well as a dozen small game cameras. Now that we have power, Liz said she could rig a wifi system up so that we would get real-time alerts."

"Wifi? But I thought the internet was down?"

"It is," laughed Stan. "But wifi and the internet aren't the same. The wifi is the local network, and the internet is what connects our computers to others in the world. Our local network, or LAN, just needs electricity, and with some of our routers, we can push that out almost 1,000 feet. The devices just need power. We were going to set these up in Vermont with batteries, but as we didn't run power full-time at the house, it didn't make sense. Now that we have dedicated electricity, we should be able to set up 360-degree electronic trip wires around the house."

"Wow," said Matt, shaking his head. "It's amazing how much we took technology for granted. As time passes, I think it's critical you really stay focused on technology, Stan. You and Liz, especially, but also LT, Juliet, and even Christopher and Laurie. We need to constantly be looking for technology that we can harness and adapt to the changing world, and we can't let our technology knowledge lapse. It's what's going to separate us from the barbarians like the Nomads and The Base going forward."

"Amen, brother. Amen." They both held up their beers in a toast before taking deep swallows.

"If it's okay with you," said Matt. "I'll put some thoughts down on paper tonight - maybe some queries and priority information requirements that I think we could use. I'm sure you have your own list, but it would be good if you, Liz, and Juliet could start working on this in the morning. I think this should be their primary task. Amey might be quite interested in helping as well."

"Absolutely, Matt. I'll try to have a rundown of new info tomorrow afternoon."

Both men turned as Marvi poked her head into the family room from the kitchen. "If you four gentlemen would care to join us all in the dining room, our first nightly feast is served."

CHAPTER 26

October 12, 11:39am

"Okay, so eight different families totaling twenty-six people? Can you go through their names and details again? I want to take notes this time. My tiny infantryman's brain takes a while to process all this," said Matt. He, Dave, and Grace were sitting in the small living room of Dave and Michelle's cottage. Matt and Grace had walked over a bit earlier to meet Dave and discuss the noon meeting with the residents of Vinalhaven. Dave had initially wanted it to just be Matt so as not to alarm everyone, but Matt had asked Grace to also come to administer the vaccines. He also thought a pretty, vibrant face would be disarming and less threatening.

"Sure, no problem, Matt. I get that it's a lot to take in at one time. I think once you meet everyone, it'll be easier to remember. Basically, there are twenty-six people in Vinalhaven, in addition to Michelle and me. Four families are year-round residents, two own property but are mostly seasonal, and two arrived after the pandemic began."

"Okay, let's start with the year-round residents. You said it was two retired couples, a lobsterman's family, and a single guy who's a handyman?" Matt asked.

"Yes, exactly. Vance and Amelia Davis are the oldest couple on the island. Vance was the CEO of one of the paper mills in Lewiston. They retired here full-time almost twenty years ago but have owned a home here for over fifty years. They live in town on Carver's Pond, and he's the chairman of the Fox Islands Electric Coop - so basically the guy who knows the most about the windmills." Matt scribbled in his moleskin notebook as Dave spoke. "The next oldest couple is the Pelletiers. They also live right in town, a few houses from Vance and Amelia. Bill Pelletier is a retired FBI agent. I'd say he's in his early-70s, and they moved here about ten years ago. His wife, Suzanne, runs a successful gift shop in the center of Vinalhaven. They're really good people; of the twenty-six, they're the only ones Michelle and I know pretty well."

"Okay," said Matt, still taking notes. "Good to know."

"Then there is Tim and Regina Philbrook and their two daughters, Mia and Harper. They are both at least second-generation Vinalhaven - I think Tim's family came here in the late 1700s. They met in elementary school and decided to raise their family here after both getting degrees from UMaine over in Orono. Tim runs a couple of lobster boats, and Regina is a teacher at the school. They live over on High Street. From what I've seen, Tim's a bit of a hothead, but also a very capable guy. He definitely makes his opinions known."

"Got it."

"And the last full-timer is Frank Oullette. He's a few years younger than Tim and Regina and a handyman by trade. We've used him here a few times for odd jobs, and he's quite good. Basically capable of fixing just about anything, and does carpentry as well as small remodeling jobs."

"Good guy?" Matt asked.

"Yeah," said Dave. "I like him quite a bit. He's very quiet. Comes off as pretty aloof and maybe even a bit slow. But he's a bright guy, keeps to himself."

"And he's single? Lives alone here year-round?"

"Yeah. I don't know his social life. I think he was dating someone, but he's definitely alone now."

"Okay. That covers the year-rounders. What about the seasonal people?"

"Yeah, two families. The Olivers and the Norgaards. There's seven in the Oliver family. Old man Earl Oliver is in his mid-eighties and comes from a wealthy family. They've had a home here since the turn of the century, the 20th century, which is basically a large estate on the northern part of the island. His son, Kent, is a pretty famous Hollywood character actor. I'd guess he's in his mid-fifties. I can't remember what he's been in, but you'll definitely recognize him when you see him. I had met Kent and Earl a few times before the cataclysm, and both are very likable. Kent's wife is named Janet. They have three young adult daughters, all between, I'd guess, eighteen and twenty-three. Lastly, there is Eleanor Steinberg. She's Kent's younger sister and is also an actress, but mostly just on Broadway. She was apparently married to some famous Broadway director, now divorced, and the only time I met her, she was kind of a pain in the ass. Complained a lot about how backward everything is here."

"Interesting. You say they live on the north side of the island? How far from here?"

"Well, their compound is up on Holt Point, maybe five miles north of the town center. We're almost exactly a mile east of town right here."

"Okay. Does anybody drive by here on their way to town?" Matt asked. Dave's cottage, and also the home the Sheridans now occupied, were on a small side street off Pequot Road, which ran along the eastern shore of the island as part of the perimeter road.

"No. Everyone is either in town or more on the western side of the island."

"Excellent. I like that."

"Yeah. It's a nice coincidence," said Dave.

"Okay, sorry for interrupting you. Please continue," said Matt.

"Yeah, so the only other seasonal residents are the Norgaards - Filip and Astrid. They're Danish, and he's a retired engineer. I assume they are quite successful, as they own a waterfront home on the island's west side. I just met him a couple of weeks ago, but he seems like a very knowledgeable, efficient guy. Both in their mid-sixties. Filip is quite handy, and Astrid comes across as an extremely nice woman."

"Okay. That's the residents, year-round and seasonal. Now you said two families showed up after the pandemic? What made them choose Vinalhaven?"

"Good question. The first family is Ferhad Agha. He's a professor at Colby, and he basically grabbed his family and fled Waterville. He got here just before the ferry stopped running, maybe a day or two before the President went public about the pandemic."

"Agha? Is he Kurdish?"

"Yeah, I guess he could be. I know he's originally from Iraq, but never asked if he was a Kurd. I don't really know anything about him. Of everyone, they keep very much to themselves. It's him and his wife, I think her name is Nasrin. I've only seen her once. They have two teenagers, boy and a girl, maybe sixteen and fourteen. Again, I've only seen his family once and have only seen him maybe three times, I think."

"You said they came on the last ferry. Do they own a place here?"

"No. They said they rented an Airbnb, but I don't know if that's true. They are staying off Dogtown Road, west of town, and right on the Reach. The Reach is the main channel on the island's south side where the ferry comes in, kind of between the mainland and Talbot and Green Islands."

"Okay. I knew a guy named Agha from Erbil. Knew him quite well. Wonder if they're related."

"We can ask. I'm not sure he'll be there today, but we could go by his place."

"Okay. And the last family."

"Yeah. Saving the best for last. The Biancos. From what they say - a pretty wealthy family from New Jersey. They were at their place on the shore, Toms River, I believe, when the nuke destroyed Manhattan. When things seemed like they were getting bad, they took the family sailboat north and landed here. They've only been here a little over two weeks. In fact, we had them quarantine for ten days before we'd let them attend the twice-weekly meetings."

"Smart. So you've only met him a couple of times."

"Yeah. Bianco always comes with his whole family. I think the guy's seen too many Soprano episodes, but he's probably not a bad guy. Short, thin dude with slicked-back gray hair, maybe sixty. His name is Tony. His wife seems okay. I believe her name is Camila, but she doesn't say much. They have two kids. A son, AJ, who's a real piece of work. Carries an AR-15 and tries his hardest to look like a Delta operator. First thing out of his mouth when I met him was that he was an Army veteran. Turns out he spent four weeks in Basic Training before getting kicked out. The daughter, Gianna, seems pretty normal. I'd say she's maybe eighteen or nineteen. I think she said she was a freshman at Penn, and they picked her up at school after the bombs hit. She seems the most normal of the bunch, always smirks whenever her brother talks."

"Interesting. Did you get all that, Grace? There's going to be a test."

"Ha ha," said Grace, deadpanning and cracking a slight smile. "It is a lot to take in. It's good background info, though, and it'll be much easier once we can put faces with the names and see their personality a bit."

"Yeah," said Matt. "Okay, Dave. Anything else we need to know before we head down there? My goal's to introduce ourselves and give them their vaccines. After that, we can play it by ear. Ideally, I'd like to meet with some of them individually, maybe over the next few days. Try to build some relationships. That's much more difficult to do in a group setting."

"Agreed. Why don't we head down there and see how it goes? I'll drive," said Dave.

"Sounds good. I'll defer to you, but I'd feel more comfortable if we go fully armed with long guns and not just sidearms. Whadda you think?"

"Yeah, I always go fully armed, but I leave the M4 in the

truck when I drive. The knucklehead Bianco kid will have his rifle, but everyone else usually comes unarmed."

"Okay. That works for me. Let's do this."

CHAPTER 27

October 12, 12:01pm

The town center was precisely one mile from Dave and Michelle's cottage. Riding in Dave's Ford Expedition, Matt took in the scenery en route to the town. It was almost exactly as he remembered it from his last visit several years prior. The exception was the lack of people. It was a beautiful October day, the autumn leaves exhibited their orange and red hues, yet not a single sole was visible outside the vehicle's windows.

Everything else about the island appeared unchanged.

The Vinalhaven school set back from the south side of the road, empty of students. The historic, brown Shingle-style Union Church stood vigilant watch kitty-corner across from the public library. Matt knew that neither parishioners nor patrons would likely have use for either building for quite some time. As Main Street curved right into the center of downtown, the sight of the Sand Bar restaurant brought back fond memories of enjoying chowder, chicken wings, and cold beer in a much simpler time. *Would we ever eat in a restaurant again?*

Dave continued into town at the slow pace of 20 miles per hour, driving past a small art gallery, two gift shops, and a restaurant Matt had not seen before. Directly across from Carver's Harbor Market, the only grocery store on the island, Dave pulled into a large, mostly empty parking lot. On the far side of the parking lot sat the Tidewater, the largest inn on the island. The Tidewater was unique because it was built on top of the stone bridge separating Carver's Harbor from Carver's Pond, an estuary fed by the harbor's tidal waters. As the tide came in, as it was now, water flowed northward under the hotel, filling up Carvers Pond. When the tide turned, as it would in several hours, the water flow shifted, and underneath the hotel became a waterfall gushing out towards the sea. The effect was visually stunning. To the left was the harbor itself, the deep blue water dotted with dozens of colorful boats bobbing on their moorings.

While Matt referred to this area as Vinalhaven's downtown, he knew the locals often called this "downstreet." It was a fond adaptation that was a more apt description of the town center, which was a mere two blocks long and contained about a dozen commercial establishments.

Shifting his attention from the hotel to the parking lot, Matt could see six distinct groups of people standing in a loose circle approximately ten yards from each other. Three groups were older couples; one consisted of two middle-aged men, and a fifth was an Arab-looking man standing alone. Lastly, the final group was a man in his mid-fifties accompanied by two college-aged women. As Dave had predicted, Matt instantly recognized this man, the actor Kent Oliver, from several movies whose titles did not readily come to mind. Kent was maybe 5'9", stocky build, wavy dark hair turning gray and wire-rimmed glasses. Matt got the impression that he had played either a disheveled professor type or maybe a defense attorney.

As Dave slowly pulled into the parking lot, several couples not standing in front of vehicles took a few steps backward, creating a spot for Dave to park that would allow everyone to maintain their ten-yard social distance. Some were wearing N95 masks or respirators, while others held them in their hands. Everyone was staring intently at the new arrivals, obviously alert to the fact that Matt and Grace were newcomers. Matt was surprised, although very pleasantly so, to see that no one appeared overly alarmed at his presence.

Coming from their experience in Woodstock with the Nomads, it was evident that the residents of Vinalhaven were not overly concerned with their security. Matt could not see a single visible weapon on any of the attendees, although Matt was pretty sure the older of the two men standing together had a pistol printing through his flannel shirt.

Dave, Matt, and Grace each opened their doors and exited the Expedition. As agreed upon beforehand, Dave immediately took the lead.

"Hello, everyone. I know you're all wondering, so I'd like to introduce my cousin, Matt Sheridan. And this is Grace Heck," said Dave, gesturing at Grace standing behind him. "They've just arrived last night from Vermont."

"What about quarantining?" Said the oldest man present, who Matt guessed was Vance Davis from his age. "Aren't you worried for your family?"

"That's the reason I brought Matt and Grace to town with me," replied Dave. "It's probably best if I let Matt speak."

"Hi, folks. It's a pleasure to meet you, and I hope to get a chance to get to know each of you in the coming weeks. The first thing I want to say is that we have several vials of the updated smallpox vaccine, and I hope we can inoculate each of you right now. And you can vaccinate your family members who aren't present as soon as possible."

Each of the small groups immediately began murmuring to each other. Amid the various conversations, Kent Oliver raised his hand and spoke up. "A vaccine? How is it possible that you have the vaccine?"

"Well, that's quite a long story. The short version is that we got it from a batch delivered to Dartmouth-Hitchcock Hospital in Hanover, New Hampshire. Sixteen of us arrived here yesterday and are staying with the Reeds, and we've all been inoculated."

"How do we know it's real? Or that there aren't side effects?" Kent followed up.

Dave answered before Matt could respond. "Kent, we

haven't spent much time together, but I think you'll agree that I've always been a straight shooter. Michelle and I received our vaccinations two days ago when Matt first came to Carvers Cove. We've had no side effects other than some slight soreness around the injection site." Dave paused to let that sink in. Matt noticed several of the murmurs had been replaced by head nods. 'And I'll add one more thing. Most of you know my background in the military and as a special agent with NCIS. I can unequivocally tell you, if there is one person I trust implicitly in this world, it's Matt Sheridan."

"Thanks, Dave," said Matt. "Look, folks, I'm not here to convince you to take the vaccine. Grace, who happens to be in med school at the University of Florida, and I want to ensure you all have an opportunity. I'm not sure how much everyone knows about what's happening worldwide. Most of the world's population is dead, killed by the smallpox over the last four weeks. It's completely up to you whether you take the vaccine, and we're happy to give you enough syringes for everyone in your family."

"Everyone? Everyone is dead?" This question was posed by the Middle Eastern-looking man Matt assumed to be Ferhad.

"From what we've been able to gather, the estimates are that between 95% and 98% of the population is gone. We drove to Camden from Vermont and did not see a single soul. There appear to be some areas where they were somewhat successful distributing the vaccine, but those are rare."

Matt was a bit taken aback by the look of surprise on everyone's faces. He was confident they all knew the death toll from smallpox was devastating, as there were only twenty-eight remaining out of more than one thousand residents, but apparently, hearing it definitively was a bit of a shock.

Grace stepped forward into the silence, holding up an N95 mask she had found in the back seat of the Expedition. "I have more than enough syringes for everyone, and I also have the vial of the vaccine. I'm happy for you to review the label on the vial if that's something you'd like to do. I can also administer the shot to you now, or I can load enough syringes for your entire family, and you can take them back and administer them yourselves. We're quite thankful to be here on Vinalhaven, and there's simply no need to live in fear of smallpox when we have the vaccine."

Matt, Grace, and Dave stood there and watched the others for a reaction. *This could go sideways pretty quickly,* Matt thought. *If they all bail on us, it'll be difficult to build trust.* Matt tried to look each individual in the eye while waiting for a reaction. Many of the small groups were whispering within their cluster.

"Okay, we're in," shouted Kent. "The three of us will get it now, and then could you possibly come out to our place to give it to the others? I'm concerned about my 86-year-old father. Will it be safe for him?"

"It should absolutely be safe," replied Grace. "My 67-year-old grandmother took it, as we all have. The only side effects we've seen are some slight swelling at the injection site, and a few people had a mild fever during the first twenty-four hours. Other than that, we've seen no adverse reactions. And yes, I believe it would be no problem for us to come out to your place. It would be a pleasure to meet your father."

Dave was a bit surprised that Kent was the one who stepped forward. While Dave liked Kent quite a bit, he had never come across as a leader to Dave. Everyone watched as Kent removed his fleece, rolled up the left sleeve of his shirt, and stepped forward.

"Oh, Kent. Did I mention the shot's not in the arm? It's in the eyeball."

Kent stopped in his tracks, his face turning white. Matt tried to keep a straight face, being familiar with Dave's dry sense of humor, but it appeared no one else appreciated the joke as they all visibly paled.

"I'm joking, Kent! I'm joking!" Dave said, realizing his joke had fallen a bit flat in the tenseness of the situation. Kent, however, realizing he had completely fallen for it, began laughing out loud. His belly laugh was followed by the laughter of his daughters and then several of the others around the loose circle of people. “Geez. Lighten up, Francis,” Dave said, primarily to himself, as he spouted the famous line from the movie *Stripes*.

By then, almost everyone was at least smiling. Kent continued forward to Grace, rotating sideways to present her with his bare left deltoid. Grace held up the vial so that he could read the label, then uncapped a syringe, filled it from the vial, and popped it smartly into the fleshy part of Kent’s upper arm. Kent never even flinched.

Turning to Grace as she swabbed the injection site, he held out his right hand. “I’m Kent Oliver. It’s a pleasure to meet you, Grace. Welcome to Vinalhaven.”

Grace shook his hand firmly. “Are those your daughters? Want me to vaccinate them too?”

“Yes. Please,” said Kent. Turning to his daughters, he said, “Emily, Charlotte. Come get your shot.” Kent introduced himself to Matt as Emily and Charlotte approached Grace to receive their injections. They arranged to drive up to the Oliver compound on the island’s north end to provide vaccines to the rest of the family.

As Grace finished with the second Oliver daughter, one of the three older couples approached Grace. “I am Astrid, and this is my husband, Filip,” said the woman, with a slight Scandinavian accent. Matt guessed she was probably sixty but could easily pass for a woman twenty years younger. She was absolutely stunning with her tall, athletic build, short blond hair, and piercing blue eyes. Matt would not have been surprised to learn she had once been a supermodel. Grace administered the shots to the Danish couple as Matt introduced himself.

“Hello, I’m Matt Sheridan,” he said, extending his hand first to Filip and then to Astrid. “It’s a pleasure to meet you both.”

“Yes, thank you,” said Filip. “It is our pleasure to meet you as well. Thank you for your consideration in providing this vaccine. We are most thankful."

Matt wanted to speak with them further but noticed that the other older couples were now standing before Grace. Dave took over talking with Filip and Astrid, as Matt introduced himself to the Pelletiers and immediately afterward the Davises. Knowing from Dave that Vance Davis was the longest resident on the island and fancied himself as the residents' unofficial leader based on his position with the Fox Islands Electric Coop, Matt gently took Vance aside. "Vance, I was wondering if I might speak with you sometime this afternoon or tomorrow. I can come by your house if that's acceptable."

"Absolutely, young man. I'd be most interested in speaking with you as well. We have much to do to prepare this island for the winter."

"Vance, that's exactly what I wanted to speak with you about. How about later this afternoon after we get back from the Oliver's? Maybe around 5 pm or so?"

"Excellent, Matt. We'll see you then. Dave knows where we live."

"Looking forward to it, Vance." Matt left Vance talking with Dave as the Pelletiers got their shot. Matt noticed the three Olivers pile into a Suburu wagon and move west across the Main Street bridge. Matt turned his head to keep an eye on the two men who, as of yet, had not made any move to get the vaccine. Matt assumed these men were Tim, the lobsterman, and Frank, the handyman, but he didn't know who was who. The two spoke in hushed tones and seemed to cast wary looks toward Grace and her syringes.

As Matt was about to call out to them, an old Econoline van with more rust than paint came barreling into downtown from the west. Matt estimated the van was doing about fifty miles per hour as it passed the Oliver's green Subaru, followed immediately by the screech of worn brake pads as the van slowed to turn into the parking lot and pulled right into the center of the informal circle the group had formed, the nose of the van about ten yards directly in front of Dave's Expedition.

"Ahoy," said Vance to the group. "The Biancos appear to have arrived."

A short man in his sixties, not more than 5'7", jumped out of the passenger side of the van and immediately turned to open the sliding cargo door. He wore boat shoes, designer blue jeans, and a Patagonia fleece zipped to the top. His thinning slate gray hair was slicked straight back over his forehead, poorly disguising a large bald area on the top of the man's head.

Tony Bianco. A legend in his own mind. Matt thought.

As the cargo door slid back loudly, two women stepped out. The first was undoubtedly Mrs. Bianco. Matt had no idea how she maintained her big hair amid a cataclysmic pandemic, but she certainly did. Like her husband, she had on jeans and a fleece but wore white sneakers instead of boat shoes. The other woman appeared college-age, athletic, with her raven-black hair pulled back in a ponytail under a baseball hat adorned with the blue-and-red split-P of the University of Pennsylvania. While her parents were dressed for sailing, the woman Matt assumed was named Gianna wore black Lululemon yoga pants and a pink Hollister sweatshirt.

As the two women stepped onto the pavement, Matt's focus was drawn to the driver's side of the van, where a young man closed the van's door after reaching for something inside. Matt tried not to laugh. This was AJ, as Dave had mentioned, and he may have watched the movie *American Sniper* one too many times. He was dressed very similar to Chris Kyle, the decorated Navy SEAL sniper with 160 confirmed kills in Iraq, but all similarities ended with the clothing. AJ wore tan cargo pants with a 5.11 tactical assault shirt - the kind where the shirt's body was tan while the sleeves were woodland camouflage. On his head, he wore a black baseball cap, on backward, and had mirrored Oakley sunglasses. Similar to noticing a person dressed in a western shirt and a cowboy hat yet not wearing cowboy boots, Matt smirked when he noticed AJ was wearing low-top Chuck Taylors on his feet. AJ stood a hair taller than his father at about 5'8" and couldn't have weighed more than a buck forty soaking wet. While AJ's appearance screamed "holster sniffer" to Matt, as Dave had warned, the fact that he carried an AR-15 rifle with a seated 30-round magazine was a bit alarming.

This guy is fucking dangerous, thought Matt, making a mental note that AJ needed to be watched.

"What's going on, Dave? Vance? And who are these two newcomers? Shouldn't they be in quarantine?" Tony said, speaking quite loudly. None of the Biancos wore a mask, but they maintained their ten-yard social distance. Noticing that Tim and Frank were distant from the others, who remained grouped around Dave's Expedition, Tony called over to them. "Hey, Tim, what's up? Seems like we missed something by being a few minutes late."

Before Tim could answer, Dave spoke. "Afternoon, Tony. Nice to see you again. I'd like to introduce you to my cousin, Matt Sheridan. He and Grace here just recently arrived from Vermont. Long story short, they brought several vials of the updated smallpox vaccine with them and are administering it to everyone on the island."

"Are you from the government?" Tony asked, addressing Matt directly. "Did they send you here?"

"Ah, no, Tony. I'm not from the government. I don't believe the government exists anymore, certainly not in any form that provides services here in Maine. I'm just a private citizen. We obtained some of the vaccine from Dartmouth-Hitchcock Hospital over in...."

"I know where it is," interrupted Tony.

Matt paused, looking at Tony sharply. Matt had little tolerance for fools and even less for those who could jeopardize his family's safety. Matt was pretty sure Tony was the former. However, the verdict was still out on whether Matt would put him in the latter category, which would not be good for Tony.

"Okay," Matt continued. "Well, I'll cut this short since you know where it is. We have the vaccine and are happy to administer it to you and your family if you'd like. It's 100%

your decision."

"How do we know where you got it?" Tony asked. "I mean, this could all be a ruse to give us smallpox or something worse."

Matt let his breath out slowly, annoyed but trying hard not to let it show. Before he could answer, Dave spoke. "Well, first off, Tony. Since the Black Pox is about 98% fatal, I'm not sure what we could put in a vial that would be worse. Second, as has Matt and his entire family, Michelle and I have taken it without any side effects."

"So you say," quipped Tony.

Now it was Dave's turn to breathe slowly. "You're right, Tony. I will give you the benefit of the doubt that you didn't just question my integrity. That said, whether you take the vaccine or not is completely up to you. There's no strings. We have it if you want it, whenever you'd like."

"Okay, Dave. I'm sorry if you thought I was questioning your integrity. I am just trying to do what's right for me...."

Tony stopped mid-sentence as his daughter strode forward directly toward Grace. Before anyone could react, she walked right up to Grace while pulling up the sleeve of her sweatshirt. "Hi! I'm Gianna. Could I please have the vaccine?"

Grace smiled, grabbed a fresh syringe and filled it from the vial. Everyone watched Tony and AJ carefully as Gianna received her vaccination. As Grace swabbed the injection site with a small alcohol pad, Gianna waved hello to everyone around the Expedition. She smiled mischievously at Matt, then abruptly turned and returned to stand beside her mother.

It was all Matt could do not to burst out laughing. While her father may be a fool, Gianna Bianco had earned Matt's instant respect.

Attempting to regain some modicum of control, Tony said, "Okay, I've had a chance to consider it, and I think we should all get the vaccine. Especially with everyone else on the island getting it." Tony gestured for his wife and son to follow him, and he walked up to Grace to receive his shot.

After getting jabbed, Tony shook hands with Dave and Vance, then turned to Matt with his right hand extended. "I'm sorry for all that, Matt. Just trying to do what's best for my family in these troubling times."

"I completely understand, Tony. It's nice to meet you, and I'm sure we'll have plenty of opportunities to get to know each other better."

"I look forward to it," said Tony.

AJ stepped forward while pulling his sleeve down. "Hey, Dave. Was your cousin in the military like us? He looks like he could be a Navy SEAL. Are you a SEAL, man?"

"Nah, man," said Matt. "I took the test, but my IQ was too high to be a SEAL."

"Ah, too bad, man. Too bad." AJ turned and walked back to the van, where his father was getting into the passenger seat. With the Biancos loaded up, AJ started up the van and departed the parking lot - heading west toward the home they were staying in.

Everyone's attention turned to the three remaining men: Tim and Frank standing together on the left and Ferhad to the right.

Dave said, "Gentlemen, there's absolutely no pressure whatsoever, but I notice none of you has commented yet. Are there any questions we can try to answer for you? Like I said to Tony, feel free to think about it. It's not like we're going anywhere; the vaccine will always be available for you."

Tim and Frank looked at each other, nodded, then both stepped forward.

Dave spoke to the taller of the two. "Hey, Tim, how are things going?"

"As good as can be expected, Dave. We don't really have any issues taking the vaccine, and in fact, we appreciate what you and your cousin are doing. I hung back cuz I wanted to ask Matt here more about what's happening on the mainland. You said no one is left?"

"Nice to meet you, Tim. And I assume you're Frank?" Matt

said, looking at the shorter of the two men. Both men were dressed identically in jeans and grubby hooded sweatshirts. "Why don't you let Grace here give you your shots while we're talking." Matt gestured to Grace, and she stepped forward as the men yanked up the sleeves of their sweatshirts.

"Well, Tim. My extended family and I traveled over from Vermont and grabbed a boat in Camden Harbor. We didn't see anyone on the journey until we got to Camden. In three days of sitting atop Mount Battie and watching the town, we saw two people - a young couple in their mid-twenties. We didn't approach them."

"That's it? What about the police? What about I-95? You must have crossed over it on your way," asked Tim.

"Yeah, we came across 95 around Waterville. Nothing, Tim."

"God damn," whispered Tim. Both Tim and Frank looked deflated. "We've all been so stressed about catching smallpox that no one has checked any of the houses here on the island. I mean, we assumed people left and even that many of them got sick and died, but thinking that everyone is gone is just crazy. Isn't it?"

"Yeah, it is, Tim. There's still people out there, just not many. Most people are in clusters where the vaccine was finally delivered. There's also some pretty bad folks out there too. We fled Vermont because a motorcycle gang had basically taken over southern Vermont and New Hampshire, maybe even parts of Massachusetts?"

"No shit? That's fucking crazy."

"Yeah," said Matt. "Yeah, it's definitely crazy."

Grace interrupted the conversation. "Tim, would you like us to come to your house and vaccinate your family? We could do that now if you like."

"Actually, could I just get three loaded syringes? My wife's a teacher, but she's also a trained EMT. It might be easier if I discussed this with her first rather than have ya'll show up unannounced. She'll be able to inject herself and the kids."

"Not a problem, Tim. Let me get those set up for you." Grace handed several loaded syringes to Tim, and the two men walked west out of the parking lot. Matt realized that none of the cars in the parking lot were theirs and they were likely walking home. The Davises and Pelletiers had departed while Matt and Dave spoke with Tim.

The only island resident remaining in the parking lot was Ferhad, who had barely spoken the entire time. He still stood just over ten yards away, standing next to a mountain bike resting on its kickstand.

"Ferhad," said Dave. "I'd like to formally introduce you to my cousin, Matt, and this is Grace. I realize you're new to the island, but I want you to know we consider you a full resident, just like everyone else. We're all in this together."

"Thank you, Dave," replied Ferhad, who spoke with a proper British accent. "It is a pleasure to meet you. Matt and Grace, on behalf of my family, I thank you for your kindness in bringing us this vaccine."

"Same here, Ferhad," said Matt. "Do you have questions?"

"Not really. I am a professor of biology at Colby College, so I'm quite familiar with the vaccination process and the smallpox virus. It's the reason we decided to come to the island before everything turned badly. I knew that many people would die from the virus, but I did not think it would spread so quickly."

"From what we've learned, it appears the virus was specifically modified to be super-virulent and contagious. It's swept through the entire world in just two weeks."

"How's your family getting along?" Dave asked. "From our previous group meetings, you were mostly silent, but Michelle and I've been concerned that you may not have enough food and supplies."

"Thank you, Dave. Yes, we're doing fine. We have supplies for at least two more weeks, and I think now, with the vaccine, we should be able to forage in neighboring homes without fear of contracting the virus."

"Okay, good," said Dave.

"Hey, Ferhad," said Matt. "I wanted to ask you. Dave said you're from Iraq and your last name is Agha. You wouldn't be from Erbil by any chance, would you?"

"Why yes, I am. I was born there but moved to Mosul for university and stayed there for my doctorate and as a professor. We came here in 2008. Are you familiar with Erbil?"

"I spent quite a bit of time in Iraq and made many trips to Erbil and Mosul. I have a good friend who shares your last name, Peshro Agha. Might he be related to you?"

Ferhad's face broke into a huge grin. "But of course. Peshro is my first cousin. He's a few years older than me, but we were close and have remained in contact. He's in Sweden with his family. How do you know Peshro?"

"Such a small world, isn't it? Yes, I visited Peshro and Amina at their home in Gothenburg last year. Peshro and I worked closely together during the war and have remained very close ever since."

"I understand," said Ferhad. Peshro was a Kurdish security forces commander with whom Matt's Special Forces A-team worked closely during a hard-fought counterinsurgency campaign. "It is my sincere hope that he and his family are some of the few that have survived, Inshallah."

"Yes," agreed Matt. "Peshro's one of the good guys. And he's a survivor. It wouldn't surprise me if he's running things in Sweden at the moment."

Grace stepped forward with a syringe as Ferhad pulled up his sleeve. "If it's not too much bother, Ms. Grace, I would like to take three syringes back to my family, similar to Tim."

"Yes, absolutely," replied Grace. "Let me get them ready for you."

"And Dave and Matt, I would be most honored if you would come by for a visit at a convenient time. It would be nice to finally speak with others and discuss how best for all of us to survive on Vinalhaven through the winter."

"Of course, Ferhad," said Dave. "We'd enjoy that very much.

I think now that we're all vaccinated, it's important that we interact more and help each other. It's going to be a long, cold winter."

CHAPTER 28

October 12, 1:52pm

They drove north from downstreet Vinalhaven by taking North Haven Road along Carvers Pond en route to the Oliver estate. As Dave described, the Olivers had a family estate with a huge home and a smaller guest house on over forty acres on Holts Point. Located about five miles north of Main Street, Holts Point was a narrow, finger-like peninsula nestled between the large expanse of Calderwood Neck to the northeast and the area of Fox Rocks and Middle Mountain to the northwest.

Matt thought about what had transpired in the parking lot and the various personalities he would have to deal with going forward. Overall, he was pleased that everyone had been present and agreed to receive the vaccine. Matt felt confident that almost everyone would be supportive of working together to do what was necessary to get them all through the long winter. The only question mark was the Biancos. While the daughter was impressive, the father and son left Matt concerned that they could become significant problems if not appropriately managed.

Dave provided a running sightseeing commentary to Grace, who had never been to Vinalhaven and was fascinated by its geography. They drove past Lawson's Quarry, one of two abandoned quarries on the island that had become popular swimming holes. As they neared the turnoff to Holts Point, Dave pointed out the three gigantic windmills off to their left.

Matt was amazed at how tall the windmills were, estimating they stood between 350-400 feet tall. Dave stopped the Expedition at the turn to Mills Farm Road and rolled down the windows.

Whump

Whump

Whump

Whump

The steady beating of the windmill's blades could be easily heard, and like a drumbeat at a concert, the deep, steady beat could almost be felt in their chests.

"Jesus. That's pretty loud. I can't imagine everyone was happy to have the wind turbines installed," said Matt.

"You got that right," said Dave. "We were supportive as it's on the other side of the island, but many people were downright angry. I've always thought it a bit funny that we're creating a terrible eyesore with a completely artificial sound profile in an effort to go green and reduce the carbon footprint."

"Yeah. Progress, I guess. But man, am I glad they went through with it. It's a complete game changer for us if we can keep these running and producing electricity."

"Absolutely," replied Dave, putting the vehicle back in gear and heading northeast up Mills Farm Road.

After a few minutes' drive, the road narrowed substantially and turned to pea stone gravel as they passed through a gap in a crumbling stone wall reminiscent of those found all over New England. Several hundred yards later, they pulled in front of an expansive cedar-shingled house so large it seemed to wrap halfway around the circular drive. To the left, Matt could see a smaller, similarly-styled home through the trees. Both houses held prime positions above the rocky shoreline, beyond which were breathtaking views along the length of the Fox Islands Thoroughfare, the body of water separating Vinalhaven from North Haven, its island neighbor to the north.

Matt stepped out of the Expedition as soon as it came to a stop. His senses were immediately assaulted by the scent of saltwater in the air, the sounds of waves crashing on the rocks as seagulls squawked overhead, and the contrasting colors of the deep blue water, green evergreens, and the purple of fall-blooming wildflowers.

"Mmmm," said Grace, also exiting the vehicle. "It smells so crisp and clean up here. What an amazing view!"

"Yeah," said Dave. "The best thing about Vinalhaven is that there are a thousand spots on the island with views as good, if not better, than this one."

"I can see why people live here, that's for sure." Before Grace could say anything else, the front door opened, and Kent Oliver stepped onto the wide veranda accompanied by a dark-haired woman his age. The woman was full-figured but athletic and, like Kent, was wearing jeans, a fleece, and Merrell hiking shoes.

"Welcome to Longview. Dave, I know you know my wife, but Grace and Matt, I would like to introduce you to my wife, Janet." Matt walked forward and shook Janet and Kent's hands at the bottom of the front porch.

"We can't thank you enough for bringing the vaccine to Vinalhaven," said Janet to them all. "We've been waiting patiently for word of whether the government would deliver it but haven't heard anything since the televisions and radio stations went off the air a few weeks back."

"We're all in this together," replied Matt. "I can imagine how difficult it's been for all of you, isolated as you've been on the island. While I'm afraid we aren't bringing good news about what's happening on the mainland, at least we have sufficient stock of the updated vaccine."

"We'd like to have a more detailed conversation with all of you," interjected Kent. "But Dad is waiting inside with my sister and daughter, and they're all eager to get the vaccine. You have no idea what a strain it's been wondering if we may have been exposed to the virus at any moment."

"Absolutely," agreed Matt. "Please, show us the way."

Kent led them into the house, where everyone was waiting in the large family room. Grace administered the vaccine injections while Matt admired the room's view and decor. While Matt estimated that the house was originally built close to one hundred years ago, similar to the place they had taken over in Carvers Cove, the Oliver estate had also been recently, and expensively, updated. Retaining its original New England charm, the home's main living area had been opened to a modern kitchen. Multiple leather sofas and easy chairs were positioned to take advantage of the views through the oversized plate-glass windows with long views down a narrow bay. North Haven could be seen about a mile off in the distance.

"It's a pleasure to meet you, Ambassador Oliver," said Matt after everyone had been inoculated. "Dave has told me quite a bit about you." Matt had been fascinated to learn earlier from Dave that the Oliver patriarch had earned a Silver Star as a Marine in the Korean War, followed by a highly-successful career as a diplomat with the State Department. He was fluent in several languages, including Arabic and Russian, and had been posted to Russia several times during the Cold War and Iraq during the first Gulf War. Kent mentioned his father was 86 years old, and Dave said he still had 100% of his wit, charm, and intelligence.

"Please. Call me Earl," said the elder Oliver. "And please, do have a seat. I hope you have a few minutes to have a brief conversation. There is much to discuss."

"Absolutely, Ambassador, ah, Earl," said Matt, sitting in one of the oversized leather chairs across from where the Ambassador was sitting. Everyone else found seats around them, and Matt noticed that even with ten of them in the room, several open seats remained.

"On behalf of my family, I would like to thank you for your generosity in sharing your vaccine with all the residents on the island. We have all lived the last few weeks in isolated fear, and I hope being vaccinated may allow us to return to a somewhat more normal life. Kent has informed me that you have traveled from Vermont. I would be most interested in hearing of your experiences since the nuclear attack on our country and what you have seen in your travels across northern New England."

"First, we appreciate the kind words, but there is absolutely no need to thank us. We were fortunate to have obtained the vaccine, and as we intend to make Vinalhaven our long-term home, it was never a question that our first step would be to vaccinate the residents remaining on the island." Matt paused as Janet Oliver set down a tray of steaming mugs of coffee, from which everyone grabbed a cup. "As for our journey, it's quite a long story."

"Please, Matt. Indulge an old man if you'd be so kind. I have nothing but time."

"Yes, sir. Well, my family and I live primarily just outside Newport, Rhode Island. I was fortunate to have woken up seconds after the bomb in Manhattan was detonated. We evacuated immediately and headed to my brother's farm in Woodstock, Vermont. While my brother, his wife, and youngest daughter were visiting Ireland, his three other children were at the farmhouse when we arrived. We had plenty of supplies, but when we learned the vaccine would be available, we decided that Grace and I would travel to Dartmouth-Hitchcock Hospital, about fifteen miles away, to get enough vaccine for the family. We happened to arrive at the same time the hospital was violently attacked by a highly-organized motorcycle gang intent on stealing the vaccine. A National Guard lieutenant fled with some of his men and a case of the vaccine, and we were able to escort them back to the farmhouse, although two of his soldiers were killed in the process."

"So that's how you have the vaccine? Very interesting. May I ask? How many doses do you have?"

Matt sipped his coffee, deciding whether to tell the Olivers the truth. "We have approximately 10,000 doses."

All of the Olivers except Earl stopped drinking and stared

at Matt. Earl seemed unfazed and continued sipping from his cup. Matt realized that forty-plus years in the diplomatic corps had undoubtedly provided Earl with a world-class poker face.

"10,000?" Kent asked. "That seems like an awful lot of vaccine. If the country is truly down to less than 5% of the population, your case of vaccine will go a long way toward keeping everyone remaining alive."

"I've thought long and hard about this. While I do think there may still be pockets of isolated individuals, the majority of those remaining alive in our country have likely already had the vaccine or are perhaps one of the less than 1% that survived their bout with the Black Pox."

"Excellent point, Matt," said Earl. "But I also suspect your case would still be extremely valuable to the right people. Thinking long term, our society likely no longer retains the capability to produce more, therefore, your case may prove priceless to future generations."

"That is what keeps me awake at night, Earl. And it's the main reason we are here right now. The motorcycle gang I mentioned, the Nomads, is intent on seizing the case from us. We've had several run-ins with them, the final one a fairly major armed engagement at our Vermont farmhouse. Our group had decided to evacuate to a place that provided more long-term opportunities for security and survivability, and we chose Vinalhaven. My wife, Clare, and I had been here several times, visiting Dave and Michelle, and this seemed like the ideal place. Everything I've seen so far has reinforced that we've made the correct decision."

"Well, we are quite happy to welcome you. I can unequivocally say, as the island's longest resident - my grandfather built this estate in the 1920s, and I've been coming here since I was a boy - that you have more than earned your right to reside on this island. Not that my approval is required in any way, of course."

"Thank you," said Matt.

"You seem a competent man, Matt. I'm aware of Dave's

military and law enforcement background. Might you have a similar background as well?"

"Yes, sir. I was an infantry and special forces officer in the Army, and for the last ten years or so, I've been managing a consulting firm working on special projects for the DoD and other government agencies."

"I see. Mostly overseas?"

"Yes, sir."

"And you mentioned your family but inferred that your group is a bit bigger than just your extended family. Is that true?"

"There are sixteen of us, Earl. Seven of us are Sheridans, but the other nine include Grace and her grandmother, our neighbors in Vermont, the National Guard lieutenant I mentioned and my niece's college roommate. More recently, a very close friend of mine from college, who was a commander in the Navy, as well as his close friend, a retired Navy captain, and their families have joined up with us prior to departing Vermont." While Matt immediately trusted Earl Oliver, he decided there was no need to be expansive about identifying Stan White and the QuAI computer terminal they had set up in Carvers Cove.

"Excellent, excellent," said Earl. "What's that bring us to, Kent? Just over forty on the island?"

"Uh, yes, that would seem about right."

"There are now forty-four on the island to my knowledge, Ambassador," answered Dave.

"Mmmmm, forty-four," mused Earl. "And to think that just over a month ago, we had over one thousand. When I was your age, we spent a lot of time thinking and preparing for doomsday scenarios as part of the Cold War. As I finally retired in 2000, I thought I would live to my end without seeing anything like this. It's painful to be so wrong."

They all sat in silence, drinking from their mug of coffee or staring out the window toward the bay.

After a moment, Earl picked up the conversation. "And what

of your drive here? Were you able to gather any information about the remaining population?"

"Very little, Earl. We saw absolutely nobody on our way to Camden. While in Camden, we camped atop Mount Battie and spent a couple of days reconnoitering the area from the hilltop."

"Smart," said Earl.

"Very smart," added Kent.

"We did see one couple. They were wearing masks, so we assumed that they were unvaccinated. They went into one of the stores in Camden and departed soon after, likely to wherever they are isolating outside of town."

"Interesting," said Earl. "Just as we learned of the vaccine, quite a few residents left to head to Portland or Bangor, thinking those were likely places where the vaccine would be distributed first. Have you heard anything about those cities?"

"Nothing so far. But Rockland and Bangor are both places we plan to investigate once we get more settled. The first priority for me, as I think it should be for all of us, is to ensure we can survive the winter as comfortably as possible."

"Agreed," said Kent. "Our family has discussed this at length, and I'm sure Dave has shared that it's something we've tried to broach with the wider group of residents. We're just all a bit unorganized, and without the vaccine, none of us wanted to forage or leave the island for fear of bringing the virus back to our families. Now, with Grace's vaccine here, we can finally take some more proactive action."

At this point, Dave spoke up. "Earl, Kent, Janet - you're pretty well situated here with your family. The one issue is that you're about five miles from town, which could become a bit of an obstacle in the winter. I know Matt has given this considerable thought, but I think over the next few days, we should all put our heads together and devise a plan to divide some of the tasks. This way, we all pull our oars in the same direction."

"Well said, David," said Earl. "Please let us know when you'd like to meet next. We are 100% supportive of your efforts."

CHAPTER 29

October 12, 3:44pm

Stan and Juliet stood at the front of the home theater in the barn's second story while most of the adults in the extended family sat in the comfortable recliners arranged in three tiered rows of four. The lights were on, and instead of a movie, Stan had projected a map of the United States onto the wall-sized screen at the front of the room.

All eyes were focused on Stan, who had called this meeting, so there was no need to get everyone's attention.

"I know you've all had a hectic day, and thanks for taking some time to hear what I wanted to say. Juliet, Liz, and I spent all day working with QuAI. Now that we have dedicated electricity, we were able to program some queries last evening, which QuAI worked on overnight. The good news is that QuAI remains uncompromised and is still connected to a variety of sensors around the world. The biggest issue for us going forward is bandwidth. Without broadband and relying solely on the satellite connection provided by the two BGANs we have, cross-leveling data with QuAI's primary data center in Virginia is a lengthy process.

"That said, based on some questions Matt provided yesterday, as well as ones Liz, Juliet, and I put together, we've been able to paint a much more accurate, updated picture of what's happening in the United States and the world.

"The bottom line is that it's not good and likely worsening. Nationally, not much has changed from what we learned in

Vermont. The federal government continues to run under President Donovan. However, his ability to exert control is limited primarily to the greater Colorado Springs area and the military enclaves around Norfolk, San Diego, Seattle, and Oahu. The total population remaining in these five areas is just over one million people. That equates to about 10% of the pre-cataclysm populations of these metro area, although some are as high as 20%."

"What about Fort Hood?" Matt asked. "In Vermont, you mentioned that Fort Hood was an enclave."

"Yes. Fort Hood is an enclave that survived with about 80% of the military and dependent population, plus many retirees from the Killeen area. QuAI estimates around 100,000 people are now protected inside the Fort Hood enclave. I didn't mention them because it appears they are no longer under US government control."

"Seriously?" Pete said.

"Yes. Apparently, the commanding general there, a one-star who took over when the original CG died of smallpox, is a guy by the name of Patton, no relation. He has broken away from Donovan's leadership and says Donovan is not the duly elected President of the United States. Therefore, he's running his little fiefdom as he sees fit."

"Patton? Not Jim Patton?" Matt asked.

Stan turned to Liz, who looked down at her notebook before replying. "Brigadier General James E. Patton. A graduate of VMI."

Matt snorted. "That motherfucker is useless. I knew him when he was a lieutenant colonel in Iraq. The spineless fucker is about five feet tall and thinks he's Napoleon. I can see him splitting off. A general like President Donovan would never stand for a guy like Patton. He probably tried to relieve him, and Patton decided to do his own thing."

"Makes sense," said Stan. "We have no information as to why the split occurred, but we do know that Fort Hood has declared itself the capital of the Republic of Texas and has split from the United States of America."

Matt laughed. "Comical, really. We're a month into the greatest moment of destruction our planet has seen since the Ice Age, and all the rats are scurrying to carve out their empires."

"Yes, that appears to be the case here. And elsewhere, which we'll get to in a minute."

"Sorry, Stan," said Matt. "I didn't mean to interrupt."

"No problem, Matt. Before moving on to more local issues, I just wanted to add that QuAI was able to identify a dozen more other areas around the country that seem to have developed into smaller enclaves, all of which continue to support the federal government in Cheyenne Mountain. These mostly surround military bases, which we know were the first places to receive the updated vaccine. Jacksonville to Savannah and Tampa to Sarasota are both areas that have well over a 10% survival rate. Columbus, Georgia, and Clarksville, Tennessee, home to significant bases with large infantry units, have also become operational enclaves. In the midwest, areas around a half dozen Air Force bases in Oklahoma, Nebraska, and the Dakotas have almost 20% survival rates.

"Wow," said Clare. "That's hopeful. Especially regarding Sarasota." Everyone knew that Matt's parents, and Kelsey, Dylan, and Derek's grandparents, lived in Sarasota. They had not heard from them since the first week after the nuclear attack but were hopeful they had survived. Clare reached over to squeeze her husband's hand.

"Okay, so that's the big picture across the United States," continued Stan. "Now let's talk about New England, particularly Maine."

Stan paused, looking around the room. "Folks, from the information QuAI has been able to gather, it's not good. Not good at all. The Base is fully in control from Massachusetts to Maryland and has partial control of Virginia, New Hampshire, and Vermont - including those three states' capital cities."

"So, the Nomads?" Clare asked. "They are definitely part of

The Base?"

"Oh yes. Most definitely."

"And you said before, Stan, that there is some Muslim affiliation with The Base?" This time it was Pete who asked the question.

"Yes. This mostly comes from intelligence out of Cheyenne Mountain and what QuAI gathered before the internet went down. Apparently, the CIA and FBI have several informants within The Base and are able to gather intel through satellite phone reports on a regular basis.

"So, in a nutshell, The Base was formed by Islamic fundamentalists here in the United States prior to the September 8th attacks. They appear to be primarily Iranian and Saudi, and have both Shia and Sunni members working together for one of the few times in history. This is a new brand of fundamentalist, and they have completely cloaked themselves as true American patriots. By doing so, they planned to recruit the fringes of American society - rogue motorcycle clubs, right-wing militia organizations, etc. By focusing their attention on states with the lowest percentage of gun ownership, bringing together these violent groups provided them with a significant firepower advantage over the population, especially in New York and New Jersey.

"So they've dropped their Islamic fundamentalism?" Pete asked.

"Yes and no. They are still privately devout but appear tolerant of all religions. In fact, part of their mantra is the complete separation of church and state."

"Fucking crazy times, huh?" Pete said. "They nuke eight cities, which basically leads to the complete annihilation of the Muslim world, and now they preach separation of church and state."

"Yes," replied Stan. "But it gets even crazier. Juliet, you've done the most research and reading on this part of things; why don't you explain."

"Thanks, Dad," said Juliet, stepping forward. Juliet was tall, athletic, and with super-model exotic looks. She stood at least 5'10, having inherited her father's height rather than her mother's, and her mocha-colored skin and delicate features were stunning. Clicking a button on a small remote in her hand, Liz changed the slide on the screen to show a map of the eastern half of the United States. The northeastern states from Virginia northward, as well as the state of Michigan, were colored red. "Think of The Base as being outwardly modeled after the Pilgrims and the Founding Fathers, but simply as a disguise for a greedy, perverted, totalitarian state. The Base has taken our unique American history and turned it against us."

Liz paused, letting that last statement sink in as she made eye contact with everyone in the home theater. "They've established a new country, calling themselves the Union of American States. They have adopted a constitution - and not just any constitution. They've adopted the original U.S. Constitution but without all of the amendments. And lastly, they have thirteen original member states."

"Jesus," said Matt. "Are you serious?"

"As a business end of a .45, Matt," replied Juliet. "They're smart, bordering on brilliant, actually. By adopting the original Constitution, they reinforce everything these militia groups have been advocating for years. Remember, with no amendments, there is no freedom of speech, no prevention of unlawful search and seizure, no prohibition of cruel and usual punishment...."

"And no abolishment of slavery," interjected Stan.

"Yes," continued Juliet. "Not only is slavery potentially legal, but only 'free' Men can vote. And these new states get to decide who is free and who isn't."

"Holy shit," said Clare. "How are they able to just do this? I mean, it's one thing for a motorcycle gang like the Nomads to harass a sparsely-populated area like Woodstock and Hanover. How are these people able to exert this level of control over thirteen states? And which thirteen? Mass to Maryland is maybe seven."

"Eight," said Juliet. "But they're also including Virginia, Michigan, and the three northern New England states of Maine, New Hampshire, and Vermont."

"But they don't have control over New Hampshire and Maine?" Matt said. "We just drove through those areas, not a single indication of The Base's presence."

"Yet," replied Stan, standing back up next to his daughter. "Matt, that's the critical piece of our briefing. They don't yet control northern New Hampshire and Maine - but they plan to. And soon. The same is true for Virginia. They control the capitals of Virginia, Vermont, and New Hampshire, and it is just a matter of time before they push outward to control those entire states. Or maybe they decide to redraw the boundaries; who knows."

"Okay, sorry to interrupt your briefing. Please continue, Juliet," said Matt.

"Okay, almost done. The bottom line is that The Base is real, they are powerful, and it doesn't appear that the US government in Cheyenne Mountain is in any position to push back against this new Union. The federal enclaves seem to all be focused on self-preservation and long-term survival, and keeping the United States intact is beyond their capacity.

"And from the intel QuAI was able to gather, the Nomads and their nightly, sadistic bonfires at Dartmouth seem more the rule rather than the exception. Women are routinely enslaved throughout this new Union, and only able-bodied men who join The Base and pledge their full allegiance to the Union are considered free men with the right to vote. Men unwilling to give up their wives and daughters or participate in some of these ritualistic, hedonistic executions are either killed or enslaved. Picture the Taliban crossed with some of the harshest dystopian fiction you've ever read - worse than Handmaid's Tale. The Constitution, in its original form, plays right into their hands. They control these thirteen states, and each of these states is now a totalitarian regime with a very small legislature of zealots. Again, don't think Islamists.

Think zealots who no longer rely on the Koran, or the Bible for that matter, but are now using their so-called patriotism as a framework for seizing total power. These new founding fathers, and that's what they call themselves, are intent on turning the northeastern United States into their own country.

"And so far, they're getting pretty close to accomplishing their goal."

"Thanks, Juliet," said Stan, taking back control of the briefing. "So what does this all mean for us? After all, that's the most important aspect of this entire briefing. Juliet," Stan nodded toward his daughter, who promptly clicked her remote. The screen on the wall changed from the northeast US to now showing a detailed map of the state of Maine, with the island of Vinalhaven colored blue. "So now that we understand what The Base is doing in general, it's critical to know what is happening on the mainland off the coast of our haven. We spent last evening feeding some queries into QuAI and then refining them this morning. Please remember that QuAI affords us a capability that no one else on Earth has. It's the equivalent of having our own NSA, NRO, and CIA all rolled into one computer terminal. For the last thirty years or more, the quality of the hardware collecting signals intelligence, often called SIGINT, has increased so significantly that we are basically able to capture almost every electronic signal on the planet in some form or another. Billions of phone calls, satellite images down to objects about six inches in size, and all sorts of radio and instrumentation signals are collected and stored in massive data centers. The issue is refining this data into something that we would call useable intelligence.

"Information is the raw data itself. Insights are the estimations that we can create based on analyzing information. And intelligence is the product of these synthesized and analyzed insights as applied to our current or future circumstances. I know this is kind of complicated, but I think you all must understand this. Think of information as a vast field of endless haystacks, a few of which contain needles of various sizes. An insight would be the analysis of which haystacks contain a needle, which type of needle it is, and where precisely in the haystack the needle is. Lastly, intelligence is processing the insights against the knowledge of which needle we need for our purposes, and creating a useful result that we can take action against - thereby finding the specific needle we need in a massive field of haystacks. Make sense?

"Yes," said Clare. "That's a perfect analogy. Thanks, Stan."

"Good, now what the NSA, NRO, and CIA do is have buildings full of thousands of analysts combing through data from tens of thousands of computers and sensors and trying to put together intelligence. We have QuAI. With the right questions, she can do all of that for us - often in seconds.

"I say all this because what I'm going to show you is not raw data but rather intelligence as provided by QuAI. It's been synthesized and analyzed millions of times over, all in her incredibly fast AI brain, and what we have is intelligence that we can use to make decisions about our security and future.

"So, with all that said, here's what QuAI's been able to put together.

"The state of Maine, as it exists today, basically consists of two cities: Portland and Bangor. The governor moved the capital to Bangor soon after learning of the smallpox pandemic. Unlike the other New England states with a fairly robust Army National Guard, Maine mostly has Air National Guard. These assets, basically an aerial refueling wing, are primarily stationed around Bangor International Airport, with a small contingent housed at the Portland International Airport.

"The pre-cataclysm population of Maine was about 1.3 million people. One million of these people live basically south of Augusta, about 150,000 live in the greater Bangor area, and the rest scattered around the rest of the state. Remember, Maine is twice the combined size of Vermont and

New Hampshire. The governor, her name is Lorraine Babbitt, by the way, and to the best of our knowledge, she's still alive. She's decided to circle her wagons around Bangor while simultaneously encouraging everyone else in the state to go to Portland to get their vaccine.

"Mighty white of her," said Dave. "Not surprising, though. She's a libtard who's not even originally from Maine."

"Yes, well, her actions, right or wrong, have created a huge power vacuum in Maine," continued Stan. "As we now know, LT, your helicopter flight out of Manchester was one of the few to get off the ground. The Base, in the guise of a rogue Massachusetts National Guard unit as well as a large group of Nomads, attacked north across the Massachusetts border and seized much of the supply of vaccine designated for northern New England. General Condretti, the 2-star adjutant general of New Hampshire, was able to flee the area with three cases of the vaccine. He initially went to Portsmouth, but when that proved untenable, he fled to Portland. QuAI believes that he sent one case to Bangor to the governor. Apparently, Condretti doesn't particularly like the Maine governor, so he is taking his commands directly from Cheyenne Mountain. The National Guard, in every state, was federalized by President Hutchinson immediately after the nuclear attacks when he declared martial law. This technically means, under the premise of martial law, that Condretti is overall in command of the state of Maine as the military has replaced the civilian government.

"Hey, LT, is Condretti a good guy? What do you know of him?" Matt asked, turning around in his seat in the front row so he could see LT who was sitting in the back row next to Grace.

"Uh, he seemed okay to me. He had a pretty good reputation, but honestly, I only met him the one time. I'm pretty sure he was an artillery officer."

"Okay, thanks, LT," said Matt. "Stan, correct me if I'm wrong, but you basically said he had three cases of vaccine. Are those the same size as ours? That would put the total vaccines at

30,000. Is that right?"

"Yes, you're absolutely correct. 30,000 doses for a population of over 1.3 million people. And that doesn't include New Hampshire. The vaccine has become the most valuable commodity in the entire world. If you'll recall, President Hutchinson told the country they had made ten million doses of the updated vaccine and planned to make up to fifty million more doses in the coming days. He lied. QuAI believes that only 6-8 million doses of the updated vaccine were ever produced. Of this, the estimate is that as much as 50% of it was destroyed or lost at some point through intentional attacks like at Dartmouth-Hitchcock, plane crashes, or losses similar to how we have our case."

"Wait," said Pete. "You're saying the entire world only has four million doses of vaccine, at most."

"Well, that's what QuAI is saying, but yes."

"How much of the vaccine does The Base have? Does QuAI have an estimate for that?" Matt asked.

"Yes, she does," said Stan. "QuAI estimates that no more than one million doses were sent to the northeastern states now under The Base's control. Remember, Boston and New York were decimated, and much of the country's refugee turmoil occurred here in the northeast. Similarly, the distribution of the vaccine was through military channels, so most of it went to the major military hubs that had already created safe havens, like Norfolk and San Diego."

"So of the million, QuAI thinks, what, maybe 500,000 doses made it into The Base's hands?"

"She estimates about 300,000 at most, with likely an additional 150,000 doses being administered through normal channels directly to the people. Condretti's 30,000 would fall into that 150,000 pot."

"So basically, we have possibly 20,000 good guys in Portland, 10,000 good guys in Bangor, and a horde of 300,000 fucking barbarians posing as the 21st-century James Madison and George Washington spread south to Virginia. Is that about right?"

"You hit the nail on the head, Matt," agreed Stan.

"Oh, I almost forgot," continued Matt. "It's likely that both the good and bad guys desperately want what we have and are likely willing to kill us over it."

"Bingo!"

CHAPTER 30

October 12, 7:06pm

Matt walked into the large family from the kitchen, holding two open beer bottles in each hand. The entire extended family, including young Christopher and Laurie, were gathered around the room. Most were sitting in easy chairs, on the couch, or in one of several dining room chairs carried in for this gathering. A few, including his young children, Dylan and Grace, lounged comfortably on the floor. Matt looked around and realized this was possibly the first time they had all gathered in one room.

Before dinner, Dave had driven Matt, Grace, and Pete over to Vance Davis' house on Carvers Pond, a few blocks north of the downtown area of Main Street. Bill Pelletier and his wife had been there as well. They all spent a half hour learning more about each other and discussing some of the most critical tasks going forward. Matt felt confident the Davis and Pelletier couples would fully support his plans for Vinalhaven.

As Matt walked into the family room where his family now gathered, he made eye contact with Stan, Pete, and Dave, holding up the beers as a silent offer. Stan and Pete nodded in acceptance while Pete shook his head as he held up a rocks glass full of amber liquid, which Matt assumed was bourbon, Pete's drink of choice. After handing his friends two beers, he returned to an empty dining room chair between his wife and Molly.

"Is that an extra, Matt?" Molly asked. "I haven't had a cold beer in quite some time."

"Of course, Molly," Matt said, smiling and handing her a cold bottle of Allagash. It hadn't occurred to him that Molly might be a beer drinker. Matt sat down and raised his remaining beer to take his first sip. As he brought the bottle to his mouth, Clare reached over and snatched it out of his hands. Before Matt knew what had happened, his wife took a long, deep swallow of the pale ale, her dark brown eyes twinkling with mischief.

"Thanks for the beer, sweetheart," Clare whispered, leaning into his shoulder and winking at him.

Matt sat there empty-handed, shaking his head but smiling as he looked at his extended family gathered around him. They were all relaxed, happy, and enjoying one another's company. *If this is the future, I can do this. We can make a life here.*

"First off, I'd like to thank everyone who had a hand in tonight's dinner. It was an absolute feast! One of the best meals I can remember. So Molly, Clare, Marvi, Kelsey, Michelle, and of course Christopher and Dylan….thank you." Matt paused to allow a smattering of applause and a round of thank you's from the assembled family members. Dinner had been lobster, steamed clams, and striped bass freshly caught from the shore by Christopher and Dylan that morning. "I'll keep this meeting as short as possible, as Kelsey has a surprise dessert for everyone after this."

Matt gestured toward Amey, sitting on the couch with a spiral-bound notebook open on her lap and a pen poised in her right hand. "I've asked Amey to be our scribe, for what we cover tonight is extremely important. We've spent the last six weeks preparing the Pomfret farmhouse to survive long-term. Now that we're on Vinalhaven, we must think through all the details to make life here safe, comfortable, and sustainable. There are sixteen of us in the family, and as you know, another twenty-eight residents are on the island. While eventually, we will begin to do more things with the others, for now, the tasks we discuss tonight are really just for our family to accomplish.

"For the next three or four days, our main effort will be to secure all of the homes on this cove and gather everything we can. Molly, Clare, Marvi, and Michelle are Team Home. You're going to stay here at the house and prepare for all of the things everyone brings back.

"Stan and Juliet, you're Team Intel. You keep focused on QuAI, as well as looking at how we improve our communications and security around the cove.

"Pete, you and Liz are Team Transport. We need at least two more king-cab pickups and two full-size SUVs. That's your highest priority. We need those vehicles to move people and supplies. You're also responsible for keeping our two boats in good working order and maybe finding us a couple more kayaks and canoes. As we go through each house, I'd like you two to examine the vehicles and take notes. Also, keep an eye out for things like mountain bikes, motorcycles, snow-plows, snowmobiles, and cross-country ski equipment.

"Everyone else, we're Team Forage. I thought of splitting into two groups, but I think it's best to stay together for now. Basically, we're going to start with the houses on both sides of this cove. Dave and I will initially clear the building. Remember, there is the slimmest potential for there to be a live person in the home, and we need to be prepared in case they aren't friendly. Also, while some of these houses are seasonal and will be empty, others are very likely to have dead bodies. Bodies that have been dead for several weeks."

"Are we going to bury these people?" Kelsey asked.

"Any bodies are going to be pretty far into the decomposition process, Matt," added Grace before he could reply to Kelsey.

"To answer your question, Kelsey, no, we are not going to bury these people. At least not yet. I think when it freezes this winter, we may decide it's a good time to clear some of the bodies as they will be frozen, and the smell won't be as bad. But for now, that's why Dave and I are going in first. LT, Derek, and Dylan, I want you three kitted up with masks and gloves, as we may need to move some of these bodies to have better access to the house. However, whenever possible, we'll just close off doors with bodies in them. Does that work for everyone?"

Matt heard a smattering of "yeah" accompanied by head bobs.

"I just thought of something I hadn't considered. Amey, I noticed some spray paint in the barn. Grab a couple of cans tomorrow, and also make sure you have your notebook. I'll teach you a quick code, but basically, we want to spray paint a few symbols and numbers on the front door to tell us which houses have been cleared, how many bodies are inside, and whether there are supplies remaining. We want to keep careful notes about each house. It's going to be impossible to gather everything, so we want to know where to look."

"What are we gathering, Matt?" LT asked. "Just food? Or are there other things we want?"

"Good question, LT," replied Matt. "Marvi and Clare put together a list of household things we need, and I've added a few things. Basically, unexpired canned and jarred goods and unopened containers of staples such as rice, flour, sugar, salt, and pasta. We will also collect all firearms, ammunition, camping, and fishing equipment. Lastly, we need to take note of special items such as woodworking equipment, power tools, and anything else we think we could use in the future but don't necessarily want to move right now."

"Do we have a plan for which houses to clear first?" LT asked.

"Yes, Dave has put a plan together for us. Basically, we're going to clear the northern side of the cove, maybe six houses. Then we're going to do the southern side of the cove and keep going around the point at the head of Roberts Harbor. There are some pretty large homes on the point there, and Dave thinks those might have a lot of supplies. After that, we'll decide how we want to tackle some other parts of the island. Make sense?"

"Yep," said LT. "Sounds good to me."

"Lastly, If you carried a sidearm in Vermont, I want you to

carry one here when we're away from the house. We just can't be too careful. Any other questions?"

"Matt, can I add something?" Clare asked.

"Sure, honey."

"The one thing we haven't discussed is pets. Michelle mentioned that they'd heard and seen some packs of wild dogs. One of the unfortunate aspects of smallpox is that pet owners have died, often leaving their dogs and cats locked in the house. Be vigilant. These animals could be starving and may attack. If possible, collect cat and dog food but leave it at that house and just note it. We're probably going to add some pets here, depending on what we find."

"Great point, Clare," said Molly. "I hadn't even thought of that."

"Yeah," echoed Matt. "That is a great point. Feral dogs may be our biggest concern when we enter these houses, so be careful. Any other questions? Please, if you're thinking it, undoubtedly someone else is too."

"What about after we clear the houses along the cove, Matt?" Dylan asked. "Are we going to go throughout the island? What about the mainland?"

"Good question. Everything is subject to change, but right now, the plan is for us to start moving farther outwards. Clearing the cove first does three things for us. First, it ensures we have secured our immediate surroundings and that we all get familiar with the cove. Second, we gather additional supplies while also identifying potential long-term accommodations for all of us. Third, it gives Team Home - Clare, Marvi, Molly, and Michelle - a chance to inventory what we have and put together a list of what we need for long-term survival and comfort.

"After those first few days, I'm thinking that we'll further split up into foraging teams. Some of you, soon-to-be experienced foragers, will target specific homes and commercial establishments to build up our stocks. We'll do this in coordination with other island residents, as we want to share the resources. A second team will go back to the mainland. We'll both recon the area for intel but also gather additional supplies and equipment that we don't have on the island. Sound good?"

"Yeah," said Dylan. "Sounds like a plan."

Molly raised her hand.

"Yes, Molly?" Matt asked.

"Do we have plans for meeting the others on the island as a group? I was wondering if it might not be a good idea to maybe have a get-together. Maybe in a lobster bake or something like that."

"That's a great idea," added Marvi.

"Yeah, I like that," Matt agreed. "Maybe Team Home can come up with some ideas, and we can send out an invitation. I'm not sure I want everyone to come here. Maybe we could do it downtown in the parking lot and see if there are grills there. Does that work?"

"Yes, Matt, thank you," replied Molly. "And I have one more question, if that's okay."

"Sure, Molly. Ask away."

"I know we've been in a rush and, until now, have been focused on security as a family. Have you given any thought to long-term accommodations? I know the younger ones have been enjoying staying in tents, but in a few weeks, it'll be way too cold for that."

"Yes, again, excellent question. One of the main reasons for clearing the cove is to see what houses we can clean up and occupy - hopefully within the next week. I'd really like to keep us all somewhat together if possible. Another option is taking over the Tidewater Hotel downtown, which Dave thinks has about 15-20 rooms and a big dining room and kitchen. My concern is that I don't know how secure that area is. I think we'll know more once we clear all the houses surrounding the cove."

"Okay, fair enough, Matt. That's all the questions I have," said Molly.

"Okay, anyone else? Anything at all."

Sitting on the floor beside Dylan, Young Christopher raised his hand.

"Yes, Chris?"

"What team am I on, Daddy?"

"Why you're with me, of course. We couldn't do this without you, buddy."

"And me, too?" Laurie asked. "I'm a big girl and can do forging just like the big kids, Daddy."

Everyone in the room laughed. "Yes, sweetheart. You're definitely a big girl. And you can do 'for-a-jing,' just like the rest of us. Maybe you can keep an eye on Kelsey for me; sometimes, she needs someone to keep her in line."

"You're funny, Daddy."

Everyone smiled. "Okay," said Matt, wrapping up the meeting. "Now, I don't want to spoil the secret, but I think Kelsey has put together a surprise for everyone. Kelsey?"

Kelsey stood up. "Okay, everyone, it's not much, but I found a few items that I think would be a lot of fun to make. Derek was kind enough to get the bonfire started...."

"What's the surprise, Kelsey?" Christopher shouted, never one to be patient when it came to dessert.

"Well, I just so happen to have found two boxes of graham crackers, a bag of Hershey chocolate bars, and a couple of packs of marshmallows in the pantry."

"Yeah!!" Shrieked Chris and Laurie, followed by smiles from around the room. "S'mores!!! Let's go!" The two children ran out the door to the patio, followed by Kelsey and Juliet close on their heels. The rest of the family wandered out after them. *Life almost seems normal,* thought Matt.

CHAPTER 31

October 14, 9:22am

Matt retired to the den after eating a hearty breakfast, wishing to have some alone time and do some research before tackling another day. The owner had remodeled the den to give it an old-school feel, complete with aged wood floors, a red leather chair and couch, and floor-to-ceiling bookshelves with a mounted wooden ladder. The den was in the back corner of the house, and sitting behind the antique writing desk, Matt could look out the window to the head of the cove toward Dave and Michelle's cottage.

Yesterday had been a full day of foraging - a strange mix of disgust, sadness, and excitement combined with a strong dose of manual labor.

They had cleared five houses on the north side of Carvers Cove and Roberts Harbor as a group. Two had been empty, but the occupants had been dead in the other three. Of these, two homes had contained older couples who had died in their beds, likely all of them getting sick and then crawling into bed when the inevitability of their sickness became clear. The third house would likely haunt Matt for a very long time, and he was thankful he was the first one to enter the home. A man, who appeared to be in his 30s, lay decomposing in his Barcalounger after taking his own life with a .45 caliber 1911 pistol that lay across his chest. Evidently, he had stuck the barrel in his mouth and pulled the trigger, spraying blood and brain tissue all over the back of his chair and the wall behind him. As Matt searched the rest of the home, he found what he assumed was the man's wife lying dead on the bed next to a little girl a few years younger than Laurie. Both had died of smallpox and were wrapped in blankets on the bed.

Matt had closed the rooms to the deceased family and let the others into the house to search for useful items. While most complained of the permeating smell of decomposing flesh, it was the sight of the dead little girl that Matt could not erase from his memory.

The five homes had yielded a significant stock of canned goods, unopened jars of staples such as peanut butter, spaghetti sauce, and a substantial supply of macaroni and cheese and microwave popcorn. Of the vehicles at these homes, Pete and Liz had selected a late-model Chevy Suburban and a high-mileage Dodge Ram pickup with a snow-plow attachment already mounted on the front. If they were to keep the roads on the island open through the winter, snowplows would be critical.

Matt told everyone to relax this morning, and they were all planning to meet at 10 am to start foraging along the south bank of the cove. Before him on the antique desk lay a printout that he had asked Juliet to provide him from QuAI's databanks. It was an annotated copy of the original U.S. Constitution from the Constitutional Convention held in 1787.

As a political science major in college, Matt had read the complete Constitution numerous times. He was curious to see how The Base had usurped what was universally considered the seminal document of democracy to further the goals of their perverse, totalitarian regime. He knew that removing the Bill of Rights, the first ten of the twenty-seven amendments to the original document, would drastically change the powers of the government and the society in which people lived. There would be no more freedom of speech, assembly, or the right to bear arms. The legal system would be oppressive without the protections against unreasonable search and seizures, the right to be represented by an attorney, and the right to a fair, speedy trial judged by one's peers. There was also no prohibition against cruel and unusual punishment. Perhaps of greatest importance, without the Tenth Amendment, the federal government could infer that any powers not listed in the Constitution belonged to it rather than to the States as enumerated in this final amendment of the Bill of Rights.

Matt took notes in the small moleskin notebook he always carried with him. After reading through the document twice, the key was in the notations. Americans in the modern age learned the Constitution as it existed with all the amendments. Without them, many of the intricacies of how the government worked were very different from what Americans were currently used to. For example, under the original text of the Constitution, Senators were elected by the state legislatures and the President by electors sent by the states, with no criteria for how those electors were chosen. Not only was slavery legal, but states had to return slaves who escaped to other states. Lastly, the right to vote was restricted to "free men," and it did not take a genius to understand how The Base would define "free men." Women would be chattel, as well as anyone who disagreed with The Base's edicts.

A final issue caught Matt's attention. Article 2, Section 4 stated that the Congress shall meet, at a minimum, yearly on the first Monday of December. Matt wondered if this were, by chance, a significant day for the new Union of American States and possibly the official kickoff day for The Base's new regime. Under the original Constitution, this would be the day that the new Congress would open up the Electors' ballots and affirm their vote for the new President. Matt realized The Base could easily install token, puppet legislatures in each of the thirteen states under its control, and then both elect Congressmen, Senators, and electors for President. If they did this by the first Monday in December, they would be in compliance with their new Constitution.

It makes sense.

But it also seems a waste of effort.

With probably only a million or so people remaining throughout these thirteen states and likely no foreign governments in existence, it seemed somewhat unnecessary to Matt for them to go through all this trouble to appear legitimate, especially to a population that was either terrified or who had already drunk the Cool-Aid.

Matt's thoughts turned to how The Base and their plans could affect his family in Vinalhaven. He realized he didn't care what The Base did as long as they left his family alone. The same went for General Condretti in Portland and Governor Babbitt in Bangor. Matt wasn't sure any of them would be allies, and all of them could cause significant harm to his family. He knew that, according to QuAI, it was simply a question of time before The Base pushed north and east to defeat the forces controlled by Condretti and Babbit.

He also knew that if any of them learned that he had almost 10,000 vaccine doses, they would not hesitate to kill everyone on Vinalhaven to get it.

Part of him wanted to simply take most of the vaccine and give it to either Condretti or Babbitt and be done with it. Bangor would be the simplest choice logistically, but without knowing anything about the situation, Matt was hesitant to place himself or other family members in danger. Additionally, he was concerned that once people learned of life on Vinalhaven with electricity, there could be a rush to take over, bringing an entirely new host of problems and dangers to his family.

No, he thought. *The best course is still to do everything possible to protect my family. In the end, nothing else matters.*

Matt looked up as someone knocked at the door to his den.

"Hey, Matt," said Dave, standing in the doorway. "D'ya have a minute?"

"Sure, man. What's up? Have a seat." Matt motioned toward the red leather sofa along the wall before his desk. Above the couch was a large framed nautical chart of Vinalhaven and the surrounding islands.

"Two things. First, Michelle and I were talking last night, and there's a property I think you should see. It's called Roberts Hill Farm. As the crow flies, it's probably less than half a mile away. However, the way the roads are, it would be about a five-minute drive." Dave turned on the sofa and put his finger on the sport where the farm was located, a point almost due south of their current location and on the broadest part of Roberts Harbor.

"Okay, what's special about Roberts Hill Farm?"

"Well, it's the only working farm on the island, and it's also right here on Roberts Harbor, although set back up on a hill overlooking the sea. We haven't been there since the cataclysm, but Michelle thinks they may have all sorts of fresh vegetables we could potentially harvest. At a minimum, they have several very large greenhouses, seeds, tools, and everything else we would need for long-term sustainability. Lastly, the farmhouse and barn areas are huge. It could easily be a B&B with maybe ten-plus bedrooms. It might be a perfect home for everyone who doesn't have a bedroom here."

"Mmmm," said Matt, thinking. "Sounds promising. Why don't we get everyone else started on clearing the southern bank of Carvers Cove? Then let's grab Michelle and Clare and go check it out."

"Just what I was thinking. There's one more thing."

"What's that?"

"I think we need to make another set of rounds amongst the residents. We're not scheduled to meet until noon tomorrow, but I was thinking maybe today we go speak with everyone individually. We can invite them to a good old-fashioned New England clambake tomorrow at noon. It would be good to involve some of them, like having Tim bring several dozen lobsters. Things like that."

"Yeah, you're absolutely right. I'm not great at the politics of these things. I was actually thinking of having you and Pete be the outreach people."

"It's definitely important, and I think Pete is the right guy.

Maybe even Stan. They have more patience than either you or I do."

"Yeah. Agreed. Let's talk about it on the way to Roberts Bay Farm. Now, let's get everyone in gear."

CHAPTER 32

October 15, 12:16pm

High tide on a beautiful October day. Colorful lobster boats bobbed in the harbor, dozens of seagulls chirped overhead, and his two children shrieked in delight while watching a family of seals swimming along the rocky shore. The cookout in downtown Vinalhaven was in full swing.

After visiting Roberts Hill Farm yesterday, the Sheridans and Reeds made the rounds of all eight families on the island and invited everyone to today's clambake. In the case of the Davis and Pelletier families, Matt had made it seem like the clambake was their idea. Everyone on the island, including the Biancos, seemed much friendlier than they had during Matt's first meeting, and all had made the trip into town for the festivities. Tim Philbrook had graciously offered to supply both the lobsters and the clams.

The surprise for everyone was the basket of fresh, golden Kennebec potatoes that Michelle had dug up from the Roberts Hill Farm's garden. Fresh vegetables had been scarce the last few weeks, and everyone looked forward to enjoying them with the lobsters and clams. Christopher and Dylan had added several striped bass they had caught that morning. It was fixing to be quite a feast, as well as a bonding opportunity. Most weren't aware of the four apple pies that Michelle had made at her cottage throughout the night, after picking a bushel of apples from the small orchard at Roberts Hill Farm. Matt's mouth was watering just thinking of them.

"Penny for your thoughts, Mr. Sheridan."

Matt turned to see his wife step up next to him, sliding her arm underneath his and squeezing tight.

"Well, Mrs. Sheridan. I was just thinking how this might be a place we can make a life for our family." He nodded toward where Christopher and Laurie were laughing at the edge of the parking lot, looking over the harbor at the seals with Kelsey and Juliet. On the other side, Dylan and LT threw a football, playing keep-a-way with Grace and Amey between them. Pete and Stan were engaged in a lively conversation with Tim, the lobsterman, and Frank, the handyman, as they all watched over the steaming pots of lobsters, clams, and potatoes cooking over charcoal grills in the downtown parking lot. Everyone else was engaged in some form of conversation, and as there was no shortage of alcoholic beverages on the island, most were feeling no pain.

"I know, Matt, right?" Agreed Clare. "It's difficult to believe that a week ago, I thought for sure one of you would be killed by the Nomads. And here we are now, living in a beautiful seaside home and having a seafood boil with our extended family and friends. It's all so surreal."

"Clambake," said Matt.

"What?"

"It's clambake, not seafood boil."

Clare laughed. "Do you always have to be the smartest person in the room, or do you just have to *think* you're the smartest person? Because when I rank everyone here, Mr. Army Ranger, you aren't going to break the top ten in terms of intelligence."

Now it was Matt's turn to laugh. "I'm teasing, honey. But don't let old Vance there, or Tim the lobsterman, hear you call it a seafood boil. That's something they do down in Savannah. Clambake is pure New England, baby."

"Well, excuse me, Mr. Yankee," said Clare, batting her lashes like the southern belle she wasn't. "But I sure do miss those seafood boils we used to do when we lived in Savannah." Clare's smile turned serious. "I'm not sure I want you guys going to Rockland tomorrow. It's a risk I'm not sure we need to take right now."

Matt looked down at his wife, knowing she bore the brunt of the worry for the entire extended family. "It'll be okay. I promise. We have an excellent plan to go places and get precisely what we need. Besides, if we don't go now, then when? You heard Stan's briefing on what QuAI estimated. The sooner we get everything we might need from the mainland, the sooner we can button up here on Vinalhaven and enjoy our peaceful winter. If these Base yahoos are hellbent on taking over Maine, then let them. As long as they leave us alone on Vinalhaven."

"Yeah, I know. I just worry."

"It's okay to worry, Clare. But it's also okay to have fun. You've done an absolutely fantastic job keeping this family together, turning every place we go into a home, and making our children feel loved and special. Now let's go enjoy the clambake!"

CHAPTER 33

October 16, 10:37am

Camden Harbor was as they'd left it.

Low tide that morning was at 7:50 am, so they had waited for the flow to fill Carvers Cove to make departing in the Hinckley less tricky. Pete and Liz brought the yacht into the pier, and the designated shore party hopped on board. Matt had decided to bring LT, Derek, Dylan, and Stan. In addition, to appease the island residents, Matt had invited Frank, the handyman, along as well.

Frank and Derek had spent the end of yesterday's clambake going to each family and writing down things they felt were needed from Rockland. Surprisingly, everyone's list was pretty basic. The primary item requested by the residents was food. While many had begun foraging their neighborhood homes now that they had been inoculated, everyone knew the Maine winters were long. The goal was for everyone to have at least six months of food at a minimum.

The other item people requested most was clothing. This was especially true of the Biancos, Aghas, and Matt's own family. These newcomers to Vinalhaven had all arrived with a minimum of outfits, and while there was undoubtedly plenty of clothing in the various houses on the island, people weren't quite ready to rummage through bedroom closets while there was often a dead body in the room.

Pete berthed the Hinckley onto the floating pier at the Lyman-Morse dock in Camden Harbor. Matt had already briefed everyone on the plan to take the Humvee and their two largest SUVs. They were all on high alert as they walked to the office, with the boys splitting off to ready the vehicles. Derek carried the M240B machine gun, as Matt planned to remount this on the Humvee to lead their convoy into Rockland. One could never be too careful.

Matt headed to the side of the building to check the SD card on the game camera they had hidden there. Juliet had provided him with an iPad and a card reader device, so he popped the SD in and scrolled to the file directory. The game cam was motion-activated, so the camera created a new file each time something set it off. It had been five days since they departed Camden Harbor, and eleven files were on the camera. Matt noticed that the file sizes were relatively small, and the longest video was only nineteen seconds. Matt opened that one first.

Five deer ambled across the fuzzy green screen. This occurred during the nighttime as the camera was in infrared mode. The deer did not appear alarmed in any way and simply wandered across the parking lot and into the backyard of the house on the corner.

Matt opened the other files to find that either animals or the wind had activated the video camera. No people. That was good.

While part of Matt was hopeful that more people had survived the cataclysm, the security consultant part of Matt knew that fewer people meant fewer threats to his family. The fact that no one had been to Camden Harbor in five days was a very good sign for Matt. It meant this location was likely to be a secure port for them going forward.

Pete had volunteered to stay with the Hinckley to ensure nothing happened to their ride back to the island. Given the lack of activity on the game camera, Matt thought of docking the boat and having Pete join them, but in the end, he erred on the side of caution. Matt checked in with Pete on the radio and gave him the all-clear to move out into the harbor, moor the Hinckley, and wait for their return later that afternoon.

The city of Rockland was ten miles due south of Camden, a straight shot down US Route 1. According to Frank, this usually took about twenty-five minutes with the speed limit and traffic. Matt estimated they would do it much faster than that this morning.

The Humvee led out with the Suburban and Tahoe right behind. Matt rode shotgun in the Humvee, with all passengers carrying handheld UHF radios. Frank was in the seat behind the driver, with Liz in the turret. Derek and Dylan each drove one of the other vehicles.

"Okay, LT, turn left onto Route 1, and then we'll just follow that through Camden and down into Rockland. Once you get through town, push the speed a bit. I'd like to keep us around fifty miles per hour or so, if possible."

"Roger," said LT.

Clicking his radio mic, Matt continued, "Okay, we're off. Everyone, keep your head on a swivel. If you see something, call it out over the radio."

Turning to face Frank sitting behind LT, Matt said, "So Frank, this is your first time on the mainland since early September?"

"Actually, man, I haven't been here since August. The end of summer's super busy for me, so I haven't been here in a while. I can't believe it's so empty. Camden's usually bustling right now with leaf peepers."

"Yeah, it's pretty crazy to see everything deserted."

"How come you guys carry so many guns? I mean, I grew up in Maine, but I've never really been a gun guy."

"Well, Frank, my philosophy has always been that you can never be too careful. We don't expect to see anyone today; if we do, we hope they're friendly. But if they mean us harm, we want to be ready."

"Yeah, that makes sense. I heard the story of your battle with the motorcycle gang. That's some wild shit."

"Definitely some wild shit, Frank. Most definitely."

Matt liked Frank. He was a simple guy but, by all accounts,

extremely hard-working and reliable. He supposedly could fix almost anything on the island and built his own house from scratch. He also knew Rockland well, having grown up there prior to moving to Vinalhaven as an adult.

They drove in silence through the ghost town of Camden, then south through the similarly vacant hamlet of Rockport. LT picked up the speed considerably after Rockport, and they rocketed down Route 1. The road was clear of obstacles, and they made great time toward their destination.

After about five miles, LT slowed, and Liz called over the radio. "Something up ahead, guys. Seems like maybe a roadblock or possibly some kind of traffic accident."

"Go ahead and stop, LT," Matt said. He yelled up to Liz in the turret. "Hey Liz, take these binos and tell me what you see."

Liz reached down and grabbed the binoculars from Matt's outstretched hands. After about fifteen seconds, Liz knelt inside the Humvee to speak directly to Matt and LT. "Definitely looks like it was some kind of roadblock. I count four police cruisers parked on both sides of the road at a stoplight. There's also probably ten to fifteen cars parked haphazardly on this side of the roadblock, possibly even more on the far side."

"Is it manned?"

"No. I didn't see anyone. And the good news is I'm pretty sure the road is wide open. Not sure why all the mess, though."

Turning to Frank, Matt asked, "Any thoughts?"

"Well, the only thing I can think of is that I'm pretty sure that intersection is the turn-off to Pen Bay."

"What's Pen Bay?"

"Oh, it's the hospital. Only one around, actually. It's got an emergency room and most of the usual stuff. Pen Bay Medical Center's the official name, I think."

"Okay. Thanks, Frank," said Matt. Turning to the others, "Makes perfect sense. With the pandemic, the first place cops would secure is the hospital. You think the road's clear, Liz?"

"Yeah. I can see all the way through the intersection. It's clear."

"Okay, let's go. Slowly, LT, just in case. Liz, unlock the M240B swivel so you can aim freely." Matt paused, reaching down to toggle his mic. "There appears to be a roadblock about three hundred meters to our front. It's an intersection with the hospital, which is off to our left. Liz scanned it with the binos and saw no signs of life. Derek, Dylan, I want you guys to stay right here in overwatch until we make it through. Once we get through, I'll call you forward."

"Roger," said Derek.

"Dylan copies," said Dylan.

"Okay, LT, let's roll," Matt said to his driver.

The Humvee rolled into the intersection, and everyone realized immediately that it wasn't deserted. A more accurate description would be that there was no one alive. On the left, next to two dark-colored police SUVs with white doors displaying the lighthouse logo of the Rockland Police, several dead bodies lie on the side of the road. At least two of the bodies were uniformed policemen. Matt noticed instantly that their holsters were empty, and there did not appear to be any firearms on the pavement near them.

"Look right, Matt," Liz yelled down from the turret as LT stopped the Humvee. "Those cars are shot to shit. Looks like they must have had quite a gunfight."

Matt looked to his right and saw several more bodies strewn across the hoods of a couple of cars, all of which had shattered windows and were pockmarked with bullet holes.

"See anyone, Liz? Anything moving?" Matt scanned to his right as he felt the turret pivoting back and forth behind him.

"Nothing, Matt. We're clear."

"Okay, LT, pull up about a hundred meters, and we'll keep an eye out until the others catch up. Once they catch up, let's head into Rockland."

"Roger," said LT, pressing his foot down on the Humvee's throttle.

Into his radio, Matt said, "The intersection is clear. Looks like they had a gunfight, but no one is manning it now. Pull your vehicles forward, and let's get back up to speed." Matt heard two separate clicks on the radio, acknowledgment of his orders.

"They're coming up behind us now," Liz shouted down from the turret.

LT pressed down on the gas pedal, and Matt kept a sharp eye on their surroundings as they continued down Route 1. They were at their first destination of the day a mile and a half later.

Matt motioned for LT to turn right at the next intersection, and LT turned the Humvee onto a steep access road that brought them up to a large parking lot. Looking to his left, to the east, Matt could see another shopping plaza below them and across Route 1. In the distance, but no more than a 1/4 mile, was the blue-green water of Rockland Harbor stretching out into Penobscot Bay.

Directly in front of the Humvee was a large Home Depot.

Matt scanned the parking lot, which was mostly empty of vehicles. Several Home Depot-branded rental trucks were lined up on the far side of the pavement, and maybe a half-dozen cars and SUVs were scattered along the first few rows of parking spots. Otherwise, the large, open lot was completely empty.

Matt opened his door and stepped out of the Humvee. Everyone else followed suit, and in a moment, the five of them were gathered around the hood while Liz stood tall in the turret. Everyone but Frank carried a holstered pistol and an M4 dangling from a sling. They also wore a plate carrier stuffed with 30-round magazines and other assorted items. While some of the rifles, like Matt's, had a Surefire tactical light mounted under the barrel, everyone also wore a small LED headlamp on an elasticized band around their heads.

"Dylan, I'd like you to grab the binos and take over for Liz in the turret. She and Stan have a specific wishlist of items they're looking for. Frank, you probably know this store well. Everyone go grab a couple of carts while LT and I take a quick look inside and clear the building. It looks empty, but you just never know."

Matt and LT made a beeline for the front sliding doors, which appeared to be stuck in the open position with the power out, while the others angled toward the row of stacked carts lining the front of the building. As he neared the door, Matt clicked on his headlamp and rifle's tac light. The inside of the building was completely dark, and Matt guessed the batteries in the emergency lighting probably gave out weeks ago.

Matt stood next to the open doorway and inhaled deeply. All he could smell was the faint scent of the ocean mixing with a musty smell coming out of the entrance. The smell of decaying flesh was absent, something Matt was expecting but now happy was not present.

"Well, doesn't smell like rotting dead bodies," said LT.

"Yeah," replied Matt. "Always a good sign. Stay ten yards behind me, and let's cut down to the center cross-aisle and then go all the way across the store. You clear the right side aisles, and I'll clear the left."

"Got it."

Matt and LT entered the Home Depot. To Matt, as his light flickered over the high shelves stacked with various home improvement items, this seemed like every other Home Depot. He looked left across the service return area and down the front cross-aisle toward the cashier stations. Nothing moved. The place was a bit messy, with carts strewn around the aisles and various boxes littered on the floor.

Matt led LT halfway toward the back of the store. His light played across a display of lightbulbs, then traversed to the right and illuminated patio furniture and lawnmowers. When he reached the middle cross-aisle, he turned left, and he and LT walked abreast. They walked steadily, pausing ever so slightly at each aisle. LT's light stayed focused on the aisles to the right, back toward the rear of the store, while Matt kept his head and rifle turned to see down the left aisles. Shelving, painting, plumbing, electrical, and eventually, the aisle containing lumber. They reached the end of the store without seeing anything but carts.

Matt toggled his radio. "All clear. Keep your eyes out, but otherwise, happy shopping."

"Hey, Matt. Unless you need me, I'm going to link up with Derek. We have a list of things we're supposed to get."

"Go for it. I'll see you out front in a bit."

LT jogged off back toward the entrance to find Derek. Matt turned and walked about halfway back along the cross aisle. Looking up, his light illuminated the aisle labels, and he turned right at the one labeled Electric. As he turned, he saw Stan and Liz pulling items off the shelves and putting them into one of the four shopping carts assembled behind them. Matt walked closer and saw that Stan was stacking tightly-wound coils of extensions onto several large boxes of CAT 6 ethernet cable already in his cart.

Liz was a section further down the aisle, loading her cart with slim white boxes. Matt played his flashlight over them and read that they were Blink wireless outdoor cameras, five to a package. Matt counted six of the slim boxes in her cart as Liz tossed in the last two from the shelf. She then stepped a few feet down and looked closely at the small selection of routers and switches in stock.

"Matt, can you take one of these carts out front?" Stan asked.

"Sure thing." Matt grabbed the front of Stan's lead cart and began pushing it toward the front of the store with Stan following behind pushing a second cart. His natural inclination was to head toward the checkout counter, but then he realized he could walk right out the front entrance as there was no need to pay. Matt walked toward the light and soon found himself in the parking lot, squinting his eyes in the bright sunshine.

"Can you take this second cart too?" Stan asked. "I want to go back in and check on Frank. He was getting all the outdoor electrical stuff."

"Yeah, no problem." Matt reached back and grabbed the

front of Stan's other cart, then awkwardly pushed the too heavily-laden carts toward the vehicles parked about thirty meters away. "All good?" He called up to Dylan in the turret.

"Yeah, Matt. All good. You guys get what you needed?"

"Yep, I think so."

Matt pulled the carts up to the back of his family's Chevy Tahoe, pulled up the rear door, and began packing the items as efficiently as possible. The rear seats had already been laid flat, creating plenty of room. There were several boxes of 1,000 feet of CAT 6 cable and more than a dozen 100-foot coils of outdoor extension cords. In the other cart were spools of rope, wire, twine, and chain. *Jesus Christ!* Matt thought. *That's why this cart was so fucking heavy.*

A rattling noise behind him caused Matt to turn, and he watched as Liz tried to push both carts toward the vehicles. She finally stopped, realizing she had to push one while simultaneously pulling the other. Soon she was at the rear of the Tahoe, and together they loaded the items from her two carts. In addition to the cameras and routers, Liz had what looked to be an assortment of computer/telephone toolkits and what looked to be at least a dozen packs of two-way radios. Matt saw the name on the clear plastic packs was Cobra, and they advertised a 35-mile range. *These will definitely come in handy creating a comms network with all the residents!*

A few minutes later, Derek and LT came out. Each pushed a traditional shopping cart, while between them, they pulled one of the low-slung metal carts that were ideal for carrying large objects. On the cart were four large boxes, which Matt knew were generators. In the shopping carts, Matt could see a couple of tall stacks of 5-gallon buckets, numerous lids, as well as axes, work gloves, and at least two chainsaws.

Matt directed Derek to load everything into the Suburban he had been driving.

Matt looked at his watch and wondered what was keeping Stan and Frank. He noticed they'd only been at Home Depot for about twenty minutes. There was no real rush, but Matt wanted to be on the road as soon as possible.

As he headed back into the Home Depot to check on them, Stan and Frank came out pushing one cart each. Frank's was loaded with electrical components such as light switches, outlets, and junction boxes. Stan's cart was stacked neatly with various hand tools and packs of Dewalt rechargeable power tools. Matt could see several packs of rechargeable lithium-ion batteries.

Matt helped stack these items into the Tahoe, filling every spare inch of cargo space. By the time they were done, Derek and LT had also finished loading.

"Staples next?" Stan asked.

"Yep. That's the plan. It's right across the street. Let's load up. Dylan, you stay in the turret, and Liz can drive the Tahoe."

Everyone loaded up, and Matt directed LT out the way they had arrived, turning south onto Route 1 and then taking a left immediately after the Bar Harbor Bank & Trust. They pulled into what was labeled the Harbor Plaza shopping center, an L-shaped plaza with a Shaw's supermarket along the long end to their left and a Staples anchoring the top end of the plaza. Like Home Depot, the parking lot was almost entirely empty, with maybe a dozen cars parked sporadically throughout.

Matt eyed the Shaws supermarket as they drove past. They planned to skip the leading supermarkets, figuring they would already have been completely stripped of useful products, in favor of first trying a specialty restaurant supply warehouse that both Clare and Marvi figured stood a good chance of having been overlooked. Seeing all of the broken windows as well as the charred left side of the Shaws simply reinforced their plan to bypass it. LT continued driving straight and pulled up in front of the Staples office supply store at the end of the lot.

Without getting out, Matt spoke into his radio. "Stan, Liz, why don't you both go into Staples and get everything you need. Derek, wait out front and keep an eye on things. We're going to take the Humvee and check something out. We shouldn't be more than ten minutes and just one block to the south."

"Roger," replied Stan. "We might want to think about getting more vehicles or unloading everything and returning. The only room left is in the Humvee."

"I'm on it. Hope to have the problem solved in ten minutes."

"Got it. We'll meet you out front."

Matt directed LT to make a U-turn through the parking lot and return to Route 1. At the main road, they turned left and then took an immediate left. Quick Chevrolet of Rockland. Unlike the Home Depot and Harbor Plaza parking lots, this lot was full and offered exactly what Matt was looking for.

As LT pulled to a stop in front of the showroom, Matt jumped out and jogged over to two black, crew-cab GMC Sierra 2500 pickup trucks. He looked at both stickers, briefly noting the exorbitant price before memorizing the stock number for each vehicle. He then walked to the open window where Frank sat behind LT.

"Hey, Frank. Could you do me a favor? Reach around behind you there and grab that Halligan tool on the floor behind you."

Frank turned and looked around. "You mean this funky pry bar thing?" When he turned back around, he had the Halligan in his hands. It resembled a pry bar on steroids, a 30-inch forged steel bar with an elongated steel fork at one end and a lever and spike at the other. Firefighters commonly used it to rescue people, but Matt had learned its usefulness as a forced entry tool while serving with the 1st Ranger Battalion.

"That's it, man. Thanks."

Matt took the Halligan and walked to the front glass doors of the Chevy dealership. He checked the door, in case it might already be unlocked. It wasn't. Turning his back to the door and shielding his eyes, Matt whipped the tool down and backward, smashing it into the plate glass below the door handle. The glass instantly shattered, and several large pieces fell to the ground. Matt turned and used the Halligan to knock out more glass and enlarge a hole so that he could easily reach in and turn the locking mechanism. With the door unlocked, he opened it and walked inside.

Phew, what was that ungodly odor? But Matt already knew. Someone was dead in here, and death's smell permeated the open showroom. Matt pulled up the buff around his neck to cover his mouth and nose, but it did little to mask the smell. *I must remember to get Vicks vapor rub when we hit the pharmacy. We're going to need it when clearing out all the houses on Vinalhaven.*

Matt turned on his headlamp and looked around the showroom. He walked to the offices along the back wall, figuring the keys to the vehicles were likely kept in one of these. He checked each one, using his rifle's light to illuminate the walls while looking for a lockbox. No joy.

He decided to walk around to the back hall and see if there was something toward the service area.

Bingo!

As he went down the hall, there was a small room to the right with a copy machine, counter, and a large lockbox mounted on the wall. Matt used the Halligan to pry open the flimsy metal cover and was rewarded with row after row of neatly labeled key fobs. It took a few moments, but Matt finally found the two key fobs matching the stock numbers of the trucks out front.

He immediately retraced his steps to the front door, exiting the building and motioning for Frank to join him beside the pickup trucks.

"Hey, man, here's your new truck," said Matt, tossing Frank one of the key fobs. Matt clicked the 'open' icon on his key fob, smiling at the satisfying chirp and flashing lights of the truck nearest him. "Guess yours is the other one. Do me a favor, Frank. Start it up, and let's see how much fuel they have. I'm guessing not much."

Matt jumped in the truck, adjusted the power seats, and pressed the 'start engine' button. The truck roared to life. Matt pushed the buttons to lower both windows as his eyes searched the dashboard for the fuel gauge. *1/4 tank. Not too bad.*

Looking out the open passenger window, Matt called to Frank. “How’s your fuel?”

“Mmmm,” said Frank after figuring out how to lower his window. “Somewhere between an eighth and a quarter of a tank. The trip computer says 70 miles remaining for fuel.” *That’s more than enough to get us to Camden.*

Derek’s voice came over the radio.

“Hey Matt, we have a bit of a situation here.”

CHAPTER 34

October 16, 11:53am

"What's happening?" Matt asked Derek over the radio.

No reply.

Matt stuck his head out of the window. "LT, Dylan. I'm going to burn rubber over there. I want you up on Route 1, at the intersection where we turned into the plaza. That's a great overwatch position. Hang tight there til I tell you what's happening. You should be able to see the front of Staples clearly." Matt turned to his passenger window. "Stay here," he yelled at Frank. "Don't move. We'll be back shortly."

Matt put the GMC truck in gear and surged forward out of his angled parking space. He accelerated out of the parking lot and onto Route 1, taking a sharp right on Glen Street, 200 meters north. Glen Street ran along the southwest side of the Shaws/Staples parking lot, and in seconds he was turning left into the parking lot, basically along the short side of the plaza's L-shape, directly in front of Staples. Immediately upon turning, with Staples thirty meters to his front, he slammed on the brakes.

Five men, four with rifles, stood thirty meters in front of him, pointing their weapons at Derek, who was now standing basically in the corner of the L-shaped building. Strike that - four men and a woman.

Derek had his rifle tucked into his right shoulder and pointed directly back at the woman who was standing in the center of her group. Matt opened his door and stepped out, leaving his rifle slung across his chest to stand in the crook made by the truck's open door. The woman said something to her crew, and two of them turned to cover Matt while the other two kept their rifles trained on Derek.

"Stan, are you watching this?" Derek said quietly into his radio.

"I got you. We have you both covered from inside Staples. We can drop all four whenever you need us."

"Roger, hold your fire."

"Hey, Derek," Matt yelled loudly enough so that everyone could hear him. "What seems to be the problem."

Before Derek could reply, the woman took a step forward and shouted, "Who are you and what do you want here?" Matt estimated the woman to be no older than her late twenties. She was athletic, wearing form-fitting jeans and a tight fleece that showed off slim legs and a large bust. Her auburn hair was chopped short and left spiky. She did not carry a rifle but was packing a pistol in a leather holster on her left hip. The men on both sides of her appeared to be her age or younger.

Matt raised both his hands, showing he meant no harm. "My name is Matt. I see you've already met Derek. We're just here gathering some supplies. We mean you no harm whatsoever."

"Oh yeah? Well, you've already put us in danger just by being here. We don't know where you've been, and how can we be sure you haven't left smallpox virus on things you've touched? You could kill us all."

"Look, we're both vaccinated. And we are not here to hurt anyone. Maybe we can put the guns down and talk this through like civilized people."

"Well, Matt, sounds good. Unfortunately, without a civilization, there really isn't the possibility of being civilized. Wouldn't you agree?"

Matt remained silent, figuring her question was rhetorical and seeing if he could draw more information from her. The more she talked the more likely this wouldn't end in gunfire.

Over the radio net came Dylan's calm voice. "In position, Matt. I have them all covered with the 240. Stan, please move to the side of the store closest to Derek so you are not in our line of fire."

Matt did not acknowledge the call, nor Stan's affirmative reply.

"Cat got your tongue, Matt?" Yelled the woman. Matt could see that the men on either side of her were getting a bit fidgety. Derek still had his M4 leveled toward them.

"What's your name? I'm sure we can come to an agreement. Maybe we have something you need. Have you considered that?"

"Well, unless you have the vaccine, the only thing we need is to be assured that you won't ever come back here. As it is, the places you've been will need to be quarantined from us for at least two weeks just to be safe."

"And your name?"

"Fuck this guy, Kim!" Yelled the guy farthest away from the buildings. "I say we waste these two for trespassing. They're probably murderers anyway."

Kim kept her eyes locked on Matt, willing him to speak first. Matt obliged.

"Kim, is it?" Matt said. "I'll tell you what. I'd like to sort this out before hothead here decides to do something stupid."

"Who the fuck you calling stupid?" The man yelled, spittle flying from his lips. He was clearly keyed up, and scared, and Matt didn't fully know the dynamics of who was in charge of this group. This could go sideways quickly.

"Okay, Kim. Like I said, I'd like to sort this out. And seeing as how I'm in a generous mood today, I'll tell you what's gonna happen." Kim watched him, her expression never changing. *Hmm, not sure I want to play poker with this one.* "It just so happens, Kim, that we do have some vaccine. I'm not sure how many are in your group, but I believe we likely have enough for all of you."

"Oh yeah? And why should we believe you?"

"Well, Kim, I can think of one very good reason."

"Why's that?" Kim said.

"Yeah, why's that, motherfucker?" Yelled the man at the edge.

"Why don't all of you take a look to your right? That's right. Up there on Route 1 next to the bank, about 200 meters. See that Humvee? The one with the man in the turret behind the very large machine gun?" Matt paused for effect. "That's why, *motherfucker.*"

The man visibly blanched, as did the faces of the other men Matt could see. Kim kept her poker face in place.

"As I said, Kim. We mean you no harm. We're trying to survive the same as you. There's no reason whatsoever we can't all get along."

"You keep saying that, Matt. But yet you lie to us. How can we be friends if you start the friendship lying?"

"I haven't lied about anything, Kim. I simply showed you that you're outgunned."

"The vaccine. You lied about having the vaccine."

"No, Kim. I didn't lie. Why don't all of us put down our weapons and we can start over? I understand the world we live in has created a security dilemma - every man or woman for themselves. Kill or be killed. Eat or be eaten. But the reality is that there's no real reason we can't get along and coexist peacefully."

"You really have the vaccine? How'd you get it?"

"Long story, Kim. But the condensed version is that we received some at a hospital before it was overrun by bad guys. We had more than enough for our group, with quite a bit left over. How many are in your group?"

"Twelve," said Kim, seemingly deciding to trust Matt.

"Where's the rest of you?"

"We're staying at the Samoset Resort, maybe 1/2 mile behind us, on the water."

"Yeah, I know it," said Matt. "I'll tell you what, Kim. Let's do this. Why doesn't everyone simply sling their weapon? We can start over the right way. I'm not going to force you to disarm. Just stop pointing them at us. Deal?"

Kim locked eyes with Matt from across the stretch of parking lot, thinking, calculating. Finally, she turned to the men on both sides and said something Matt was too far away to hear. All four men lowered their weapons, two letting them hang from slings and two slinging their rifles over their shoulders.

Without waiting to be told, Derek let his weapon fall onto his 2-point sling, holding his empty hands apart.

Matt toggled his radio. "LT, bring down the Humvee. All clear. Stan, come on out."

Kim and her group watched as the Humvee drove down into the parking lot and sped toward them. Dylan had the weapon pointed skyward, but the sight of the armed vehicle was still pretty threatening. Stan and Liz quietly walked out of the Staples, and as they came into view of Kim's group, they were visibly startled.

"Jesus," said Kim. "Who the hell are you guys? You act like goddamn special forces."

"Well, Kim, that's a pretty good guess. As I said, I'm Matt. Derek is the one you initially cornered, and this here is Stan and Liz. They've had you covered from inside Staples since the beginning."

"Okay. You can't be from Rockland? We would have seen you before."

"True. We're not from Rockland. We are just passing through and gathering a few critical supplies."

"Do you really have the vaccine?" One of the men in Kim's group asked.

"Yes," said Matt. "Just one sec."

LT had pulled the Humvee up behind Matt's new GMC Sierra pickup, and Matt walked to the passenger side and grabbed his assault pack from the back seat. He reached in and pulled out a small canvas bag Grace had packed with one new vaccine vial along with fifty syringes. Matt took the small, zippered pouch and walked halfway toward where Kim stood with her group. He placed it on the ground, then purposefully turned his back and walked back to stand next to Derek, Stan, and Liz. Matt wanted Kim to know he didn't fear turning his back on her.

"In that bag is an original vial of vaccine, complete with seal. There are also fifty syringes. You can read the dosage on the vial, and if you do it right, there are fifty doses in that one vial."

"My god," one of the men exhaled. "It's a fucking miracle. You're literally our savior."

"Hey, I've been called a lot of things in my life, but savior isn't one of them," laughed Matt. "Seriously. Kim. These are for you. No strings attached. We want you to survive, and we want to consider you allies. Whadda ya say?"

Kim walked forward, knelt, and grabbed the case. She stood up, yanked on the zipper, and peered inside. She thought for a moment, pulled out the vial and one syringe, then walked back and handed the bag to one of her men. She examined the small bottle of vaccine closely, then expertly flipped off the syringe's cap, plunged the needle into the vial, and withdrew some of the liquid. With her other hand, she yanked up the sleeve on her fleece, exposing a well-defined bicep and deltoid on her upper arm. Without hesitation, Kim took the needle in her opposite hand and injected herself.

They all watched as Kim spoke quietly to her group and instructed them on how she would give them the vaccine.

"Matt, this is Frank, over."

Shit! In all the excitement, Matt had forgotten entirely about Frank.

"Ah, hey, Frank. It's all clear. Can you drive over to Staples? You'll see us in the parking lot."

"Will do. Frank, over and out." Matt smiled at Frank's amateurish attempt at proper radio procedure.

By the time Frank pulled up a minute later, Kim had finished inoculating the four others in her group. She walked straight up to Matt, sticking out her right hand. "My sincerest apologies, Matt. Thank you for what you've just done for us, and we are happy to be allies."

Matt shook her hand. Suddenly everyone was shaking hands and introducing themselves.

"So, Kim, how'd you end up at the Samoset? And why just twelve of you?"

"Well, I'm a professor of coastal science at the Woods Hole Oceanographic Institute. I was leading a research program up here for three weeks when the nuclear attack hit Boston. The program I teach is a joint Woods Hole - MIT program, so we were basically stranded here without any path to get back to either Boston or Cape Cod."

"Jesus. I don't know if that's good luck or bad luck," said Matt.

"Well, I'll count it as good luck. I'm still here and talking to you, while 99% of the population isn't."

"Yeah," said Matt thoughtfully. "That was kind of insensitive of me, wasn't it?"

"Don't worry about it. You make a good point. Who's to say how things would've turned out if I were in Woods Hole when everything went down."

"So these four are your students? Same with all eleven?"

"Well, three are research assistants from Woods Hole, and eight are graduate students from MIT. The guy you bantered with is one of my research assistants. The other three here are MIT students."

"How are things at the Samoset? I stayed there years ago. Nice place for a vacation and round of golf, but I have no idea how it is during a cataclysmic pandemic," said Matt.

"Honestly, we've made out pretty well. The one thing about having MIT students, I'm surrounded by geniuses. Literally."

Matt laughed, and Kim joined along. After the tenseness of a few minutes ago, it was nice to let their guard down.

"How about you, Matt? You never mentioned where you're from or where you're at now."

"Fair enough. Quick story, my home is Newport, Rhode

Island. We fled to Vermont, just outside Dartmouth, when the bombs went off. About a week ago, we were forced to flee Vermont. We selected the island of Vinalhaven. There are sixteen of us, most of them my extended family or very close friends. There are another thirty or so residents on Vinalhaven."

"And the vaccine? How'd you get access to that?"

"As I said, it's a long story. Short answer is we got it from a U.S. military delivery to Dartmouth-Hitchcock Hospital."

"And how much do you have?"

"Enough," said Matt.

Kim eyed him quizzically, understanding that there were things each was likely keeping from the other party in their new friendship.

"Listen, Kim. I'd like to stay in touch and help each other if we can. I think we likely have some capabilities that your group may be lacking, but I also think you have plenty to offer our group as well. What do you think?"

"You mean like machine guns and snake-eater, special forces shit?" Kim asked, smiling with both her mouth and eyes.

"Exactly," replied Matt. "You wouldn't happen to have a satellite phone, would you?"

"We do. We also have a marine VHF radio if that helps, but I'm not sure if Vinalhaven is in range."

"Okay, let's exchange numbers and stay in touch. Our phone is monitored 24/7. What are you doing for power?"

"We have generators that run the portion of the resort we've taken over. We've been working toward providing long-term survivability. We've stockpiled plenty of food, fuel, wood, and comfort items."

"Good. And security? Any problems so far?"

"Not really. No one has come to the resort. We've run across a few stragglers in town but have scared them off. We thought your guy here, Derek, was it? We thought he might be a straggler."

"Be careful, Kim. There are some evil people out there."

"Okay," said Kim, and from her tone, Matt wasn't sure she fully understood the depths the human race had sunk. Now wasn't the time to educate her.

"How about others in the area? Are there more people in Rockland?" Matt asked.

"In Rockland, no. But there is a small group, seven, I think, down on Owls Head south of the city. We've met with them a few times. They're two families now living together. Nice people."

"That's it?"

"Well, they told us that there is a larger group out in Thomaston near the state prison. They don't come this way cuz they're on a different inlet off Penobscot Bay which naturally takes them south. They also mentioned an even bigger group over in Damariscotta. At Lincoln Academy."

"How many in each group? Any idea?"

"I think they said about twenty in Thomaston and maybe as many as fifty in Damariscotta. We haven't seen any of them, and it doesn't make a ton of sense for them, or anyone really, to come here."

"Okay, excellent," said Matt. "We have a few more errands to run, and we need to be back before dark. We're going to the other side of town and then to the harbor, so we won't bother you here. And other than what Stan has in his carts from Staples, we won't take any food from Shaws here, okay?"

"Thanks, Matt. And truly, thanks again. It still hasn't fully sunk in what you've just done for us with the vaccine. It changes everything for us. We could venture farther out now and maybe seek out other groups."

"Kim, I'd really caution you on that for a bit. The extra vaccine you have is yours to use how you see fit. But be very wary of others. We've seen some barbaric things that you wouldn't even believe were possible. Trust me. Please."

Kim looked Matt in the eye, realizing the gravity of what Matt was trying to tell her. "Okay, Matt. We'll be careful."

"I'll check in with you tomorrow by sat phone."

Everyone said their goodbye's and Kim and her group walked back around the corner of Staples, heading in the direction of the ocean and the Samoset Resort. Matt turned toward everyone in the group.

"Well done, everyone. I mean that. Derek, good job staying calm and keeping the situation from escalating. Stan and Liz, outstanding that you were monitoring what was going on and getting in a position to provide covering fire without them even knowing. Dylan, LT, always great to have you on overwatch."

"They're from MIT," said Dylan. "I'm just glad they didn't do anything stupid that would have forced us to kill them."

"Agreed," replied Matt. 'Stan, were you able to get what you need in Staples?"

"Yes, that and more. I like your new ride, by the way. Yours too, Frank!" Stan said, nodding at the two large, black pickup trucks. "We have four full shopping carts inside the main door. Anybody care to help us load them up?"

The group spent the next ten minutes loading everything into Frank's pickup truck. In addition to several laptop computers, laser printers, and boxes of paper, the majority of items seemed to be related to computer networks, hard drive storage, and video cameras.

"Liz, why don't you hop up in the turret, and everyone else drive your original vehicle? Frank will drive one of the pickups, and Stan, I'd like you to drive this one. I'll ride shotgun in the Humvee, and we'll lead out. We're gonna continue south on Route 1, past the harbor, and then turn right on Park Street, which is still Route 1. Got it?"

No one bothered to reply verbally. Instead, they all began to silently move to the correct vehicle. His team had gelled over the last few weeks, but Matt made a mental note to set aside at least part of every week for military training. Despite the relative security Vinalhaven offered, Matt knew their situation was far from secure.

Matt directed LT to head south. They had two stops remaining, and he wanted to get back to the Hinckley as soon as possible.

CHAPTER 35

October 16, 12:22pm

Their five-vehicle convoy rolled down Route 1. Matt had LT keep it to about thirty miles per hour. They could sense and smell the ocean off to their left, and in just over a mile, they could see glimpses of it as they drove. Claws lobster shack appeared on their left, and soon after, a stretch of road offered unobstructed views of the harbor. Route 1 paralleled the harbor's shore, and they could see dozens of sailboat masts behind the buildings between the road and the harbor.

Just north of downtown Rockland, Route 1 became one way in each direction, with the southbound lanes splitting off to the right before turning back south and paralleling northbound Route 1, albeit one block to the west. Wishing to stay in view of the harbor, Matt directed LT to keep heading south but to stay in the northbound lane. Matt was pretty confident no vehicles would be traveling in the other direction. Within two blocks, the left side of the road was completely open to the harbor, with a series of large parking lots occupying the several hundred yards between the harbor and Route 1. The ferry terminal was at the south end of these parking lots, and Matt knew from experience that this was where one boarded to take the ferry out to Vinalhaven.

They continued several more blocks through the heart of downtown Rockland. Stores, coffee shops, barbers, and restaurants lined both sides of the street. The last time Matt had been here, the place was bustling with people. Like

Woodstock in Vermont, Rockland was a quintessential New England town. Today it was empty.

Matt carefully examined the stores as they rode past. Almost all of them simply looked deserted. There were no broken windows, scorched roofs, or dead bodies in the street. It was as if everyone had simply closed up shop one afternoon and never returned.

They neared the intersection of Main and Park Streets, and Matt decided to call an audible. Matt motioned for LT to stop the Humvee and then toggled his mic. "Listen up, quick change in plans. Just on the southeast corner of this intersection is the Maine Sport Outfitters shop. LT will stop right here, with Derek taking over the turret. Liz'll jump out here to go with Dylan, Derek, and Frank to the outfitters. Liz knows best what the ladies need regarding clothing, and Dylan has a list from the Biancos and Aghas. There's plenty of room in Frank's pickup for everything. One of you stay outside as a lookout at all times. Understood?"

"Roger," said both Derek and Dylan into the radio.

"LT, Stan, and I'll take the Humvee and the other pickup and head down to the restaurant supply store. It's less than a half mile down Park Street on the right. When you're done, head down and link up with us. We'll likely need help loading and packing everything in the truck. Call us on the radio if you need anything."

Another chorus of "rogers" came over the radio.

Liz jumped out, LT turned the Humvee onto Park Street, and Stan followed in the new Chevy Sierra 2500. In about sixty seconds, they were pulling into the parking lot in front of Rockland Restaurant Supply. QuAI had suggested this place, and Kent Oliver had confirmed it as a warehouse store used by all the local restaurants for their food. Matt figured a place like this would have the best chance of not being looted, as many people would assume it was more equipment than food. Additionally, its food items were likely larger, making them easier to transport and store in the bulk quantities they hoped to find.

LT jumped up into the turret as Stan and Matt made entry through the front glass door using the Halligan tool. Inside, the smell was not nearly as bad as Matt had feared. A rotting odor of spoiled meat emanated from the back of the store, where Matt could see some walk-in refrigerators and freezers. The store was not especially large, maybe the size of a basketball court, with tall ceilings, open ductwork, and five long aisles running from front to back. The front of the store was half-lit from the sun pouring through the large plate-glass windows, but the farther back one went, the darker it became.

Matt and Stan turned on their headlamps and grabbed a couple of carts each. They stuck together, wanting to ensure they got the needed supplies and didn't miss anything. As they walked down the first aisle, the shelves appeared about half stocked with goods.

"Looks like much of this stuff has already been taken, but let's see what's left. It might just be that they haven't been resupplied."

The first aisle catered to all types of international cuisines, with sections for Mexican, Italian, Chinese, and Japanese spread along both sides. Matt grabbed several one-gallon jars of salsa and six #10 cans of refried beans, while Stan added three one-gallon jugs of soy sauce. At the Italian section, they filled an entire cart with #10 cans of tomato sauce, stewed tomatoes, various large jars of minced garlic, and cans of breadcrumbs.

As they approached the back of the store, the smell of rotting meat became considerably worse. Matt started gagging and rushed to put his buff over his mouth and nose. Stan didn't seem as bothered, but they turned into the second aisle and headed back toward the front of the store before the stench became unbearable.

In the second aisle, they found staples. This was what they wanted the most. Flour, sugar, salt, and peppercorns went into the cart. Fifty-pound sacks of rice were stacked on the bottoms of each of the four carts. Large 20-pound boxes of pasta, each containing twenty 1-pound smaller boxes, filled another cart. Fettucine, linguine, spaghetti, elbow macaroni and ziti - all tossed into a cart. Jugs of olive oil, vegetable oil, and canola oil. Condiments such as ketchup, mustard, and relish. Assorted packets of gravy, muffin, pancake, and cornbread mix. Cases of condensed milk and 5-pound tubs of powdered milk. Matt recited the variety of everything in his head, and for a moment, he felt like the characters in Forrest Gump listing all the types of shrimp: *pineapple shrimp, lemon shrimp, coconut shrimp, pepper shrimp, shrimp soup, shrimp gumbo, shrimp stew, shrimp salad.*

As they loaded a cart, one would push it forward to the front of the store. As they started down the third aisle, Derek called over the radio to say they had finished at the outfitters and were on their way to meet up.

"Hey guys," Matt said in reply over the radio. "When you get here, you'll see full carts at the front of the store. Please start loading them in the truck."

Matt and Stan continued down the third aisle, which consisted of canned and jarred vegetables, then proceeded back up the fourth aisle - mostly kitchen supplies. The last aisle contained items specific to running a restaurant, with items such as tablecloths and all sorts of mixers and toothpicks for alcoholic drinks.

It was almost 2 pm when they had everything loaded. There were hardly any places for everyone to sit, and all the vehicles sat low upon their springs.

Two more stops until they could head back to Camden and stow everything on the Hinckley.

They drove east on Park Street toward the ocean. Right before the intersection with Main Street, where the outfitters were located, Matt directed LT to pull into the Walgreens. He could already tell from the parking lot that the place had been looted, as all the windows along the front of the store had been smashed. They parked their five vehicles in the middle of the parking lot, and everyone stepped out of the vehicles.

"This place is probably pretty picked over, but there's undoubtedly still some things remaining," said Matt to his assembled group. "Derek, your turn in the turret. Everything seems calm, but keep an eye out.

"Liz, here's the list Clare, Marvi, and Grace made up last night. You and Dylan try to get everything on the list. It's mostly feminine products, first aid, and over-the-counter meds. Stan and I will go to the pharmacy and see what's left."

"What about me?"LT asked. "Should I stay out here with Derek?"

"Nope, you and Frank are in charge of sundries."

"Sundries? What're sundries?" Frank asked.

"Candy! Potato chips, cookies, gum, playing cards," said Matt. "Whatever goodies you can get. I'm not sure what'll be left over, but find the garbage bags first and then start filling'em up. Any questions?"

Everyone shook their head. "Okay then," said Matt. "Let's do this."

They walked to the front door. The Halligan tool in Matt's left hand proved unnecessary as the front doors were propped wide open, despite all the glass in the doors having been completely shattered. The store was dark, with a faint sour odor. Unlike the restaurant supply warehouse, which stank of rotten meat, Walgreens' scent was more reflective of spoiled milk.

Matt and Stan made a beeline for the back of the store, where their headlamps picked out the overhead sign for the pharmacy. The others scattered down various aisles scavenging for the items on their list.

Stan was ahead of Matt and came up to the pharmacy counter first. There was a metal security shutter that had once been secured from the ceiling to the top of the counter. At some point, someone had pried a corner of it loose and pulled it open. While an opening to crawl through the mesh shutter remained, Matt noticed that the intruder had been kind enough to unlock the door leading back to the pharmacy.

The open door makes it easier for us to gain entry, but it also means that looters have probably taken every pill of value.

Matt carried a list of medicines he and Grace had put together last night. Clare's focus was collecting medicines the family might require for sickness, while Matt wanted drugs for emergencies, such as gunshot wounds. The list included antibiotic pills and ointments, EPIPENs, prednisone, NSAIDs for inflammation, Silvadene cream for severe burns, and other items to cover health situations Grace felt were possible. Matt knew that narcotics like OxyContin and Percocet would have been the first things looted, but he hoped he could find some lesser-known painkillers that drug addicts might not be as aware of.

Through the door, the pharmacy looked like a tornado had hit it. Large bottles and containers littered the floor, thousands of pills were scattered everywhere, and paper littered the ground.

"Check the customer bins," said Stan. "Looters and addicts aren't going to waste their time, but if you think about it, prescriptions filled for people are exactly the types of medications we're looking for."

"Great point, Stan. I'm gonna just sweep everything into one of these big bins and take it with us. We can sort it out later. Check the shelves there - see if it's alphabetical or maybe organized by type of medication."

Matt looked at the dozen bins labeled with alphabet letters, each containing one to a dozen small paper bags of filled prescription meds. Matt dumped them all into one big bin, then moved over to help Stan search for the medications on their list. It took them about ten minutes, but they were able to find pretty much everything they were looking for.

Gathering up their two bins, Stan and Matt headed back to the front of the store. The others were finishing up as well, and they all exited pretty much at the same time. Liz and Dylan lugged an overstuffed garbage bag between them. Frank and LT each carried a full garbage bag while LT munched on a

Payday candy bar.

"Load up, everyone. Find room for those bags, and let's get going."

They tied them off and then stuffed their bags into the back of the pickups.

"Wait a sec! Forgot something," yelled Dylan as he scrambled back into the store. Everyone watched, wondering what he had forgotten. Thirty seconds later, Dylan came trotting out the door, three full cases of canned soda cradled in his arms. "Figured the kids might appreciate this, Uncle Matt."

"They don't usually drink soda, Dylan," Matt said, shaking his head and smiling.

"They do now," said Dylan, dumping the cases in the back seat of the pickup.

"Okay, listen up," Matt called out to everyone as they stood near each of their vehicles. "We're going to swing by Rockland Harbor. Just a quick peek. Everyone can stay in their vehicles except Stan and me. Let's go."

Matt led the heavily-laden convoy north on Main Street for one block. Downtown Rockland was truly beautiful but also a security nightmare for a convoy. Both sides of Main Street were lined with three-story brick buildings that created an alley-like feeling as they drove down the deserted street. With wide sidewalks, numerous shops, museums, and restaurants, the tree-lined street was a delight for the casual shopper on vacation. However, with all of the uncertainties in this post-cataclysmic world, all Matt saw now were potential sniper hides and ambush spots.

They took a right onto Tillson Avenue, and the commercial district was replaced by two blocks of parking lots, warehouses, and buildings catering to the commerce of boating and fishing. They drove by several boat repair shops, with blue mobile gantries on oversized wheels and numerous sailboats parked on stands, some stripped down to expose bare hulls.

After a few blocks, the warehouses on the right were

replaced by an actual pier, with several commercial fishing boats tied up alongside. Rockland harbor was quite a bit larger than Camden's, and Matt could see dozens and dozens of small and large boats moored in the bay. As they continued, Tillerson Avenue abruptly ended at a small parking lot on top of a pier, the open harbor beyond.

As soon as LT stopped the Humvee, Matt jumped out. Turning around, he told LT to get all the vehicles turned around and be ready to roll in five minutes. Stan, at the rear of the convoy, pulled his pickup into a parking space and stepped out to join Matt on the pier.

"Whadda ya think?" Matt asked, looking southward at several small docks behind the pier. "I think we're outta luck."

"Yeah," said Stan. "These are just harbor patrol boats. I was hoping one of their small or medium cutters would be here. They probably pulled everything to either Portland or Bangor."

This part of the wharf belonged to the US Coast Guard. Matt had hoped there might be a cutter in port that would give them some maritime options should the need ever arise where they were forced to leave Vinalhaven. The Coast Guard had a 154-foot Sentinel Class Patrol Boat that Stan said would be perfect for their needs, allowing them to travel as far away as Europe or Florida and carry up to thirty people.

No joy.

All that remained at the wharf were two 29-foot small response boats and one 47-foot medium boat. QuAI had provided them with information that one such large cutter was in Rockland as recently as September 6 but had no information after that date. It was very likely that the Coast Guard had moved some of its assets after the nuclear attacks.

"Oh well," said Matt. "You can't win'em all. I'd say all-in-all, we've had quite a productive day."

"Agreed. Let's get back to Camden."

"Hey, what's that?" Matt said, pointing off to the south. Stan turned, and they both shielded their eyes from the afternoon sun. While the ferry terminal and many of the harbor's moorings were behind them to the north, to the south were several commercial marinas catering mostly to pleasure craft. About five hundred meters across the harbor, a large, white super yacht sat docked at the Safe Harbor marina in front of a small bayside park. "That's a pretty big yacht for Rockland."

"Agreed," said Stan. "I'd put her at 200 feet."

"Something to keep in mind. Do you think you could drive her?"

"It's called piloting, Mr. Airborne Ranger. You drive a tank; you pilot a yacht. And yes, if I could captain a Navy destroyer, I should be able to figure out that yacht."

"Wanna go check her out?"

"Nah," said Stan. "She's not going anywhere, and we need to get back to Vinalhaven. Anything else you want to show me?"

"Nah, let's get back home."

CHAPTER 36

October 16, 10:34pm

Matt lay in bed, his left arm wrapped around Clare as she nestled her head on his chest. The mid-October nights were getting colder, but the kids still seemed to enjoy living in the tents in the yard. The master bedroom faced southeast onto the cove, and with the blinds up, Matt could see the light from the flickering bonfire still smoldering below.

Matt's back and shoulders were sore but in a good way. After leaving Rockland harbor, the trip to Camden had been uneventful. Pete was waiting for them at the dock, and it took them over an hour to load the boat. Matt wasn't sure everything would fit at one point, but in the end, they had sufficient room. Luckily the weather was sunny, although the wind picked up and the seas were higher than their previous trip. Matt wasn't sure if his sore back was from the heavy lifting or the forty-five minutes of pounding as Pete pushed the Hinckley 35 through the choppy seas.

Everyone was extremely pleased with their team's haul from Rockland. Molly and Marvi smiled incessantly as they directed the younger ones to where to store their extensive food supplies in the barn. Frank took his tools, a generator, a portion of the food, and the clothing and agreed to deliver them to the appropriate resident who had requested each item. After the initial unload, Stan, Liz, Juliet, and Amey sequestered themselves in the room above the barn to work on putting all of their new electronic toys together. When Matt had gone up to bed a few minutes previously, they were still hard at work.

"Quite a day you've had, Mr. Sheridan," said Clare quietly, her head still on Matt's chest. Like him, they were mesmerized by watching the flickering firelight through the bay window.

"All for you, Mrs. Sheridan. It almost seems like things are becoming normal."

"Yeah, I'm not sure I've seen the kids so happy and full of energy. There's something to be said of being surrounded by family. I just wish it were under different circumstances."

"Mmmmm," agreed Matt.

"Hey, I almost forgot," said Clare, pulling her head off Matt's chest, lying back on her king-size pillow and turning to face him. "I promised Molly I'd talk to you about Robert's Hill Farm."

"What about it?"

"Well, Michelle, Molly, and I spent most of the day over there today. We were shocked they still had so much food that hadn't yet rotted. In the basement, we found stores of canned and jarred vegetables, fruits, and preserves. Michelle said they had a very successful shop and also went to the farmer's market in Rockland. There was enough to last us probably for nearly a year."

"That's great, Clare. Amazing. So what'd you promise Molly you'd talk to me about?"

"Well," said Clare, pausing to find the right words. "She'd really like to move to the farm. And she'd like to bring anyone who'd like to go with her, including us, if we want. There's something like ten or twelve bedrooms. Not to mention several barns, greenhouses, and a two-bedroom cottage at the front of the property right on Roberts Harbor."

"Okay," replied Matt, intentionally noncommittal - biding some time. "What do you think?" If there was one thing Matt had learned as a husband, it was to always get his wife's opinion first before providing his own. Happy wife, happy life.

"Honestly, I think it would be great. For her and all the young adults, I mean. I want to stay here, Matt. This house and the property are amazing, and here's where I want to live as a family. Dave and Michelle are right next door."

"What about the Whites? And Pete and Liz? Where would they go?"

"It's totally up to them. They're welcome to stay here or go to the farm. Or they could pick any of the other houses here on the cove."

"Okay," repeated Matt.

"You don't like the idea. Just say so." Clare sat up in bed, facing him.

Ah, Jesus. And the night had started so well. Now we're going to have an argument, right when I was ready to fall asleep.

"No, Clare. I didn't say that at all."

"But that's what you're thinking. I know you. If it's not your idea, then you don't like it."

"Clare, stop for a sec. Please." Matt also sat up, propping himself on the stack of king-sized pillows on the plush bed. *Who in their right mind would want to leave this house?* "You're making assumptions that simply aren't true, sweetheart."

"So you agree that Molly's idea is a good one?"

"Yeah, I do. It's maybe a tad farther away than I'd like it to be, but otherwise, I think it's perfect."

"I think all the kids would be happier there together. We have eight between seventeen and twenty-four. Molly would be like the house mother. Plus, they can all work the farm in the spring and spend all winter getting things ready."

"Have you and Molly spoken with any of them about this? What do they think?"

"Well, it was Kelsey and Grace's suggestion in the first place. When we described Roberts Hill Farm to them yesterday, they knew instantly it was an ideal spot for them. They know they can't sleep in tents all winter, and despite how large this house is, it would be cramped to fit everyone in here."

"I'm on board. We can start talking with everyone in the morning and get the ball rolling. Honestly, if we're going to do this, doing it sooner rather than later would be much easier."

"Thank you, honey. I knew you'd think it was a good idea."

Clare leaned over and kissed him. She pulled her head back, maintaining eye contact. Then she leaned forward again for a much deeper kiss, all thoughts of Roberts Hill Farm forgotten.

CHAPTER 37

October 22, 7:59am

The radio on Matt's hip squelched as he sat at the dining table finishing his breakfast.

"Matt, this is Stan."

"Go ahead, Stan," replied Matt, pulling the radio off his belt and pressing the push-to-talk button. When on any operation, such as the trip to Rockland, Matt typically wore an earpiece with the radio where he could simply push the toggle on the cord clipped to his shirt. Around the house, though, Matt usually removed the earpiece and turned the volume to a level he was sure to hear while wearing it on his hip.

"Would you mind coming up to the theater? There's something we'd like to show you. Grab Pete and Clare if they're around."

"Will do."

"This is Pete," chimed in Pete over the radio network. "I copied. Be right over."

Matt took a few more bites of his eggs and a last sip of coffee. The previous week had been a flurry of activity as well as change. Everyone was excited about taking over Roberts Hill Farm and making it the home base for the young adults and Molly. Well, everyone except Christopher and Laurie, who were heartbroken to learn their cousins were moving out. 11-year old Chris had even made a pitch to be allowed to live at the farm, and Clare had compromised by allowing Molly to designate one of the many bedrooms to be Chris and Laurie's on the occasions they were allowed to sleep over.

The other saving grace with the kids had been that Pete and Liz decided to remain at the main house, which everyone was now referring to as "Carver Main." Dave and Michelle's nearby cottage was named "Carver Cottage," while the small home Stan and Marvi had moved into had been christened the "White House." The White House was a hundred yards from where Matt now sat, situated east on the other side of the long stone pier. Like many of the waterfront homes on Vinalhaven, the three-bedroom house Stan and Marvi had chosen had been recently updated and offered tremendous views of Roberts Harbor and the islands at the harbor's mouth.

The first couple of days occupying Roberts Hill Farm had been a ton of hard work and had also taken some emotional toll. They found six dead people in several locations in the main farmhouse and four other people in two of the small cottages on the property. Pete and Derek had volunteered, so along with Matt, the three wrapped each of the bodies and carried them outside. The farm had several working tractors, and Dylan had dug a mass grave large enough to lay all nine side-by-side, at the rear of the property. Kelsey and the kids had used spray paint to decorate a large rock that had previously lined the pea gravel driveway as a memorial headstone, and Dylan used the tractor to emplace it over the grave.

With crisp and cold weather, they opened all the windows and let the house air out completely for 24 hours. The tents had all been repositioned from in front of Carver Main to a grassy area in front of the farmhouse, and after that first day, all of the young adults plus Molly had resided at the farm.

Roberts Hill Farm was about two miles away by road, but the kids had appropriated some mountain bikes, and the distance was almost exactly a half mile by cutting through various yards and using some long unpaved driveways. Either way, driving or biking between the two locations took just over five minutes. In the winter, they could plow the road and also create a shorter path for snowmobiles.

The farm itself proved an even more significant find than Clare had described. Not only was there a substantial amount of fresh and preserved food, a portion of which Marvi had begun distributing amongst all the Vinalhaven residents, but there was an incredible woodworking shop as well as tractors, tools, and other items of outdoor equipment. Possibly more importantly, the farm had an enormous cache of seeds. All types of seeds for just about every flower and vegetable you could imagine. Lastly, the farm had chickens. Matt would have preferred cows for their meat, but the large coop of hens provided the entire island with a steady supply of fresh eggs.

Kent Oliver had mentioned that North Haven, the neighboring island to the north, had a substantial farm with pigs, sheep, and cows. Matt added this to the list of things to check before winter. He had begun initial discussions with Clare and Molly about hosting an all-island Thanksgiving in November. One of the three barns at Roberts Hill Farm had been recently renovated, and Michelle said the owners had plans to use it as an event venue. There were tables and chairs inside for more than sixty guests, and they all agreed it would be ideal for future all-island gatherings.

While most of the extended family had been working diligently to get Roberts Hill Farm in working order, Stan, Liz, and Juliet spent all their time at Carver Main's barn working with QuAI. As Matt took a last sip of coffee, he assumed that QuAI was responsible for whatever Stan wanted to see him about now.

Clare walked in the back door as Matt stood up. She had biked with the kids over to the farm so the kids could spend the day there, and she'd just returned.

"Hey, honey. Everything good at the farm?"

"Yeah, if we're not careful, they're going to turn into a little commune," said Clare, smiling.

"Stan called down and asked me to come up and bring you if you're not busy. He has something he wants to show us."

"Let's go then."

They both walked out of the kitchen, through the mud room that connected the house to the barn and then up the stairs. As they crested the top stair, they could hear Stan and Pete talking in the theater room, so that's where they headed.

"Morning, Clare, Matt," greeted Stan. "Thanks for coming up. Please, have a seat."

Matt and Clare entered the theater room, where Pete, Liz, and Juliet were already seated in the front row.

"So, whadda ya got for us, Stan?" Pete asked after Clare and Matt took seats in the second row.

"When I got up here this morning around 7 am, Liz and Juliet had already been here for over an hour. As I've explained before, we normally posit our questions in the evening based on our lack of bandwidth connecting us to QuAI's data center. QuAI provides the answers almost immediately, but depending on the quantity of data we are asking for, doing this allows her to download the info to our remote terminal throughout the evening hours."

"What kind of data takes that long to send?" Matt asked.

"It's mostly graphics that she wants us to see or that we ask for. QuAI does almost all of the intel analysis within her own data center, and what she sends us are finished reports in text form - these are transmitted almost instantly, even over satellite.

"So to continue, when I arrived this morning, there were several documents and some graphics that QuAI had marked as urgent for me to see. Here. Let me pull it up on the screen. Juliet, would you mind pulling up the first slide?"

Juliet grabbed a remote control, bringing the theater's wide projection screen to life. Another click and the screen showed a map of northern New England, from Boston north to the Canadian border. The screen was large enough to make out a lot of detail, including numerous graphical symbols and arrows superimposed on the geography. Matt sat up a little straighter in his seat. The map looked like the campaign maps he'd seen countless times in tactical operations center briefings in Iraq and Afghanistan. This was a war map.

"This is a map of northern New England, but as you can see, QuAI has added additional graphics. You've all seen these maps before from your time as military officers. Blue icons represent the good guys - in this case, those assets allied with the state and federal governments. Red symbols are for The Base.

"To jump right to the point, The Base is on the warpath. They've consolidated their hold on their territory from Richmond, Virginia to Burlington, Vermont. The only portions of the mid-Atlantic and New England they don't control are southeast Virginia and Maine. And as you can see from this map, they are focusing their next move on capturing Maine."

Stan used a laser pointer to highlight numerous military symbols on the map near Portsmouth and two areas farther north in New Hampshire: North Conway and Gorham.

"Wait a sec, Stan. We were just in Gorham a little over two weeks ago. There were no assets of The Base there. There wasn't anyone there at all," said Clare. "Are we sure QuAI's intel is accurate?"

"You're 100% right, Clare, and that's exactly why I wanted you to see this right away. The Base is pushing its forces north into New Hampshire and staging them along the three major roads that would allow them to decapitate the entire state of Maine completely."

"Stan, when you say 'forces,' what exactly are you talking about? I can read the map there, and the symbols you have up there are for platoon and company-sized elements. Looks like infantry, cavalry, MP, and artillery units," said Matt. "Can that be right?"

"Yes, that's correct. And we have no reason to doubt the veracity of QuAI's intel. In fact, we have every reason to believe it, as there is no possibility of human error. She's collecting data, collating and analyzing it, and using her artificial intelligence capabilities to render informed intel estimates on what is happening and, more importantly, what is most likely to happen. The unit symbols are mostly based on equipment, as obviously The Base forces aren't likely to be trained Military Police or Cavalry. However, they do have the equipment from those units, and in the case of artillery, this is important."

"And what does QuAI say is most likely to happen?" Matt asked.

Stan paused a second to look at the group. "QuAI states that within 48 hours, forces loyal to The Base will move upwards through Maine with the intent of destroying all forces loyal to General Condretti and Governor Babbitt. The Base has marshaled most of its forces near Portsmouth and Kittery and will first attack upwards along I-95 to seize Portland. At the same time, a few cavalry units will move eastward from New Hampshire along Route 302 and Route 2 to fix any of Babbit's forces in Augusta and Bangor. When the main effort has completed seizing Portland, they will continue northward along I-95 to seize Augusta and Bangor."

"And does QuAI make any estimates on how The Base will fare in these attacks?"

"Yes," continued Stan. "QuAI says, with a 94.2% probability, that The Base will be successful within 72 hours of initiating their attack."

Matt and the others sat in stunned silence.

"Well, there's still a 5.8% chance," said Pete in an attempt to lighten the mood.

"Actually, QuAI says there is a 5.8% chance the attack could take as long as 96 hours."

"So basically, she's stating with 100% certainty that Maine will belong to The Base in the next few days?"

"That's exactly what she's stating," answered Stan.

"Any good news for us today, Stan?" Clare asked.

"Well, I do have one small point that QuAI believes is relevant and positive to us, and I also have one more piece of information that is important for you to hear."

Everyone waited for Stan to continue.

"Okay, the small, positive piece is that QuAI believes The

Base will expend minimal effort, possibly none, along Route 1 from Brunswick to Belfast. They are extending their forces for this attack, drawing on captured National Guard units and equipment from Massachusetts and New York and using a considerable amount of their fuel stocks. QuAI believes The Base leadership simply wants to remove any vestiges of the old state government. They will install a puppet regime in Portland with a small legislature supporting the ratification of the new Constitution of the Union of American States. So bottom line for us, there's nothing in this part of the Maine coast that The Base wants."

"Except us," said Matt.

"Yes, but they don't know we're here, Matt," said Liz, standing up to speak. "That's our first priority information requirement, or PIR, that QuAI is looking for. And as of now, QuAI's come across no information that The Base knows we're here.

"Well, that's certainly a relief," said Clare sarcastically.

"Juliet, would you please advance the slide," said Stan in an attempt to regain control of the briefing. The map on the screen widened to a view of the United States from New York down to the Carolinas. Norfolk was colored in blue, while the rest of Virginia, plus Maryland, Delaware, New Jersey, and New York were all in red.

"There have been several fairly intense skirmishes between The Base and active-duty military forces from the Norfolk Naval Base. The standard engagements have all been won handily by the US Army. However, as we saw in Iraq and Afghanistan, The Base has exacted some toll through snipers, IEDs, and booby traps. Perhaps of even greater significance, The Base has rounded up extended family members of the Norfolk leadership. In particular, they have the Admiral's two adult daughters and his mother, who all resided on Philadelphia's Main Line. Philadelphia was one of the cities that received early shipments of the vaccine. QuAI's intel is that The Base is holding about fifty people hostage, most of them relatives of military leaders in Norfolk. They are threatening to execute them in Independence Square while ringing the Liberty Bell for the first time since 1846."

"Holy shit," said Matt. "These fucking Base guys are something else. Jesus. How has the Admiral reacted."

"Well, the Admiral has said that should any of those hostages be harmed, the reprisal will be swift, severe, and completely beyond anything The Base could imagine. So far, none of the hostages have been harmed. At least as far as we know."

"Stan, let me ask you," said Matt. "What's the federal government doing about any of this? Does President Donovan have his head in the sand, or do they have a strategy for dealing with The Base?"

"Good question, Matt. One interesting blindspot with QuAI in the post-cataclysmic world is that we have very little information about discussions or decisions made inside Cheyenne Mountain. On the one hand, QuAI has millions of times more capacity than the current federal government. The NSA, NRO, DIA, and a myriad of other 3-letter agencies are all gone - what remains is just the slice of these organizations that fled to either Cheyenne Mountain or Norfolk. While many of their sensors remain intact and in place, their ability to crunch this data and analyze the information has been severely restricted. It's a function of reduced personnel as well as access to computing power. Remember, Fort Meade was abandoned - they scuttled much of that computing power. While they do have extensive analysis capability, the best in the world other than QuAI, it's a fraction of what it was three months ago.

"All that said, QuAI believes President Donovan is loathe to take on The Base directly. He desperately wants to avoid the killing of more Americans, especially by other Americans. But he does have a small human intelligence network, and the intel that is feeding back to him about The Base is horrific. QuAI believes that the federal government will strike out directly against The Base at some point, but in what form, we don't know.

"How about the Navy, Stan? How operational are they?"

"Yeah, that's something we've recently been querying QuAI about. The Navy is somewhat intact, but its capability has been significantly degraded. To give you some quick figures, the US Navy operates about 240 warships with over 100,000 sailors on board. About 1/3 of these ships are roaming the ocean at any given time. The rest are based at their home port - although some of these home ports are in places like Japan, Guam, and Bahrain. More than 60% of these 100,000 sailors are assigned to one of twenty ships: one of the 11 aircraft carriers or the nine amphibious assault ships. This became important when the pandemic hit.

"After the nuclear attack, the Navy ordered most of its ships to return to defensive positions off both coasts of the United States. Contrary to popular belief, the Navy doesn't just drive around in circles alone in the middle of the ocean. They are constantly sending planes and helicopters to the mainland for supplies, mail, transfer of people, et cetera. When the pandemic hit, smallpox got on board most of the Navy's surface ships and decimated them.

"What about the vaccine?" Clare asked.

"Yeah, what QuAI learned is that all Navy personnel on ships received the initial vaccine. It didn't work against the Black Pox - but no one figured that out until it was too late. With hundreds, in some cases thousands, of sailors crammed onboard these ships, the virus spread like wildfire. Once a ship became exposed, there was nothing to be done. So QuAI estimates that about 85% of onboard Navy personnel died of smallpox. The 15% are basically submarines and some solo ships that happened to have no contact with anyone."

"Jesus," said Pete.

"The good news, if any, is that the ships in port fared somewhat better. Well, I should say the people didn't fare better, but with the ship in port, there was more ability to get sick people off the ships. So, the condensed version is that QuAI says the Navy has control of about 60% of its ships but only has the personnel to operate about 20% of these. Almost of these ships are located at one of the safe havens such as Norfolk, San Diego, or Oahu. The other issue is fuel. The remaining aircraft carriers and some submarines have been tethered to port to provide an electrical power grid using their nuclear reactors. Aviation has come to a complete standstill. What aviation fuel they have remaining is being reserved for emergency use."

"So what's that mean for us? Are they moving any ships to help Maine? Or just staying put," asked Matt.

"No. We don't know where the subs are, not even QuAI. But we know that all surface ships remain in a defensive posture around the various enclaves.

"Well, Stan, good talk. Just the way I wanted to start my day," said Matt jokingly. He stood up and fist-bumped Stan. "Hey, I know we don't say this enough, but this is incredible work. All of you. Liz, Juliet. I mean it. What you guys are doing is keeping us alive. The whole reason we're here is because of your ability to manage QuAI. Please keep doing what you're doing."

Clare walked up from behind Matt and kissed Stan on the cheek. She then went to hug Liz and Juliet. "This is hardest on you three. It's difficult enough hearing about all this, but you three are the ones who have to be the messenger. It's never easy. Thank you."

There was some additional small talk, and then the room broke up, with everyone heading back to their original plans for the day.

CHAPTER 38

October 24, 6:12am

The knock on the bedroom door startled Matt, but he was instantly awake.

"Come in?" Matt said, knowing it was either Pete or Liz, as neither of his children would ever bother knocking. Clare stirred awake beside him.

The door opened a crack, and Liz poked her head in. "It's me, Matt. Sorry to wake you. The attack on Portland is going down. I woke my dad, and now you. I figured I should call Stan on the radio, but wanted to check with you first."

"Yeah, definitely wake him up. He'd be upset if you didn't tell him right away. He's probably already up anyway. Why are you up so early?"

"One of us tries to be up by 6 am. Today was my turn. Got up a half-hour ago and went to the barn to check on QuAI's overnight activity. Looks like the attack just started."

Matt looked out the shadeless bay window and saw the faintest hint of dawn creeping in from the east. It would be light enough to see in about fifteen minutes. "Okay. Call Stan on the radio. I'll get dressed and will be right over."

Liz closed the door, and Matt stood up to throw on the jeans and long-sleeved Georgetown t-shirt he had thrown over the armchair next to the dresser. Clare also got out of bed and started walking to the room's ensuite bathroom.

"You don't need to get up, honey. It's not like we can do anything."

"Yeah, I know. But we get up with the sun, and it'll be too light to sleep in less than a half-hour anyway. I'll make you guys some coffee and bring a loaf of the pumpkin bread Laurie and I made yesterday."

"Can't wait. See you over there." Matt closed the bedroom door behind him and padded down the stairs in his socks. He put on his shoes in the mudroom and headed straight over to the barn's second floor.

Liz handed him several sheets of computer paper, and he sat on one of the couches in the large recreation room. Pete was sitting on another couch reading what looked like the same report. The first two pages were formatted almost like a ship's log, with QuAI providing a running commentary of things happening in the United States that she felt met one of the numerous priority intelligence requirements provided by Stan's team. Stan had explained previously that QuAI had access to an incredible number of raw information sources, which Stan often referred to as sensors. These included access to many US government and private sector satellites crisscrossing the sky hundreds of miles overhead. The Hawkeye 360 system, which the family had used weeks previously to identify the locations of radio signals, was a key sensor. Additionally, QuAI had access to satellites with visual targeting - letting her see what was on the ground, synthesize various objects using her incredibly fast AI, and then draw conclusions about what was happening. There were also sensors that captured satphone and radio communications, analyzed weather patterns, and a myriad of other things.

According to the report in his hand, at 4 am this morning, QuAI detected a massive increase in radio traffic in the Portsmouth and Kittery areas where The Base had marshaled much of its force. Twenty minutes later, at 4:20 am, QuAI noted related radio activity in Goreham and North Conway. At 4:30 am, those radio transmissions in northern New Hampshire began to appear as pings moving eastward along Routes 2 and 302. Matt inferred that this was the fixing force moving out, and as they had a much farther distance to travel, they would leave first.

At 5:00 am, according to QuAI's report, The Base's main force crossed into Maine on I-95 and began speeding north. Given the distance, Matt knew driving from Portsmouth to Portland took about an hour. He had no insight into The Base commander's plan, but he assumed that he was planning to attack just after first light. Matt looked at his watch: 6:20. Looking out the window, he could see the sky brightening considerably. It was that period between dawn and sunrise that the Army had always taught was one of the most likely times for the enemy to attack. Major Robert Rogers, considered by the 75th Ranger Regiment as the first true Ranger, learned during the French and Indian War that Indians were most likely to attack at dawn. *If I remember correctly, Roger's Standing Order #10 was "Don't sleep beyond dawn. Dawn's when the French and Indians attack."*

Matt knew General Condretti was not an Army Ranger, but as Rogers' Rangers were from New Hampshire, Matt sincerely hoped he was following Rogers' Standing Orders.

Stan walked up the stairs, carrying a tray of coffee mugs. Matt could see the steam rising from each cup. Behind him followed Clare, her hands full of a large plate of pumpkin bread. They each placed their trays on the ping-pong table and grabbed a seat on the couch; Clare sat next to Matt and handed him a mug of coffee.

"Morning, Stan," said Matt. "Here's the report that Liz handed me. Looks like The Base is hitting Portland right now. No more detail than that."

"Okay," said Stan, showing no reaction. He began reading the report while sipping his coffee.

"I feel like we should be doing something. I hate just sitting here."

"I know. You're a man of action, Matt, and that's what makes you such a great leader. But right now, there's nothing for us to respond to. It's a waiting game, but it's also one of preparation.

Liz and Juliet have been working on their surveillance system. I recommend we make that the main effort for today. Hopefully, we can have it up and running by this afternoon."

"Are these the networked video cameras you mentioned the other night?" Pete asked.

'Exactly. Liz, Juliet, and I spent most of yesterday reconning the island's west side. We found two points, Dog Point and Browns Head Light Station, that would be ideal surveillance points. We grabbed almost twenty extended-range routers at Home Depot and Staples the other day and combined with some slight modifications and soldering, we should have more than enough capability to stretch across the island."

"So are you building like a bunch of wifi hotspot circles that all overlap?" asked Clare.

"That might be a bit of an oversimplification, Clare, but essentially yes," answered Liz, who, until this point, had stood silent in the doorway of the QuAI computer room. "Not to bore you with the details, but we are modifying these extended-range routers to be more unidirectional than omnidirectional. Basically, we can focus the antenna's power to push outward in a narrower pie slice than waste its energy pushing out 360 degrees. By setting these up in the upper stories of homes across the island, we can build a continuous chain of wifi signals for several miles."

"And this wifi will let us do what?"

"Video surveillance. The other thing Stan and I focused on getting in Rockland were video cameras. We'll set up several cameras and link them to the wifi system. So we'll be able to see what's going on. For example, Browns Head Light is a lighthouse on top of a home on the island's northwest corner. It's a navigational aid for mariners, but for us, it's a perfect lookout spot to view West Penobscot Bay. These cameras will see any boat approaching from the mainland."

"Those webcams have visibility that can see the mainland?"

"No," interjected Stan. "That's the genius of this surveillance system. We don't have high-resolution long-range cameras. But we do have QuAI. She can monitor all these cameras 24/7 and use her AI to identify the change in pixels to extrapolate information impossible for the human eye to discern. A speck on the video might seem like nothing to us watching it, but the AI would detect a movement pattern by that speck that would be interpreted as a boat. QuAI could then notify us in real time and provide early warning. So instead of having to post a full-time sentry with binoculars, we can use QuAI."

"Sorry for all the questions," said Clare. "I'm not a skeptic, just interested. It sounds amazing."

"Yeah," said Stan. "I think it's a game-changer as far as security goes."

"And how long do you think it will take to get set up?" Matt asked.

"I think we could probably have it ready today, Matt," answered Liz. "Emily and Charlotte Oliver have volunteered to help. They know the island's north side well and have already picked out the houses we'd need to set up the routers. If Juliet and I go this morning, I think we could have this in place by dark, at the latest."

"Okay," said Matt. "Well, Stan, it's your team. But I think this is a very high priority. If The Base is going to control Maine, as QuAI says is imminent, then we need to know if anyone's coming across to Vinalhaven by boat."

"I second that," said Pete.

Stan and Clare were both nodding as well. "Agreed," said Stan. "Liz, take a vehicle and go grab Juliet. She stayed over at the farmhouse last night. Your main focus is getting this up and running. If you need help with labor or anything, call on the radio, and we'll get what you need."

"Okay," replied Liz. "I'll go now. I'll see if LT and Derek will go with us as well. They can help clear the houses, and also, if we need to do any heavy lifting with the ladders."

"I love it when a plan comes together," concluded Stan.

CHAPTER 39

October 24, 12:44pm

Marvi, Michelle, and Clare sat at the dining room table in Carver Main after enjoying a delicious lunch of beef stew while Matt did the dishes. Michelle and Dave still had a large freezer full of meat, and Clare had made a beef stew with fresh potatoes and carrots from Roberts Hill Farm. Pete, Dave, and Stan had departed a few minutes prior - Stan to head up to the barn while Pete and Dave went out to add some improvements to the two yachts moored in the cove.

Matt enjoyed washing the dishes and found himself relaxing while scrubbing the stack of bowls before him. Things on Vinalhaven were coming together. Roberts Hill Farm was turning out to be a huge success, and the island's residents were beginning to work together. Tim had helped ready two more lobster boats in Carver Harbor and was teaching the Biancos and Aghas about lobstering, crabbing, and fishing. The Norgaards, the family from Denmark, had proven especially helpful. Filip was an engineer and was working closely with Vance Davis to ensure their windmill generators were serviced correctly, while his wife Astrid was teaching Molly all about efficient ways to grow fruits and vegetables in the greenhouse in winter. Janet Oliver and her oldest daughter routinely assisted Molly and the others at the Farm, while the younger two daughters had hit it off with Julia and Liz - all four of which were now hard at work on the island's new surveillance system.

"Matt, can I talk to you for a sec?" Matt looked up to see Stan standing in the back doorway leading to the mudroom and the barn.

"Sure thing," said Matt, turning off the water and wiping his hands on a dishtowel. Stan turned and retreated into the mudroom, so Matt followed. When Matt got to the mudroom, Stan handed Matt the heavy zip-up fleece Matt often wore, as Stan himself slipped into an old Barbour jacket.

"Let's go for a quick walk. I want to check something out and figured we could kill two birds with one stone."

"No problem, let's go."

They walked out the rear door of the mudroom and followed the crushed stone pathway around the back of the barn and then onto the gravel road that led a hundred yards to the stone wharf and the cottage where Stan and Marvi were staying.

"So what's up, Stan? Any updates from QuAI on The Base's attack on Portland?"

"Yeah, that's partly what I wanted to discuss."

They sauntered along the road following the north edge of Carver Cove, heading toward the ocean to their east. Immediately to Matt's right, Pete and Dave were aboard the Hinckley moored in the middle of the cove. Matt gave them a quick wave which Dave promptly returned before refocusing on whatever task he was doing in the yacht.

"The situation in Portland is dire," continued Stan. "QuAI's been able to tap into real-time satellite imagery, a satellite phone, and other high-powered radio communications. Simply stated, The Base is routing Condretti's forces."

"How big of a battle are we talking, Stan? You had all those symbols on the map yesterday, but the largest-sized element I saw was company-sized. That's normally about a hundred to a hundred and twenty soldiers. What size force does The Base have attacking Portland?"

"QuAI says 3,500 attackers. About 3,200 of them hit Portland this morning, with 300 or so as the fixing force crossing over from northern New Hampshire to put roadblocks on I-95 around Augusta and Waterville to prevent Bangor from sending reinforcements."

"Any mechanized infantry? Bradleys or anything like that?"

"No. It is all-wheeled vehicles in the form of Humvees, LMTV transport trucks, civilian pickups, SUVs, and buses.

"And how many defenders does Condretti have? You said he likely has 20,000 people in Portland."

"Had, you mean? Condretti is dead."

"Shit. That's not good."

"No. He was apparently killed before the battle began. The Base infiltrated Portland and wreaked havoc on the command staff before they even woke up."

"So, are the defenders putting up a good fight?"

"Again, past tense, Matt. Yes, some of them put up a good fight. Especially the two batteries of 105mm howitzers that Condretti brought from Portsmouth. They're now mostly dead. Others fled, and even more just capitulated."

"Not the outcome we were hoping for."

"That's an understatement."

"And I assume The Base is now continuing up I-95."

"Yes, but not all of them. QuAI estimates they kept 1,000 or so of their forces back and sent about 1,500 north to Augusta to link up with their forward element."

"1,500? That leaves 700 unaccounted for out of the 3,200."

"Dead."

"Oh shit. That's some serious fucking carnage this morning. So if they won, they must have killed at least two or three times that."

"3,000 minimum. Possibly more. QuAI is intercepting reports of mass killings, rapes, you name it."

"Fucking barbarians," said Matt. "Any good news, Stan?"

"Maybe. QuAI has intel that a platoon plus of Marine reservists escaped and headed back to their armory, which is in Brunswick. That's on Route 1, not I-95. So they're basically providing a blocking force for us in case The Base wants to head up Route 1. The Marine platoon would just be a speed bump, but QuAI would know The Base is coming."

"Okay, well, at least that's something. Poor fucking jarheads, though. Jesus, 3,000 defenders killed in six hours. That's a lot, Stan. Like a fucking bloodbath."

"Yeah, it is." They had reached Stan's cottage, but Stan showed no inclination to stop. "C'mon, let's keep walking. I wanted to show you this next house." They both continued slowly walking along the gravel road, which turned slightly to follow the curve of the cove. Roberts Harbor opened up before them, with Sheep Island directly to their front, protecting the small harbor from the rolling waves of the Atlantic Ocean.

"I also want to discuss something else with you," continued Stan.

"That doesn't sound good."

"It's not."

"I'm a big boy, Stan. What is it."

"Over the last two days, QuAI has detected someone probing into her activities."

"You mean someone has gotten into her underground bunker? I thought you said that was impenetrable?"

"No, not probing her physically. The bunker in Charlottesville is completely impenetrable, and there are no indications of tampering other than people entering the main office building, which is nowhere near QuAI's data center."

"So what do you mean by probing."

"Well, let me try to explain it." Stan stopped as they were standing in front of a small cottage near the water's edge. The view from this spot was incredible. Not only could they see the entire bay opening up to their southeast, but their slight elevation allowed them to see past Narrows Island to the east, all the way to Isle Au Haut, about eight miles away due east. Anyone approaching Vinalhaven from the eastern side would easily be spotted from this spot. "As I've told you before, QuAI has some pretty incredible access to a wide range of sensors because of our military and civilian contracts. She could see things that the NSA didn't have access to on the commercial side, even before the cataclysm. And like I mentioned the other day, with the human analysis power severely depleted from what little remains of the US intelligence agencies, QuAI's ability to analyze data and use AI to produce intelligence estimates far surpasses anything Cheyenne Mountain or anyone else in the world is capable of."

"Yes, you said that yesterday. What does that have to do with probing?" Matt asked.

"QuAI has detected someone in Cheyenne Mountain trying to gain access to sensors that QuAI has access to but that Cheyenne Mountain does not. The best example is the Hawkeye 360 satellite system which provides us with incredible data on RF signals worldwide. My company had a business relationship with the Hawkeye team. In fact, we were an early investor, but the USG only had partial access to the system, which disappeared when the power went out. Headquartered in southeast DC, there is no Hawkeye office to call to renew their subscription. See what I'm getting at."

"Yeah. Sort of. How much more can we see than what Cheyenne Mountain can see?"

"Mmmmm, maybe 100 times more? Maybe 1,000? It's hard to quantify. For example, Cheyenne Mountain can still control some Keyhole satellites and maneuver them into the orbit they want, et cetera. QuAI can see everything they can see. They can't turn us off because they no longer have access to those permissions, and the people formerly responsible for that are likely dead of smallpox. But QuAI can see Hawkeye 360 and a dozen other commercial systems that the US government can't. But even more importantly, like a million times more importantly, QuAI does the analysis for us.

"Cheyenne Mountain may have several schmucks sitting in the bunker looking at hi-res satellite images of Portland right now and trying to figure out what is happening. Someone at another desk, in another part of the bunker, is possibly analyzing RF data or querying the database of recently collected satellite calls. Or maybe that person is on a ship in Norfolk or a submarine in Oahu. They lack the ability to put it all together.

"While QuAI uses AI to put it all together, almost instantly," said Matt, finishing Stan's thought.

"Exactly!"

"Okay, I get it. But what's relevant about the probes?"

"QuAI believes someone in Cheyenne Mountain is on to us. That they know we have this capability. A capability that is exponentially greater than theirs."

"And this is bad? I thought we had contact with Cheyenne Mountain?"

"Well, we do. Kind of. I've spoken with a couple people I know who survived and are now part of the National Command Authority staff. I've hesitated to tell them that the entire QuAI system is still functioning and that we are tapping into it. They just think we have a good computer system, as they do, and are using it on our own, but without the massive artificial intelligence capability and the largest data center remaining in the world. Now someone is trying to follow our access through some of their systems and to see what we're looking for and how we're using it."

"Okay," said Matt. "So, like The Base, you think they may want what we have?"

"Exactly."

"Okay, that's definitely something to think about..."

"There's more," interjected Stan.

"Great. There's always more."

"QuAI is pretty certain that the person in Cheyenne Mountain is collaborating with The Base."

"You're fucking kidding me? How could QuAI possibly know that?"

"I told you, Matt, but I know it's almost impossible to comprehend. QuAI is not just data; she's AI. For example, you might see a guy holding a rifle and another person loading a truck. QuAI puts everything about those facts together with everything else in her databanks, and she draws conclusions. For example, she might estimate that those people are readying to go on an offensive, while your conclusion is simply that there are two people, one with a rifle and one loading a truck."

"Okay. I get it. So you're saying, based on everything QuAI knows, she thinks this person is in communications with The Base."

"Exactly. And likely more than one person."

"That's definitely not good."

"No. No, it isn't."

CHAPTER 40

October 24, 9:18pm

Matt walked up the stairs to the barn's second floor. Stan and Juliet sat on couches reading reports. As he crested the top step, Liz walked out of the QuAI server room with a sheaf of papers.

"Hey, Matt. How's it going? Great dinner, by the way."

"My pleasure, Liz. I'm the man with a plan when you need a gourmet meal."

Liz rolled her eyes at Matt's comment. He had cooked dinner for the eight of them that evening - a specialty of Spam, baked beans, and a side of canned mixed vegetables. It was far from gourmet, but no one complained, and several people asked for seconds. They were limited in their fresh food options, and everyone wanted to take a night off from seafood. *Who would have thought we'd be sick of eating lobster?*

"Just checking in with you guys. What's the word on Bangor?"

Stan looked up from the papers he was reading. "Still holding out, surprisingly."

"No shit?"

"No shit. Their commander is a guy named Scott Barsin, 19th Special Forces Group out of the Rhode Island National Guard."

"Scotty Barsin, huh? I know him - pretty well, actually," said Matt. "He's a Major. Sharp guy. Led an A-team in 3rd Group in the 'Stan, then went into the Guard. What's he doing in Bangor?"

"That, we don't know. But apparently, he's there now and

has been put in charge by Governor Babbit of the defenses for all of Bangor and Castine."

"No shit?"

"You keep saying that," said Stan, smiling.

"Yeah, I'm trying to imagine Scotty Barsin defending an American city against a horde of barbarians who happen to be fellow Americans."

"I know, it's a lot to take in. Everyone always thought in terms of World War III. What we really have is Civil War II."

"So, how's he holding out? Did they build solid defenses?"

"No. Almost the opposite. He built kill boxes and used two things The Base didn't count on."

What's that?" Matt asked.

"Artillery and helicopters. First, he put up obstacles on I-95 that vectored the initial Base columns into chokepoints that he had dialed in with artillery. Seems as if Condretti sent a battery of six towed 105mm howitzers north before The Base attacked. Barsin had them sighted in on several key boxes. When the enemy vehicle entered, they let loose. These Humvees are mostly unarmored, but even the armored ones can be immobilized by artillery. Troops in pickups and Greyhound buses were decimated."

"Wow. Smart."

"Yeah, but then the artillery ran out of ammo, and The Base kept coming."

"So helicopters? UH-60s? I can't imagine the National Guard here has Apaches."

"Yes. UH-60 Blackhawks. There are at least two detachments there in Bangor at the airport. He had his defensive positions hold what they could, and every time they were about to be overrun, he put up a helicopter with door gunners. The M240 door gunners would shred the attackers and then the helicopter would disappear before the Base could return fire. The Base has no anti-aircraft capability, it seems."

"So, what's the situation now?"

"Stalemate," said Stan.

"Not for long," said Liz. "Here, I was just bringing you QuAI's latest estimate."

Stan took the two pages of computer paper from Liz and quickly read through it. "Shit."

"What?" Matt and Juliet both asked simultaneously.

"QuAI reports that helicopters are moving north from Fort Devens toward Portland. She estimates that these are four Blackhawks that will stop at the Portland airport, now under The Base's control, to refuel. After topping their tanks, they'll fly north to Bangor to take on Barsin's helos."

"Wow. Air-to-air combat using M240 machine guns in helicopters," said Matt. "And does QuAI predict a winner?"

"Of course, she does, Matthew. Have I taught you nothing about QuAI?" Stan paused. "She estimates that The Base's helicopters will surprise the defensive ones. They'll either catch them unaware in the air or, more likely, will strafe them on the ground while they sleep. She estimates that Bangor will fall by 10 am tomorrow morning."

CHAPTER 41

October 25, 08:40am

Stan walked into the downstairs den, which Matt had turned into his sanctuary to get away and think about things. He was currently looking at some nautical charts.

"Bangor has fallen."

"Okay," said Matt, a bit sadly. "I guess we knew the outcome. Any word on survivors? Casualty estimates?"

"Yeah, but not as precise as Portland. Estimates are 600-800 attackers killed and about 1,500 defenders, including those who fought and people hunkering down in Bangor."

"Damn. Any word on Barsin? How about Governor Babbit?

"Barsin, no word, but QuAI did provide some interesting info that I'll get to in a sec. Babbit was captured. There's no word on what they'll do with her, but QuAI posits the likelihood that they will bring her to Philadelphia at over 60% probability. Interestingly, unlike Portland, where the people mostly surrendered, those in Bangor simply melted into the countryside. Barsin had provided some preparation, and when the signal was given, there appeared to be a mass exodus from the city. Several dozen large boats headed down the Penobscot River at high speed, while other RF signals indicated that people drove vehicles north, possibly heading for Canada."

"Did The Base pursue?"

"No, actually. They torched some things, summarily executed many of the remaining people, and appear to now be moving southward along I-95," said Stan.

"You mentioned Scott Barsin and some additional information?"

"Yes. I did. QuAI noted that most of the fleeing boats went all the way down the Penobscot River and turned northeast toward Southwest Harbor; their final destination was likely Canada. Two of the boats, however, capable of carrying a total of about thirty people, stopped at Fort Knox."

"Are you referring to that huge granite fort from the 1800s? The one right on the side of the river by the Penobscot Narrows Bridge?"

"Exactly. QuAI believes this is likely Major Barsin and some of his military personnel. They use the same radio frequencies to command the battle in Bangor through the night. These radios are now stationary inside the old fort."

"Interesting," said Matt. "We'll have to keep that in mind. Any indications that The Base is moving down Route 1?"

"None at all."

"Okay, Stan. Thanks for the update. Need anything from me? I'm still trying to wrap my head around everything you told me yesterday. As peaceful as it seems here, everywhere else seems to be hanging on by a thread."

"Yeah, I couldn't agree more. I'm going to keep plugging along up in the barn. I'll let you know if we hear anything new."

"Hey, how's the surveillance system coming?"

"Good. I'm hoping to hear from Juliet soon over the radio. They've installed all the cameras and are working with the Oliver girls to get all the wifi extenders in place and tuned into the right network. The plan is to troubleshoot it today and hopefully have everything working by this evening. I'm working right now on having QuAI learn to identify anything approaching the island."

"That's cool. Let me know if I can help with anything."

"Will do."

Stan departed, and Matt returned to the charts on his desk. Looking at his watch, Matt reached over and picked up the satellite phone on his desk. It was plugged into an external antenna to be used inside the house. The ringer was at full volume to alert anyone in the house should someone ever call. Matt picked up the phone and pressed speed dial #1.

Ring, Ring

Ring, Ring

Ring, Ring

"Howzit, mate? Good to hear from you. How are things on your side of the pond?" It was great to hear his friend Rob's voice. They tried to speak weekly, but with all the uncertainty, Matt was never sure if Rob was still alive until he answered.

"Interesting, man. Definitely interesting."

"Yeah? Pretty dull here, I have to say, bru. Lots of work on the farm, cookin' a braai every night. Almost becoming normal."

"Island life so far has been good too. We took over a small farm, and our group and the island residents are starting to come together. Can't complain, really. But on the mainland, it's getting a bit crazy."

"Yeah, I'm hearing similar things as well. These Base fuckers are quite somethin' else."

"Hey, you still talk to Roy Brownley? Or anyone else in Cheyenne Mountain?"

"Yeah, I do. Just about every week. I talk to him and Chris Harbinson. Remember him?"

"Yeah, I think so. South African guy who joined the Seals? Was DEVGRU before going to Langley?"

"The one and only. He actually left Cheyenne Mountain and is in Oahu now. Seems like the government's main effort is building up Oahu. Everything there is intact, and they have the infrastructure to support pretty much everyone left."

"Interesting. What's he doing in Oahu?"

"He's been tasked with setting up the intel center there, especially the maritime focus. But he says it's kind of a goat rodeo at Cheyenne Mountain; lots of conflicting guidance. He was just happy to get to Oahu."

"That supports some of the things we've been hearing as

well. It's one of the reasons I called, other than to make sure you hadn't been ass-raped by a bunch of wild gorillas."

Rob laughed loudly into the phone. "Hey, bru, you know me. If there's any ass-rapin to be done, I'll be the on the giving end, not the receiving."

Now it was Matt's turn to chuckle. "Seriously, Rob. I'm very interested to hear if Roy's heard anything about what's happening in Maine. And in particular, if he's heard anything about our group here on Vinalhaven. We're trying to stay under the radar as much as possible."

"Okay. I can definitely ring him up, bru."

"Ring him up, bru? Rob, do you realize how much you sound like a native South African? You do know you're American, right?"

"Yeah, yeah," replied Rob. "I quite like it here, if you can get past all the end-of-the-world-as-we-know-it bullshit. But when everyone around you speaks English with an accent and uses funny words, I guess you naturally just pick it up. Lucy is teaching me Afrikaans. Pretty soon, I might not even speak English!"

Matt laughed before getting serious again. "So you'll talk to Roy Brownley?"

"Yeah, straight away. I'll try him now. He doesn't always answer, but I'll keep trying throughout the day. I'll let you know what he says."

"Oh, and Rob. Tell him we've heard rumors The Base may have some infiltrators in Cheyenne Mountain. Possibly on the intel IT side."

"Got it. I'll pass it along. Talk to you soon."

"Take care, Rob. Say hi to Lucy for us."

Matt disconnected the call and placed the sat phone back on his desk. He picked up the nautical chart in front of him: a detailed map of Vinalhaven and the surrounding islands, including water depth, channel markers, and other critical maritime information. A plan was brewing, but he wasn't quite sure it was either feasible or the right thing to do. *Time will tell. If I've learned anything in the last six weeks, it's better to be safe than sorry.*

CHAPTER 42

October 25, 7:39pm

Clare and Christopher sat on the floor trying to finish a jigsaw puzzle featuring Gillette Stadium, while Liz and Laurie played a game of cards. Matt sat in the oversized leather chair reading a hardcover Stephen King novel he had found on the bookshelf in his office. Having electricity allowed them to enjoy these quiet evenings as a family, and Matt thoroughly enjoyed these relaxing evenings.

The day slipped away as a whisper like they all seemed to, but the afternoon was memorable. Molly had hosted the first all-island dinner party, which was a big hit. It was another clambake. In addition to scores of lobsters provided by Tim and his new team of fishermen, his wife Regina had made a massive pot of absolutely delicious clam chowder using potatoes, carrots, and celery from the Farm. Kelsey and Amey had baked several delicious pies from the preserves in the farm's basement.

Everyone seemed to get along well except for the Biancos and Aghas. Edris Agha, Ferhad's 16-year-old son who went by Eddie, was a shy, skinny, introverted boy who mostly kept to himself. AJ Bianco, who still insisted on carrying his AR-15 rifle everywhere, had turned out to be a bit of a bully and was often giving Eddie a hard time while they were helping Tim out with lobstering.

Matt was not a big fan of AJ, having been forced to counsel him and his father several times to ensure AJ kept his rifle unloaded while he was around other people. AJ had had an accidental discharge several days before, and some residents felt he shouldn't be able to carry a gun. Anthony had initially pushed back in support of his son, but Matt had shut that down. He thought everything had been sorted, when he saw AJ push Eddie during a game of horseshoes the kids had been playing before dinner.

Eddie had picked up the game of horseshoes quite quickly and had become a fan favorite with the other kids. Matt liked the unassuming teenager but could see how the unpopular, know-it-all AJ would single Eddie out as a target for his bullying. Anthony Bianco was a bit of a loudmouth. At the same time, Eddie's father, Ferhad, was a quiet, thoughtful man who, as a biologist at Colby, had proven extremely valuable in helping Molly with winter planting and preparing seeds for spring.

As AJ began pushing Eddie, Matt's first reaction was to rush over and intervene. Ferhad, who Matt was talking to at the time, had witnessed the bullying as well but placed his hand on Matt's arm, holding him back. Ferhad wanted to let his son resolve the situation, and Matt's opinion of Ferhad continued to rise.

Most of the gathering families were impervious to what was happening in the horseshoe area, but several young adults were watching intently. They were too far away for Matt to hear what was being said, but it was clear that both Dylan and LT were telling AJ to knock it off. Eddie attempted to ignore AJ and bent down to pick up a horseshoe from the ground. AJ stepped forward, shoving Eddie off-balance and causing him to fall. Eddie jumped up, anger etched on his face, and the two young men squared off. As LT rushed forward to intervene, Eddie moved with a quickness Matt didn't think possible. Eddie feinted to his left, then stepped forward and slammed his fist into AJ's mid-section with a blistering uppercut. AJ buckled at the waist, and Eddie performed a simple leg sweep causing AJ to collapse in a heap on the ground, where he lay groaning and attempting to catch his breath.

Tony Bianco started yelling and ran over to help his son, verbally berating Eddie for hitting his son and chastising the others for letting this happen. Ferhad walked over calmly, took his son aside, and whispered in his ear for a moment. Matt had also walked over, wanting to make sure things didn't get out of hand, while the remainder of the island's residences looked on from where they stood or sat in the open barn.

Eddie walked away from his father and strode up to AJ. "AJ, please accept my apologies for striking you. It was wrong of me to do so, and I'm sorry."

"Go fuck yourself, you fuckin' haji pussy," AJ hissed, still being comforted by his father. "You're lucky our dads are here, or I'd fuckin' kill you."

Eddie stood there solemnly, unwilling to take the bait.

Instead of scolding his son and forcing him to apologize as well, Tony continued to pat his son's back and turned him around to walk toward their parked car on the other side of the barn. "C'mon, Gianna, go grab your mother. We're leaving," said Tony.

Standing in a group with Kelsey and the eldest Oliver daughter, Gianna made no move to comply with her father's directive.

"Let's go, Gianna. Now," Tony said sternly.

"I'm gonna stay, Dad. I'll get a ride home with the Olivers."

Tony looked coldly at his daughter. For a second, Matt thought Tony would walk over and grab her, but Tony shook his head in disgust and continued leading his son toward the car. Camila Bianco, holding a glass of wine and watching from the barn with the residents, was embarrassed and unsure of what to do. After hesitating, she placed her wine glass on the table, apologized to those around her, and shuffled off to join her husband and son as they got into their vehicle and drove off.

Everyone seemed to look around at each other for a few moments. The spell was broken when Christopher shouted for Eddie to continue the horseshoe game. The dinner party returned to normal, with the Agha family stock rising considerably amongst those in attendance.

As Matt now sat in the living room, the hardback novel resting on his lap, Matt thought he would have to speak with Tony Bianco about AJ and weapons. It was probably necessary to have the young man go unarmed for the foreseeable future.

Matt's reverie was interrupted by the shrill ringing of the satellite phone from his office on the other side of the house. Before Matt could get up, Liz sprang to her feet. "I'll get it!" She said and dashed out of the room.

In seconds, Liz was sprinting back into the living room, holding the satellite phone in her outstretched hand, her face ashen. "Matt! It's for you. Hurry!"

Matt jumped up and grabbed the phone from Liz, placing it immediately to his ear. "Hello? This is Matt."

"Matt?" Yelled a panicked feminine voice. "It's Kim! They're here! What do I do!" She hissed on the verge of hysteria. Through the phone, Matt heard a stuttering of loud noises in the background, which sounded like automatic gunfire.

"Calm down, Kim. Deep breaths. There you go. Deep breaths. Now tell me, what's happening?"

"I don't know, Matt! Three jeeps just pulled up and started shooting. They've killed some, and they have Judy tied to the hood, her shirt's ripped off. They're coming now, Matt!"

"Okay, Kim. Stay calm. Do what you need to do to stay alive. Just go along, Kim. We'll be there as soon as we can. Okay."

"Hurry!" The phone went dead.

Matt looked up, and everyone was staring at him. They could tell by Matt's side of the conversation that something terrible was happening. "Someone is attacking Kim at the Samoset Resort. She said three vehicles, and my guess: it's three Humvees from The Base. We need to help her."

"Matt, wait a second. Before you go running off, let's think about this for a minute. You don't need to go rushing off and getting killed. We hardly know those people and certainly don't owe them anything," shouted Clare.

Part of Matt knew she was right, but the other part knew that the right thing to do was help. "Clare, listen. We need to go. If it's The Base, I want to deal with them in Rockland and not here on Vinalhaven. We could be their next target if they get any of Kim's group to tell them about us here on the island. And we know what they do to women. We can't just let it happen. We can't."

"Matt, please. Think about your family. This isn't your fight."

"It is, Clare. I know you think it isn't, but we can't let them occupy Rockland. If they do, we will live every moment in fear. Please trust me. I've thought this scenario through dozens of times before this even happened. We need to go."

"Okay," said Clare, capitulating. "I do trust you. Completely. What can we do."

"Liz, go get Pete and your dad in the barn. Tell them what's happening and that the A-team leaves in ten minutes. Then run over and get Dave. Clare, please call the Farm on the radio. Alert the A-team. Tell them we need them here in less than ten minutes."

"Can I go, Daddy?" Christopher asked, wanting to be a part of all the excitement.

"Hey, buddy. Not this time, okay. But I do need your help, and it's super important. While I'm gone, I need you to watch over your sister and mom. Okay?"

"I'm on it, Dad. I won't let you down."

Matt rushed upstairs as he heard Clare grab the radio handset from the kitchen counter and call the farmhouse. Over the last week, with everyone living in a few separate locations, Matt had briefed his extended family on several contingency plans that he felt were most important. One of these was the creation of the A-team. In addition to Matt, this included Pete, Stan, Liz, and Dave, who lived in houses around the cove, and Grace, LT, Juliet, Derek, and Dylan, who were staying at Roberts Hill Farm. Everyone thought the term A-team referred to the 12-man unit used by Special Forces, but Matt had really named it after the renegades-turned-heroes of the 80's television series with Mr. T and George Peppard.

CHAPTER 43

October 25, 8:53pm

Matt sat in the front-facing passenger seat of the Hinckley 35 as they eased closer to shore. High tide was exactly 9:27 pm, so Matt couldn't have planned the timing any better. Matt had already briefed the team, and everyone on the yacht sat silently, reviewing the tasks they were each responsible for and visualizing how it could all play out.

Everyone had assembled as fast as possible, and within ten minutes of receiving the call, Matt was handing out weapons and magazines from the room on the barn's first floor, which served as their armory. Matt kept his vest fully loaded with everything he usually carried, grabbed his M4 and the M320, and a bandoleer of 40mm grenades. Most everyone already had their M4 and assault kit with them, but Matt handed the three Remington 700 sniper rifles to Liz to carry to the boat. LT grabbed the M240B, while Derek and Dylan grabbed several boxes of linked 7.62mm and a rucksack full of 30-round magazines for the M4s. Grace had the first aid kit she always carried, but she also grabbed the trauma kit they had put together. Lastly, Matt tasked Juliet with grabbing several dry bags for waterproofing their night vision goggles and scopes.

While the loadout was happening, Pete and Dave readied the Hinckley and positioned it alongside the stone pier so everyone could board. They had to be slow and careful navigating Roberts Harbor at night, but once they reached the open bay, Pete showed everyone why the Hinckley was a million-dollar boat. They cruised easily at over forty knots per hour, the boat surging on a following swell as it sped toward Rockland Harbor.

Stan had downloaded maps of the Samoset Resort and satellite images and passed them around as soon as they boarded. Kim had briefly explained to Matt in a previous conversation where her group was set up in the resort, so Matt used that to form the basis of his plan.

Rockland Harbor was shaped like a huge C, with the opening facing due east into Penobscot Bay. The bottom of the C extended out a bit farther than the top and was named Owls Head. At the same time, the Samoset Resort was located at the very tip of the top part of the C. Jutting out from the Samoset Resort, pointing directly southeast and extending almost halfway toward the other lip of the C, was a 4,000-foot long breakwater. The breakwater had been built entirely of granite blocks in the 1890s and had withstood the pounding of the Atlantic Ocean for almost 130 years. At the end of the breakwater was a lighthouse, whose solar-powered light still shown brightly even though all power on the mainland had been out for almost six weeks.

The Samoset Resort itself, while positioned at the top of the C, faced outward toward Penobscot Bay north of the breakwater instead of facing inward toward Rockland Harbor. The resort's southern boundary was a narrow lane called Samoset Road that led from the Staples store on Route 1 back to the Rockland breakwater. The north side of the road was the resort's southern boundary, while across the street to the south was a row of single-family homes on tree-filled waterfront lots.

Inside the long, granite breakwater and immediately adjacent to the homes off Samoset Road was a floating pier connected to land by an aluminum walkway that moved up and down with the tide. This was their destination, and they were currently on final approach about two hundred meters out. Matt was still in awe at how quiet the Hinckley's twin outboard engines were, and as they cruised toward the dock, everything seemed eerily silent. The remainder of the harbor was dark, the far shoreline visible as a shadow in the faint light of a quarter moon.

Liz and Dave moved to the bow and stern of the yacht to tie it to the pier once Pete expertly maneuvered the boat alongside. As soon as they were firmly tied up, everyone moved toward their assigned position. Like every successful raid, Matt had split his force into two teams: assault and overwatch. His initial plan had been to drop the overwatch here at the pier and then have Pete speed around the breakwater to drop Matt and his assault team onto the bayside beach, which would have been a great angle to approach the resort. However, while this often worked in the movies, the reality was that it was the end of October with a nighttime air temperature of under forty degrees and the water temp probably being about the same. Matt knew from experience how being wet and cold could instantly sap all of your strength and make a person combat ineffective within minutes.

His current plan was much simpler and offered the most versatility while still being easy to command. Both overwatch and assault elements would exit the boat at the pier. Stan was to take his overwatch element - Liz, Derek, and Dylan - and find a position on the north side of Samoset Road that allowed them to look down into the resort's pool area and along the front of the hotel. Matt and his assault element of Dave, Pete, Juliet, LT, and Grace would swing around to the east along the shoreline, then move back toward the hotel at a 90-degree angle to the overwatch team. A basic 'end around' maneuver. This allowed the overwatch to place accurate fire onto the objective and shift fire to the left as the assault element bounded across the objective. Keep it simple, stupid.

That was the plan anyway - a plan Matt had made while bouncing along in a boat without knowing anything about what was happening at the resort.

Matt and Clare had stayed at the resort several years prior, so Matt felt he knew it somewhat well. Samoset Resort sat on 230 acres along the north side of Rockland Harbor. The resort's main buildings and conference center were arranged in a semi-circle, with three 4-story hotel buildings built as spokes off the semi-circle pointing toward the ocean. Adjacent were three additional and separate four-story buildings containing hundreds of hotel rooms. All the buildings were set back approximately 150 meters from the rocky beach, with several holes of an 18-hole golf course filling the area between the hotel buildings and the water. On the southern edge of the hotel, closest to Rockland Harbor, was a large resort-style pool with a snack bar and dozens of patio loungers. Tucked around the pool were three small bungalows built in a stand of trees.

From a brief conversation with Kim on the sat phone a few days prior, Matt understood that Kim's group primarily occupied the ground floor of the hotel nearest to the pool, while Kim and a couple of teaching assistants occupied the bungalows. They used the snack bar at the pool as their common area, as it was between their two occupied areas and had a fireplace and outdoor grills for cooking food.

Matt assumed Kim's group and the attackers would likely be in this outdoor area. If he had to enter the hotel's main lobby, his entire overwatch plan would be useless.

Matt had already fastened his night vision goggles, referred to as NODs, onto his head, and he clicked the tubes down over his eyes as he exited the Hinckley and walked up the pier. Dave, who was also very familiar with the Samoset, was bringing up the rear of the assault team. Matt walked briskly, almost at a trot. They had a lot of ground to cover, and every second counted in a situation like this. In addition to being loaded for bear, everyone had a handheld radio on their vest and an earpiece that allowed them to listen silently.

Matt led the assault element east to the breakwater, then cut northward, staying along the edge of the golf course closest to the rocky shoreline. The easterly wind cut across Matt's face and sliced frigidly through his cargo pants. *Man, am I glad I didn't go with Plan A and swim ashore! I'd have a severe case of shrinkage and would be shivering my brains out right about now.*

When Matt reached a point about a hundred yards north of the breakwater and directly seaward of the three bungalows, he brought his team to a halt, lay down, and kneeled in some sand bunkers on the golf course. Matt remembered playing this hole #4 - a par-5 dogleg that hugged the shoreline. Matt recalled that he had put two balls in the water off the tee, and hoped they fared better this evening than he had that day on the links. Looking up through his NODs at the looming hotel buildings in the distance, Matt detected light coming from where he knew the pool to be. He couldn't tell what was creating the light.

"Stan, this is Matt. We're at the release point."

"Roger, we're getting into position now. I should have eyes on in a sec. Wait one."

Matt was confident that Stan would execute his two tasks with precision. His first task was emplacing the family's two best sharpshooters, Liz and Dylan, in a position where they could use their sniper rifles to provide everyone with details of the objective. His second task was to find a good spot for Derek with the M240B machine gun - where Derek could rain accurate machine-gun fire onto the objective should it be needed.

Although one of the most challenging things to do while commanding an operation, Matt waited patiently in the sand bunker. Calling Stan on the radio would not make him do his job faster, and it would only make everyone more anxious than they already were. Instead, he looked around at his assault team and gave everyone the thumbs up and a quick nod.

Without Matt saying anything, Dave had positioned LT and Grace to face northward and protect their right flank. As a Ranger-qualified paratrooper and former NCO, Dave played the platoon sergeant role well, which allowed Matt to focus on tactics and decision-making.

"Matt, we have eyes on. I'll let Dylan describe it."

"Assault, this is Dylan. It's bad," came Dylan's voice through the radio. Matt could instantly tell that whatever Dylan was about to describe was something his young nephew should never have had to see. "All activity centers around the resort pool, where they have a lantern. I see four women standing, each tied to the columns of the pool's snack bar. There are six men, all armed with sidearms and some with assault rifles. There appear to be several, maybe as many as six, bodies floating in the pool. Facedown and not moving."

"Roger, Dylan," said Matt into his throat mic. "What are they doing now? Are they all awake."

"Yes." There was a noticeable pause in the transmission. "They are raping two of the women. One is tied up, and the other is pinned down atop one of the tables."

"Okay. Do you see any sentries? Can you see their vehicles?"

"No sentries visible," replied Dylan.

"Matt, this is Derek. I'm in overwatch just to the north of Dylan. I can see three hardshell Humvees parked in the parking lot. Lights off. No one visible in any of the vehicles."

"Roger. Wait one," said Matt.

Matt hissed, and everyone immediately gathered around him. "Listen up. We're going to assault right now. We can't afford to wait until they're asleep. We're all going around the left side of the bungalows; that way, we're not shooting back toward our overwatch. The satellite photo shows a couple more sand bunkers about thirty meters, just shy of the pool area. You four drop off there and cover us. Pete and Juliet, focus on covering the main hotel buildings. Grace and LT, you take the left side. Dave and I will try to get as close as we can right up the middle. Hopefully, we can get close enough to drop everyone without hitting any of the women. Be alert for squirters heading toward the hotel to our right and also for anyone we might not have seen. They could be in the bungalows or in the hotel. Got it?"

Everyone nodded their heads affirmatively.

"Overwatch, this is Matt." Matt paused, organizing his

thoughts to ensure his next words were clear and concise. "Assault element will move forward quietly and stop short of the pool. Snipers, each select one target and then alternates. Do not fire until you see us fire or if the enemy reacts to our approach. Dave and I each have lasers on our rifles. You'll see the targets we will shoot first, so shift your primary target to someone else. Derek, do not fire into the pool area because of the hostages. Focus on the area between the pool and the Humvees. Take out any fleeing enemy or anyone in the Humvees. Stan, please keep an eye on the hotel. Three Humvees could hold twelve people, and we've only accounted for six."

"Overwatch copies," replied Stan.

"Let's go," said Matt.

He hopped out of the sand bunker and jogged across the fairway to the left side of the bungalows. He knew they were out of sight of the pool, so speed was of the essence. He saw the double sand bunker he had pointed out from the satellite image and vectored the group toward it. They were about thirty yards short of the concrete apron for the pool. A low chainlink fence surrounded the pool area, but that didn't concern Matt. This fight would be won or lost from outside the wire.

"At the bunkers," Matt whispered into his radio. A single affirmative click came back as a reply. Stan was watching their progress.

Matt touched Dave's shoulder and leaned over to whisper in his ear. "There's no need to get closer. We can drop these guys from here."

"Agreed."

"Take the rapist by the pole. I'll get the one on top of the woman," Matt whispered to Dave, then toggled his mic. "We'll take the two rapists. Firing in ten seconds."

Matt clicked on his laser and moved it directly onto the man raping the woman on the table. Matt was close enough to feel confident in a headshot and didn't want to risk hitting the woman. He noticed Dave's laser center mass on the man assaulting the woman by the column. He had her hands tied around the pole, standing behind her and holding her from behind. Before Matt's blood began to boil, he refocused on his own target. Matt slowly took up the slack on his trigger, pressing ever so gently, the laser dot unmoving on the back of the man's head.

Breathe in.

Breathe out.

Bang!

Matt fired, then shifted his aim to the other man standing by the table, holding onto the woman's head. Without thinking, he squeezed the trigger and watched the man drop. Matt immediately pumped two more rounds into the man's crumpled body, then shifted back to his first target, who had fallen on top of the woman he was raping. Matt pivoted his aim but saw no more living targets in the pool area. All six men were down. Matt flicked up his NODs.

Matt heard screaming and watched through his ACOG as the woman on the table shoved the man off her and slithered onto the ground. Matt knew this man was dead as his brains were all over the place, but he fired two more rounds into his head on principle.

Matt flipped his NODs back down and scanned the area. The women had all dropped to their knees while still tied to the columns and were shielding themselves as best they could.

Boom.Boom.Boom.Boom

Boom.Boom.Boom.Boom.Boom.Boom.

Boom.Boom.Boom.Boom.Boom.Boom.

Derek was pounding away on the M240B, and Matt could see his rounds streaking behind the pool area and up into a ground floor room of the hotel.

Boom.Boom.Boom.Boom.Boom.Boom.

Boom.Boom.Boom.Boom.

Boom.Boom.Boom.Boom.

Matt watched as Derek's six-to-nine round bursts

obliterated the open hotel room door and shattered the plate glass window. Matt could see one dead body lying in the doorway. Flashes from automatic rifle fire burst from the darkened room behind the open curtain now blowing in the wind. Derek followed with a sustained fifteen-to-twenty round burst aimed directly at the muzzle flashes. The room went silent.

All Matt could hear was the screaming of a woman with sobbing from others in the background.

"Cease fire! Cease fire," Matt said into his radio. Turning to his assault team, Matt shouted, "Dave, Pete, LT, go clear that hotel room and secure the building. Grace, Juliet, come with me."

Matt got up and began walking toward the pool. His NODs were down, and he continued to scan for threats. He could sense Grace behind him and to his left.

He toggled his mic again. "Overwatch, assault element moving to clear pool and the hotel room. Shift your fires to cover the parking lot. Any movement at the Humvees?"

"Negative," replied Derek immediately, instantly relieving Matt's worrying mind. Matt's biggest concern in the assault was whether any crew-served weapons on the enemy Humvees had been manned. They would have chewed up his assault element hiding in the sand bunker.

Matt refocused his attention on the pool area.

The scene before him was unlike anything he'd ever seen. Absolutely horrific. Like right out of some BDSM snuff film. The women were all naked and shivering, four tied to the columns and one crouching behind a chaise lounge. Matt counted five dead bodies floating in the pool, in various states of undress. He was about to try to climb over the waist-high chain link fence when he noticed a latched gate immediately to his right. He pivoted toward it, opened the gate, and motioned for Grace and Juliet to go first. "Check on the women tied to the columns. I'll get the female on the ground," he said, recognizing that woman.

Matt flipped up his NODs and approached the woman slowly, his M4 dangling from its sling and both hands held up, empty and unthreatening. He knelt next to the woman. "Kim? Kim? It's Matt. You're safe."

She looked up at him, her eyes locked in a terrified, hopeless expression that Matt hoped never to see again as long as he lived. It took Kim a second to focus on his face in the darkness, and then she flung herself at him, wrapping her arms around his neck and sobbing uncontrollably.

"It's okay, Kim. I'm here. You're going to be okay." He stroked her back, hugging her tightly, unable to imagine the horrors of her last hour.

"Are they…are they dead? All of them?"

"Yes, Kim. They're all dead. They can't hurt you anymore."

Matt realized she was shivering wildly as she continued to cling to him. Matt looked around, hoping to find some towels. He was hesitant to release his hug as she clung to him so tightly, so Matt continued to kneel there and tried to comfort her. He took one hand and reached for the toggle switch of his mic. "Liz, please come to the pool. Stan, you have control of everything outside the pool. Let me know when it's clear."

Matt continued to hold Kim, not knowing what else to do. Grace and Juliet were cutting the cords that bound each woman to the columns, giving them a hug and leading them to sit in one of the pool chairs. In seconds, Liz appeared at the gate and entered the pool deck. She walked directly to Matt. Even in the dark, Matt could see the look of horror on her face.

"Liz, check out that door there. See if there are any blankets in there or some towels. These women are freezing. We need to keep them from going into shock."

Liz returned in seconds with a large blanket and a handful of towels. Matt took the blanket and wrapped Kim as fully as he could, trying to separate himself from her grasp.

"Don't leave me," she whispered.

"I'm not going anywhere, Kim. We need to get you warm. You've been through a lot, and we need to keep you from going into shock. Okay?"

"Okay. Just...just don't leave me." She wrapped her arms around him again, squeezing him tightly.

After a few more minutes of consoling her, Kim calmed down considerably. She accepted a bottle of water from Liz and was able to take a seat next to her friends.

"Matt, Pete. Hotel room is clear. Two enemy KIA. One friendly KIA and one traumatized. I'm going to walk her down to you. Dave and LT are clearing the main parts of the hotel.

Jesus. What the hell did they do to these women?

Matt assured Kim he wasn't leaving but got her to agree to allow him to step a few feet away. "Roger, Pete. Thanks for the update. Break. Stan, how's the parking lot look? Coordinate with Dave, and let's get those Humvees cleared.

Pete walked up with a young dark-haired woman wrapped in what looked to be a comforter from the hotel bed. He handed her off to his daughter, who, along with Juliet and Grace, was rendering aid and comforting the women sitting in lounge chairs.

"What a fucking nightmare," said Pete, standing close to Matt and speaking low so the women wouldn't hear.

"What happened?"

"Looks like a couple of these ass clowns brought two of their captives up to the room for a little fun. I think we attacked before the festivities began, at least for her - she said her name was Elizabeth. Once the shooting began, she ran into the bathroom and dove for the tub. One shithead was killed outright, and it looks like the other stabbed the second woman in the heart with a fucking bayonet. Derek then tore that guy in half with the 7.62. If you ask me, he got off lightly."

"Jesus," said Matt. "Looks like they killed five of 'em and tossed them in the pool. Kim had told me they had twelve in their group, so that accounts for everyone."

"We need to be sure."

"Yeah, let me ask her. Why don't you get with Stan and see if everything is clear? If it is, maybe take Dylan to the Hinckley and get it ready."

"You gonna bring them back to Vinalhaven?"

"Yeah. I can't think of any better solution, can you?"

"No. Let's get them home and safe. Then they can decide what they want to do."

"Okay, go ready the boat." Matt turned and motioned for Grace to come to him. "Hey, Grace, what do you think?"

"Honestly, it's almost all mental trauma. Some cuts and bruises and one woman might have a broken nose. Other than the obvious trauma, no one's too physically injured."

"Were they all raped? Or just the two we saw?"

"I didn't ask, but I think it was just the two. We can figure that out tomorrow."

"I'm thinking of bringing them back to Vinalhaven. I don't think we can leave them here. What do you think?"

"Definitely. We can't leave them."

"Okay, I'm going to talk with Kim, who's their leader. Can you talk to the others and figure out where their stuff is? Let's get them clothes and pack up whatever we can carry."

"Will do."

"Thanks, Grace." Matt took a few steps back and sat down next to Kim. She was huddled in her blanket, drinking a bottle of water. Matt put his arm around her, not quite sure what to say. Kim beat him to it.

"Thanks, Matt. I owe you my life."

"Kim, I'm so, so sorry this has happened. We got here as soon as we could. I'm so sorry we didn't get here sooner."

"It's not your fault. I'm just so thankful you arrived. All I could think of was that I would end up in the pool like the others." Kim shivered.

"We want to take you back to Vinalhaven. You'll be safe there, and we have plenty of room. Are you okay with that?"

"Yes. I'd like that. I'd like to stay with you if you don't mind. This whole thing has really fucked me up, and I just know that things will be okay if you're there."

"I'm sure we can figure that out when we get to the island.

We have several places to stay, and my wife Clare will help you figure out where everyone should sleep. Does that sound okay?"

"Okay. As long as you're there."

Matt knew she was psychologically attaching his presence to her continued safety. He didn't know what the psychology textbooks called it, but he had seen something similar on the battlefield with wounded soldiers.

Grace was gathering up the women and herding them toward the back gate. She took a few steps over toward where Matt sat with Kim. "Hi Kim, I'm Grace. We're going to take everyone back to the bungalows to get you dressed and get some of your things. Would you like to come with me? You'll feel better when you're dressed."

"Yes. Thanks, Grace. Thank you for everything." Kim stood up and began walking with Grace. She suddenly stopped, turning toward Matt. "Matt? Would you mind coming with us? Please."

Matt looked at Kim, then to Grace, who simply shrugged her shoulders, unsure what to say. The wounded look in Kim's eyes broke Matt's heart. "Sure, Kim. I'll walk with you and wait outside while you get everything."

Kim hugged Matt again. "Thank you."

They walked down to the bungalows. While Matt waited outside, Stan called over the radio. "Matt, this is Stan. Resort is secure. No signs of anyone else. I'd like you to come up and see what we have here."

"Roger, I'll be up in a few. We're getting the women dressed and packed, and then I'll have them escorted to the Hinckley."

"Roger. Pete and Dylan are at the Hinckley. I'll keep everyone else up here until you get here."

Matt waited patiently for about ten minutes, talking with Stan, Pete, and Dave over the radio and ensuring everything was secure. When Kim walked out of the bungalow, she was dressed similar to when they first met at Staples - cargo pants and fleece; although she wore a light-green Helly Hansen hooded shell over the fleece. She carried a large rucksack with several items clipped to the outside. The hurt from her eyes had disappeared, replaced with the same fierceness he had seen outside Staples.

"Okay, Matt. I'm ready. I'd like to get my Glock if possible. The last I saw it, those fuckers tossed all our weapons behind the bar at the pool."

"We'll get it. Is everyone else ready?"

"Not quite. Maybe ten more minutes. But Grace said you needed to leave to go see the Humvees. I'd like to go with you."

"Ah, Kim." Matt wasn't sure exactly how to respond to this request. "Kim, look. I think it might be best for your team if you stay with them. You're their leader."

"No, Matt, I'm not. You're their leader. I'm not a puppy dog; you won't break me. I just feel safer with you. Is that okay?" Matt hesitated, not sure what to say. Kim took a step closer to him. Lowering her voice, she pleaded, "Please, Matt. I'm barely holding things together right now."

"Okay."

"Thank you," said Kim, standing taller and more confident.

"Hey, Grace?" Matt shouted, unsure if the bungalow women were still getting dressed.

"Yeah, Matt," she replied, poking her head out the nearest bungalow door. "What's up?"

"I'm going to take Kim up to the Humvees. Can someone grab her backpack and walk everyone over to the Hinckley? Pete's waiting there with Dylan. If you need help, call on the radio, and we can send someone down."

"No problem. I'd estimate about ten more minutes before we're ready to go."

Matt turned and motioned for Kim to drop her pack and follow him. They walked up to the pool, and Kim found her pistol in a pile of weapons strewn behind the bar. She holstered it in the holster already on her belt. She also picked up an AR-15 with a 2-point sling and slung it overhead, cinching it tightly to the front of her body. Without a word, Kim led Matt around the snack bar and up to the parking lot.

When they arrived, Stan and Dave stood in front of the three Humvees parked haphazardly in the parking lot. Matt immediately noticed the armaments on the top of each vehicle. One had an M240B mounted, identical to the weapon they already possessed, but the other two vehicles carried different weapons. One had a .50 caliber M2 machine gun, while the other mounted a Mk 19 automatic grenade launcher. Matt also noted numerous jerry cans of fuel strapped to the outside of the vehicles.

"Wow," said Matt to his two friends. "Please tell me they have lots of ammo."

"A fucking shit ton," said Dave. "Like twice the normal combat load, maybe three times. Plus tripods and pintles for both weapons."

"Nice," replied Matt.

"Even better, they also have two SAWs, an M320, with lots more ammo for both."

"Excellent. Anything else of note?" Matt asked.

"Yeah," said Stan. "They have a few maps. They appear to show their attack plan for Portland and Bangor and have some notations about where these guys were from. They're apparently from Connecticut."

Matt turned and looked at the front bumper, briefly shining his flashlight to see 3-71 CAV stenciled on the bumper. "Connecticut? Are you sure? 3-71 CAV is out of Fort Drum, in upstate New York. This is an active duty Army vehicle, not National Guard."

"Interesting," said Stan. "That does make some sense. The 10th Mountain Division out of Fort Drum was almost entirely deployed to help with containment and refugee control after the nuclear bomb hit Manhattan. They were decimated by smallpox based on their close contact with displaced people. Dave, you said the two in the hotel were gang-affiliated?"

"Yeah. The two fuckers in the hotel room were definitely gang bangers. Hispanic, lots of prison ink. Latin Kings, from the looks of it. One guy had a Hartford tattoo on his forearm, so that supports your Connecticut assessment. They 100% were not soldiers," Dave answered. "Did you check out the punks at the pool, Matt?"

"No, I didn't get a chance to search them," said Matt. "Maybe you could go down there, Dave? You have the most experience with this kind of stuff anyway. See what you can find on them."

"Roger. I'll take LT with me." Dave and LT trotted off.

"Anything else, Stan?"

"Ah, yeah." Stan looked at Kim uncomfortably. "Could we have a private word?"

"Yeah, sure," said Matt. Turning to Kim, he said, "Kim, I'm just going to be right over here, okay?"

"Sure," said Kim. "Matt, I'm okay. I just feel better when I'm with you, but it's not like you can't be twenty feet away, okay?" She said, smiling for the first time.

"Got it." Matt walked over to the other side of the Humvee with Stan. "What's up?"

"These guys were reconning Route 1. I found a task list for them with route instructions. They apparently never went to Bangor. They were part of that fixing force that went to Augusta. Then they cut down here to Rockland. They were supposed to confirm that no one was here, then head south on Route 1 to Damariscotta to await linkup."

"Okay, what about after that?"

"It doesn't say. I'll feed this into QuAI when we return, but I'm worried The Base will send more people this way."

Matt took a second and thought about what Stan's information could mean. "Hey, Stan, I want to run an idea by you. I haven't told anyone about this, not even Clare, but now may be a good time."

For the next few minutes, Matt and Stan talked.

CHAPTER 44

October 25, 10:27pm

Matt huddled with Pete, Dave, Stan, Grace, and Kim. The three Humvees were now parked at the end of Samoset Road, and all of their armament and supplies had been loaded aboard the Hinckley. The five women from the Samoset Resort were now on board as well.

"Are you sure?" Pete asked. "I mean, I love the idea, but is tonight the night to do it?"

"Yeah, I think it is. Look, it's going to take us several hours to get it ready. High tide tomorrow is just before 10 am. If we wait until tomorrow to come back, we'll be here all day; for all we know, that could be too late. These guys had no night vision, so most likely, any more of them will arrive in the daylight. I'd like to be gone before they arrive."

"Okay, fair enough. You know I support you," said Pete. "So you'll call Clare on the sat phone?"

"Yes, I'm going to call her right now using Kim's phone. I'll let her know what's happening and to expect you. Head to the dock at Roberts Hill Farm. They'll be waiting for you."

"Okay, I'll go tell Liz. She'll be up in a minute."

"I'll go with you, Pete," said Grace. "Good luck, you guys. See you in the morning. Ready, Kim?"

Kim made no move to leave. "I'd like to go with Matt. I think I can be useful."

"Kim," Matt said. "Are you sure you wouldn't be more comfortable heading back with your team? You're their leader."

"As I said, Matt. You're their leader now. I'm confident the best place for me is with you. Do any of you have a Master Captain's license up to 100 gross tons? I have a lot of recent maritime experience, and I captained our 60-foot research vessel up here from Woods Hole. I think you could use my knowledge and experience."

Everyone looked at her and nodded their heads. She had a point. "Okay, Kim. You got it."

Grace and Pete walked down the dock and onto the Hinckley 35. In moments, Liz walked back up and joined them.

"Okay, Stan, Dave, and I will drive the other vehicles as we've driven Humvees before. Liz and Kim, you ride shotgun. Let's do this."

Matt wore his NODs and led the three-vehicle convoy up Samoset Road, then turned left on Waldo Ave, keeping the harbor to his left. Matt turned south at the intersection with Route 1, and they retraced the path they had taken on their previous visit to Rockland. They placed the Humvee's lights in "black-out drive," with infrared light paving their way. Matt kept his speed up above thirty miles per hour. He wasn't expecting anyone, but if they came across anyone, he wanted to blow past them before they knew what was happening.

In minutes they were through downtown Rockland. Matt turned left onto Water Street, then another left onto Ocean Street, after the Rockland Harbor YMCA. He slowed down and turned into the parking lot above Sandy Beach. The spot provided a clear view over the southern portion of Rockland Harbor. He had a phone call to make while the others kept watch.

Everyone stepped out of their vehicle and looked out over the harbor in the dark. Matt pulled out Kim's sat phone and walked twenty meters away to make his call, which he was not looking forward to. Kim watched him the entire time, always keeping him within eyesight.

In five minutes, Matt returned to the group.

"How'd she take it?" Dave asked.

"About as you'd expect, Dave. Probably about as well as your wife is going to take it when Clare tells her. You too, Stan. When I called, Clare, Michelle, and Marvi were all sitting in the living room at Carver Main."

"Oh shit," said Stan. "Glad it was you who called and not me." The three had a quick chuckle.

"In all seriousness," continued Matt. "Clare's on board. She was slightly miffed at why we needed to do this tonight but she also understood. And right now, she's most worried about the young women about to arrive. The three of them are taking the kids and heading to the Farm. She was calling Molly on the radio, and everything will be ready by the time Pete docks the Hinckley."

"Thank you," said Kim. "All of you. We really owe you our lives."

"You're welcome," said Stan.

"No worries," added Dave, trying to lighten the situation a bit. "Stick with us long enough, and we'll all owe each other."

"Everyone ready? I take it nothing is moving out there?" Matt asked.

"All clear," said Dave.

"Okay then. Let's get this show on the road." Matt flipped down his NODs and walked up the parking lot toward a small building. From the overhead imagery he had studied, he knew there was a walkway around to the right of the building that led out to a long dock. Kim fell in behind Matt, followed closely by the others. Kim had taken Grace's night vision, so the entire party walked quickly using NODs.

Matt stepped onto the long dock that led down to the boats tied up on the cross-piers. This was a private marina, and the docks were shaped like a backward-facing capital F. Several twenty-to-fifty foot boats were tied along the short stems of the F. Matt paused, taking a long look at the reason for their trip.

Tied up along the backbone of the F was a super yacht

at least 200 feet long. Matt could see its three full decks rising above the waterline, with even taller radio/radar masts towering over the highest deck. From the parking lot, the vessel was completely dark, although as they approached, Matt's NODs showed a faint glow of light from the lower portholes. He held up his right arm, elbow bent, palm open in the universal sign for "stop."

Dave walked forward, passing Kim, and leaned into Matt's ear. "I see it too, bro. You and Kim walk forward slowly. I'm going to have Stan and Liz stay here in overwatch. I'll catch up to you in a sec."

Matt nodded and continued walking slowly. He brought his weapon up to the low ready position and continued to walk steadily down the pier toward the ship. With the help of his night vision, Matt could read the yacht's name painted across its stern in the moonlight. "The Irish Rover" was a fitting name, and Matt's sense of karma clicked in. *This was definitely the right boat.* Matt also noted the yacht's home port was George Town, Cayman Islands. *Interesting.*

The gangway was in the downward position, allowing anyone to walk onto the boat. With the naked eye, the boat was completely dark. Matt stopped at the gangway and leaned over to put his hand on the yacht about six feet above the waterline. A slight vibration could be felt through his palm. Something mechanical was running on this ship.

Matt toggled his radio, whispering into his throat mic. "There's something mechanical operating on the boat. I can feel a slight vibration. Other than the faint lights we see through the NODs, it's completely dark."

"Let's clear it, Matt," Dave said, standing right behind him and whispering. "There could be someone living on board exercising great light discipline."

"Wait," said Kim. She was also whispering but from a few feet away on the dock. "It could just be the generator. If they had full fuel tanks, a generator would last for months, maybe almost a year."

“Seriously?” Dave asked, shocked at the statement.

“Yes.”

“Okay, Dave. You and I clear it; we’ll start on the back deck and see if the door opens.” *Damn, wish I had brought the Halligan tool. Although, on second thought, I can’t imagine taking a Halligan to what is probably a $60 million yacht.* Matt clicked his radio mic. “Stan, Liz, we’re moving in to clear it. Nothing threatening on the outside, so why don’t you move down here and follow behind us with Kim.”

One click - meaning affirmative.

Matt nodded, and Dave walked up the gangway, holding his rifle up and ready to fire. Matt was stacked up behind him. Kim waited on the dock, keeping him in sight. The gangway put them on the aft part of the yacht, onto a wide walkway forward of the open rear deck. The two of them walked toward the stern. In the green glow of the NODs, Matt could see an oversized couch with plush pillows wrapping around the stern, facing several coffee tables and then four chairs that looked to be made of rattan. A large sliding door faced forward back into the first deck of the yacht. It was closed.

“Okay, see if it’s open, Dave. And let’s go white light once we’re inside.”

Dave slowly took a few steps forward, staying to the side of the large sliding door. He put his hand on the handle and shoved it away from him. Indicative of the quality of the yacht, the door slid open easily and quietly. Dave pushed it more, opening it about three feet, easily wide enough for both of them to walk through.

Matt squeezed Dave’s shoulder once.

Dave immediately walked into the open door and broke to the right. Matt was right on his heels and kept the barrel of his weapon facing forward, sweeping the room for targets. Matt stopped immediately, and Dave did as well after two steps.

The smell of death was unmistakable.

No one was living here with that smell. No one.

Matt pulled up his buff over his nose, flicked up his NODs,

and clicked the Surefire tactical light on the end of his M4. The powerful light illuminated what could have been the nicest sitting room Matt had ever seen. He didn't even know how to describe it. Dark, lacquered wood tables, overstuffed gray fabric couches, and chairs, all sitting atop an immaculate white rug. Matt was hesitant to keep walking for fear of soiling the carpet.

Dave clicked on his light. "All clear," Dave said into the radio. "I'd wait outside. There's at least one person dead in here."

Matt heard Kim, Stan, and Liz walk up the gangway onto the back deck. Kim came inside, but Stan and Liz remained on the back deck. Kim seemed impervious to the smell.

"Zip your fleece up all the way and cover your mouth and nose," Matt suggested.

"I've smelled worse. You forget I'm a Ph.D. in coastal marine sciences. We smell some pretty awful stuff on a regular basis."

"Suit yourself." Turning to Dave. "Okay, buddy, I guess we follow our nose. I have no idea how one of these things is laid out. Any guesses?"

Kim spoke up. "This deck likely has a dining room past that living room up ahead. Beyond that is probably some kind of central foyer, usually with a staircase going down and up. Down will be the guest cabins. Up will be the next deck."

"Okay, you heard the lady," said Matt. "Let's go."

They both walked forward with their flashlights on, still stacked just in case. Kim was almost right. The foyer came first, and the dining room was off of that. The smell became considerably more intense the further they walked in.

"Let's go down. Cabins are down. That's the most likely place for someone to die of smallpox," said Matt.

Dave led the way down a wide spiral staircase. It was fully carpeted, and their steps were silent. They knew they were in the wrong place as soon as they got to the bottom of the stairs. The smell wasn't nearly as bad.

Without speaking, Matt simply reversed, and now Dave was stacked behind him. They got to the top of the stairs where

Kim was standing.

"Definitely not down there. Barely stinks."

"Okay. Why don't you try the crew quarters?" Kim stated.

"Where?"

"Mmmm, probably up ahead. Look for the kitchen. When you find a less nice place on the boat you'll know you're in the crew area. Look for another staircase down."

"Let's go," said Matt. Dave led out again, and their flashlights clearly showed an amazing dining room with an inlaid mahogany table and enough cloth-covered chairs to seat ten. A door led left off the dining room, and Dave entered the galley area. The two followed a couple of twists and turns and found themselves at the top of another spiral staircase heading down. *Goddamn! The smell is worse.*

Dave smelled it too and immediately started down the stairs. At the bottom, a narrow hallway led toward the yacht's bow. They walked through another galley with a built-in seating area, and then the hallway continued forward with multiple doors on each side. One door stood open.

Dave walked forward and shined his light into the room. "Found him."

Matt shined his flashlight on the wall and found an electrical plate with several light switches. He flicked them all upwards. Surprisingly, the lights all came on instantly, illuminating the entire kitchen area and hallway.

"Kim was right," said Matt. "There must be a generator still running."

"Well, this will certainly make doing this easier with the lights on," said Dave. "Here. Come give me a hand."

Matt stepped forward and looked into the room. The crew cabin was not much bigger than a walk-in closet, with built-in bunk beds along the right, a dual wardrobe on the left, and a small desk and changing area. The body of what appeared to be a young man was lying on its side in the bottom bunk. A sheet and comforter covered the bottom half of the body, but the top half was exposed. The man had not been wearing a shirt when he died, and the upper torso, neck, and face were a dark red turning to black. The bedsheet underneath the man was stained black with dried blood and other bodily fluids. Matt imagined that at one point, the body was quite bloated, but it had progressed past that stage of decomposition as it appeared almost all of the body's fluids had drained onto the sheet. *Small pox is definitely not a pleasant way to die.*

As a police officer and NCIS agent, Dave had significantly more experience dealing with dead and decomposing bodies. While over the past few weeks, they had removed quite a few bodies from houses on Vinalhaven, in all of those cases, they could open the windows and let the place air out. The confined space of this below-deck cabin was an entirely new experience for Matt. "C'mon. Let's roll him up in the bed linen and get him out of here," said Dave.

Dave stepped in and pulled the comforter off of the top bunk. Matt squeezed into the room behind him. With barely enough room for the two of them, it was quite tricky to wrap the comforter around the body. Ultimately, they covered the young man and tried to roll him into the comforter. The result was somewhat satisfactory as they were at least able to pick up the partially-wrapped body and move it out of the room and onto the linoleum floor of the crew galley.

"Go grab the sheet off the top bunk, will ya?" Dave asked. Matt stepped back into the small cabin and pulled off the top sheet. When he brought it out, he and Dave laid it on the floor and placed the wrapped body on the sheet. They tugged at the comforter to cover the entire body, then used the sheet as a final layer, rolling the body several times so that it was completely enshrouded.

"Take that end, Matt. Let's get this guy upstairs and overboard. Then we can air this place out." Matt grabbed the ends of the sheet at the body's feet, and together, they picked it up. The body was much lighter than Matt expected, but then Matt realized the human body was mostly fluid - so when this drains out, there's not much weight remaining. When they got to the first deck, Stan was waiting and used his white light to lead the way to the open back patio area, where they lay the body on the deck.

"What are you gonna do with the body?" Liz asked.

"I don't know. We could either toss him overboard or carry him up the dock and set him on the ground up there."

"I vote overboard," said Dave. "We don't have a shovel, and to paraphrase the outlaw Josie Wales, fishes gotta eat, same as the worms."

"Stan?" Matt asked. "Do you have an opinion?"

"Overboard. He was a mariner. Let his eternal rest be in the sea."

"Okay, overboard it is," said Matt. "Liz, check the side there. We can just throw him over the side, but check to ensure there's nothing below."

Liz walked over and angled her white-lens flashlight over the side of the rail. "Hey Matt, there's another boat down here. It's tethered to the side."

Kim walked over to have a look. "That's the yacht's tender. They secure it to the hip here when the yacht is moored." Matt and Dave lowered the body to the floor and walked over to have a look.

"That's a pretty big tender," said Matt. "I thought a tender was like a Boston Whaler."

"Maybe on some 80-foot yacht down in Florida," said Kim. "This mega yacht is at least 200 feet long. I bet that tender cost close to a million bucks on its own. Look, it has three 350-horsepower outboards and probably seats fifteen or more people. A yacht like this probably has a smaller tender underneath where we're standing."

Matt had to admire the boat tied alongside the large yacht. It was a center console with a hard-top cover over the pilot and rear seating areas. The front, however, was completely open, with cushioned bench seating. Matt estimated the boat had to be 35-40 feet long, but it looked tiny against the hull of the super yacht.

"Okay," said Matt. "Tossing him off the side isn't an option. Dave, let's carry him down the gangway that we initially walked up. Once on the dock, we can set him down in the water away from the boat. I don't know if he'll sink or float, but it doesn't matter."

"Let's do it." They both picked up the body, maneuvered it onto the dock, and lowered him gently onto the water, letting go of the end of the sheet simultaneously. The body sank silently into the dark, midnight waters of Rockland Harbor.

CHAPTER 45

October 26, 3:01 am

Matt sat on the couch on the second deck, which Kim informed them is called the "owner's deck," holding a flashlight and reading the ship's log. Stan and Liz were down in the engine room while Dave looked through the kitchen and storage areas to start inventorying some of the supplies.

Kim lay on the couch opposite the chair where Matt sat, curled up in a blanket they had found folded across the rear of the sofa. She had shadowed Matt while they toured the boat, and her knowledge of yachts had proven extremely helpful. She was now sound asleep, and Matt saw peacefulness on her face for the first time this evening. He half-expected her to toss and turn with nightmares, but she slept soundly.

This yacht was everything he had hoped for and then quite a bit more. Not only did it have every creature comfort known to man, but it was fully fueled and completely stocked with provisions. The crew area had a large walk-in refrigerator inside of which was a door leading to an equally large freezer. The generator appeared to have been running constantly since the young man died in bed. The yacht could comfortably carry twelve passengers with a crew of sixteen, and Dave estimated there was enough food for at least sixty days, if not more.

The first thing they did after removing the body was attempt to air out the crew area. The portholes in the rooms didn't open, but Liz found two escape hatches that opened up and let some air circulate through the crew area. As they toured the boat's upper decks, they opened up the large aft-facing sliders on each deck to air everything out. Sitting on the owner's deck, two decks above the crew area, Matt could no longer detect the smell of death. Or maybe he'd just become inured to it.

They had all agreed not to turn on the lights on any of the upper decks. It was one thing for minimal white light to seep through the below-deck portholes, but having a blazing white-lit yacht tied up in the harbor was not a risk anyone wanted to take. Matt was pretty confident that no other people were in the town, but there was no sense in taking unnecessary chances.

It took them more than an hour to tour the yacht, but the layout was relatively straightforward once they had walked everywhere. The main deck, where they had initially entered, had a large patio on the stern separated by a sliding glass door into an enormous living room. This area consisted of a sitting area followed by a large bar, beyond which was another sitting area. The sitting areas had multiple couches and chairs and were decorated with the highest quality furniture and accents. The bar was a dark, lacquered mahogany, while the rest of the parlor was accented in lighter-colored birch wood. At the center of the yacht, amidship as Stan and Liz had pointed out, there was a large foyer with a spiral staircase and a bathroom. Downward, the staircase led to four elegantly-appointed guest bedrooms, all en-suite. Taking the stairs up led to the owner's deck, which would be the second of the three upper decks. Still on the main deck and traveling beyond the foyer, a formal dining room led to a hallway off which was the main galley. Turning toward the bow, the hallway led past the captain's quarters and office and up a short flight of a half-dozen stairs to the bridge. The bridge was unlike any ship Matt had ever seen, with a half-dozen large screen monitors and dozens of instruments and controls. While Matt was in awe, he was quite relieved to see that both Stan and Kim felt right at home. Stan took a few minutes to look at each instrument and panel.

"So you think you can drive this thing, no problem?" Matt said to Stan.

"First, it's not drive; it's pilot. And yes. The United States Navy saw fit to allow me to captain several of her ships, including a destroyer and a guided-missile cruiser. I believe I'm fully capable of piloting this yacht wherever we'd all like to go."

"I thought all you Navy guys did was stand watch and drink coffee, swab and paint the deck, and train to put out fires?" Dave added jokingly.

"Well, Mr. Paratrooper, I'm sure we can find a job commensurate with your naval skills. Swabbing is definitely a task you would enjoy." They all had a chuckle. "Actually, Dave, I could use your help. The engine room is the most important thing in our ability to use this vessel. A yacht like this, I would expect it to be in pristine condition. I think we should check that out next."

"Sounds good," said Dave. "Let's go."

They had all gone down to the engine room, located amidship between the guest quarters and the crew compartment. It was indeed pristine. Matt could not recall ever having been in an engine room of this size before and could only imagine what an engine room aboard a large US Navy ship would be like. Matt had expected to see oil and grime with many pipes running everywhere. Instead, when they turned on the lights, Matt was amazed at how new and clean everything looked. The room ran the entire width of the ship, more than 30 feet, and was about the same length. In the middle of the room, eight feet down a metal flight of stairs sat two large Caterpillar engines encased in spotless chrome. On each side of the engines were two large generators painted white. Each generator was a rectangular box approximately five feet wide, five feet tall, and ten feet long. Matt had no idea how many kilowatts each generator was, but Stan said that each generator could easily run all of the ship's electricity requirements on their own, and were typically alternated as primary and backup. To the left was a small control room with dozens of neatly organized panels with switches, meters, and diagrams and a built-in desk with manuals and laminated checklists.

"First class," said Stan, looking through a window built into the control room that looked over the entire engine room. "This truly is a world-class boat. They have everything you could ever want on a yacht like this, and it's all perfectly organized."

Kim looked at some of the manuals while Liz and Dave wandered around the main engines. "Oceanco built this."

"Is that good?" Matt asked.

"Yeah. Like one of the best yacht builders in the world."

"How do you know this stuff, Kim?"

"Well, as I've said, I spend a lot of time at sea, but I've also spent quite a bit of time on yachts. I know Oceanco because I'm pretty good friends with a woman whose billionaire husband owns a mega yacht bigger than this one that Oceanco built."

"Wow. I had no idea."

"Well, that's what three degrees from Stanford will get you. My friend's husband, Felix, is also a Ph.D. from Stanford - but he decided to start a huge hedge fund rather than do research. Smart move on his part. I've been on their yacht quite a few times. It's incredible."

"That's awesome. I mean, not just that you spent time on a mega yacht. But you probably know more about this yacht than any of us. Why don't you show me the top decks while these guys mess around with the engine?"

"Sure, let's go," said Kim.

"Hey Stan, we're going to tour the upper decks. Call me on the radio if you need anything."

Stan, still engrossed reading the engine room log, simply gave him a thumbs up.

When they went up to the main foyer, instead of going down to the guest bedrooms, they went up. The staircase opened to another small foyer, immediately across from what looked like a home office, complete with a mahogany desk, plush black leather chair, and built-in bookcases. The entire outboard side of the office was floor-to-ceiling windows. Matt could faintly see the harbor through these windows and imagined the amazing view one would have in the daylight. Forward of the foyer was a huge master suite, complete with a private balcony and an outside sitting area facing the bow of the ship. Aft of the office and foyer was another large living room. This large room had a bar with two outboard-facing sitting areas, each containing a couch and three chairs facing the floor-to-ceiling windows. Behind these seating areas was more of a family room, with sofas and chairs that could easily seat ten people, all facing an 84" flat-screen television mounted on the wall. The sliding glass doors to the family room's rear opened to a covered dining area with a table large enough to seat fourteen.

Matt and Kim left the sliders fully open and explored the top deck, more appropriately termed the "sun deck," as Kim explained. The sundeck had a covered bar and dining area amidships, with large open-air seating areas fore and aft. The centerpiece of the aft seating area was a square jacuzzi hot tub surrounded by plush bench seating. Matt estimated the sun deck could have a party with fifty people and still not feel crowded. The view from the top was incredible, and in the quarter moon, Matt could make out distant islands beyond the harbor.

The tour complete, Matt and Kim went to sit on the couch on the owner's deck. It was relatively warm compared to the outside, but the open slider provided some fresh air to clear out the faint scent of decomposition. Kim almost immediately fell asleep, and Matt wandered off to grab the ship's log from the bridge.

The log was a handsome, navy blue, leather-bound binder that measured 14" x 9" and was about an inch thick. Matt leafed to the last page with writing and noted the date as September 23rd. Instead of reading backward, Matt decided to start in August and read through to see what had happened with the Irish Rover pre- and post-cataclysm.

From reading the pages from the 8th to the 15th, Matt concluded that the Irish Rover had been in Camden since early August with the owner and his family onboard and vacationing in Maine for the latter part of the summer. The owner departed on August 31st, with the last guest leaving on September 4th, which Matt knew was Labor Day. The yacht's staff were given an opportunity for leave, and planned for a skeleton crew to remain onboard until September 21st, when the entire crew would reassemble and depart for the Caribbean, where the Irish Rover would remain for the winter.

Things changed on September 8th after the bombs went off, while only five crew remained onboard: the 1st officer, engineer, two deckhands, and one cabin staff. On September 9th, there were two entries. First, the yacht received a scheduled delivery of 90,000 liters of AGO diesel fuel at 1020 hours, which according to the log, maximized their onboard full storage supply at 140,000 liters. The second entry, at 2225 hours, was about the yacht's owner, who informed the 1st officer of a change in plans. Instead of the yacht traveling empty to the Caribbean, the owner now wished to travel with it and would be bringing eight guests. He would be arriving on the 18th and wished to depart the next morning for St. Kitts.

The entries for the 10th through 15th of September consisted of preparations the Irish Rover's skeleton crew had made to ready the boat for departure. A flurry of emails and telephone calls were placed to all crew to return to the ship as soon as possible. Of great concern, no one had heard from the yacht's captain, who had gone to New York City to visit family and was feared dead in the nuclear blast that decimated Manhattan. Many of the crew also remained unaccounted for. Despite all this, the five crew onboard worked diligently to prepare the yacht. They went to the same restaurant supply store Matt had gone to and purchased a substantial amount of meat, vegetables, and alcohol from various vendors in Rockland.

On the 16th, the 1st officer, one of the deckhands and the

female cabin staff member departed at 0705 to head for LL Bean. The renowned outdoor sporting goods store in Freeport, Maine was famous for being open 24 hours a day, 365 days a year, so the trio thought they would get an early start. They borrowed a courtesy car from the marina and left with a list of outdoor gear and other supplies they wanted for the yacht. Only the engineer and a deckhand named Jackson remained on board. At 1800, Jackson noted that the 1st officer and crew had not yet returned.

At 0600 on September 17th, Jackson noted with concern that the 1st officer and crew had still not returned. At 0900, he noted that he went to check with the marina staff to see if they had heard anything about their vehicle. At 1500 he noted that he and the engineer had conducted an electrical systems test and a test of both main engines and that all systems were operating fully.

At 0900 on September 18th, Jackson wrote that when he went to the marina's office to check if they had any information about the crew or the marina's vehicle, he found the office closed with a note stating it would be closed indefinitely. At 1420, he wrote that the engineer had taken ill with the flu and was sleeping in his cabin. The next entry in the log, posted at 0540 on the 19th, stated that the engineer had become increasingly unwell during the night, was vomiting blood, and that Jackson had transported him to the hospital in a courtesy vehicle he found in the parking lot with the keys in the ignition. At 1800 on the 19th, Jackson noted that no one had returned to the Irish Rover and that the owner had not arrived as originally scheduled.

Entries for the 20th through the 22nd consisted simply of Jackson entering the times that he did the rounds of the boat. One entry stated that he was shutting off all of the lights to the yacht at the main electrical box in the engine room, leaving power only to the bridge and the below-deck area.

The final entry in the log was dated 1010 on September 23rd. Jackson stated that he had started exhibiting signs of a cold the evening before, with a fever, runny nose, and chest congestion. He further noted that this morning he was feeling much worse and that he was going to sleep in his cabin and would be unable to complete his scheduled rounds.

CHAPTER 46

October 26, 7:12am

Matt stood on the bridge and scanned the horizon beyond the mouth of Rockland Harbor. *There!*

"I got him. Just off Owls Head and heading straight for us," said Matt.

"Good, I'm ready to see what this thing can do," replied Stan. Ten minutes earlier, Stan and Liz had been down in the engine room and communicating up to the bridge on their handheld radios. The ship had two dozen handheld UHF radios, but the team felt more comfortable using their own. Stan had spent several hours studying the engine room and bridge and placed a laminated checklist in front of Matt and Kim before heading down to the engine room. Stan started the engines from within the engine room, and Matt felt a gentle rumble start in the bowels of the yacht. Once it seemed to be running smoothly, Stan came up to the bridge and began working through checklist items while speaking with Liz down in the engine room. Now they were good to go.

"Let me see how Dave and Kim are getting along," Matt said. He walked out the starboard door of the bridge and looked down. Dave was on board the tender, which in the daylight turned out to be a 37' Midnight Express. Kim was assisting him in unhooking the fiberglass rods that tethered the tender to the hip of the super yacht. Matt could hear the low rumble of the Midnight Express' trio of outboards and noted it was a bit louder than the Hinckley. Once unhooked, Dave waved to

Kim and gently engaged the throttles and rudder to move the tender away from the Irish Rover. Everything to the starboard side was open seas, so Dave turned the boat into the harbor.

"Matt, this is Pete. In the harbor now."

"Roger, Pete. We see you. Dave is in the Midnight Express heading your way. Link up with him, and we'll move away from the dock and meet you in the middle of the harbor."

"Roger. I see Dave now. Looks like you guys've been busy. Everything that you hoped it would be?"

"Yes. And then some. We'll talk in a few when we see if this thing actually works." Matt walked back into the bridge, where Stan stood looking down at all the controls and monitors. "All good, Captain?" Matt asked.

"Yeah. All good. I see the tender's clear."

"Yes. What else do you need?"

"From you? Just stand out on the starboard wing there, leave the door open. I know there's no obstacles that way, but when I maneuver us away from the dock, just keep an eye on the starboard side of the boat and let me know if we get close to anything."

"I can do that."

Stan engaged the mic on his radio. "Liz, I have set all engine controls to remote, so I have control here in the wheelhouse. Please come up to the main deck, help Kim secure the gangway, and prepare to cast off."

"Coming up now," replied Liz.

"Liz, I'll meet you on the back deck," Kim stated a second later.

Stan looked down at the controls and then at his checklist. He read a few dials and flicked a couple of switches. It reminded Matt of watching UH-60 Blackhawk pilots preparing to take off. Satisfied, Stan walked out the port door and onto the walkway that went around the outside of the entire deck - basically opposite where Matt now stood on the starboard side. Stan stood before a glass-topped fiberglass box identical to the one Matt stood next to. Stan reached down to the latch at the front and pulled the top upward, similar to opening the top on a gas grill. The lid locked upward into place, revealing a set of controls including a throttle, rudder control, several joysticks, and a dozen other small gauges and switches.

"Listen up," Stan commanded into the radio. "The tide is still coming in, so should keep us pinned to the dock. We'll cast off the bow line, then the stern, to allow you both to get on board. Liz, I want you on the bow with Kim on the dock. Kim has a bit more experience with lines. Ready?"

Matt couldn't see what was happening as everything was occurring on the far side of the boat. In a few seconds, Liz and Kim replied that they were ready.

"Standby to castoff port bow line," said Stan.

"Port bow line ready," replied Kim.

"Cast off port bowline."

"Casting off port bow line," said Kim. "Bow line clear."

Matt could picture Kim tossing the rope up to Liz on the bow, then both scrambling back to the yacht's stern.

"Cast off port stern line when ready."

Matt heard Kim say, "Casting off port stern line; stern line clear."

A few seconds later, Kim said, "All crew on board. All lines clear."

Matt watched as Stan looked over the side of the boat to both front and rear. With his hands on both the throttle and joystick, Stan moved the controls slightly. Matt felt the deck shudder underneath him as the boat was put into gear and then watched as the boat started sliding directly away from the dock. Matt figured Stan was using the bow thrusters and the rudder to push the boat away.

Matt couldn't see the far side of the boat. When he looked to the stern, he saw they were already more than thirty feet from the dock. The deck under Matt's feet shuddered slightly again as Stan put the yacht's engines in forward gear. Stan put his hands on a different joystick and pushed the throttles slightly forward, and the Irish Rover was now underway.

Stan reached up and closed the port side control box lid. He walked the few steps into the bridge and put his hands on the throttle and the rudder control device, which almost reminded Matt of a dash-mounted computer mouse.

"Good job, Stan. I guess the Navy did teach you something."

"Piece of cake, Matt. It's like riding a bike."

They stood side by side, watching out the wheelhouse's front windows as Stan pushed the throttles forward and steered the yacht into the center of the harbor. A half-mile ahead of them, inside the breakwater, the Hinckley and Midnight Express awaited their arrival.

"So whadda ya think?" Matt asked.

"I think you picked a great boat, Matt. Seriously. I liked your initial idea of trying to take a Coast Guard cutter, but I think this is a much better solution for our purposes."

"Yeah, I agree. Hopefully, this is just a backup contingency we don't need, but it's nice to know we have it."

"100%. We work well together as a family, and I like how you're always thinking strategically, several steps ahead."

"Yeah. The Irish Rover is the last piece in the jigsaw puzzle. So far, we've taken advantage of the opportunities we've been given to improve our security and survival. This is the capstone piece that puts us over the top."

"How's she ride, Captain?" Pete's voice came over the radio.

Stan replied, "Well, she's no DDG, but she'll do."

"What's a DDG?" Matt asked.

Stan laughed. "It's an *Arleigh Burke-class* guided-missile destroyer. 7,700 tons of pure destruction."

"Got it," said Matt. "Squid humor." They both laughed.

Kim and Liz joined them on the bridge, and they all watched as they cruised toward the Hinckley 35. Matt noted they were doing 12 knots. "How fast does this thing go, Stan?" He asked.

"This is about it. She's built for cruising, not for speed."

They were floating through the harbor, and Matt couldn't help but notice how comfortable the yacht was riding. "Is there anything we need to do, or can we head right for Vinalhaven?"

Matt asked.

"Let's head right into our portage. I'll play around while we go, but it's probably at least 90 minutes in the Rover," replied Stan.

Matt toggled his radio mic. "Pete, this is Matt. Are we all good with the Olivers?"

"Yes, all set. Michelle and a couple of the boys should already be there. They'll be waiting for us."

CHAPTER 47

October 26, 4:48pm

"Matt?" Clare nudged Matt lightly on the shoulder as she sat down on their bed in the master bedroom. "It's time to wake up. Stan called a meeting for 5 pm, and I wanted to talk to you before we all got together."

Matt blinked a few times, taking a moment to get his bearing, and then he was fully awake. Clare handed him a stainless steel water bottle from which he took a long gulp. "What's up? Everything okay," said Matt, sitting up in bed to talk face-to-face with his wife.

They had spent the morning moving the Irish Rover into position. Matt did not want to anchor it in the central Carver Harbor and instead had carefully selected a spot on the north part of Vinalhaven east of Holt Point and west of Calderwood Neck. Located on Mill River, the deep water anchorage was completely protected and was at least 22 feet deep at low tide, more than sufficient for the 12 feet of draft required by the Irish Rover. Matt had been leery of putting the yacht in the main harbor for two reasons. First, he didn't want to advertise it to the island's residents or anyone else who might happen upon Vinalhaven. Second, the anchorage in the north offered several deep water avenues of departure to the north and east that provided options in case his extended family needed to evacuate. The entire purpose of acquiring the Irish Rover was to provide one more contingency for his family in unforeseen circumstances.

The anchorage was a few hundred meters east of the Olivers, and Kent and his family had agreed to watch over the yacht. They had all spent the morning exploring the yacht, and when Matt had departed, Stan was still giving instructions to Kent and his daughters. With Kim accompanying him, Matt had made for Roberts Hill Farm, where he met up with Clare and Molly. Over lunch, they filled him in on the status of the five newcomers, four of whom were MIT grad students, and the fifth was one of Kim's research assistants. They were doing surprisingly well, and there was plenty of room at the farmhouse for them all.

Kim had insisted on returning to Carver Main with Matt and Clare. Matt could barely keep his eyes open and opted to nap for a few hours, leaving Kim and Clare drinking coffee at the dining room table.

"Yeah, everything is as good as can be expected. I wanted to talk to you about Kim. She seems to have a bit of an obsession with you; have you noticed?"

"Yeah, it's been kind of hard not to. She won't let me out of her sight." Matt rubbed his hand over his face, pinching the bridge of his nose, and not sure what else to say.

"She's had an extremely traumatic experience. About as traumatic as one can have. Being forcibly raped while also having to watch your friends and people you're responsible for brutally executed in front of you and casually tossed in a pool."

"I know. I watched it happen."

"Jesus," said Clare. "That's absolutely horrific."

"I know. But I also don't know what to do. She says she only feels safe when she's near me."

"Yes, she told me the same thing."

"She did?"

"Yes. Don't get your hopes up, buddy. It's not as if you're some super stud. I'm not concerned there's anything sexual. If I had to guess, I'd say she bats for the other team. But it is quite obsessive."

"Yeah. What do you suggest?" Matt knew from experience

that the key to a healthy marriage was always asking your wife's opinion and then usually following it.

"Well, we had a very long talk while you were sleeping. I really like her, and obviously, I feel horrible for her. So I've invited her to stay here with us. I'm putting Chris and Laurie in the same room, and Kim can have Laurie's room."

"Ah, okay. You sure?"

"Yes. I wanted to make sure you're okay with it. Two weeks ago, we were all living under one roof. Just because we're now separated doesn't mean she must sleep at the farm automatically. Plus, as far as I'm concerned, she's proven to be a valuable member of the team, and if being near you brings her some peace of mind, then I think it's the least we can do."

"Okay, then I agree as well," Matt said.

"Yeah, like there was ever any doubt of that," scoffed Clare. "Now get your butt out of bed and come downstairs. They're probably all waiting. I'll get you some coffee."

Clare departed, and Stan got up and put on his shoes and a fleece over the t-shirt he'd been sleeping in. When he arrived downstairs, everyone was gathered around the large dining room table. The chair at the head had been left empty, and as Matt was the only one not seated, he took that chair. Around the table were gathered what Matt thought of in his head as the "adult council." This consisted of Stan and Marvi, Dave and Michelle, Pete, Clare, and Molly. Matt made a mental note to add Kim to the list, as she was now sitting next to Clare.

"Good afternoon, everyone. Stan, did you and Liz get a chance for some sleep. How about you, Kim?"

Kim answered, "Yeah, thanks. Clare set me up in Laurie's room, and I caught a few hours' rest. Thank you."

Stan shook his head, adding, "I haven't had the chance, but I just sent Liz upstairs for a nap. We've been working with QuAI since after lunch."

"Okay, well, we need to get you some rest, Stan. You're the oldest one here by about twenty years. We don't want you stroking out on us."

"Ha, Ha," said Stan, deadpanning but then finally cracking a smile. Molly was the oldest, while Stan was less than ten years older than Matt and even closer in age to Dave and Michelle.

"So what's the occasion to keep you from your beauty sleep?" Matt asked.

"The Base. QuAI provided some new estimates overnight and into today. She believes our position here could be at risk based on new information she has gathered, including satellite imagery analysis, RF mapping, and eavesdropping on communications networks."

"What's at risk?" Pete asked. "Haven't we always been at risk?"

"Yes, but this is different. QuAI believes, with over 85% certainty, that The Base will send at least a platoon-sized element to Rockland. They have occupied the capitol in Augusta with approximately two hundred people, and QuAI has indicators that they plan to dispatch a fairly strong patrol directly to Rockland. As you know, Augusta is less than an hour's drive from Rockland."

"For what purpose? Does she believe they know we're here?" Matt asked.

"She does not have information on a specific purpose other than scouting," replied Stan. "Currently, there is no indication that The Base in Maine is aware of our presence or is actively searching for us. But QuAI has estimated there is a significant possibility, not probability, that this patrol may remain in Rockland long term. And the longer they stay, the more likely they are to visit the outlying coastal islands."

"Okay. Does she have an estimated time of arrival for this patrol?"

"Yes. Not earlier than tomorrow morning, but not later than tomorrow evening."

"Shit," said Pete.

"Exactly," agreed Stan. "That's why I called this meeting."

"Stan," asked Marvi. "Does QuAI offer any suggestions for what we should do?"

"No. I guess we could feed those requests into her machine learning, but to date, we've only used her to gather and analyze intelligence. We have not asked her for tactical advice."

"Yeah, honestly, Stan, QuAI is invaluable, but I'm not sure I'd take her tactical advice," said Matt. "That's for us to decide as a group."

"I agree completely," said Stan.

"So what do you suggest, Matt?"Asked Marvi.

"Well, I've thought about this quite a bit. First, Stan, how's the surveillance system Juliet and Liz were installing with the Oliver girls? Is it up and running?"

"Actually, it is. We have it up and running upstairs in the barn, and QuAI is also monitoring it. I think they emplaced 12 video cameras, several with infrared capability. If you think of Vinalhaven as the face of the clock, we have coverage from 3 o'clock clockwise all the way around to 11 o'clock. All approaches from the mainland are covered."

"Great," said Matt. "So Marvi, to answer your question. As I see it, our greatest vulnerability is someone coming to Vinalhaven from the mainland intending to harm us. If we're confident we can identify their approach, then our most significant vulnerability is how much force they can bring to the island. I've been thinking about this quite a bit.

"We have considerable defensive capabilities here. My biggest concern is The Base's ability to bring Humvees to the island with mounted crew-served weapons. The only way they can do this is the ferry. How many ferries are there in Rockland, Stan? Two? Three?"

"I'm not sure," said Stan. "We could query QuAI or review the most recent satellite imagery."

"Two," said Kim. Everyone turned to look at her.

"Are you sure, Kim?" Matt asked.

"100% positive. I mean, I don't know how many total ferries they own, but I'm certain there are only two docked in Rockland Harbor right now. Our Woods Hole boat, the Tioga, is docked one dock over, right with a couple of big schooners. I know exactly where they are."

"Okay, great," said Matt. "So we know there are two. Pete, would you mind getting on the radio and calling Tim and Vance? Tell them there are two car ferries in Rockland Harbor and ask them if they know of any more. Those guys would know exactly how many ferries there are." Pete stood up, pulled the handheld radio from his belt, and left the room to make the calls.

"So as I see it," Matt continued. "We could either move the ferries someplace The Base, or anyone else, can't access them. Or we can scuttle them."

"Scuttle?" Michelle asked.

"He means sink them," said her husband, Dave.

"Well, maybe not sink them, but at least disable them," confirmed Matt. "What do you think, Stan?" Not that everyone's opinion wasn't valid, but Stan had by far the most maritime experience of anyone in the room; plus, as their *de facto* intelligence officer, Matt strongly valued his thoughts.

"I think it would be very difficult for us to move both ferries, and I'm not even sure where we'd take them. We don't even know if they run, and I doubt they'd be in as good a condition as the Irish Rover. For me, moving them is too risky. So I think we need to disable them, but I'm not sure exactly how to do that quickly and easily."

"Couldn't we just take the keys?" Marvi asked.

"Yeah, honey. We could do that," said Stan. "But they could also hotwire the ignition. We could try to do something like remove the fuel pump, but it's not a simple task on diesel engines of that size. Anything we could do mechanically, if they had the right people, they could probably undo."

Pete walked back into the room. "Okay, I spoke to both Tim and Vance. Vance said there are four ferries, two big ones, and two smaller ones. One of the big ones got pulled on September 1st to dry dock, and he says there's no way anyone could get it back in the water. Tim said he knew that the "Captain Neil Burgess," one of the smaller ones, is currently docked in the

North Haven harbor. Apparently, the captain of that boat has a home on North Haven, and he brought the ferry over. Tim thinks he's probably dead, as he hasn't seen any signs of human life on North Haven in all his fishing trips."

"Okay, thanks, Pete," said Matt. "So that jibes with our estimate of two ferry boats in Rockland Harbor. Kim, does one big one and one smaller one sound right?"

"Yes, that's what's there."

"Okay, so correct me if I'm wrong, but to sum it up. We have an inbound patrol from The Base that could arrive as early as tomorrow morning, and we have two ferries capable of allowing them to bring their Humvees over here."

"That sums it up."

"But Matt," asked Molly. "Even if we disable the ferries, there are dozens, maybe hundreds, of boats they could easily use to get to Vinalhaven. It seems risky to disable two boats when they could just choose others to use."

"You're absolutely right, Molly. We can't prevent them from coming here. However, I think what's critical is that we try to prevent them from being able to bring their crew-served weapons over here mounted on top of vehicles. If it is ten guys on a speed boat, we can deal with that, especially if our new surveillance system detects them early and shows us where they'll come ashore. But if they can dock a ferry in Carver Harbor and offload four Humvees with .50 cal machine guns, we're going to be in a world of hurt."

Molly nodded, realizing how vulnerable they still were, and Matt could see from the solemn look on everyone else's face that they were thinking the same thing. Matt liked that living on Vinalhaven provided everyone a sense of normalcy and thoughts of a peaceful future. Still, he also knew the horrors of last night at the Samoset Resort could appear on their doorstep at any moment.

"Okay, this is not a big deal, and the best thing about this is that Stan and QuAI can give us plenty of warning. Pete - you, Dave, and I have a quick mission tonight. Everyone else, let's keep doing what we've been doing. I don't think it's helpful if everyone worries about The Base all day. Pete, Dave, and I will go disable the ferries, and we'll be back in a couple of hours."

Everyone around the table nodded, and other than Clare and Michelle, they seemed a bit more relaxed. Matt knew Clare and Michelle would be worried sick until they returned safely from Rockland.

"There's one more thing I wanted to discuss," said Stan. "It's important."

"Stan, please don't tell us the Canadians are invading from Nova Scotia," joked Dave, trying to lighten up the situation.

"No, not exactly."

"Not exactly?" Dave asked, a bit of worry creeping into his voice.

"The Canadians aren't capable of invading anything, to my knowledge. But QuAI believes that the federal government will launch a war against The Base. This would be launched from the Norfolk enclave."

"No shit?" Pete said.

"No shit, Pete. QuAI estimates, with extremely high probability, that this attack will occur within the next 72 hours. It will likely be a two-pronged attack. Ground forces will initially strike outward from Norfolk and seize Richmond, potentially pushing as far as Charlottesville and Lynchburg. While important, this is really a feint. The main attack would be carried out by ship, with at least one aircraft carrier and amphibious assault ship, as well as accompanying destroyers and cruisers, moving up Delaware Bay and the Delaware River to seize Wilmington and Philadelphia."

"Jesus. Do they have that capability?" Pete asked.

"Yes, they do. Remember, most of the 82nd Airborne Division and the 2nd Marine Division were moved to Norfolk once the pandemic started. While they definitely took some losses before the updated vaccine was distributed, QuAI estimates they are both around 30-40% strength. So that is at least two full brigade combat teams, maybe three, plus the firepower of the navy ships. Littoral combat ships can make it up the James River and will support the attack on Richmond."

"And why invade Philadelphia? Because it's The Base's capital?" Matt asked.

"Partly," replied Stan. "But also the refineries. Philadelphia has the only oil refineries on the east coast. They're not currently operational, but if we're to build the country back up, those refineries will be critical."

"All right. Any impact on us in the short term?"

"Not as far as I can tell. QuAI does estimate that it could force The Base to collapse northward into New England, which might eventually lead to more people on the Maine coast, but this is not something we need to be concerned about at the moment."

"Okay, thanks for the update, Stan. What's the tide schedule tonight, Pete?" Matt asked.

"High tide is just after 10 pm," answered Pete.

"Perfect. Pete, if you and Matt could help me in the barn for a few minutes, we'll depart at 9 pm. Everyone else, try not to worry. Let's be thankful QuAI gave us some early warning."

Matt stood up and left everyone around the table to say their goodbyes. He walked into the kitchen and over to a wine rack built into the kitchen wall, containing at least thirty bottles of wine, their tops all facing forward at a downward angle. Matt started pulling bottles out, running his hands over the glass, then putting them back.

Pete and Dave walked over while Clare said goodbye to everyone at the front door. "What are you up to, man? Is this going to be a true road trip with wine? Personally, I'd prefer bourbon, and I think Dave would like beer," said Pete.

After pulling out and looking at a few more bottles, Matt yanked out two bottles and handed them to Dave. Matt then grabbed a bottle opener from the drawer underneath the wine rack. Dave looked at the bottles. "Turnbull Cabernet Sauvignon. Nice!"

"These aren't for drinking. You guys follow me, and I'll

teach you a new trick."

The three walked out to the barn, and Matt immediately went toward one of the three large rooms off the far side of the first-floor garage area. The middle room was their armory, but the left room where they now were was the tool room. It had a high, deep wooden workbench in the center of the room, with a sink on the left wall, cabinets to the right, and tools hanging everywhere.

"Do me a favor, Dave. Take the opener and empty both bottles into the sink."

"Isn't that a waste of good wine? Shouldn't I offer it to Clare at least?"

Matt chuckled. "Yeah, good point. Maybe you should open those in the house and pour them into a decanter. Tell Clare. Maybe she and the ladies would like a few glasses." Dave walked out with the bottles, and Matt opened drawers, looking for something specific.

"What are you looking for? I know this room better than anyone," said Pete. Matt stopped, realizing this was true. Pete had become their handyman and spent considerable time in the toolroom.

"A glass cutter. I'm sure they have one. For fixing window panes."

"Yep. They have several. I know right where they are." Pete walked over to the right wall and pulled open a drawer. He reached in and pulled out a red glass cutter. It was the size of a fountain pen, with a small metal ball on one end and a tiny spinning metal wheel on the other. "This what you need?"

"Perfect," said Matt. "I'll be right back, but you know what I could use? Could you find six dowels for me, maybe 1/2" in diameter and at least a foot long? Also, when Dave returns, ask him to bring the electric kettle from next to the stove in the kitchen."

"Will do. Plenty of dowels in that bin over there."

Matt walked out of the shop room and over to the room they used as their armory. He was amazed at the armaments they had accrued. On the left wall, Pete and Dave had nailed a series of large hooks on the wall. M4s hung from slings on the hooks, while underneath were neatly stacked plate and fighting load carriers. Each person had their designated hooks and kept their kit assembled for quick access should a call-out be necessary. On the back wall was a portable, red Craftsman tool bench with drawers, and next to this, the crew-served weapons were laid out: 2 M240B, an M2 .50 cal, and a Mk19. Their tripods and pintles were leaning on the wall behind them, and Matt noticed three M320 grenade launchers hanging from the wall. Next to this were some open shelves, upon which Matt could see numerous rifles and pistols on separate shelves. Lastly, ammunition boxes were stacked almost six feet high to the door's right. It was on this wall that Matt focused his attention, finally zeroing in on two large wooden crates stacked to the side. He opened the clasp on one of the crates and lifted the lid. *Bingo!* Reaching in, he grabbed four green cellophane-wrapped packages approximately two inches high and deep and eleven inches long. Each package was stamped with yellow lettering: Charge Demolition M112. He reached into the second crate, pulling out two spools of green cord. He took all these items and placed them on the workbench. Reaching down, Matt opened a tall drawer below the bench, pulling it open and looking at the boxes inside. He reached in and pulled a few items out. These included a box of blasting caps as well as several fuse igniters.

Walking back into the tool room with his arms full, Matt saw Pete and Dave standing around the large workbench in the middle, two empty bottles of wine on the table with a half dozen long, wooden dowels.

"Oh, this is going to be good," said Dave, noticing the various items Matt tossed onto the table.

"Jesus!" Pete exclaimed, also noticing the blocks of C4 explosive. "Shouldn't you be careful with that shit? You could blow us all sky high."

"Relax, Pete," said Matt. "This stuff is harmless until it's time for it not to be harmless. Now, Dave, fill up that kettle and boil some water. Pete, I'm now going to show you how to make a shaped charge that will blow some pretty big holes in the bottom of each of those ferries."

CHAPTER 48

October 26, 9:14pm

Pete pulled back on the throttles and steered the Hinckley directly toward the US Coast Guard station on Crockett Point on the western shore of Rockland Harbor. They had sped through West Penobscot Bay, around the Rockland Breakwater, and were now forced to slow down to safely navigate through the minefield of moored boats and lobster buoys. They all wore NODs, so the obstacles in the harbor were easy to discern in the eery green glow of their night vision optics.

Matt sat in the forward-facing passenger seat next to Pete while Dave and Kim sat on the row of bench seating behind him, each cradling a backpack with the improvised explosive device Matt had made in the barn. Matt had built similar field-expedient shaped charges in training and combat, although mostly smaller ones used for breaching or larger ones used for cratering.

After cutting the two wine bottles in half around their center, Matt had packed a complete block of the C4 plastic explosive, 1.25 pounds worth, into the open end of the wine bottle. He had specifically chosen these bottles of Turnbull as they had the deepest and most conically-shaped indent in the bottom. This indent, called the punt, provided a perfect mold for the plastic explosive, and Matt had tamped it in like playdough. Once each stick of C4 had been molded, Matt cut three 1/2" dowels in half, giving him six 18" long pieces of wood. Using black duct tape, or 100 mph tape as they called it in the Army, Matt secured three dowels to each bottle, wrapping it tightly to ensure they would not move. The result was a rudimentary but stable tripod, with the top being the bottom half of a wine bottle filled with enough explosives to blow up a car, the open end facing up and the punt facing downward.

This specially shaped charge placed on the bottom deck of each ferry, next to the main engines, would blow a fist-sized hole directly through the steel of the hull. *At least, I hope so!*

They approached Crockett Point, and Pete angled north and around the point. The point mainly consisted of warehouses with commercial boats tied to their piers. The Hinckley was oriented straight at the Maine State Ferry Terminal as they rounded the point. With the NODs, Matt could see the two large gantries that worked the automobile loading ramps for the ferry boats, beyond which was the expansive parking lot and then Route 1. Pete slowed to a crawl, the Hinckley virtually silent as they crept through the harbor's inky black waters. There were no lights to be seen anywhere in Rockland, the silhouettes of the downtown area buildings appearing as a ghost town. Matt was confident they were alone in the city.

Pete turned the Hinckley hard to port, heading due south along the backside of the ferry terminal and into a small inlet surrounded on three sides by wharves and piers. Ahead, two ferry boats sat tied to the pier as if they were parallel parked on a city street. The larger of the ferries was first, with the small one tied behind it. Pete idled past both vessels, then turned sharply to the right and expertly placed the Hinckley alongside a wooden dock floating perpendicular to the tied-up ferries.

"Let's go," Matt said to Dave and Kim. Turning to Pete, he said, "Turn this around and pull up to the long wharf directly in front of the large ferry. I'll have Dave waiting for you to tie you off."

"Roger," said Pete. "Be careful."

"Always," said Matt, grabbing his lightly filled assault pack, turning, and stepping off the side of the Hinckley and onto the dock. Dave and Kim wore the rucksacks on their backs, all carrying their M4s at the low ready. With the NODs on, they rapidly walked down the dock, turned right, and headed to the lead ferry.

"Hey Dave, wait here and help tie off the Hinckley when Pete brings her around. This shouldn't take long, and we'll meet you back here in a few." Dave gave him a thumbs up.

There was a gangway on the side of the large ferry, so Matt walked up it slowly. "Any idea how to get to the engine room?" He asked Kim.

"Can we turn our flashlight on? It's probably in the tower there, should be a clearly marked door somewhere."

"Sure." Matt flipped up his NODs and turned on the tactical light at the end of his M4's barrel. Kim did the same. Using the light to guide their way, they walked along the steel decking of the ferry until they got to the main superstructure, shaped like a large tunnel that allowed automobiles to drive completely through and enter and exit from either end of the boat. An open door on the left showed a stairwell, going both up and down. Kim led the way and started down the stairs. Unlike the Irish Rover, there was no smell of death. There was, however, a strong smell of diesel fuel and engine oil that was not entirely unpleasant.

At the bottom of the stairs was a narrow hallway leading to a narrower doorway and a metal ladder heading down into a large room. This was clearly the engine room. There was nothing spotless about this engine room. It was a light shade of green, with two large Caterpillar engines. Unlike the Rover, though, there was nothing chrome on these engines.

"Is this the actual hull we're walking on?" Matt asked.

Kim pointed her light onto the floor, showing perforated metal decking. "No. This is some kind of planking to keep everything even. The actual hull slopes downward. We should be able to see some access panels, like maybe a D-ring on the floor."

They both walked around, shining their lights. "There!"

Matt said, kneeling and pulling up a circular ring recessed in the floor, the outline of an access panel clearly visible. Matt pulled up on the ring, dislodging the panel. He then stood up, bent down, and yanked even harder to lift the panel out of position and slide it to the left. This created a three-foot square opening into which Matt and Kim shined their flashlights. This was clearly the hull, which curved slightly downward toward the vessel's centerline. At the very bottom, they could see a bit of dark, oily water.

"Shit!" Matt said, beginning to look around the engine room.

"What is it? Something wrong?"

"Yeah, the angle is too steep. I need to be able to set up the charge on those three legs, and this won't really allow for that. Do me a favor. Take off the pack and pull out the charge."

Matt continued to sweep the floor and sides of the engine room with his light, clearly looking for something. He walked over to the far side of the room, tapping the barrel of his rifle against the wall right around knee height. "Hey, Kim. Is this the hull? The actual outside steel? Like, water is on the other side of this?"

Kim walked over and examined the wall with her light. "Yes. This is definitely the hull. See how it's curved outward going up? It curves downward as well, and when we pick up the floor, that's what we're seeing."

"Okay. And we're definitely under the water level down here, right?"

"Absolutely."

"Excellent. Please hand me the charge." Kim handed him the wine bottle with three dowels. He took it and found a spot between two pipes that ran along the edge of the hull, below knee height. Some mechanical box was about a foot from the hull, and Matt was able to wedge the charge in so that it lay at about a forty-five-degree angle, with the bottom of the wine bottle pointed directly at the hull from about a foot away. Matt pulled out a folding knife and used it to cut one of the dowels off of the charge. He then took a roll of black 100mph tape from his assault pack, placed the dowel upright on the floor but against the bottle, and secured it tightly in place with the tape. To be sure, he pulled off several three-foot lengths of tape and wrapped it around the entire charge and the pipes supporting it. The result wasn't very pretty, but the improvised device was now securely fastened to the side of the hull.

Reaching back into the bag, Matt pulled out one of two coils of M700 time fuse that he had prepared in the barn. He had already conducted two test burns on two-foot-long sections and knew the fuse burned consistently at forty seconds per foot. Each coil was twelve feet long, providing eight minutes between ignition and blast. Matt pulled a small green case from his pack, slightly thicker than a pack of cigarettes. He flipped open the lid to reveal two rows of five M7 non-electric blasting caps. Selecting one, he slid the open end down onto the end of the fuse as far as it would go. Holding his index finger on the end of the blasting cap to keep it pressed into the fuse, Matt reached back into his pack and pulled out what looked to be a weird set of pliers but was really a military-issue crimping tool. He then placed the jaws of the crimping tool around the base of the blasting cap.

"Why don't you take a step back and turn away for a sec? I've never seen one of these go off prematurely, but if it's going to, it's going to be when I crimp it."

Kim stepped back and stood behind one of the giant Caterpillar 750-horsepower diesel engines while Matt squeezed his hand on the crimping tool and fastened the blasting cap to the time fuse.

"Okay, that's the only scary part. You can come out."

"All done?"

"Yeah, pretty much. There's one more piece, but I'm not going to do that until we blow it. Let's go." Together they exited the engine room and went up the stairwell to the main deck of the ferry. Matt looked out the front end of the boat and could see the Hinckley 35 tied to the wharf thirty meters to their front. 'Okay, Kim. I'd like you to stay right here. Keep an eye on things while Dave and I set up the charge on the other boat."

"Can't I come with you?"

"No. I want to set that up, then leave Dave down there to pull the fuse igniter at the same time I pull this one."

"Okay, I understand. I'll be right here."

"Thanks. This shouldn't take but a few minutes."

Matt walked down the gangplank to where Dave and Pete stood on the pier. "Okay, I think we have that set up well. The hull is curved, and the bottom is full of water, but I improvised."

"Improvise, adapt, and overcome, Gunny Highway," said Dave.

Matt and Pete chuckled. "You watch too many movies, man," said Pete.

"I know," said Dave. "I know."

"Let's go, Dave. This should only take a few. Pete, when we get back, we'll be ready to roll. I'll have Kim get on the Hinckley; then we'll be right behind her. Keep your radio on; we'll do this all over the radio."

"No fear of setting off those blasting caps by using the radio?" Pete asked.

Matt chuckled again. "You've been hanging around too many Navy Seals, Pete. Those guys could probably fuck this up, but we're using non-electric caps and time fuse. Radio frequencies can't set them off."

"Ah, okay. Good."

"Let's go, Dave. We'll be back in a few, Pete." Matt and Dave turned and walked to the second ferry, maybe two-thirds the size of the first one, with a much smaller superstructure. The larger ferry was built to house dozens more people in an upstairs seating area, whereas the smaller ferry only had a wheelhouse in its structure. Passengers on this ferry were likely forced to stay in their vehicles or sit on the open deck.

In under ten minutes, Matt came walking back onto the dock. The engine room of the second boat was much smaller but had a similar layout. Matt didn't bother with the bilge and instead secured the explosive charge in the same manner he had the first time. He was confident it would blow a sizable hole in the hull below the waterline.

"Pete, we're all set. Why don't you get the Hinckley ready, and I'll send Kim down to prepare the lines. You'll hear Dave and I activate the charges, but when we come running, we're going to have less than eight minutes to get out of here. It's not like the boats are gonna blow up or anything, but I want to be in the middle of the harbor when they go off."

"Got it. We'll leave as soon as you get on board."

Pete walked off toward the Hinckley while Matt walked up the gangplank of the lead ferry boat, where Kim stood in the middle of the deck. "All good?" He asked.

"Yep. All good. What do you need me to do?"

"I need you to go to the Hinckley, drop your pack, and prepare the lines. When Dave and I come running, we're gonna want to leave immediately."

"Sure you don't need me down below?"

"Yep. Just the lines, Kim. We'll be there in two minutes or less."

"Be careful."

Matt walked into the stairwell and used his rifle's light to navigate down the stairs and the metal rungs into the engine room. He walked over to the charge and pulled an M81 fuse igniter out of a pocket on his vest. He had used these too many times to count and, at one point, even used an expended one as a key ring. The fuse igniter was the length of a pen but as thick as your finger, maybe 1/2" in diameter. One end had a circular ring, identical to ones found on a grenade or standard key chain, and on the end was a green screw cap with a hole in the end and a rubber plug in the hole. Matt found the loose end of the M700 time fuse that he had laid carefully along a large metal pipe. He loosened the cap on the fuse igniter, then slid the time fuse into the opening. Once pushed all the way in, Matt tightened the cap, securing the fuse to the igniter. Matt set the stopwatch countdown function on his watch for eight minutes.

"Dave, this is Matt."

"All set here, Matt," replied Dave.

"Pete, this is Matt. All ready for the getaway?"

"Roger, Matt. We're ready."

"Okay, Dave, confirm that you are ready to pull on the count of three. Remember, we will have eight minutes from the time we pull the igniters."

"Affirmative, Matt. Fuse igniter is in my hand, cotter pin is removed, and I'm ready to pull."

Oh shit! I forgot the cotter pin! Matt reached down and pulled the small cotter pin, which held the end with the pull ring in place. Matt looked at his watch and pressed the tiny button to start the countdown.

"Okay. Three, two, one, FIRE IN THE HOLE." Matt pulled firmly and sharply on the pull ring, extending a narrow metal rod approximately three inches before Matt heard a loud pop.

"Fire in the hole!" He heard Dave repeat over the radio.

A bit of flame and smoke puffed from the end of the igniter, and the fuse began to burn. Looking around to ensure he hadn't left anything, Matt walked slowly to the ladder and up the stairs. A part of him was urging him to run, but Matt knew this was the time to remain calm and deliberate. This would be an inopportune time to slip and fall on the stairs, to say the least.

When he got to the gangway, Dave was approaching from the rear ferry. "Any issues?" Matt asked.

"Nope. Let's get out of here." They picked up their pace and trotted the thirty meters to the Hinckley. Kim was in the stern of the boat, holding a line that secured the stern to the dock. Matt and Dave stepped on, and Kim released the rope from around the cleat on the dock.

"Line clear," she shouted to Pete. Pete calmly put the Hinckley in gear and steered them just above an idle out of the channel and toward the open harbor. Turning right to edge around Crocketts Point, Pete nudged the throttles forward to where they were doing about ten knots.

Matt looked at his watch. The countdown was at 5:37 and counting. Sitting in the passenger seat, Matt pointed out several moored boats in their path to be sure Pete saw them. Everyone had NODs on. Pete accelerated to twenty knots, and in four minutes, they were three hundred meters off the light at the end of Rockland Breakwater.

"Let's stop here, Pete. Make sure things work as planned." Pete pulled back on the throttles, and the Hinckley surged to a stop in the middle of the harbor. The engines were virtually silent at idle, and they could hear the waves smashing into the breakwater to their front. Matt and Dave both looked at their watches.

1:04

1:03

1:02

"How much time?" Kim asked.

"About sixty seconds," answered Dave.

"Yeah, give or take," confirmed Matt.

"So, is this going to make the boats explode? Like, shoot flames up in the air fifty feet? What should I be looking for?"

"Well, I'm not exactly sure. I've trained to blow up ships in scuba school, but I've never actually blown one up," said Matt. "If I had to guess, we'll see a flash of light, and that's about it, then a big boom. Diesel will burn, but it won't explode. Depending on how much gasoline is in the generators, that could explode in a fireball, but I'm thinking it probably won't."

"Thirty seconds," said Dave.

"Should we take our night vision off?"

"Up to you," said Matt. "It's so far away; even an explosion won't white out your NODs."

They all watched silently, scanning the horizon and focusing on the part of the harbor where they knew the ferries were docked.

:10

:09

:08

A flash of light lit up the sky. Matt was wearing NODs and knew the flash was likely significantly increased through the night vision goggles. He flipped them up and could still make out a lightening of the sky over Crockett Point. Then another flash, quite a bit larger than the first, lit up the sky.

BOOOOOM!!!!

The sound wave washed over the boat about five seconds after the flash, reaffirming that light does travel much faster than sound.

We did it! Both boats should not be seaworthy.

BOOOOOOOOOOOM!!!!!!

The second wave was louder than the first, and Matt guessed that this charge must have ignited generator's gasoline when it blew.

CHAPTER 49

October 28, 6:56pm

Matt sat on the couch in the Oliver's great room, listening to Ferhad Agha and Earl Oliver discuss the finer points of pan-Arabism and the failed United Arab Republics of the 1960s and 70s. Matt took a sip of his bourbon, forcing himself to keep a straight face. While he loved the idea of a good bourbon, and the one in his hand was undoubtedly top-notch, he had never acquired the taste. He felt the same about single-malt Scotch and red wine. A cold beer, whether it be an award-winning craft or a cheap Natty Light, would make him smile every time.

The Olivers had invited the Sheridans and Aghas over for a good old-fashioned Yankee pot roast dinner. Tim Philbrook and Ken, the handyman, had gone to North Haven two days prior and had butchered a cow. According to Tim, the large farm on North Haven had plenty of healthy livestock, and Tim and Molly were trying to devise a plan for how to maintain the farms on North Haven and Roberts Hill Farm. Tim and Ken had been kind enough to deliver cuts of fresh beef to all the families on the island, and the Olivers decided to throw a small dinner party.

Matt knew that at this very moment, Stan and Pete were standing in front of a barbecue at the farm, under Molly's supervision, and grilling hamburgers for most of the extended family. Although he hated to miss the cookout, Matt and Clare felt that socializing with their neighbors was more important. Matt used the evening to check on the Irish Rover on his way over and was happy to see how well the Olivers were serving as caretakers. The yacht was not visible from their estate, being several hundred yards to the east in a deepwater anchorage, and the two families had all agreed to keep the existence of the Irish Rover amongst themselves. The Aghas remained unaware of its presence.

"Yes, there is no doubt that Saddam was the power behind al-Bakr for many years before ousting him." Matt heard Earl Oliver say to Ferhad. Matt could tell Ferhad wanted to change the conversation but, out of politeness, was humoring the former ambassador to Ferhad's native homeland of Iraq. Matt looked across the great room and saw Laurie and Christopher playing a board game with Ferhad's teenage children and the two youngest Oliver daughters. At the other end of the room, beyond a large island separating the sitting areas from the kitchen, Matt could see Clare, Kim, Janet Oliver, and Nasrin Agha chatting away while dishing something onto numerous plates. Behind them, Kent and his sister, Eleanor, washed the dishes.

It was such an ordinary evening that Matt had difficulty processing that global civilization had ended as they knew it. His extended family and these new friends were now forced to secure their futures and forge a new society.

"Who wants cake?" Janet shouted to all in attendance. "Come and get it. You can eat it anywhere you like." The kids jumped up from their game and rushed to the kitchen counter. "Dad," continued Janet in Matt's direction, "you, Ferhad, and Matt stay right where you're at. We're all coming to join you and will bring your cake with us."

"PINEAPPLE, PINEAPPLE, PINEAPPLE." Blared from everyone's handheld radio, of which there were six in the oversized room. Matt recognized Liz's voice, and her stress was evident.

"PINEAPPLE, PINEAPPLE, PINEAPPLE. This is not a test. Boat approaching at high speed. Estimated docking location is Carver Harbor. ETA one five mikes."

Everyone in the room stopped what they were doing and looked at Matt. Pineapple was the code word for imminent danger, and everyone was to turn off their lights and shelter in place until further instruction.

"What do we do?" Kent asked first.

"Is this real?" Kent's youngest daughter, Charlotte, asked from across the room at the game table.

Matt held up a finger to signal pause, then pulled the handheld radio from his belt. He changed the channel from the all-island frequency to the one the greater Sheridan family used for internal communication. As soon as he switched, he could hear Stan talking to Liz. "..you're at. I'll get ahold of Matt, and we'll decide on the next steps. Keep us posted."

"Stan, this Matt," said Matt as soon as Stan ended his transmission. "Whadda we got?"

"Looks like a boat headed this way, at least four individuals on board. Currently south of Brown's Head Light and approaching Dog Point. Probably headed for the south side of the island, likely Carver Harbor." While Stan was talking, Janet Oliver walked over and turned off all the lights in the room except a small table lamp near Earl and Ferhad.

"What kind of boat? Did it come from Rockland?"

"Appears to be some form of lobster boat. Yes, it appears to have come from the direction of Rockland Harbor."

"Okay, Stan. Where are you now?"

"I'm at the farm with everyone besides Liz. She stayed back and is in the barn."

"I assume you all have your kit?"

"Roger," replied Stan. Matt's standing instructions were for everyone to carry their basic kit when they left the house, just in case. In Matt's truck, he had his M4, NODs, and FLC with a full load out. Kim and Clare also had their kit in the back of the pickup.

"Bring the A-team, minus Liz, and head to the Union Church. We can talk more en route. I'm leaving now, but probably almost ten minutes away. Everyone else should head over to Carver Main. I'd like the extended family all in one place. Get everyone going."

"Roger. See you soon," said Stan, signing off.

The beauty of handheld radios was that everyone in the room had heard both sides of the conversation, so Matt did not need to explain everything again. He stood up, putting the radio back on his belt opposite the holstered Glock 19 he always carried. "I have to go. I'm going to take the truck. Clare, maybe you should stay here with the kids."

"I'd really like to get back to Carver Main, Matt. Everyone else is headed there."

"Matt," interrupted Kent. "I'm happy to take Clare, Kim, and the kids back to your place on Carver Cove. We can take Round The Island Road past the airfield and be at your place in ten minutes. This route keeps us well away from Carver Harbor. Ferhad, you and your family are welcome to stay here for the night or until this is resolved."

"Thanks, Kent," said Matt. "I really appreciate that. Clare, is that okay with you?"

"Yes. Thank you, Kent."

"I'm coming with you, Matt. My kit's in the truck," said Kim. Matt looked at her and knew there was no arguing.

"I wanna come too, Dad," said Christopher, having wandered over to the sitting area from where he'd initially been at the game table. "You might need me."

"Buddy, what I really need from you is to take care of Mommy and your sister. Can you do that for me? Make sure they get home safely?"

"Sure, Dad. I can do that."

Matt started for the door, then stopped and looked at his hosts. "Janet, Kent, and Earl thank you all for your hospitality. I hope we can finish dessert sometime soon. Please stay monitoring the all-island frequency, and Liz will keep everyone posted." Matt then turned and rushed out the door, followed closely by Kim and Clare. When they got to the truck, Matt reached into the bed and pulled Clare's weapon and plate carrier. "Here, Clare. Please keep this with you. I'm sorry to leave."

Clare leaned over and kissed him on the lips. "Go," she said. "I love you. Be careful!" Clare grabbed her rifle and vest and turned to walk back to the house. Kim had already grabbed her kit, slung her plate carrier on and buckled it, and jumped in the front passenger seat. Matt threw on his stuff and climbed into the driver's seat. He adjusted the PVS-14 night vision goggles over his eyes, then drove the pickup around the Oliver's circular driveway and headed south for downstreet Vinalhaven.

CHAPTER 50

October 28, 7:22 pm

Matt and Kim lay prone atop the flat roof of the Camden National Bank, across and down the street from the Tidewater and the big parking lot they used for public gatherings. The nights were definitely getting colder, and Matt could easily see his breath. He watched through the NODs as the lobster trawler wove its way into the harbor, dodging moored boats. He knew Stan and the rest of the A-team were already in position to the east. Dylan, Derek, and Stan were in overwatch at the Snack Bar, a perfect spot for enfilade fire down the length of Main Street, as well as being able to cover the entire harbor. Matt had no doubt Dylan had the boat's passengers in the crosshairs of the scope on his Remington 700.

Dave had led the remainder of the A-team to take up covered positions on the other side of Main Street, between Carver's Harbor Market and the Star of Hope Lodge. Their position was in line with Matt's about 120 meters east on Main Street. With Stan's overwatch element on the other side of the street, they had the makings of a perfect L-shaped ambush.

Now it was a waiting game.

Matt watched the approaching boat, trying to discern who the occupants might be. According to Liz, QuAI believed these were members of the patrol The Base had sent to Rockland. Matt thought about opening fire while the boat was basically a duck in a barrel but knew his conscience would never forgive him if maybe this were an innocent family seeking refuge at

Vinalhaven, as his own family had done several weeks prior.

"Stan, this is Matt. Does the sniper see anything?" Matt asked through the radio, his and Kim's earpieces now in place to allow for silent communications. Matt knew he could call Dylan directly, but wanted to leave him to focus on the target, knowing Dylan could whisper to Stan without taking his hand off his rifle to toggle his mic.

"Sniper reports five individuals. Some, if not all, are armed. He thinks one is a woman - at least the person has a ponytail, so he's not 100% sure."

"Roger, everybody, hold fast."

"Matt, Stan. Dylan thinks they have one night vision scope. One of the men keeps raising his rifle and scoping the harbor. Dylan thinks it's infrared. No one is wearing NODs." Matt clicked once to acknowledge.

That is interesting. Matt continued to watch the boat slowly approach. *C'mon, head for the public boat ramp. Or are you fuckers going to go for the dock at Hopkins Boatyard? The tide was pretty low, and if it were me, I'd head for Hopkins.*

Matt instinctively dropped his head as a bright white light flicked on from the hardtop roof of the lobster boat. The light illuminated about fifty meters directly in front of the boat. Matt raised his head back up, watching as the boat made a slight turn to port. *He's heading for Hopkins Boatyard and not the boat ramp.*

"Listen up. Looks like he's heading for the Hopkins' dock. This puts him two blocks west of my position, which is not ideal. However, if they want to go anywhere on the island, they are going to have to walk down Main Street right into our ambush. I'll call it as they approach."

Two single clicks told Matt that Dave and Stan acknowledged.

The boat did not glide into the dock gracefully. The driver came in at too steep an angle, and despite trying to reverse rapidly, he hit the dock quite hard with the boat's bow. The co-op dock was about 200 meters to Matt's right, and he watched through his scope as several people jumped out of the boat and tied it to the dock. From their uncoordinated movements, they did not appear to have much experience as mariners.

Five individuals exited the boat and began walking up the sloped ramp leading up to the dock.

"Five individuals departed the boat, four male, one female. No one remained on the boat," Stan said over the radio.

Matt lost sight of them as they walked around the far side of the boatyard's building and in front of the Riverside and Pizza Pit restaurants. The four turned and began walking east along Main Street, directly toward Matt's position.

"Keep your head low," Matt whispered to Kim. "We're not silhouetted up here, but I still worry about that guy with the night vision scope."

"Okay."

"Definitely looks like The Base," Stan said quietly over the radio. "Dylan says he can distinguish facial tattoos on at least two people. They do not look friendly."

"Roger," whispered Matt. "They're approaching my location. We're going to let them pass. Once they reach the Tidewater, Stan, you have the call to initiate. Kim and I are almost in your line of fire, so we're going to duck down behind the brick wall. We can handle anyone who heads back to the boatyard. How copy?"

"Roger," said Stan, followed immediately by a similar reply from Dave.

As the group approached, Matt put his arm on Kim's shoulder, and they both ducked below the level of the wall atop the roof so there was no possibility they'd be seen. Interestingly, they could hear the group talking, as they were clearly making no effort to keep quiet.

"I told you motherfuckers we should have waited til daylight. This plan is so fucking stupid."

"Shut the fuck up, Hector," said a woman's voice. "We just need to check out this little downtown area tonight. Then we can hole up and eat. Damien will be here with the others at first light, and we can search the rest of the island. The reward is too good to pass up."

The group kept walking. They were not especially tactical, but they were somewhat spread out across the breadth of the road, which was likely why they were talking so loudly.

"Just passed us," Matt whispered into the radio. Two single clicks followed. Matt raised his head slightly, assuming the group was facing east and away from him. The group was now directly in front of the Tidewater, not more than fifty meters from Dave's assault element.

"What the fuck?" Kim whispered, tugging hard on Matt's sleeve. As Matt turned to look at her, he heard a loud voice below him in the street, maybe twenty meters to the right of where they were on top of the bank.

"Ahoy, there, mates. What brings you to Vinalhaven?"

Matt looked on in horror as he saw Tony Bianco and his son, AJ, standing in the middle of the street. AJ's AR-15 was slung across his chest as usual, but he and his dad had their hands empty. That didn't matter. The group of five turned around looked at the two Biancos, and immediately opened fire. Tony took several rounds to the chest while AJ dove to the ground, then scrambled to the north and between two houses.

"Initiate now," said Matt over the radio. A volley of fire erupted from Matt's left. He pushed Kim's head down below the wall just before he heard multiple rounds smack into the brick siding of the bank building. Derek opened up with the M240B, and Matt knew that Dylan was carefully picking out targets with his sniper rifle.

The fire died down in seconds, and Matt felt it was safe to pop his head up. Four bodies lay unmoving in the street. Where was the fifth guy?

Matt flipped down his NODs and looked around. *There! Hiding behind the Tidewater.* A lone figure was cowering at the side of the Tidewater hotel. He was protected from view by both Dave and Stan's teams, but unlucky for him, he was directly in front of Matt.

Matt aimed his rifle, squarely bringing the man's chest into the center of his ACOG reticle.

Bang, Bang, Bang, Bang.

Four rapid shots were fired from the bank's roof but weren't from Matt's rifle. Before he had a chance to squeeze the trigger, Kim had loosed off four quick shots. Matt looked over and could see the man writhing on the ground.

"I'm hit. I'm hit! Stop shooting! I give up! You fucking shot me!" The man kept shouting, his hands gripping his legs in an attempt to stop the bleeding. Matt looked at Kim and, despite the darkness, could see the shock on her face.

"I shot him," Kim said.

"Yes, Kim. Good job. Now do me a favor. Keep your rifle aimed at that guy, but don't shoot me. I'm going down to check on him."

Kim stared at the guy.

"Kim," Matt hissed, snapping her out of her trance. "Look at me. You did great. Now cover me, okay?"

"Yeah...yeah, okay," she said.

"All elements, four down, one injured behind the hotel. I'm going down to check on him. Dave, bring the assault element up to search the bodies."

Dave sprinted back across the small rooftop and down the outside ladder. As he rounded the building, he could see the man on the ground, still writhing in pain and talking to himself. NODs down, Matt activated his laser and kept the infrared dot centered on the man's torso as he walked forward slowly.

"Drop your weapon! Place your hands in the air."

"You shot me, you fuckah. Fuck you!"

"I'm going to shoot you again if you don't put your hands up. Last warning before I put a bullet in your face." The man put one hand in the air but kept the other pressed tightly against his thigh.

As Matt got closer, he flicked his NODs up and turned on his rifle's tac light, bathing the man in white light. Matt could see the man had been shot at least twice in his legs. A bullet had shattered his shinbone, and the lower end of his left leg hung at an awkward angle. Another round penetrated the man's right thigh, where his hand was clamped. Matt saw the blood surging through the man's fingers, immediately thinking the man's femoral artery may have been clipped.

"Help me," the man begged.

"Got a tourniquet?" Matt asked.

"What? No, I don't have a fuckin' tourniquet. Now help me, you fuckah." The guy had a wicked Massachusett accent. *A fucking Masshole. Figures!*

"Too bad. I'd say you have about three minutes, maybe four, until you bleed out."

Juliet came running up to Matt's side. "What can I do, Matt? Need help?"

"Yeah, Juliet. Thanks. Can you grab his rifle and see if he's got a pistol? I don't see a holster."

Juliet stepped forward and yanked the man's rifle over his head. She pushed him to his side, checking to see if he had a pistol in his pockets. "All clear," she said, stepping back away from the guy and slinging the guy's weapon over her back.

"So who are you, Mister?"

"Help me. Don't let me bleed out, and I'll ansah any of ya questions."

Matt reached into a pouch on his vest, pulled out a small tourniquet, and tossed it into the man's lap. "Put that on."

"How...how do I put it on?"

"Open it up. It's a loop with velcro. Wrap it around your thigh above the wound. Then cinch it down." The man clumsily did what Matt instructed. "Now take that little plastic stick, put it right in that ring, and start twisting."

The man started twisting, then screamed and stopped. "It hurts."

"Yeah, it'll do that. But it'll stop hurting when you're dead. Your call. Twist it or bleed out."

The guy twisted more and more. "How much?" He gasped.

"Until the bleeding stops," said Matt. The man twisted two more times and then was satisfied that the bleeding had slowed.

"Okay, now tell me," said Matt. "Who are you, and why are you here?"

Matt looked over and saw Dave walking over, a grim look on his face. The rest of Dave's element had searched the bodies and were dragging them over to the side of the street. As Dave got to Matt, he reached down and toggled his radio mic, "Stan, this is Dave. We need you up here in front of the Tidewater."

"What's up?" Matt asked Dave. Dave thrust out a single sheet of paper and held his handheld flashlight so Matt could read it. The paper had been folded in quarters and had some blood on the bottom edge. Matt's breath stopped as he looked at the paper, which appeared to be a photocopy. On it was an image in black and white, a picture of him and LT standing in the Woodstock Sheriff's office. Matt remembered the day well; it was right before his wife had stormed the building and killed the fake Sheriff Tate and his imposter deputies. They must have taken a cellphone image of Matt and LT before the shooting, and someone found their cell phone later. Below the picture was handwritten "HUMVEE NH ARNG C/3-172 IN."

"Fuck!" Matt said softly. "This is bad. Hey, can you get someone to check on Bianco. He's in the middle of the road, about a block down." Matt turned to the guy on the ground. "Answer my fucking question. I don't have time for you. Who are you, and why are you here?"

"I, um, I'm part of a group from The Base. We just got to Rockland yestaday, but I'm from Springfield, Mass. Honestly. We was just here seein' if there was any survivahs. Maine's now unda the protection of The Base."

"So you're here to protect us?"

"Yeah, that's right. Just to see if ya need any of our help."

"Look, man," said Matt. "I could sit here and play games with you all night. We have a surgeon back at the house, and she can fix you up good as new if you're honest." Matt dropped his weapon to hang from his 2-point sling. He reached down with his right hand and pulled his Glock 19. "If you lie, however, even once, I will put a bullet in your kneecap. Do you understand?"

"Yeah, yes."

"And add a fucking R every once in a while. I'm already sick of your accent."

"Uh, yeah. Yeah. I can do that."

"And I'm going to keep asking questions, and every time I think you're lying, even just a little, I'm going to put a 9mm round into one of your joints. So it's really your choice. Get fixed up, or die here in excruciating pain."

"Okay," sobbed the man.

"Why are you here?"

"We're checking out the island, but we're also looking for a man. I think it might be you, but it's hard to see you in the dark."

"Why are you looking for this man?"

"He supposedly has a supply of vaccine. Honestly, that's all I know. We have about ten of these sheets of paper with guys' pictures on them. We'ah supposed to keep an eye out for them. We just happened to find the Humvee, and it matched one of the papers."

"And what are you supposed to do when you find the man?"

"Kill him and take the vaccine. There's a huge reward for the team that finds him."

"What's the reward?"

"Uh...," the man hesitated, looking up at Matt. "I'm not sure, exactly."

Matt looked at the man, then shot him in his right kneecap. The man shrieked in pain, writhing on the ground. There was little blood, as the tourniquet had already stopped the flow to his entire leg, but Matt could see shards of white bone now protruding through the man's pants. *Shouldn't have lied.* Matt looked around and saw Stan, Dave, and Kim watching him.

"Don't lie. What's the reward."

"Three slaves from the next auction," the man said through gritted teeth.

"Three what?" Matt asked.

"Three slaves. Women or men if you want."

"Are you fucking serious?"

"Uh, yeah. You told me not to lie." *Jesus Fucking Christ, these guys are selling fucking people!*

"How'd you end up with The Base."

"I, uh, I don't know, man. It just happened." Matt raised his pistol, aiming at the man's ankle. "Okay, stop. I, uh, I was a CO at Hampden County Correctional Center. I got linked up with them there."

"Continue. Are these other guys correctional officers as well?"

"Ah, no. They, uh, they're inmates. The three guys're from Hampden County, and the woman came from Western Mass Women's Prison. All outta Springfield."

"And The Base recruited you?"

"Well, I wouldn't say recruited. They just, ah, they just showed up. The jails were locked down, so the pox didn't spread much. I thought it would be the safest place. Everyone else outside died, but then The Base came and gave us vaccine."

"How'd you end up in Maine."

"We, uh, we got put into a larger group under a guy named Damien. He's a gang leader in some other prison - I think upstate New York. Then we helped storm Portland and take that over, then moved up to Augusta. It was pretty wild, man."

"Yeah, I bet," said Matt. "So why'd you come here tonight? Did you know this guy you're looking for was on the island?"

"No, uh, not really. We, uh, we got to Rockland yesterday. And today, we drove around the various towns north and south on Route 1. My team went to Camden, and we messed around a couple of stores then went to the harbor. We broke into a warehouse on the harbor, and one of the guys saw this Humvee. The letters on the bumper matched what was on the photocopy. Damien thought there was a chance the guy was hiding on these islands." The guy was doing his best, but harbor and bumper still came out sounding they were spelled with no R's.

"What did you do with the Humvee?

"Whadda ya mean? We didn't do nothin. Just left it. We had our own."

"So why tonight? Why take a boat out here in the dark?"

"Well, we wasn't sure the guy was here. So Damien sent us five ahead and said to find a place to wait, and he'd bring the rest of the team over in the morning. He didn't want to ride into a harbor in daylight without some cover. So we were gonna hide out and cover them in the morning when they showed up."

"Okay, you're doing good. How many guys in your entire group? How many are with Damien."

The guy thought for a second, then said, "Nine."

Matt shot him in the ankle.

"Ahh, you fuckah! I'm not lyin'. I'm not lyin'! There's fuckin' nine more of us!"

"How many vehicles do you have?"

"Three Humvees and two four-doah pickups. I sweah. There's fourteen of us total. Five came tonight. Nine, including Damien, are comin' tomorrow."

"Where are you staying in Rockland?"

"Ah, some hotel in town. I don't know the name..." Matt raised the pistol again. "Wait! Seriously! Look, fuck, man, I don't fucking know the name of the hotel. It's across from some museum, right near the harbor. It, ah, it, it has this like lighthouse thing in the big parking lot. We brought a bunch of mattresses down to the dining area off the lobby. Didn't stink too bad."

"Okay, I believe you, buddy," said Matt. He turned to Stan and Dave. "You guys have any questions before we get this guy to the surgeon?" Both Dave and Stan shook their head. Matt turned back to the guy on the ground, looked at him disgustedly, and shot him in the forehead.

Stan and Dave both had grim looks on their face. Matt didn't care if they approved of his tactics, there was no way they were leaving this guy alive, and he'd be dead from his wounds in a day or two anyway.

"Bianco is dead," said Dave. "Took three or four rounds to the chest. Likely dead before he hit the ground."

"Yeah, I watched it happen. AJ was with him. He took off running to the north. Any sign of him?"

"No, he hasn't come back."

"Matt, this is some serious shit," said Stan. "These guys have your picture. This isn't going to just go away. If this Damien guy called it in, we have a significant problem."

"Yeah, let me think for a sec. Is everyone else okay?"

"Yeah, went like clockwork. Once we saw them start shooting, Dave's team took them all out. They weren't yet in the support team's field of fire, but the assault team dropped them all within seconds. From what Juliet said, Dave took out three himself. He's fast as shit with the M4."

"Yeah. He's had lots of practice. Definitely, a guy you want on your side in a gunfight. You find anything interesting on any of the dead?"

"Nothing," said Dave. "I sent LT and Grace down to check their boat. Make sure they didn't have anything there that might tell us more."

"Which one of them had the paper with LT's and my photo?" Matt asked.

"The woman. She took a 5.56 round to the throat. It was folded up in a pocket on her vest," said Dave.

"Okay," said Matt. "So, as I see it, we basically have two options. We can wait here and set up an ambush for Damien and his friends when they arrive in the morning, or we can go take the fight to them in Rockland right now. It's not even 8:30 pm, so we have a couple hours to plan either way. What do you guys think?"

Stan and Dave both thought for a second, neither one appearing to want to be the first to respond. "My first thought is to go with an ambush," said Stan. "This is our island, we should be able to see them coming on the surveillance cameras, and we have all night to find perfect spots to lay in our ambush. All nine will likely be in one boat, and we could even bring in the .50 cal if we wanted and blow them to bits in the harbor."

"Okay," said Matt. "Dave, what do you think."

"Well, I like Stan's plan. But honestly, I think we have to take it to them in Rockland right now."

"Why?" Matt asked.

"The variables," said Dave. "There's just too many variables. What if they don't come? What if they come ashore somewhere else on the island? What if they call in reinforcements? What if they leave someone behind to sound the alarm when they don't return? If we conduct a raid on their hotel tonight, we can control more of the variables, and we can also react and adjust. Most importantly, we're taking the fight to them and preserving this island's sanctity as much as possible."

"Stan, what do you think of that?" Matt added. "Dave brings up some very good points."

"Yeah," replied Stan, trying to rapidly think things through. "Yes, he makes some excellent points. I don't know, Matt, I think either option could work, but they could both also go terribly wrong."

"Okay, let's do this. Dave, see if we can find a sheet or a blanket, and let's wrap up Tony and maybe secure him in this warehouse or something. I see you've already stacked up the others, so you can just add this fucking degenerate to that pile," said Matt, referring to the guy he had just shot. "Load up their weapons and ammo. Stan, you take everyone back to Carver Main. Get everybody fed and reloaded. Plan as if we're going to Rockland in two hours, but we can decide when Dave and I return in about thirty minutes."

"Where are you two going?" Stan asked.

"Yeah, where are we going?" Mimicked Dave.

"To tell Camila and Gianna that their father is dead and to see if AJ is okay. I don't think he was wounded, but you never know."

CHAPTER 51

October 28, 9:51pm

The trip to inform Camila Bianco that she was now a widow went about as well as Matt expected - lots of tears and a bit of hysteria. The adult council now sat at the large dining room table in the Carver Main house, the blood-stained paper with Matt and LT's picture lay face up in the center of the table. The rest of the extended family, which now totaled twenty-four people, including the Samoset Resort group, were upstairs in the barn watching something in the theater room. Everyone here at the table had been briefed on the situation and the two options: ambush or raid.

This wasn't a democracy, and Matt did not want to take a vote. He did, however, want to gather all the information he could, including anyone's opinion that wanted to contribute.

"I know many of you feel like an ambush here at the harbor is the simplest, safest course of action. I don't disagree, but I also worry that it doesn't account for a lot of the variables that exist right now. Rockland, while providing more uncertainty, also allows us to control and adapt to the situation more than just waiting here for them to arrive. Any other thoughts or comments? Clare, you've been silent so far."

Matt hated putting his wife on the spot in front of everyone, but she was also the one person whose opinion he valued above all others. She had as much tactical experience as anyone other than Dave and Matt, but she also saw the bigger picture that included the entire family. She looked at Matt, her mind still processing.

After a moment, she spoke. "Yeah, Matt. I do have some thoughts." She paused, looking around the table. "I think the answer is pretty clear when we factor in the worst-case scenario, which, as my husband will always tell you, is one of the most important considerations for reducing risk in any plan. If we wait to ambush them, and it goes horribly wrong, then worst case is that we have perhaps a dozen armed intruders running free on the island with maybe our ambush team all wounded or killed. It would be extremely difficult for the rest of us to defend ourselves, and it would just be a matter of time before we're all killed or perhaps given away as slaves. For the raid, our force is bringing the fight to the mainland. Worst case, they're all killed; the rest of us here are still safe and secure on the island. We have the surveillance system, and we can more easily defend ourselves against an attack. So given that, I recommend we kill those fuckers tonight in Rockland."

Everyone looked at Clare, most of them nodding their heads in agreement. The worst-case scenario was always challenging to plan for, as it meant accepting that many of you would die, but it was a necessary part of any good planning process.

"Thanks, Clare. That was very insightful." Matt paused, looking around the table and fully gathering his thoughts. He knew what he was about to say may not be too popular with everyone. "Here's what we're going to do, and please, let me finish before any comments.

"We're going to raid Rockland, and we're going to leave in thirty minutes. It will be the same team as the Somoset Resort rescue, except we are adding Kim. We are also leaving Stan, Juliet, and Liz here at Carver Main."

"Wait just a sec," said Stan.

Matt held up his hand. "Please, Stan, let me finish. As I said, there will be eight of us on the raid. Stan, Juliet, and Liz are needed here for two reasons. First, any info that comes in from QuAI can immediately be relayed to us. Second, you three are critical to the survival of our extended family. Stan and Liz can pilot the Irish Rover, and the three of you add a defensive capability for the island that would be severely missing in the worst-case scenario. QuAI is our most valuable asset, not the vaccine, and the three of you are instrumental in keeping QuAI functioning. If everyone thinks about it for a moment, you'll all agree.

"Another change. I want Grace to bring the case of vaccine with her. She should leave a few vials and maybe 200 syringes so you have at least a couple of hundred doses here. However, I want to bring the rest of it with us. Worst case, if the raid is unsuccessful, then The Base will find the vaccine. There would no longer be a reason to search Vinalhaven, as they'd have me, LT, and the vaccine - the things they're looking for."

Matt paused again, looking around the table. He could see that everyone was beginning to get on board. That last part about the vaccine made it all click. They were planning for success but also to survive should the worst case happen.

"Okay, that's settled. We leave at 10:30 sharp. We're not going to go straight into Rockland. We're going to Camden, which we know well. Grab the Humvee and a couple vehicles, and drive quietly into Rockland. We'll approach the hotel on foot. Stan, was QuAI able to pinpoint their location in town?

"Yes," replied Stan. "That scumbag was telling the truth. QuAI picked up multiple RF signals all from one spot. They're at the Trade Winds Inn, on Park Drive, across from the Maine Lighthouse Museum. I'll give you the imagery before you leave."

"And we have one of the walk-talkies those guys were using? So we can listen in when we get closer?" Matt asked.

"Yes," continued Stan. "They are shit radios, so probably only work within 1-2 kilometers. However, we assume you would be able to hear them when you get closer if they're using the radio. Hopefully, they're all asleep."

"Okay. Any questions? Otherwise, Pete, go get the Hinckley ready. Dave, let's head to the barn and ensure the raid team has everything we need."

Matt, Dave, and Pete exited the dining room, leaving the rest of the council to plan how they would spend the next few hours.

CHAPTER 52

October 28, 11:49pm

Matt had all three vehicles pull over on Pleasant Street, several blocks from the harbor. They had made great time in the Hinckley flying across West Penobscot Bay, and had no issues retrieving their vehicles at the Camden harbor.

With the raiding party loaded up in their vehicles, Matt navigated them under black-out drive down Route 1 toward Rockland. At the north end of town, instead of keeping straight on Route 1, Matt detoured west a 1/4 mile and took Route 1A south, bypassing the downtown area of Rockland to the west. Route 1A intersected with Park Street, not too far from the restaurant supply warehouse, and Matt continued south a couple of blocks to Pleasant Street. Turning east toward the harbor, Matt parked the vehicles on the road. They were about six hundred meters southwest of the Trade Winds Inn, and Matt planned to approach on foot from this point. He directed Derek to remove the M240B from its mount in the turret, and everyone else loaded up all their equipment.

Like all of Matt's plans, he attempted to keep this as simple as possible and briefed everyone on the boat ride over. The eight of them were split into two teams. Matt would lead the overwatch element, taking Derek, Dylan, and Kim with him to find a position, ideally on top of the Lighthouse Museum. From the satellite imagery, the flat roof looked like an ideal position to rain death and destruction on the first floor of the hotel. Dave, along with Pete, LT, and Grace, would form the assault element. The hotel was huge, a four-story wood structure that had clearly suffered multiple additions over the years. The main wing with the entrance, lobby, and restaurant ran north-south, perpendicular to the harbor, with another wing zigging to the right, then the third wing zagging back north to the left. The shape was similar to a Z turned on its side.

Everyone had a radio with an earpiece, and the plan was for the overwatch element to walk down Pleasant Street and wrap around by the park in front of the Rockland Yacht Club, turning north until they ran into the Lighthouse Museum. The terrain by the park was much lower than the hotel, which sat significantly higher than the harbor, so Matt was confident they would be able to approach unobserved. Dave and his assault element would move forward to an objective release point approximately one hundred meters due south of the hotel. Matt would call the assault force forward into position once the overwatch element was firmly established on top of the museum.

Approaching the museum, Matt spotted an external ladder through his NODs. The museum was two stories on the side facing the harbor, but due to the slope of the hill, the building was only one story on the side closest to the hotel. Matt had his overwatch element wait at the bottom while he scaled the metal ladder as quietly as possible. Once on the roof, Matt noted with satisfaction that there was a two-foot high wall surrounding the roof, which would offer the perfect cover for his team. He could see the four-story hotel directly across Park Drive, not more than seventy meters away. The bad news was that the roof was a bitumen roof covered in a layer of crushed stone. His team would have to be patient in quietly high-crawling across the roof, and he steeled himself for some bloody knees and elbows. All part of the game.

Matt toggled his mic. “Okay, come up slowly. Dylan, Derek, then Kim. Make sure you sling your weapons on your back, and don’t let anything metal hit the ladder. We have plenty of time, so take your time.”

He watched as Dylan slowly ascended. Helping Dylan onto the roof, Matt pointed to the left side and whispered for him to crawl slowly. Derek was next, taking much longer as he diligently ensured the large machine gun strapped to his back didn't accidentally bang into the ladder. Finally, with Kim on top, they all crawled slowly into place. Dylan and Matt on the left with both sniper rifles and Derek and Kim in the center with the machine gun. Matt also had an M320 grenade launcher which he laid carefully beside him, along with a half dozen gold-tipped 40mm HEDP grenades.

"What do you see, Dylan?" Matt whispered.

"One man standing at the main entrance, smoking a cigarette. I actually think it might be a blunt from the way he's holding it. No other movement that I can see anywhere else. With infrared, you can make out a faint light in those windows to the right of the entrance. I'm guessing that's the restaurant area, and they have some kind of battery-powered lantern or something."

Matt looked out and could see the entire parking lot. There were four cars scattered throughout the lot, but in front of the hotel's middle section were three Humvees and two oversized pickup trucks. Both trucks had big tires and lift kits, and one had a roll bar with a half-dozen spotlights mounted across the top. The hotel itself was as Matt expected from the imagery. As he looked, he pinpointed the faux lighthouse extension on the side of the building, and a sheet metal sculpture of a lobster the size of a car sitting in the median between the parking lot and the street.

"Okay, keep looking." Matt toggled his radio, whispering. "Dave, this is Matt. We have one sentry at the main entrance. Why don't you begin moving up? Because of the sentry, instead of stacking along the south wall of the hotel, I want you stop short in that little park between the hotel and the bank. That puts you fifty meters back instead of twenty, but I think you can cover that ground quickly, and it's not worth the risk of getting too close."

"Roger. Moving now."

Matt looked to his left, watching for signs of the assault element. From studying the imagery, he knew that Dave would walk up through Chapman Park, cross Park Drive to the Camden National Bank, then walk twenty meters toward the hotel and stop in Winslow Holbrook Park. Chapman Park was the size of a city block, with an enormous flagpole in the middle, but Holbrook Park was a 1/4 that size, consisting simply of several trees and benches. Two minutes later, Matt watched as four people slowly crossed the intersection, taking their time so as not to alert anyone with sudden movement. They were distinct in that each person wore a combat helmet. They only had a half-dozen Kevlar helmets back in the arms storage room, but Matt insisted the four members of the assault element wear them for this mission. Clearing a building was much more complicated than assaulting a large outdoor objective, and Matt wanted to ensure his overwatch element could identify the good guys from the bad guys.

"Assault in position."

"Roger. Standby," said Matt, whispering. Matt quietly crawled over to Derek. "Hey, I'm going to have Dylan drop the sentry. When that happens, you are cleared hot. Focus your fires on those windows to the right of the entrance. Remember, they'll all be on the ground, so put your rounds into the wood below the windows - these 7.62 will go right through the walls. I see you've already linked two belts, but Kim, your job is to link another belt if he needs it. Good?"

They both nodded their heads in the dark. "And Kim, you're the lookout. Keep your eyes on the entire building and call out any targets. Remember, once we start shooting, there's no need to whisper or use the radio; just yell."

Matt silently shuffled back to his original position. He had already loaded a grenade in the M320 and ensured his other HEDP rounds were within easy reach.

"Assault, go ahead and break chem lights." Dave had given each team member a mini-chem light, which they now broke to activate and placed in the back of their helmets. With his NODs, Matt could make out a glow coming from the park down the street.

"Chemlights activated," whispered Dave.

"I'm giving Dylan the green light. When you hear his shot, move up to the corner of the building. When I see you pop the big orange chem light, we'll shift fires. Give us at least thirty seconds of sustained fire. I'll call targets over the radio if I can."

One click and Matt knew Dave was ready to go.

"Okay, Dyl," whispered Matt. Drop that sentry when you're ready. Put at least two into him, then shift to other targets. You have the 2nd Remington 700 right here if you need it. Faster than reloading yours."

"Okay," said Dylan.

Matt picked up the M320 and aimed it at the far right edge of the first-floor windows. He planned to work back toward the lobby entrance to keep people from scrambling deeper into the hotel.

On the end of Dylan's Remington 700, the suppressor muted his shot, but it was still quite loud to those on the roof. Matt was aware of the sentry collapsing, then Derek opened fire with the M240B and all hell broke loose. Matt pulled the trigger on his grenade launcher and watched the 40mm grenade shoot forward across the parking lot. *Shit! I didn't account enough for the height of this building. That one's going to be high.*

Matt opened the breach of the launcher, ejecting his spent casing to the side, and immediately slammed in another and locked it in the breach. The first grenade exploded harmlessly on the balcony above the window he had been aiming for. Adjusting slightly downward, his next round went cleanly through the appropriate window and exploded in a shower of flames and debris. Over the next few seconds, Matt furiously loaded, fired, and reloaded three rounds through the restaurant windows.

Derek was rocking and rolling on the 240. Keeping to six-to-nine round bursts, his rounds were chewing up the front of the hotel.

Bang. Bang. Bang. Bang. Bang. Bang.

Bang. Bang. Bang. Bang. Bang. Bang. Bang. Bang. Bang.

Bang. Bang. Bang. Bang. Bang. Bang.

Bang. Bang. Bang. Bang. Bang. Bang. Bang. Bang. Bang.

Matt counted three muzzle flashes from the first-floor windows, and each time a muzzle flashed, Derek put a burst into that spot. Matt picked up his M4 and fired an entire 30-round magazine at where he had seen two of the muzzle flashes.

An orange chem light flared at the front corner of the hotel.

"Shift fire!" Matt yelled to his team. Dylan stopped firing, and Derek traversed to the right and fired several bursts into the far right side of the restaurant.

Matt watched as Dave's 4-person assault team, which had moved up to the front corner of the hotel during the initial shooting, now cut across the front in and moved swiftly toward the main entrance. Matt could see the chem lights in the back of their helmets as they stopped just around the corner from the entrance. A pause, and two of the assault element pitched M67 fragmentation grenades into the foyer and front windows of the hotel. Two seconds later, the night light up with near simultaneous grenade explosions, follow by two assaulters going forward and two breaking right into the restaurant.

A quick flurry of firing came from the hotel, the flashes from the muzzles lighting up the now mostly-shattered windows along the front.

"I'm heading down there," Matt yelled to his team as he dashed for the ladder. "Keep watching. Shoot anything that moves in that parking lot that isn't me." Matt swung his feet over the ladder and headed down as fast as possible. He ran up the hill along the side of the museum and sprinted across the street and into the parking lot, kneeling behind one of the few cars parked haphazardly in the lot.

"All Clear! All Clear!" Dave's voice boomed through the radio. "All enemy down. No friendly casualties." The tension in Matt's body that had built up over the last few hours seemed to immediately wash away. He stood up and looked across the parking lot with his NODs. He could see the four members of the assault element, each with their barrel-mounted flashlights, searching throughout the restaurant's first floor.

"How many KIA, Dave?" Matt asked. "What's the count."

"Trying to get it now. Some of these guys are in pieces. I think you hit one guy in the nuts with a 40 mike mike."

"Matt, this is Kim. I thought I just saw something move over by the Humvees. It could just be an animal or my imagination."

"Roger, I'll check it. Keep in overwatch."

"Assault, I'm moving across the parking lot. Just to let you know." Matt stood up and began walking across the parking lot to the Humvees and monster trucks parked twenty meters to his front right.

"Roger," said Dave. "Right now, we count eight. Counting again."

Eight? There should be nine.

Matt walked slowly forward, his mind wondering if the guy on the island had lied or if they had one enemy unaccounted for. To his right, he heard a scuffle and what sounded like a muffled scream. Matt immediately took four steps to his right to shine his rifle's light into the space between the two pickup trucks. Kneeling on the ground, tears streaking her dirt-encrusted face, was a woman in her thirties - completely naked. Her body had numerous cuts and scabs, and her breasts were so bruised they looked purple.

What the fuck? How the fuck did this woman get here?

The woman started to scream as Matt sensed a rush of movement from his left and heard a suppressed shot from the museum behind him and a scream over his radio. Instinctively, instead of turning to look, Matt dove toward the movement, hoping to use his body to sweep the rushing attacker off his feet. Matt felt a searing pain along his left side as he rolled onto the ground. Before he could get to his feet, an incredibly strong man jumped on top of him. Matt found himself pinned on his back and, through sheer luck, had caught the man's right arm with his own left hand. Matt could see the blade of the knife pointed directly down at him, and it was taking all his strength to hold the knife up just inches from his face. Luckily, Matt was left-handed, but as strong as Matt was, unfortunately, this guy was quite a bit stronger. Matt could feel the man's abdominal muscles as he lay on top of him, and he knew he couldn't hold out for more than a couple of seconds.

The guy slid his left knee inward in an attempt to crush Matt's testicles. While this move gave the man more leverage with his knife hand, it also did something else, something that would prove fatal. By moving his knee between Matt's legs, he opened up Matt's right side, allowing Matt to reach down and swiftly pull out his Glock. Holding the barrel against the side of the man's chest, Matt pulled the trigger five times in rapid succession. These five 9mm hollow points entered the man's chest cavity and liquified his heart and lungs, blowing an exit wound on the other side of his chest bigger than Matt's fist.

Still gripping the man's wrist, Matt easily tossed him aside, where he lay listless on the pavement.

Matt stood up before noticing the pickup truck speeding in reverse through the parking lot with the naked woman at the wheel. She screeched to a halt, swung the wheel hard to the left, and sped forward, attempting to exit the lot along the same road that Dave's assault team had just entered, bringing the truck right in front of the hotel's entrance.

Oh Shit! "Don't shoot, don't shoot!" Matt yelled into his radio, but it was too late. Derek opened fire with a long, sustained burst of the M240B; simultaneously, two of the assault team rushed out of the main entrance and began firing into the windshield of the speeding truck. The 5.56 and 7.62 rounds shattered the vehicle's windshield and driver's area, causing it to swerve sharply to the right and crash head-on into the front of the hotel, about fifteen meters to the left of the main entrance.

Matt sprinted across the parking lot, realizing again that he had an extremely sharp pain in his left side, above his hip. He ran to the driver's door, pulling the bullet-riddled door open by the handle. Inside, the naked woman lay gasping, her head thrown back into the headrest by the exploding airbag, which had now deflated.

Her eyes looked at Matt, scared, pleading. Matt could see several bullet wounds, both entrance and exit, in her chest and arms. From how she sat, Matt figured her spinal cord might be severed as she didn't appear to be moving anything. He stepped up on the door's step to lean in and better assess her wounds. He heard footsteps rapidly approaching behind him and saw Grace and LT running up. They had likely been the shooters at the entrance, thinking this was a fleeing Base member and not a captive woman.

"It's okay," Matt said soothingly. "You're going to be okay." The woman tried to speak, but blood started dripping from her mouth.

She tried again. "They...they...they killed my family. My children..."

"Shhhh," said Matt, reaching up his hand to stroke her matted hair and brush it from her eyes. "We'll sort all that out later. Just keep breathing. You're going to be okay."

Matt kept eye contact with the woman as she struggled to breathe. "What's your name? We'll get you patched up here in no time," said Matt soothingly.

"Thank...thank you." Matt thought he saw the woman briefly smile; then, the life simply disappeared from her eyes. Her chest stopped moving. Like a whisper on the wind, Matt knew she was gone.

He stepped back down to the ground. He felt nauseous and thought he might throw up. *What a horrible life this woman must have had over the past few days and weeks. Her children murdered and then ravaged by these barbarians. And we fucking killed her. We didn't mean to, but we did.*

Grace and LT stepped forward, noticing it was a naked woman, not an enemy combatant.

"Oh my god!" Grace whispered, while LT looked on, stunned. "We had no idea, Matt. We thought the truck was escaping, so we fired." Grace started to cry.

"Grace, Grace," Matt said, wrapping his arms around her to calm her down. "Listen to me. You did everything right. There's nothing you could have done. She was dead the minute they killed her kids and took her captive. This is not your fault. It's none of our faults."

Dave and Pete walked up to the truck. "All clear inside, Matt. Nine accounted for, including your guy in the parking lot. Pete and I did a quick sweep of the hotel, and it seems clear. No signs of anyone else." Dave peaked into the truck's cab, immediately understanding what had happened. "Ready to roll, Matt? Still want to go through with the plan to ditch the Humvee?"

"Yeah, let's go. Did you guys find anything interesting in the hotel?"

"A few things," said Pete. "We put everything into a bag, and we can sort through it when we get home."

Dave called the overwatch team down from the museum roof while Pete, LT, and Grace jogged down to the parked vehicles on Pleasant Street.

"You're bleeding," said Kim, looking down at his left side. She pulled a flashlight from a pouch on her vest and shined it on his torso. "Jesus, Matt. You're seriously hurt." She reached out to touch it, and Matt felt fire burning along his entire left side.

"Please!" Matt said, jumping back a step. "That really hurts."

"Matt, your entire left side is drenched in blood," Kim said. Hearing her, Dave walked over to look for himself. Kim gently pulled back Matt's torn fleece to get a better look.

"Jesus, Matt. Is that from the guy in the parking lot? He got you good. Looks like a slice and also a puncture wound."

"I'll be okay. Trust me, let it bleed for a bit. I'll have Grace patch it when we get to Camden."

In a minute, their vehicles pulled into the parking lot, where they cross-loaded all of the ammunition and weapons from The Base vehicles. Grace fussed over Matt's injury, but he fended her off. He wanted this wound to bleed.

Instead of heading back north to Camden, Matt directed LT to head out Park Street, which was Route 1 South. Matt could feel his side and back sticking to the cloth seat of the Humvee, a sharp pain shooting through his side with each movement or bump in the road. After a mile, they passed a Walmart and a Lowes but kept driving southwest. After about five miles, the road curved, and they entered the outskirts of the town of Thomaston.

"Stop here, LT. Right here on the side of the road. Just turn off the vehicle, and take everything you need." Matt gingerly climbed out of the Humvee. He had already directed Derek not to mount the M240B and to take a seat in one of the pickups. There was nothing else in the Humvee that they wanted. Matt walked over to the lead pickup, where Pete was driving. "You got it?"

"Yeah," said Pete, handing Matt the folded-up photocopy of the image of him and LT in Woodstock that they had taken from The Base female KIA on Vinalhaven. Matt took the paper, crumpled it up, and threw it on the floor well of the passenger seat. He then walked to the front of the vehicle and fired an entire magazine into the Humvee - aiming for the windshield, the tires, and the engine block. He had already confirmed that the cloth of the passenger seat was soaked through with blood.

Matt returned to the pickup's open rear passenger door, where Grace sat on the other side and held up a large military bandage. "Get in, Matt. Let me stop that bleeding."

After Matt had gingerly climbed aboard and shut the door, with Grace bandaging him up, Pete pulled a U-turn, and the two pickups sped northward on Route 1, heading for Camden harbor.

"Think they'll buy it?" Pete asked.

"Who knows? Can't be sure anyone will even stop to look

at it, but if another patrol does come by, maybe they'll spot the bumper # and check the inside. Hopefully, they'll conclude that I might be wounded but that we fled south on Route 1 rather than back to Rockland and the offshore islands."

CHAPTER 53

October 29, 2:33pm

Matt sat in the overstuffed brown leather chair in the family room of Carver Main, a chair that had become his purely because he always sat there. Christopher sat next to him, dealing cards onto the small side table between them, upon which sat a cribbage board. Kim had recently exposed Christopher to the game of cribbage, and he now challenged anyone who had the time to a game.

Matt took a sip from his cold bottle of beer and picked up his cards, automatically rearranging them in his hand by suit and number. He was enjoying this time playing cards and letting the stress of the morning and previous evening drain away. His side hurt from where Grace had clipped him with a half dozen surgical staples to close up his knife wound, and he was exhausted from the evening and morning's activities. But he'd rather play cards than take a nap.

They had returned early this morning, around 3 am, and Stan, Michelle, and Clare were waiting for them at the pier in Carvers Cove. The benefit of the long boat ride back to Vinalhaven was that everyone had a chance to get the adrenaline out of their system and unwind. Matt, Dave, and Pete chatted quietly in the cockpit while the others mostly dozed on the seats behind them.

Rising at 8 am, Clare told Matt that Stan had headed downtown earlier, along with Dylan, Liz, and Juliet. They were going to bury the bodies of The Base intruders. Also, they planned a small burial ceremony for Tony at 10 am at the John Carver Cemetery north of downstreet Vinalhaven, overlooking Carvers Pond.

At nine, as Matt and Clare were about to head into town to meet with everyone before Bianco's funeral, Stan called over the family-only channel of the radio.

"Matt, this is Stan."

"Hey, Stan, we were about to head your way."

"You're about to get a visitor. Gianna Bianco. She's driving and should be with you momentarily. Please don't leave until you speak with her. It's sensitive, and I'm not sure I want to broadcast it over the radio."

"I understand. I'll see you after I speak to her."

"Matt, is Clare there?"

"Yeah, Stan, she's right here."

"Good. You'll see in a minute."

Three minutes later, the old Econoline van the Biancos had been driving since arriving on the island pulled into the driveway behind Carver Main's barn. Matt and Clare walked outside to greet their visitor. Gianna Bianco was dressed as usual in yoga pants and an oversized sweatshirt. However, Matt noticed she was now wearing a pair of Merrells they had picked up for her on the team's first trip to Rockland.

"Hey Matt. Hey Clare. Could I have a word with you, please?"

Matt could immediately tell that Gianna had been crying. Although her face was now dry, her eyes were puffy, and her cheeks a splotchy red.

"Sure, honey," replied Clare. "Let's go sit down inside. Can I get you something to drink? Warm tea, maybe?"

"No, thank you." Gianna followed Clare into the house and sat on the sofa where Clare gestured. Matt sat in "his" easy chair while Clare sat beside Gianna.

"I'm sorry about your father, Gianna," said Matt. "It's a terrible situation. As I said last night, anything we can do at all, just ask."

"That's why I'm here. My mother's dead, and my brother's

gone. And I'd like to live here with you, or maybe at Roberts Hill Farm. Would that be okay?"

Both Matt and Clare sat forward, alarmed at Gianna's statement. "Whoa, Gianna. Could you back up a bit, please?" Matt asked. "I just saw your mother last night. She's dead, you say?"

"Yes, my brother killed her. About thirty minutes ago."

Matt sat forward in his chair while Clare slid over on the couch and wrapped her arms around Gianna. The young woman began sobbing, burying her head in Clare's shoulder while Clare stroked her hair soothingly.

"It's okay, Gianna," said Clare. "Why don't you tell us what happened."

Over the next few minutes, Gianna outlined a story right out of a horror movie. Unable to sleep after her husband's death, her mother drank through the evening, finishing two bottles of wine. When AJ awoke, her mother started berating him, accusing him of failing to protect his father and going so far as to say he was responsible for his father's death. The alarming part was that her brother sat calmly listening to it all while eating his breakfast. He then asked his mother if she was done talking, and when she said yes, he pulled out his pistol and shot her. He kept pulling the trigger and shooting her until the magazine was empty. Gianna was sure her brother would have killed her as well, but he was out of bullets. He then ran out of the house.

Matt called Stan to inform him. Stan and Dave rode out to the Bianco's house and confirmed Gianna's story. Having been sent back to Carver Main by Stan, Liz confirmed thirty minutes later that AJ had taken one of the lobster boats moored by the Bianco's house and appeared to be heading for Rockland.

Matt and Clare spent an hour talking with Gianna, who Matt had always admired at how she stood up to her parents, and Clare had taken her to the farm to get her settled in with Molly and the rest of the crew. Stan and Dylan had buried Tony and Camila Bianco without ceremony.

Just another day of drama on Vinalhaven.

Matt sipped his beer and selected two cards to lay away in the crib. "You go first, buddy." Matt was looking forward to spending at least an hour playing cards with his son, then maybe seeing if Laurie wanted to do something. Then possibly a nap.

Matt heard someone enter through the mudroom at the back of the house, assuming Clare was returning from the farm. Stan walked into the room.

"Hey Matt, I'm sorry to interrupt, but can I see you for a minute? It's important." Matt looked up, and Stan looked like he'd seen a ghost. Matt knew right then that something was very, very wrong.

"Sure thing. Hey buddy, why don't you wake Uncle Pete upstairs? He loves cribbage more than I do."

"Okay, Dad," Chris replied, used to having his father pulled away. Matt followed Stan as he walked out the mudroom door, and up the stairs to the room above the barn. Matt walked in and immediately sat on the sofa while Stan remained standing.

"What's up, Stan. You look like you've seen a ghost."

Stan paced a bit back and forth. "I don't even know where to begin, Matt."

"Try the beginning. I've never seen you like this, Stan. What happened?" Matt was beginning to become very concerned. Matt had never seen Stan rattled.

"General Donovan was assassinated two hours ago in Cheyenne Mountain. The Vice President has already been sworn in as President."

"Holy shit! Are you fucking serious?" Matt was incredulous. "Jack Donovan is dead?"

"Yes, shot on his way to lunch in the cafeteria."

"By who?"

"By an intel analyst. They have already found this person had ties to The Base."

"Jesus. So Todd Moravian is now President of the United

States? Or what's left of it?"

"Yes, he is."

"And you know him, right? You didn't have anything good to say when you learned Donovan had appointed him as the VP."

"No, he's a worthless human being, and I don't use the term lightly. I wrote him his last fitness report in the Navy, and I am proud to say that evaluation was likely why he resigned his commission. I had no idea he'd be elected to Congress from Arizona and turn into a right-wing extremist."

"Yeah, I never liked the guy's politics. I always liked that he was a veteran, but he also seemed slimy to me. The whole eye patch thing kind of bothered me as well."

"You mean the fact he lost his eye in a motorcycle accident, yet let's everyone believe he was a Navy Seal and lost his eye in combat? He was a logistics officer in the Navy. He ran the concessions on my ship - like he was literally the guy in charge of our equivalent of a 7-11 store."

Matt chuckled. "Politicians."

"Yeah, well, that politician - he just started Civil War II."

"Seriously?"

"As a heart attack. QuAI confirmed that the 82nd Airborne has launched a two-pronged attack along both sides of the James River to seize Richmond. One brigade is moving up along I-64 through Yorktown and Williamsburg, while another is charging along Route 460 through Petersburg. Littoral combat ships and guided missile destroyers are supporting the attacks from the James and York Rivers as much as possible."

"Wow," said Matt. "You mentioned the other day that QuAI said this would happen, but I didn't really think through the ramifications."

"That's not all. An aircraft carrier, the USS George HW Bush, according to QuAI, is leading another front to seize control of Philadelphia. What remains of the 2nd Marine Division is on board, supported by a fleet of destroyers, cruisers, and littoral combat ships. They will be there by midnight. QuAI estimates that much of Philadelphia will likely be destroyed and that The Base will sabotage the oil refineries. In fact, QuAI believes the oil refineries have likely already been sabotaged."

"Damn. Looks like Moravian isn't messing around."

"That's the thing, QuAI isn't sure Moravian is leading this. She thinks the Norfolk admiral launched this as soon he learned of Donovan's assassination. While the government may have planned and prepared to conduct this offensive, Donovan was loathe to attack fellow Americans on such a large scale."

"So what's all this mean for us? Is this bad for us or good for us?"

"Well, normally, I'd say this is pretty good for our situation here on Vinalhaven, at least in the short term. Should the Base choose to fight back, which it looks like they'll do, it will likely focus all its attention and assets on fighting the federal government. That leaves less potential for someone to come looking for you. Long term, however, it could be the opposite. If Norfolk pushes The Base out of Virginia and eastern Pennsylvania, those barbarians need somewhere to go. They could push west or head north and reinforce New England."

"Okay. That makes sense. Any timeline for this?"

"Well, for us, it should be after spring, worst case. Winter should cut us off from just about everyone if they aren't pushing into Rockland in the next six weeks. It's not like the roads are going to be plowed. And the older the stored fuel gets, with no options for replenishment, the more conservative people will become in using their shrinking resources to explore new territory."

"I like the sound of that. So, we just need to make it to mid-December when the snow will likely accumulate for the winter, and we should be safe until March. Right?"

"I think that's a pretty safe assumption."

"I'll get everyone together before dinner, and we can let everyone know. I'll go downstairs and tell Pete right now and

Clare if she's home, then maybe walk over and let Dave and Michelle know. Dave can tell the other residents on the island." Matt got up to leave.

"There's one last thing, Matt. It might be the most important."

"What's that," said Matt, sitting back down.

"Remember when I said someone at Cheyenne Mountain was trying to follow our activity within the DoD intelligence sensors to see what we were accessing?"

"Yes, I do. You said QuAI thought it was a sympathizer for The Base. Did you find out more?"

"Sort of. That individual left a message."

"For QuAI?"

"No, for me."

Matt did a double-take. "What do you mean, Stan? How did they leave a message for you?"

Stan handed Matt a sheet of paper with one sentence typed on it:

Stan White, we want to talk about sharing
QuAI. We know where you're located.
Contact us immediately. QuAI will know how.

"What's this mean, Stan? How does QuAI know how to contact them?"

"That's the genius of the message. If it were interrupted by anyone but me, with control of QuAI, I'd have no clue how to reply. But when I asked QuAI, she knew exactly where to leave a message."

"Have you replied?" Matt asked.

"No. I don't know what to say."

"Fuuuuck," said Matt in exasperation.

"Exactly.

"Why do they want you so bad, Stan? What do they hope to gain?"

"As I said the other day, QuAI is the most powerful data analyzer in the world, and with her machine learning capability, we have thousands, maybe even millions of times more processing power than what is left of the entire world combined. Before the cataclysm, QuAI was the most powerful AI computer on earth. That's why I was worth seven billion dollars. I was too busy working to spend it, and Marvi and I are pretty down-to-earth people so that net worth was meaningless above a certain amount. But QuAI is potentially the world's future - at least she's the world's best hope for rebuilding."

"So, have you considered giving access to the government?"

"Yes, I have. Marvi, Juliet, and I talk about it quite a bit. Almost every night. I liked General Donovan, and I felt I could probably work something out with him that would give me assurances QuAI wouldn't be used for the wrong purposes. With him dead, I'm not so sure. Moravian is a lunatic. Not only is he not very bright, but he's also dangerous. And I've heard similar things about the Norfolk admiral, a guy named Cryover."

"Yeah, I can see that. There are no more checks and balances or the rule of law. If you gave them access to QuAI, you would absolutely lose control of it without recourse. Is there any way anyone could gain access without you?"

"No. Right now, the only access is through that terminal in the room next to us. Only I can get into the main bunker in Charlottesville."

"What if something happens to that computer terminal next door?"

"Technically, myself, Marvi, or Juliet would be able to gain access through a different computer, but it would be a long process and require some special verification as well as the fobs we carry. Remember, QuAI is an artificially intelligent super-computer. In layman's terms, she has some capability to think for herself. She is programmed to accept guidance from me, Marvi, and Juliet - and if we are able to make contact with her by any means, she would have the process to validate our authenticity."

"Okay. Makes sense. So what do you think we should do?"

"Right now, nothing. I'm just scared shitless, Matt. You've had the Nomads and The Base chasing you, but learning that what remains of the federal government wants what I have, and knowing they are willing to take it from me by force, scares the hell out of me."

"I feel you, Stan. I do. You tell me what I can do to help, and we'll do it. You're part of this family, and whatever I can do or any of us can do, just let us know. Okay?"

"Yeah, thanks, Matt. I already knew that, but it's nice to hear. I'll keep you posted. I think we need to let everyone know about Donovan and the Civil War, and I'll update you as I learn anything."

CHAPTER 54

October 29, 4:02pm

Matt sipped a glass of iced tea. Clare had made a batch from a powdered can of sweet tea, and honestly, it wasn't bad. Grace had come by and finished changing Matt's dressing, and she, Kim, and Clare were joining him in the family room for iced tea and MRE cookies.

It had been an hour since he'd left Stan upstairs in the barn, and Dave and Pete had decided to make a trip around the island and let everyone know about the President's death and outbreak of Civil War. The adult council, as Matt still referred to it, was planning to meet at 6 pm, and Matt was going to grill lobsters while Michelle was bringing a pot of clam chowder.

As Matt took another sip of iced tea, the satellite phone in his office began ringing loudly. Matt got up and walked to his office to retrieve it, wondering who was calling. The Olivers had a sat phone, but they would typically use the radio. Rob was the other possibility, but it was a bit too late in South Africa for him to be calling.

"Hello, this is Matt."

"Matt, it's Rob."

"Hey, man, good to hear from you. How are things in South Africa."

"Good, Matt. Listen, I don't know any other way to say this, bru. You need to leave Vinalhaven now. Tonight. They are coming after you and Stan White. They know about the computer and the vaccine and want both."

"Woah, back up a sec, Rob. Who's they?" As Matt asked this, he heard a commotion in the mud room down the hall from his office. He could hear Stan yelling his name and Clare calming him down and telling him that Matt was on the sat phone.

"Cheyenne Mountain, and the new president. Moravian. They've dispatched a ship to get what they think is theirs."

Matt's head reeled, and Stan poked his head in the doorway. Matt covered the phone receiver, "It's Rob, and it's bad. Get the adult council here, now."

"Yeah, Matt. They're sending a Navy ship to Vinalhaven. For you and me." Matt could tell Stan was a bit panicked, but like all good leaders, he quickly calmed himself down.

Matt uncovered the phone. "Okay, Rob, anything else you can tell me?"

"No, bru. Roy Brownley just called. He didn't have your contact, but I had told him about you previously. You know he's a guy we can trust with our lives, and he called me to tell you to run. As far and as fast as you can. And to run right now."

"Okay, Rob. I appreciate the warning. We thought something like this might happen, and we have a contingency."

"Stop!" Rob shouted. "Don't tell me. These sat phones are nothing more than radios talking to satellites. You never know who's listening."

"Roger, good point. I'm sure I told you where my sister-in-law's family was from. That's where we're headed."

There was a pause on the line, and Matt could almost see Rob racking his brain trying to recall that conversation. In five seconds, Rob replied, "Got it, Matt. Good luck, bru. Seriously. If you can make it here, we have plenty of room. For all of you. Be safe, my friend."

"Thanks, you too, Rob." Matt disconnected the call and laid the phone back in its cradle. He turned to walk back to the family room when the phone rang again.

"Yeah, Rob, what'd you forget?" Matt asked.

"Matt, it's not Rob. This is Roy Brownley."

"Hey, Tex. I was just speaking with Rob, and he told me what you told him. How are you?"

"As good as can be expected, which is way better than 98% of the world's population, so I can't complain. So you know about Moravian? And the littoral combat ship?"

"Yeah, Rob told me."

"Okay, man. I gotta go before someone tracks this call. Give my best to Clare and your family."

"I appreciate it, Tex. I really do. I know you're sticking your neck out for us."

"It's what we do for brothers in arms, Matt. I'm here if you need me. Take care."

The call disconnected.

Matt entered the kitchen and saw everyone sitting at the dining room table. He took his place at the head and, looking around, noticed that everyone from the adult council was present except Pete and Dave. Before he could ask, Clare said that they were expected within minutes.

"Okay, Stan, why don't you fill everyone in on what you learned earlier this afternoon. We can discuss the most recent activity when Pete and Dave arrive."

Stan spoke to everyone for about five minutes, wrapping up as Pete and Dave walked into the room and sat down. "Okay, now that everyone is here," continued Stan. "There've been some recent developments that require some immediate decisions on our part." He paused and looked around the table. "About ten minutes ago, QuAI alerted that a Littoral Combat Ship had been dispatched from Norfolk Naval Station en route to Vinalhaven. Their task is to apprehend Matt and me and confiscate all vaccine doses and components of the QuAI computer system."

"What the fuck," exclaimed Dave. Everyone else around the table looked stunned, shocked even. Clare and Marvi were both deathly pale. It was difficult to hear that the federal government had dispatched a warship to collect your husband against his will.

"I'd like to add that I just got off the phone with Rob in South Africa, as well as a senior member of the CIA who now works at Cheyenne Mountain and who I worked alongside quite extensively in Iraq. Both are men I have previously trusted with my life and I now trust implicitly. They each called to warn me and to tell me to flee, and I quote, as fast and as far as I can."

"They can't do this," said Michelle. "You've done nothing wrong."

"It's not about right or wrong," said Matt. "It's about power. We have something they want, and they believe they have the power to take it. Honestly, it's no different than The Base. A bit less barbaric, but still as counter to the ideals of democracy and common decency as you can get."

"Is this the new president?" Marvi asked. "For those who don't know, Stan almost kicked the new President out of the Navy when the guy was a junior officer."

"Yes, love," answered Stan. "He's likely behind this. There's something else at play, but we're not quite sure what it is. In any case, we don't want any part of it."

"Is there some way to work this out?" Molly asked. It was rare for her to ask a lot of questions.

"No," said Matt. "We're beyond the discussion point. I think right now, the discussion needs to be about what we are going to do. Usually, I would prefer to get input from everyone and then put together a course of action with group consensus. We simply don't have that kind of time. I'm going to put out a contingency that I've been thinking through for weeks but haven't shared with anyone but Clare since it seemed unnecessary.

"We commandeered the Irish Rover for one reason - so we could flee in the Irish Rover if things became untenable on Vinalhaven. Stan, what is the earliest that navy ship can be here?"

"QuAI estimates about 8 am tomorrow. But the ship also has a helicopter, which could arrive as early as 6 am."

"Thanks. Pete, how about the tides? It looks like the cove is getting low."

"Low tide is just after 6 pm, in less than two hours, and high tide is a bit after midnight. 12:22 am, to be exact."

"Great. Thanks, Pete. So my plan is simple: pack up everything we can and depart on the Irish Rover at midnight's high tide."

"Where would we go?" Molly asked.

"Kinsale, Ireland."

"Wow, Matt. That sounds incredibly specific."

"Molly, I think we've known each other long enough for you to know I'm always thinking of contingencies. And yes, it is extremely specific. Not only is that our destination, but I have already had Liz print out all the necessary charts and information we might need to get us there. There'll be plenty of time on board to explain why I chose Kinsale, but I believe it is the ideal destination for the future success of this family."

"Can we leave in eight hours, Matt?" This time it was Marvi asking the questions.

"It doesn't matter if we can. We must. If not, Stan and I will end up in a brig in Norfolk, at best, and we will have lost our two biggest assets."

"I thought all of us were our biggest assets?" Molly said.

"You're 100% correct, Molly. And that's exactly why we're fleeing. I only have one goal, and I think you know me well enough to agree. The only thing I think of, day and night, awake or dreaming, is how to keep this family safe. And fleeing to Ireland is the best option to do that. In my opinion, anyway."

"I agree," said Clare. "Let's move on to what we need to do."

"I'm in," Kim added.

"Us as well," said Michelle, speaking for her and Dave.

"We're in," said Marvi, with Stan nodding.

Everyone looked at Pete and Molly. Pete raised his hands. "Hey, I didn't think I even needed to say anything. You're our family."

"Molly, before you say anything, I'd like to add something," said Matt. "I think if Stan and I leave with our families, I'm very certain that the government people coming here, who I assume will likely be Navy people with maybe someone from the civilian side of the intelligence or DoD, will leave you alone. They will leave almost immediately and let the residents of Vinalhaven live in peace. I consider you part of the family, and I am not asking you to leave the home you've spent the last month building. We will all support your decision 100%."

"Matthew, I do feel like I know you quite well, and I think of you as a son as well as the patriarch of this wonderful, extended family that we have all put together over the past few months. I'm 67 years old, and I never once anticipated anything like the cataclysm could ever happen. But you all are my family. It never crossed my mind not to go with you."

"Okay, that's settled. Anyone want to add anything before we get to taskings and responsibilities?"

No one said anything. Matt gathered his thoughts. He had thought through this contingency many times and knew exactly what he would say. "As it currently stands, there are twenty-five of us if we include all of Kim's folks and Gianna Bianco. The boat has beds for twenty-five. However, it can fit probably double that if we wanted. I am going to go around the island and speak with all of the residents. I'll offer them passage, but I'm not going to tell them our destination. I am not sure anyone will come, but we should be prepared. I've thought through what needs to be done, so here's how we divide the labor. We can then discuss, agree, and move out. This meeting should end in ten minutes or less.

"Molly, you and I will return to Roberts Hill Farm and brief everyone there. Some will be tasked to help others, but most will stay and help you. Your primary responsibilities are two-fold. First, get everyone packed and bring everyone's essentials. Second, load all of our non-perishable food items, like MREs, canned goods, et cetera, plus as much fresh food you think will travel well and get them to the Oliver estate. That is our staging point from where we will load the yacht. There's a walk-in fridge and freezer on the boat.

"Stan, you're in charge of dismantling QuAI and transporting all components to the yacht. Take every IT thing we can take. I'd like to leave the surveillance system in place, but if we can condense it and take those WiFi extenders, we should. Once you get everything to the staging point, get yourself aboard the yacht and get things ready to roll. Liz and Juliet are your mates to get started. So other than QuAI, you are focused on captaining the Irish Rover.

"Pete, your task is the two boats I think we should take: the Hinckley and the Midnight Express. There's gear on the Irish Rover to tow both boats, and I know super yachts do that all the time across the Atlantic. Fill the boats with the fuel they need, as many gas cans as possible. We can also store some supplies in the berth of the Hinckley.

"Dave, you're responsible for armaments. I will send LT and Derek back to assist you. Get everything loaded up, and then when you get up to the yacht, figure out the right way to store them so we can access what we need en route."

"Got it," said Dave.

"Clare, Marvi, and Michelle. You have the most important jobs. Make sure we have everything we need to live on the yacht and especially after. Blow-up beds for the journey, bedding, clothing, extra household items, friggin' European outlet adapters, anything you can think of. Lastly, think of everything I'm now forgetting to do, and task someone to do it. Molly has more than fifteen people at her disposal. Task away. Okay?"

"Yes, Matt," replied Clare, with Marvi and Michelle nodding in assent.

"Kim, I didn't forget about you. You should come with Molly and speak to your team. Then you can come with me to the Olivers. I'm going there first before speaking with anyone else. I'm going to leave you there, and you're going to be the marshal for this load out. I want you standing on the back of the yacht, identifying and noting everything we're loading and telling them where to load it. Grab a couple of your students to help you. You know that yacht better than us, so tell us where to put everything. Get a look at what's being stacked in the staging area, and then have a plan. We need to have started loading by 9 pm at the latest. Any questions?"

Kim shook her head.

"Anyone want to add anything?"

"Let's do this!" Dave said. Everyone smiled and stood up.

"You're right, Dave. Let's do this." Everyone moved off to execute their assigned mission.

CHAPTER 55

October 29, 11:47pm

Matt stood in the Vinalhaven Fisherman's Co-Op parking lot in Carver Harbor. He was two docks down from where The Base had docked their boat the night prior. *This is way better than trying to load in Mill Creek. Thanks, Kent!* After briefing everyone at Molly's, Matt and Kim had driven directly to the Olivers to inform them of the decision to flee and to elicit their assistance in loading the yacht.

Once he explained the situation, Kent and Earl strongly suggested we move the yacht to Carver Harbor and load it from the Fisherman's Co-Op dock. It was long enough for the 205-foot Irish Rover and would allow them to drive loaded vehicles almost to the pier, then walk or use a dolly to move all their supplies and equipment. The anchorage in Mill River would force them to load everything on a dinghy or tender and then transfer it to the yacht while tied alongside. Using the pier at Carver Harbor was going to be much easier.

Stan and his team had started the Irish Rover's engines, performed twenty minutes of checks, and then pulled anchor and motored the yacht around the west side of the Island and down to Carver's Harbor. They had left just after 8:30 pm and arrived here at 9 pm. Kim was waiting with her crew of marshals, Bonnie and Avery, and they noted every item and identified where it should be stored on the yacht. Matt hoped this would provide a solid inventory so they would know what they had aboard.

None of the island's residents had opted to join them on their one-way cruise. Both the Agha family and the Norgaards had seriously considered Matt's offer. Still, in the end, they felt that the *status quo*, with electricity and ten miles of Penobscot Bay as a buffer, was enough to keep them in place. Everyone had wished them well, and all had offered to help. Not wanting to give away their destination or the contents of their equipment and supplies, Matt had asked everyone not going on the cruise to stay home after saying farewells.

The exception was Kent Oliver and his wife Janet, both currently standing in the gravel parking lot next to Matt. Matt had come to enjoy Kent, even though he kept thinking of him as the defense lawyer he portrayed in a popular television series.

"We're sad to see you leave, Matt," said Kent. "You made a big difference for all of us. We can't ever properly thank you."

"There's no thank you necessary, Kent. It's been an absolute pleasure getting to know you and your family. We wish you nothing but the best."

"You know, Matt," said Janet. "We seriously considered joining you. Earl was adamant against leaving, but we really felt the girls might have the best chance at a normal life if they went with you. Ultimately, it was too much risk and not enough certainty."

"Janet, I completely understand. And for the record, were I in your shoes, I would make the same decision. You have a sat phone, and we expect to communicate regularly with you. If things work out as we hope, we can always come back and get you. It's not that far when you think about it."

Kent and Janet smiled. He realized that this was difficult for them. The Sheridan extended family had provided a blanket of comfort, security, and normalcy that was about to be yanked away from them.

"So, if anyone asks, tell them we went to Canada, either Nova Scotia or Newfoundland. Then if they really ask, tell them you think we were faking the trip to Canada and planned to swing around to the east and then head south for the Caribbean. Everyone will want to believe we went south, which makes the most sense."

"Will do, Matt," said Kent, extending his hand. "We should get going and leave you to it. Best of luck to you and your family." Matt shook Kent's hand and then leaned in to give him a man hug. Janet then stepped in and hugged Matt so hard his wounded side barked, but he hid it well.

"Goodbye, Olivers. We'll talk soon."

Matt watched as they walked up to the main road and got into their vehicle. He then turned and refocused his attention on loading. As far as he knew, all of the items they were taking were currently stacked on the dock or piled high in the backs of several pickup trucks they were using to transport everything.

Before coming to the dock, Matt had done a last walk-through of the Carver Main house. Clare had already grabbed everything there was to take, so it took Matt less than five minutes to conduct the walk-through. He said his goodbyes to the house and the cove - a special place he wished they could have stayed longer.

Juliet had created a manifest with the names of the twenty-five passengers who now made up the extended Sheridan family. Half the team had already boarded, and Kim's staff had them hard at work stowing things on board. On Matt's last walk-through of the yacht a few minutes before the Olivers had arrived, he had been a bit shocked to see that Dave had set up the Mk 19 automatic grenade launcher and the M2 .50 cal machine gun on the sun deck, one facing the bow and the other the stern. Matt understood Dave's logic, but it was the four-high and two-deep revetment of sandbags that Dave had also added, filling them from a stock the Co-op had for use during floods, that made Matt smile.

A half-dozen of the younger ones, including Dylan, Derek, LT, Grace, and Kelsey, were hard at work loading and transporting everything on the dock up the gangway to the main deck. Once deposited there, Kim's marshals directed a half-dozen others where to take and store it. The pile of items on the dock dwindled quickly under the combined effort.

"Hey Derek, remember to load those three dollies onto the yacht. They might come in handy for the offload."

"Good point, Uncle Matt. I'll make sure they get on board."

Rather than watch the loading, Matt decided the best use of his time would be to make another quick tour of the yacht. He didn't want to micro-manage, but he also knew it was important for someone to always keep the big picture in mind. He walked up the gangway and onto the main deck. A narrow staircase spiraled down from the rear of the main deck, but Matt had already been down there. That stairwell led down to the swim deck, which contained a huge garage and a small fitness center. They had designated the fitness center as the ship's armory, loading most of the extra weapons and munitions there. With everything gathered over the past few weeks from The Base, they had tens of thousands of rounds of ammunition - enough to win a war. This garage also included two jet skis as well as a small tender. Pete said this tender would hold about twelve people and had a front end that lowered to allow guests to walk out right onto a beach.

Up on the main deck, the back area had been left as a living room, while the internal sitting areas had been turned into major storage centers. Leaving from the co-op had also been a boon to their storage organization. Someone had had the incredibly bright idea of using the large blue crates that lobsters were stored in as storage containers aboard the yacht. Choosing the clean ones that had aired out over the past two months, dozens of these containers were now stacked in rows on both sides of the sitting room amidship. On the side of each bin was a piece of tape with a description of the contents.

Continuing forward through the foyer, Matt turned left into the galley area. Amey and Kelsey were organizing many of the utensils and pots they brought with them into the items that were already present. Matt could hear a lot of commotion down below, most prominent of which was Molly's voice directing people where to store things. Matt didn't want to interfere, and as the crew area was already cramped, he didn't feel he could add anything.

Matt nodded to Kelsey, who walked over and hugged him. "Thanks, Uncle Matt."

"Don't thank me, Kels. If anything, I'm the one making us move again."

"Move again? Matt, this is incredible! We're living on a superyacht!" Kelsey and Amey both started laughing.

Matt laughed with them. Oh, to be young again and always up for an adventure!

Matt walked down the hall and up the stairs to the bridge. Stan stood looking through some checklists and fiddling with several displays.

"All good, Captain?" Matt asked.

Stan turned to face him. "Yeah, Matt, we're all set. I'm a bit shocked we're actually doing this so fast. How's it look out on the dock?"

"I'd say we'll be fully loaded in another ten minutes. It'll take many hours to store everything, but we can get underway here shortly. You need anything?"

"Nope. Liz is in the engine room, and I've got the helm. I might use you again to watch the port side while I use the starboard controls. That okay?"

"Sure, I'll be up when everyone is on board. I'm going to grab Pete and Dave now and have them get into the Hinckley and Midnight Express. We'll have them lead and trail us until we're around to the north of North Haven, then we'll hook them up. That still work for you?"

"Yeah. Pete, Liz, and I already put the yoke on the stern. Each boat has its tethers in place. I think you're right that using the jet ski is the best way to do that, and Derek seems to have the most experience on those. Won't be that simple at night, but I think we can get it done."

"Okay, Stan. I'll see you in about ten."

Matt returned the way he came and bumped into his wife as

he walked into the foyer. She was coming down the stairs from the owner's deck. She was sweaty, but she also looked vibrant. "What do you think, honey?" He asked her.

"Well, if we have to flee, this is certainly the right way to do it. That owner's suite is off the hook. I've set up blow-up beds for Chris and Laurie, and Chris had already taken over the owner's sundeck as his personal sentry position."

"Do we have enough beds for everyone?"

"Yeah, plenty. We had eight blowup mattresses between Carver Main, Michelle, and the Farm. Plus, we have so many damn couches I can't even count them all."

"Okay, that's good. We're gonna shove off in less than ten minutes. Pass the word."

Matt walked back out on the rear of the main deck, where Kim stood checking this off. He saw she had a manifest of everyone's names and had checked off those already aboard. Matt looked out and saw Derek, Dylan, LT, and Grace left on the dock. The original four musketeers from the Pomfret farmhouse.

"All set, Kim?" Matt asked.

"Yes, Matt. Everything is going well. They have maybe two more trips each with the dollies; then I think we're done."

"Okay, so it's just those four who aren't on board?"

"Yes."

"Sounds good. I'm heading down to the dock. I'll be the last one on board."

Matt walked down the gangway in between Grace and LT with their dollies. Derek was pouring sweat, even though the October evening temperature hovered just above forty. "Hey, Uncle Matt. One more trip, and I'm staying on board. You need anything else?"

"Nope. Great job, Derek. We couldn't have done this without you. All of you."

"No problem, Uncle Matt. We're excited. I'm keeping my fingers crossed, and I think we'll see Mom, Dad, and Kirstie in ten days. I just know they made it through this. I can't wait to see the look on their faces."

"Yeah, I can't wait either." Matt didn't quite share Derek's optimism that his brother Donald and his wife Tracy were still alive, but he was certainly hopeful.

Dylan nodded as he went by with the full dolly. Matt walked over to the pickups and checked the beds - all empty. A few more boxes stood on the dock, and Grace and LT came down with their dollies to load them up.

"This is it, Matt," said LT. "I'm bringing on the last box."

"Okay. I'll follow you two up. Then we'll haul in the gangway and get out of here."

Matt helped Grace stack the last of her boxes on her dolly, and she tilted it back and pushed it forward up the gangplank, with LT right behind her. Matt looked around, appreciating the empty dock, and followed them up.

At the top of the gangway, a group had gathered in the seating area of the rear deck. Clare, Marvi, Michelle, and Kim were all standing there, as well as Derek, Dylan, Grace, and LT. Matt pulled the radio off his belt as Kim maneuvered the gangway into the closed position. "Pete, Dave, this is Matt. Are you guys in the boats?"

"Roger, Matt," replied Pete. "I'm in the Hinckley, and Dave is in the Midnight Express. We're out in the harbor already."

"Roger. Standby." Matt turned to Kim. "Everyone on board?"

"Aye, aye. All twenty-five on board and accounted for."

"Stan," Matt said into the radio. "I'm heading up to the bridge. We can leave as soon as I get there."

Matt walked forward through the yacht, their yacht, and made his way to the wheelhouse. He took his position on the port side, toward the open harbor. He could see the Hinckley and Midnight Express idling several hundred yards out into the mouth of the harbor. Stan had lifted the top of the starboard control box. "You ready, Captain?"

"All ready, Matt. Let's do this."

"All on board, this is Matt. Next stop, Kinsale, Ireland."

ACKNOWLEDGEMENT

I would like to personally thank all of you who have taken the time to leave a review on Amazon. The goal of any author is to have more people read their books, and by leaving a quick 5-star review on Amazon this greatly impacts the algorithms that allow new readers to find this book. So I would like to personally thank all of you in advance for taking the time to leave a quick rating.

Another huge thank you to all my extended family and friends who have encouraged and supported me on this journey as a novelist.

I have the fortune to live quite near Stephen King and often see him walking his dog, exchanging the occasional wave hello as we pass. I've read his novels and short stories voraciously since I was in junior high school, but just very recently I was given his book, On Writing, as a Father's Day gift. The level of understanding that he brings to the craft of writing is truly astounding, and I found it quite humbling. I don't know if reading this book has made me a better writer, but it has certainly made me feel like a better writer, with a clearer picture of how to do what is most important: tell a good story that people enjoy reading. Thank you for your insights, as well as many evenings lost in one of your memorable tales.

While I have attempted to make this work of fiction seem as real as possible, any factual errors are entirely mine. In some cases the errors are intentional, while others are likely due to ignorance - but in all cases, the fault lies entirely with me.

A special thank you to Donald, Tracy, Kelsey, Derek, Dylan, and Kirstie for letting me borrow your names, your house in Vermont, and to some extent your personalities. I hope you had as much fun reading this story as I did writing it.

Dave and Michelle - I'm sure you never imagined being part of a novel when you invited us to visit your home on Vinalhaven so many years ago. It is a special place, and thanks for letting us experience it with you.

Butch - your support and encouragement are instrumental. Keep the new ideas coming. Bret - I would not have had the time necessary to write without all of your dedication and hard work. Thank you.

Matt Robbins was instrumental in providing considerable insight into the operations of superyachts as well as helping with the early drafts of this story. I need to thank him not only for his assistance but also for just being one of those great friends that is always there when you need them. Thank you to Ray and Jeanne Conrad and the crew of their amazing yacht, Lucky Lady. I would never have had the knowledge necessary to tell the story of Matt Sheridan's liberation of the Irish Rover and fleeing Vinalhaven if not for the patience and assistance of Captain Scott Barsin and 1st Officer Chris Harbinson of the Lucky Lady, true professionals with extensive experience in the yachting industry. They both have earned a special thank you and it was my pleasure to name characters in this story after them.

Thank you to my parents for their encouragement and for passing on their love of reading.

Thank you most of all to my wife and children. They have endured many evenings with my office door closed while I attempted to capture this story in writing, as well as listening and commenting on new ideas and characters. Your love and support are what make everything worthwhile.

ABOUT THE AUTHOR

Robert Cole

Robert Cole is a former infantry officer in the U.S. Army who has worked as a consultant on classified government projects similar to those outlined in this novel. In addition to having served with some of the Army's most elite units, Robert is also a successful entrepreneur and college professor.

To learn more about Robert please visit his website at www.officialrobertcole.com. Robert is currently at work on the third book in the Matt Sheridan series, as well as an international thriller.

Made in United States
North Haven, CT
08 June 2024